Gold Mountain

KAREN J. HASLEY

Karen J. Hasley

outskirts
press

Denver, Colorado

Donaldina M. Cameron
Beloved "Lo Mo"
Mother to Many and a Remarkable Woman of Purpose

July 26, 1869 — January 4, 1968

Chapter One

A wounded sigh for these folks: paupers gone begging on a mountain of gold.
from "Hymn on the Way" by Kuan Hsiu [832 - 912]

Johanna and I left China on an April morning so clear and beautiful that the horrors of the past twelve months might have been only a delusion, a trick of memory—or of nightmare. Surely no place so lovely in blue and green could have spawned the crimson violence and death of the past year.

As the ship pulled away and the harbor faded, I looked down at my young companion's face, pale and pinched from silent grief, and placed an arm around her shoulders to pull her close.

"I predict your grandmother will be waiting for us on the dock in San Francisco, Johanna. Her wire to Father was—"

"Imperative? Dictatorial? Autocratic?" Johanna gave me a slight smile as she spoke and in unexpected intimacy did not immediately move away from my casual hug.

"I was going to say decisive, but I can't argue with any of your choices." Then, resolved to take advantage of our rare closeness, I continued in a conversational tone, "I don't recall that your mother had any such similar air about her."

"No, she didn't," agreed Johanna and pulled away from my touch to step closer to the rail as if she wanted to get a better look at the now distant coastline. I knew better, however. Her posture told me that she was not yet willing or ready to talk about her family. Perhaps because I reminded her of them too much, she would never be able to do so with me. Perhaps it would take new surroundings and an unknown grandmother to allow Johanna to heal and start to live again. Poor child. Orphaned a year ago and haunted by frightful dreams that awakened her—awakened both of us—in the night. Nevertheless, bad dreams or not, I knew Johanna Swan well enough to believe that she would one day be whole again. The girl was made of strong stuff.

Johanna and I traveled aboard the *Solace*, an ambulance ship with an itinerary that necessitated an extended Pacific voyage before we reached our destination of San Francisco, which was one of the complaints Johanna's grandmother had wired to my father. Had my father been a different sort of man, Mrs. McIntyre's demanding tone that bordered on the scornful—*"Your years apart from your extended family in so rustic a part of the world may have caused you to forget a family's natural and urgent desire to be together. Why else would you consider putting my grand-daughter on an ambulance ship? I assure you cost is not an issue."*—might have been offensive. Fortunately, my father had spent his early years in China being pelted by unkind names and shrieked at by terrified children so a few sentences from a Chicago society matron never fazed him.

"She could at least have said thank-you," I remarked indignantly after reading the lengthy wire.

"She is grieving and worried," my father replied, understanding the feelings behind her words and as always more sensitive than I. "I sympathize with Mrs. McIntyre's impatience and wish I could do better than the *Solace*, but it's all I can arrange and it will have to do. You're content with the vessel, aren't you, Dinah?"

I wanted to tell him that it was the idea of the trip itself, not the vessel, that caused me dismay and sadness, but I couldn't say the words. He had asked me to accompany Johanna to California, I had said yes, and thus the deed was as good as done.

"Perfectly content, Father." I kissed him on the cheek. "I can't wait to see Ruthie and because *Solace* is an ambulance ship, Johanna's interest in medicine should keep her occupied the whole trip. Time will speed by."

"Not fast enough for the McIntyres, I fear," my father responded, glancing once more at the paper in his hand, "but the *Solace* is the best trans-Pacific ship available at the moment. You'll explain that to Mrs. McIntyre when you see her, won't you?"

"Of course," I agreed but, in fact, never had the chance to do so.

As predicted by my father and feared by Mrs. McIntyre, the *Solace* docked in both Yokohama and Honolulu before it finally arrived in San Francisco, a trip of six weeks that had we been aboard another ship—the USS Oregon, for example, or another military vessel—would have taken only half that long. Such ships were not available at the time, however, and truthfully, neither Johanna nor I minded the lengthier voyage. As I had predicted, Johanna spent a great deal of time with the *Solace*'s doctors, nurses, and patients, observing what she was allowed to observe and absorbing as much medical information as she possibly could.

I spent my time observing Johanna, watching the color come back into her cheeks, surprising sudden smiles, and listening to her interested chatter about wounds and injuries, illnesses and treatments. I drew the line at certain topics—"Johanna, I do not share your interest in the symptoms or effects of gangrene. As far as I'm concerned, there is such a thing as too much knowledge."—but on the whole felt the voyage was a blessing of rest and health for both of us. Why I was surprised by that fact I didn't know. *Solace* was an ambulance ship, after all, purposefully intent on the recuperation of its passengers. Perhaps my father, in typical understated wisdom, had planned it so all along.

The *Solace* docked at Mare Island, the naval shipyard north of San Francisco, at daybreak, and Johanna's and my bags were transferred to a tug that, once the morning fog completely burned off, carried us to a wharf in San Francisco Bay. I felt a mix of emotions: relief at our safe arrival and eager anticipation to see my younger sister, certainly, but worry on Johanna's behalf and a powerful reluctance—now that the moment had almost arrived—to give the girl up. She had wept in my arms at the news of her family's murders and together we had experienced weeks of intense fear, fatigue, and fighting in a siege that none of us expected to survive. We had seen the bodies of dead friends in the streets and spent many nights holding the hands of young men shattered by terrible wounds. Such shared experiences strengthened our bond of affection so that the thought of parting made me feel suddenly protective and tender toward my young friend.

"I see my sister Ruth and her husband," I told Johanna, pointing out a fair young woman dressed in green and the young man beside her, both of whom stood on the dock waving wildly. I raised my hand in a return greeting.

"I imagine that is my grandmother standing next to your sister, then. She looks exactly as I expected."

I couldn't tell from Johanna's voice if she was speaking of Mrs. McIntyre or Ruth and was dismayed by her unemotional tone.

"Johanna, as you lost a mother so your grandmother lost a daughter. I know she loves you and longs to have you with her. You have nothing to fear. And I've given you Ruth's address so we can stay in touch."

Johanna turned to face me fully, no smile on her face and the expression in her unusual amber eyes as serious as death.

"I'm not afraid, Dinah. I'll never be afraid of anything again. But I don't delude myself. My grandmother has never met me so how can she love me?"

"Oh, Johanna." I took both of her hands in mine. "You know better than most that people are capable of loving God, whom they've never seen, quite fervently, so why should you question if they can do the same with their fellow humans? Especially if the person carries the memory and reflects the image of one dearly loved." Then, spoiling the effect of my little speech, I choked on emotion and made a sound somewhere between a hiccup and a snort. "Now you've made me weepy, confound it! You know how I hate that." But I grinned when I spoke and she responded with a chuckle.

"Yes, I know. I've learned from you to prefer action over emotion."

"That doesn't mean emotion is bad," I retorted, suddenly fearful I'd ruined the girl for life by my preaching about the value of independence and my scorn for the weaknesses stereotypically ascribed to women. "I hope I haven't taught you to fear your feelings or doubt your honest emotions, Johanna. If I've set a bad example for you, please forgive me." Johanna gently withdrew her hands from my grasp.

"There is no one living I admire more than you, Dinah. I've learned more from you than you'll ever know, and I appreciate it all. You are my best friend. I expect you always will be." We turned shoulder to shoulder to gaze once more at the people waiting on the dock, then clutched the rail for support as the tug bumped against the wharf with a thud. "Life is just a series of good-byes." My companion said her concluding words so quietly that I almost missed them.

I looked at the group of people standing on the dock, most of them waving and smiling and eagerly trying to pick out the object of their welcome among the few military and civilian passengers that waited with us by the ship's rail.

"I know sometimes it seems so, Johanna, but there are moments of welcome, too. Don't dwell on the farewells with such intensity that you miss the warmth of homecoming." Then the gangplank was lowered and she and I were being escorted off the *Solace* and it was too late for more confidences.

My sister, followed by her husband, hurried forward as soon as I set my foot on land, elbowing her way through the small crowd with a ruthless intent that was totally unlike her usual docile temperament.

"Oh, Dinah! I've been worried sick forever! How could you and Father treat me like this?!" At those accusatory and totally unreasonable words, she threw her arms around me and burst into tears. Behind her, her husband, Martin, ineffectively patted her shoulder. I hugged Ruth to me, surprised by the powerful tug of emotion I felt at seeing her, and gave Martin a smile of greeting over his wife's shoulder.

"I refuse to take the blame for the Boxer insurgency, Ruth, either in total or in part." She gave a weak laugh.

"You know very well that when we were children, you were the one with the harebrained ideas that got us all into trouble, and I was the one who fretted and worried because of it. How could I not think that your mischief had something to do with the conflict?" I held her away from me to take a good look.

"You might give me credit for maturing over the last three years." Then I took a second look at her. "Ruth, are you—?"

She blushed a rose-pink that contrasted charmingly with her fair hair and blue eyes. "Yes, but now is not the time to discuss it." She cleared her throat and stepped back. "Dinah, here are Mr. and Mrs. McIntyre."

The couple—an elegant woman with brown hair threaded through with gray and a bearded man of about her same age—stood at a distance looking past me. At Ruth's words, they turned simultaneously to face me, and the woman immediately put out her hand.

"How do you do, Miss Hudson? My husband and I don't have the words to thank you for the kind escort you provided our granddaughter." Her gaze slid past me to Johanna again, and I stepped aside.

"I was happy to have the company," I replied, then placed a hand on Johanna's arm. "Johanna, here are your grandparents."

I wanted to give them as much privacy as was possible on the busy wharf, but neither the couple nor Johanna seemed to need the consideration. Mrs. McIntyre stepped close enough to take Johanna's chin between her thumb and forefinger and tilt the girl's face so the two could meet eye-to-eye.

Now there are two peas in a pod, I thought, seeing the same firm mouth and unflinching gaze in both of them, regardless of the difference in generations.

"You favor your father, child," was all Mrs. McIntyre said before her husband stepped forward to sweep Johanna into a more traditional embrace. The next thing I knew, Mr. McIntyre was off in search of Johanna's baggage, and his wife, one hand firmly on Johanna's arm, was leading her granddaughter away.

I turned to follow them, determined not to lose Johanna so quickly, and the moment my sister put a hand on my arm to hold me back, I noticed a ragged group of Chinese girls huddled together at the edge of the wharf's rough boardwalk. Something about their posture—shoulders bent, eyes downcast, hands clutching each other for support—made me focus on them more intently and when one girl, small and pale, lifted her head our eyes met squarely. I could hardly believe what I saw.

"Mae Tao!" I called.

At my cry, all the girls raised their heads to look in my direction and with that concerted motion the man standing with them grasped the arm of the girl I recognized and barked in Chinese, "Come now." The girl tried to take a step toward me, her instinctive action making me even more certain that I was right to recognize her, and the man gave her arm a rough yank, repeating harshly, "Come now I said." She hesitated long enough for him to hiss something at her in a tone so low and savage she tried to back away from the malevolence she heard there. His words seemed to startle her enough to make her forget my presence, and as he pulled her along, the other girls, all still holding hands as if on a school outing, followed them down the wharf toward a busy street.

I picked up my skirts intending to try to catch up with them when from behind me I heard Johanna cry, "Don't forget to write, Dinah! You promised!" Suddenly caught between two imperatives, I turned around in time to see Johanna give a quick wave before she briskly walked away flanked by her grandparents.

"I will," I called. "I promise I will." I waved at Johanna in return, although by then she wouldn't have seen the gesture, conscious of a lump in my throat that for a moment kept me from further speech. After she and the McIntyres disappeared into the crowd, I looked back to locate the small clutch of Chinese girls I had recently seen, but they—like Johanna—had also disappeared. The spot where they had stood was filled instead with members of the crew of the vessel from which the Chinese girls appeared to have disembarked.

"Wait!" I called to the closest man as I brushed away Ruth's hand and tried to push myself through the busy press of people. "You! You there, from the—" I glanced at the name of the docked tramp steamer "—Pandora! I want to speak with you for a moment!" At the name "Pandora" called in my loudest, most peremptory voice, the men stopped talking and watched me approach, my gait still unsteady from the past days at sea. When I stood before them, one of the men, taking on the role of spokesperson, had the good manners to remove his hat.

"Yes, ma'am?"

"I want to ask you about those girls."

The man with longish, dark brown hair and a pencil-thin mustache didn't blink. His brown eyes held my gaze in a brash look that seemed too bold for the occasion, but I was used to the politely dropped gaze of the Chinese, so perhaps I reacted too strongly to normal American self-assurance.

"What girls would that be, ma'am?"

"The Chinese girls. The girls who were standing over there just a few minutes ago." I pointed in the general direction of the boardwalk. "The ones who came off your steamer."

The speaker shook his head, rebutting my words. "Sorry, ma'am, but we didn't carry no Celestials in, girls or otherwise. If we had, we would've notified the immigration officer, and he'd have those girls in hand as we speak. Importing Celestials is against the law so if you did see Chinese girls, they didn't come off the Pandora."

I knew he was lying as surely as I knew the sun was shining.

"I know what I saw: six young Chinese girls standing right over there and they had clearly just gotten off your vessel."

"With all due respect, ma'am,"—he imbued the word *ma'am* with faint but unmistakable mockery—"San Francisco's got so many Chinese living here, it's a second China. You could have seen six hundred for all I know." He paused purposefully before finishing, "But no girls came off the Pandora. No, ma'am. You'd be making a serious mistake to suggest that."

As he spoke, I felt vaguely threatened, certain that his words held an ulterior meaning he wanted me to be sure not to miss. In response, I glared back at him.

"I did not make a mistake——" I retorted firmly, but my brother-in-law, who had come up behind me, interrupted.

"Come along, Dinah. Ruth is feeling faint and needs to sit down. I don't know what this is all about, but let's resolve it later. You'll spoil your homecoming." Martin touched the brim of his hat dismissively at the man who had been speaking and placed a hand on my arm. "I have a carriage waiting, and Ruth is anxious to have you with her at home. Please, let's go."

I didn't want to leave just then. Something told me this was a matter important to pursue, that I truly had seen Mae Tao and that the instinctive but hazy unease I had experienced at the child's reaction to the man who had taken her and the other girls away was significant and not to be disregarded. At the same time, I could see from where I stood that Ruth had paled in the past few minutes and looked on the verge of being seriously unwell.

"All right," I answered Martin, adding for the sake of the man from the Pandora who still stood in front of me, "but I intend to start a search for Mae Tao as soon as I'm settled in. I'm quite sure I saw her just now, and I can't imagine why she would be in San Francisco. Something doesn't seem right and I won't forget about her." I spoke the final five words with distinct emphasis, then smiled pleasantly at the sailor. "Thank you, sir. You were more helpful than you could possibly imagine," using a tone that implied an ulterior message of my own. I don't think he missed my intended meaning, either, because his eyes narrowed as I spoke and his insolent grin faded as he continued to study me. My steady return stare encouraged the man to realize that having survived the prolonged, murderous attacks of furious renegade Chinese, I was not a woman to be cowed by one lying sailor. Point made, I turned around in a leisurely fashion, went back to Ruth's side, and took her arm. "I'm sorry to make you stand in the sun, Ruthie. Are you feeling awful?"

She gave a wan smile. "It's early days, I'm afraid, and I do feel awful a great deal of the time, but I'm assured the worst is almost over. What was that commotion all about?"

I explained as she and I, followed by Martin and a man pulling a small cart that carried both Johanna's and my baggage, walked slowly down a side street to a waiting carriage.

"I know I saw Mae Tao. Do you remember her, Ruth? Her mother, Ping Lee, came to work at the mission when you were still there. Mae Tao was six years old at the time." Ruth responded with an apologetic shrug.

"I don't remember either of them, Dinah. I'm sorry. It's been too many years."

"You were also desperately in love, as I recall," I replied, teasing her and trying to take her mind off her discomfort, "so I'd be surprised if you remembered anything except wedding plans from your last year in China." I leaned forward to unfasten my sister's jacket. "Now take off this jacket and remove that fashionable hat, please. You'll be more comfortable. It's only Martin and me, after all, and you don't have to impress either of us. You wrote about the delightfully *temperate* climate of San Francisco, but if this is temperate, I'd hate to think what California heat feels like."

"The weather's been unusually warm," Martin interjected, keeping an eye on his wife's face. "Ruth was right to praise our climate because it is delightful. Most of the time."

His quick response had a touch of the defensive in it and I said quickly, "I'm sure it is, Martin. Ruth will tell you that this heat would be considered almost polar for a Chinese summer. Now that was a sweltering experience!"

My innocent words, intended as simple conversation, evoked a sudden hodge-podge of sights and sounds and smells from last year's summer: the unremitting and oppressive heat, the moans of the wounded during sleepless nights, the unmistakable stench of death. For a moment I faltered. How clearly and worse, how unexpectedly, memories could surface!

Concerned at my abrupt silence, Ruth spoke my name and I smiled in response, immediately back in the present.

"Sorry," I murmured and changing the subject asked, "Now tell me, have you started thinking about names for the baby?"

"Victoria," my sister announced firmly at exactly the same time Martin said, "Clementine." All three of us laughed out loud.

"Apparently the subject is still under discussion," I remarked, and we spent the rest of the trip in casual conversation.

When we arrived at my sister's house, Martin settled Ruth and me inside and then left to accompany Johanna's baggage to the train station.

"I didn't realize Johanna was leaving for Chicago this very day," I said with dismay. "I thought they were just taking her to get settled in their hotel. Couldn't they have stayed here long enough to take in some of the sights of California?"

"I did suggest that," Ruth replied, "and offered them the hospitality of our home for their stay, but Mrs. McIntyre knew what she wanted and what she wanted was to be on the next train east. She's not the kind of woman to change her mind and she would not hear of any other plan. Your poor Johanna may find her grandmother to be more than a little intimidating."

I recalled the similarity to her grandmother in the stubborn set of Johanna's mouth and her unflinching gaze.

"Johanna can hold her own. She's come through the fire."

"Unburned?"

"No," I answered thoughtfully, "but stronger for being seared."

"Poor child," murmured my sister, but I could never apply the adjective *poor* to Johanna, not materially—with her mother's family as wealthy as they purportedly were—and certainly not poor in temperament or outlook or intelligence, either.

"Johanna is a young woman of strong opinions, who is destined for the exceptional," I told Ruth.

"She has not escaped your influence, then."

I couldn't tell if my sister was praising or chastising me and chose not to pursue the matter. That was old ground for the two of us, and I was in no rush to bring up our differences. No doubt there would be plenty of time for that particular discussion later. As soon, in fact, as I began to search for Mae Tao in earnest. I had been perfectly serious in the words I'd spoken to the cocky seaman earlier that day: I was sure I had seen Mae Tao and I would not forget about her.

Chapter Two

The birth of the first of the next generation of Hudsons was the initial topic of conversation over the breakfast table the next day. "Have you let Father or David know?" I asked my sister.

"I was waiting for your safe homecoming before I wrote. That way I could send them good news in duplicate." Ruth paused in her explanation to ask, "Dinah?" My sister, used to my mental *drifting*—as she called it—and used to calling me back to a conversation if I became distracted, must have recognized a familiar expression on my face.

"Sorry. I was just thinking about whether California really constitutes a homecoming for me," I said. "You're here, of course, but other than that, except for getting off a train and onto a ship fifteen years ago, I have no bond to California at all." Ruth leaned toward me, her expression sincere and animated.

"You'll love it here, Dinah. I know you will. The climate is lovely and the city exciting. There are all kinds of cultural offerings, including musical and dramatic ventures that I know you'll love. And because of Martin's work—" Ruth smiled proudly and looked over at her husband, who was quietly eating breakfast as the two of us conversed "—we've met some of the most prominent citizens of the city so our social circle is both prestigious and interesting," concluding nonchalantly with, "I've met several very eligible bachelors, any of whom might end up being the perfect man for you."

"I suspect God broke the mold for the perfect man after Martin was born," I replied, hoping to forestall the matchmaking gleam in my sister's eyes. Ruth knew me well enough to understand my intention but couldn't resist the tempting opening, especially when Martin modestly began to disagree with my expansive statement.

"Martin is a wonderful husband and a good provider. He's been promoted to chief teller at the bank with increased responsibilities and a matching increase in salary, all just in time for our new addition. According to Mr. Gallagher, the bank's owner, bank manager will be the next step." Her tone continued to display pride and affection for her husband as she rested one hand lightly on her increased waistline. "But Martin is also very busy and he works long hours. That's why I'm so glad you'll be here for the birth, Dinah."

Startled, I responded, "But I hadn't planned to stay that long. I only made the trip to accompany Johanna and check up on you. I told Father eight weeks at the most."

"Well, you'll have to write and let him know it will be six months at a minimum. He would never expect you to leave before the baby comes." Ruth set down the delicate teacup she had been holding. "I admit I'm a little surprised that you're so ready and willing to return to China after what you've been through. Was it as terrible as the newspapers made it seem?"

"I didn't read the papers," I answered calmly, "so, of course, I don't know how the situation was presented in print, but it was certainly terrible. Worse for some than others but all around and incontrovertibly terrible."

I could never describe what it had been like to find the hacked bodies of friends in the streets or see a man die in front of me, picked off by a sniper mid-sentence. I carried heavier burdens, too, shadows that lurked at the edge of my consciousness, memories I couldn't share. If I were as sensitive as my sister or had her same delicacy of feeling, I would have been plagued by bad dreams as Johanna had been, but happily for me, I possessed a pragmatic nature and the ability to subjugate past experience to present necessity. That combination usually allowed me to force unwelcome memories into a distant corner of my mind, shutting the troublesome creatures into a locked cage where they crouched untouched and undisturbed. Sometimes they would stir ominously when roused by a sound or smell that blazed a quick picture across my mind with the same brilliance and suddenness of a photographer's flash. Fortunately, the moment usually passed as quickly as a flash, too, and the beasts would settle once again into their fitful slumber. Looking into Ruth's blue eyes fixed with such concern on my face, I realized I could never share all the details with her about those horrendous weeks. I knew, recalling the time our mother had died, that my sister was more susceptible than I to dreams and memories, and with her present condition, I imagined she might be even more sensitive to any thing I told her about my experiences during the siege of Pekin. And some things I couldn't have spoken out loud, regardless of the sympathies of the listener. I feared that wrapping memories in words would give them such power that I would never be able to lock them away again.

As if to fill the sudden silence around the table, Martin stood, folded the newspaper he had been reading, and kissed his wife lightly on the cheek.

"And what plans do the two of you have for the day?"

"I thought we might go shopping," my sister suggested. "The stores are wonderful and—"

"We may do anything you like," I interrupted pleasantly, "after I make a visit to the Pandora Transport Company."

"Are you still convinced you recognized a Chinese girl on the dock yesterday?"

"I'm absolutely certain, Ruth, but I can't imagine why Mae Tao would be in San Francisco. She should be with her mother in Pekin, caring for her little brothers and sisters, exactly where I last saw her."

"You were at a distance, Dinah, and they all look alike. If you've seen one Celestial, you've seen them all."

My brother-in-law's observation was offensive on several levels and brought the conversation to a standstill. I stared at Martin, momentarily made speechless by the casual scorn and disgust in his tone and sentiment, and either my look or my silence caused a touch of defensiveness to creep into his voice.

"I meant no disrespect, but it's not as if there's the same variety of features you find in Americans. They all have yellow skin and their eyes slant. You could easily have mistaken any Chinese girl for this Mae Tao."

To control my temper, I took a deep breath before speaking. I did not pretend to know my brother-in-law well. We had not spent much time in each other's company, and I understood that when Martin had met my sister in China, he had been there only temporarily for business reasons. At that time, the country was no longer foreign to us because it had been our home for years, but Martin had not lived among the population or experienced our opportunity to appreciate China's art and culture and rich variety of people. Nevertheless, to hear all the inhabitants of a great country lumped together under a dismissive description that used only two physical features annoyed me a great deal.

"I was not mistaken, Martin. I have lived among the Chinese for over half my life and I find a great deal of variety in the Chinese face. In fact, some Chinese—this may astound you—do not have yellow skin at all." Martin flushed, sensing the rebuke behind my badly veiled sarcasm.

"I told you I meant no offense, Dinah." Relieved to change the subject, he continued, "I have a general idea where the office of The Pandora Transport Company is located, and I don't advise you going there. It's in a part of town into which unescorted women should not venture." He turned to look sternly at Ruth. "My wife is not going to accompany you to such a location."

Ruth opened her mouth to respond, caught his eye, and remained quiet.

"I wouldn't dream of asking her to do so," I rejoined, although that had been my exact intention until just a moment ago. "Perhaps you—"

"I am leaving for work now and will not be home until supper time, I'm afraid." The satisfied smugness in Martin's tone caused me to feel a quick flare of dislike for my brother-in-law. He hadn't seemed so priggish when I'd known him in China.

"I see. And you're sure that where Pandora is located is in a part of the city that's not safe?"

"The alleys behind the Broadway Dock are no place for you, Dinah. You'll have to trust me. I know the city better than you."

"Very well, then, Martin. Of course, I trust your judgment." I took a sip of tea and smiled at him. "I hope your day at work goes well." He looked grateful, if somewhat surprised, that our discussion had ended so abruptly and so amicably.

"Thank you. I hope you ladies enjoy your shopping today," adding by way of concession, "Mr. Gallagher has some contacts in Chinatown. When I next see him, I'll ask if he has any suggestions about locating this Mae Tao."

Ruth walked with Martin from the bright breakfast room into the hallway, and I heard their murmurs of conversation before she returned to stand in the doorway studying me.

"Tell me I'm misunderstanding the look on your face," she said finally.

"What look would that be?"

"The look that says you intend to do exactly as you please and you didn't mean a word you said to my husband."

"I do intend to do as I please—in this matter, at least—but that doesn't mean I was prevaricating to Martin. Not entirely." At her skeptical look, I grinned. "I do find a great variety of expression in the faces of the Chinese and I wasn't mistaken about Mae Tao."

"But Martin has forbidden me to accompany you to that steamship office, Dinah, and I won't disobey my husband!"

Ruth looked sincerely distressed, and I had to squelch the familiar feeling of guilt I always felt when upsetting my sister or leading her into a mischief for which she had no true inclination. As the elder sister, I had too often taken unfair advantage of her pliability and the poor girl had occasionally shared in the unpleasant consequences of actions that should rightfully have fallen only on me. I rose to give her a quick kiss before sidling past her through the doorway.

"You are an exemplary wife, and I would never ask you to disobey your husband."

"Dinah, you heard what Martin said! Pandora is located in a part of town into which unescorted women should not venture. He said you were not to go." I turned to face her as she followed me down the hallway.

"You are confusing issues, Ruth. It's no doubt commendable that you are such a tractable and respectful wife, but Martin is not my husband and I have every intention of visiting the Broadway Dock. It was very kind of Martin to tell me where the office was located."

My sister said my name with the touch of reproof I remembered from our childhood and continued, "You haven't been in San Francisco even one complete day. You don't know your way around the city. Why can't you entertain the idea that you might possibly be mistaken about this girl? You haven't changed one little bit, you know. You always have to be right!"

"I know," I rejoined, grinning at her again, "but don't look so worried. I understand that the trait of stubborn disobedience skips a generation, so it's unlikely your little one will inherit any of the bad characteristics I seem to possess." Because she continued to look worried, I added, "I'll hire a cab so I don't get lost, and I'll be back before you know I'm gone. We can shop all afternoon. It's amazing how impervious to danger one feels after living through a violent rebellion, Ruth, and spending a few minutes in a rough part of town isn't going to hurt me. Believe me, I learned how to be careful. I promise everything will be fine. I just can't rest until I find out where Mae Tao is. I need to be sure she's safe and in respectable hands. I can remember when she was born. I watched her grow up, and I need to assure myself that she's all right. I can't for the life of me figure out why she would be in San Francisco. Her mother worked at the girls' school and depended on Mae Tao to take care of her little brothers and sisters."

As I pinned on my hat, I thought how easily Ruth and I had slipped back into old patterns. My parents, my two older brothers, my sister, and I had traveled to China fifteen years earlier, fresh from the tree-lined streets of Cleveland, Ohio, none of us—not even my father, the only one with any foreknowledge that such a move might inevitably and permanently transform us as a family—really comprehending how profoundly the transition would affect us. We were an idealistic, hopeful, generous group of benevolent amateurs, intent on doing good and changing lives, and it turned out that it was our lives that changed long before we were able to better the day-to-day existence of the Chinese poor. Eventually we did make a difference, set up a hospital and a school, brought hygiene, hope, and happiness to some, but not before our mother died of a virulent fever and my elder brother, Joseph, abruptly and unexpectedly left home to join the Navy fourteen months after our mother's death, never to return.

At the time Father attributed Joe's departure to grief—my brother had been very close to Mother—but from his first letter home, it was obvious that Joe loved the Navy, loved the sea and ships and sailing, the broad expanse of horizon and the sound of waves slapping against the hull. I knew he had found his destiny and was a little envious of his ability to answer the call of adventure. I felt the same passion as he for the water and understood the siren voice that would eventually take his life as he died with 265 other men aboard the USS Maine when it exploded in Havana Harbor one February night in 1898. My clear-eyed brother, who possessed a gift for enthusiasm that was even brighter than his eyes, still lay at the bottom of Havana Harbor, forever twenty-six, smiling, and wearing a jaunty sailor's cap, exactly as he appeared in the black-draped photo hanging on the wall of our parlor in China.

Joe had been the instigator of all mischief and I had been his eager accomplice, both of us thorns in Ruth's side, poor girl. After Joe's enlistment, I had taken upon my shoulders the mantle of his exuberant love for adventure and daring tomfoolery and because David was already a serious divinity student, had only Ruth as collaborator. Admittedly, an unwilling and unappreciative collaborator, bemoaning my lack of feminine instinct and wishing with all her heart that a miracle would occur to spare her the uncomfortable mixture of affectionate exasperation and dread that haunted her conscience whenever she and I were left to our own devices.

The miracle for which Ruth prayed showed up one Sunday morning at the Presbyterian Church in Pekin and his name was Martin Shandling. Since that fateful morning meeting, Ruth had become a wife, moved to San Francisco with her husband, set up housekeeping in comfortable affluence, and now awaited motherhood. We had been apart for over three years and yet, within twenty-four hours of reunion, I had forced us back into old and familiar behaviors. She had matured. Apparently I had only grown older.

My sister lived in what appeared to be a new home in a fledgling neighborhood on Grove Street just east of a main thoroughfare called Van Ness. Her house along with all the houses in that area seemed poised, both geographically and economically, on the edge of prosperity, not mansions but the house in which one lived just before moving into a mansion. Martin must be doing very well indeed.

When I left the house, found a cab, and gave the driver my destination, I turned into the quintessential country mouse come to the city. My father's medical clinic was located in Tung Chow, not an especially prepossessing city, but as a teacher I had spent a great deal of time at the Presbyterian Home for Girls in Pekin and thought I was accustomed to the sights and sounds of a large city. Turning onto Market Street, however, I caught sight of some of San Francisco's extraordinary buildings and realized that nothing in Pekin could have prepared me for this particular city. Yesterday I had been busy chatting with my sister and reacquainting myself with my brother-in-law so I had not spent any time observing my surroundings. Alone and without distraction on this trip, I could only look out the carriage window with my mouth hanging open in admiring astonishment. What a wonder of a city with its broad streets filled with the chaos of pedestrians, cable cars, hand carts, horse cars, and even a few automobiles! I hoped Johanna had had a chance to see some of San Francisco on her hasty way to the train station and hoped even more that her new home of

Chicago would be kind to her. I would write once she had a chance to settle in and we could compare cities.

We curved onto Third Street, passing through the reek of slaughter houses, and leisurely moved south. I could see the broad expanse of the Bay and knew from the sights and sounds that I was nearing my destination. Frankly, my surroundings didn't look all that bad, despite Martin's dire warning. The area teemed with both street and foot traffic, congested and noisy and filled with a variety of people coming and going, but it held nothing ominous or threatening.

I thought the cabbie intended to drive us straight into the Bay, but he pulled up before we were dunked and called out, "Here's the Broadway Dock then. You want I should wait?" He had a broad, bald head and an engaging grin. Irish from the lilt of his speech.

I eyed the alley's incline before replying, "Please, if you don't mind. I won't be very long."

Hearing my answer made him ask, "You're not Irish then, are you?" apparently surprised I didn't have a brogue to match his.

"Not a drop, despite the hair," I answered, laughing. "But you're not the first person to think I should be."

"Imagine not." He eyed my hair with such admiration that from a self-conscious reflex I reached up to reposition my hat. "No disrespect meant, miss," he added, noticing my discomfort and suddenly embarrassed himself.

"No disrespect taken." I took a few steps up the alley, then turned back to ask, "What's your name?"

"Casey."

"Well, Casey, you remember this red hair. I'm new to the city and looking for the office of the Pandora Transport Company. If I'm not back in a reasonable time, I could be lost. Do you know if this is the right alley?"

"It is. You greet that Jake Pandora for me. Tell him it were Casey's cab that brought you. You'll be safe enough."

I couldn't tell if my safety was guaranteed because I would be talking to Jake Pandora or because I had arrived with Casey. Either way, Martin's fears for my well-being seemed to be handled.

Despite its impressive name, The Pandora Transport Company was nothing but a small storefront, flanked by a liquor distributor on one side and a small beer garden on the other. Those bookends made me smile. Mr. Pandora certainly had no excuse for being thirsty. When I stepped inside, I saw a young man—fifteen at the very oldest—sitting at a tall wooden desk. He had an open metal box next to him and a stack of papers next to that. I watched him take a paper from the top of the stack, read it, make a note in an open ledger book on his desk, place the paper in the safety box, then reach for the next paper. He had his method of operation down to a *t* and didn't notice me until I cleared my throat.

"Mr. Pandora?"

I startled the poor fellow so much that he inadvertently knocked the box off the table, causing him to pronounce one very coarse phrase as he grabbed for—and missed—the box, which clattered onto the floor. The contents of the box fluttered down to the floor like so many large, paper snowflakes. Even in the dim interior I could see the young man's face color. The words he'd just spoken with vehemence and precision weren't usually used publicly or in polite society. Because I didn't miss much, hadn't even as a child, and had spent considerable time on ships and around sailors besides, I recognized the colorful phrase and didn't bother acting shocked.

"Beg your pardon, ma'am." He was apologizing for his language. "Didn't see you there."

"I should apologize for sneaking up on you," I replied, feeling bad about his obvious embarrassment. His cheeks were suffused with such a deep crimson color, I thought blood might start spurting out of his pores at any moment, a mental picture with enough recent memories to make me uncomfortable. I needed to move the conversation along. "Are you Mr. Pandora?"

Behind me a male voice spoke. "No. There's no Mister about him. He's just Eddie. I'm Jake Pandora."

I turned around to face the speaker, who stood behind me in the open doorway, and found myself facing the most beautiful man I had ever seen. Nothing effete or feminine about him but beautiful in the classical sense, golden olive skin, black hair curling against a perfectly shaped head, straight nose, full, firm mouth, and dark brown eyes. He could have been a Michelangelo statue come to life. Of medium height with a muscled build and a face that was flawless. Conscious that I was staring, I stepped back and dropped my gaze but not before I saw a glimmer of understanding in those deep, dark eyes. No doubt he had experienced such a reaction from a woman before. A female would have to be dead not to appreciate—even envy—the perfection of his appearance. Then I immediately thought *poor man* and wondered if stares—even stares as appreciative as mine—grew tiresome after a while.

Prodding me to speak, the man repeated, "I'm Jake Pandora. The only Mister Pandora in San Francisco as far as I know. What can I do for you?" His slightly amused tone brought me to my senses.

"It's about your steamer."

"I have several steamers, Miss. Which steamer would that be, exactly?"

Any residual good humor I felt from his aesthetic attraction rapidly disappeared under the impatient, slightly patronizing tone I heard in his voice. Too bad, I thought, that his manners were not as appealing as his face.

"The one that docked yesterday morning, Mr. Pandora. It had the numeral two painted on the side, right after the name of your company. Does that help?"

I saw him take in my appearance, my outdated dress and unbecoming hat, and recognized the exact moment he decided I was not there on any business that would put money in his pocket.

"Yes, ma'am. It does help. What about it?"

"You carried a passenger I recognized and I'm trying to find her. I thought you might be able to tell me where she's staying."

Jake Pandora stepped farther inside the small office and tossed a coin to the young man at the table. "Eddie, go find lunch while I talk to this lady." When the young man left, Pandora motioned to the chair. "You can sit down if you'd like."

"I don't need to sit. This shouldn't take very long."

"I agree since I carry freight, not passengers."

"You carried passengers yesterday."

"No, ma'am, I didn't."

"Yes, sir, you did." I mimicked his tone and inflection. "A group of young Chinese girls got off your number two steamer and I recognized one of them. I'd like to find her."

"I don't carry passengers," he repeated as if I hadn't spoken, "and even if I did, I wouldn't be dealing in that trade."

"I saw a girl I knew when I lived in China. Her name is Mae Tao. I recognized her and I believe she recognized me. I want to find her."

That I ignored his previous declaration with the same glib assurance he had used to disregard my words added a short-tempered irritation to his tone as he spoke.

"You may have seen someone you recognized on the dock yesterday and she may have been a Chinese girl, but she didn't get off any of my steamers."

"I have made mistakes in my life that I deeply regret, Mr. Pandora, but in this instance I am not mistaken." I spoke the final words through teeth that had begun to clench of their own volition and paused to take a relaxing breath before continuing so my words would come out sounding reasonable instead of hysterical or threatening. "If you fear I will report you to the authorities for illegally transporting Chinese, please be assured that I have no intention of doing so. I only want to find Mae Tao. Your business, while deplorable, remains your business."

"Yes, it does remain my business. Thank you for stating the obvious. Now I repeat, Miss—"

"Hudson," I supplied. "Miss Dinah Hudson. And yes, before you say it, I'm fresh off a boat myself, but I assure you I am not mistaken in this particular circumstance."

"Now I repeat, Miss Hudson," he continued, "no girls, Chinese or otherwise, got off any of my boats at anytime, yesterday or last month or last year." He stepped to the side, giving me a clear path to the door. "I don't traffic in females. Never have. Never will. Now if that's all, I need to be going."

You really need to be going, he meant, and I glared at him, recognizing that I was at an impasse and resenting the helpless, frustrated way his words and attitude made me feel. Familiar emotions, the same I had experienced trapped inside a city for eight weeks, held against my will and furious at the stupidity of violence all around me and the ignorance and prejudice shown on both sides of the conflict. I attribute my unacceptable exit from the office of the Pandora Transport Company to that unpleasant miasma of memory.

Walking past Jake Pandora, I stopped directly in front of him, much too close for courtesy or propriety, and placed my right forefinger against his chest. He wore a common costume of the docks, collarless shirt and informal dark coat and pants, and I tapped my finger—hard—against his collarbone that showed just above his shirt. From his expression, he was clearly taken aback by my gesture and physical proximity and more than a little angry at my continued defiance.

"And I repeat, Mr. Pandora: I am not mistaken in this particular circumstance. I will find Mae Tao and if she has come to any harm, I will make sure you are held personally responsible for it to the fullest extent of the law. The fullest." I repeated the words with undisguised relish. "You would be making a serious mistake to underestimate my determination when I know I'm right." I tapped his chest methodically as I spoke, giving one final, forceful jab as I concluded. "If your memory suddenly returns, you can send a note to Grove Street, where I'm staying with my sister and brother-in-law, the Shandlings."

Aware that he had retreated into the shadow of the doorway and stood watching me, I stepped into the alley and strolled away at a pace to indicate I didn't have a care in the world, out for a leisurely and recreational excursion and in no hurry whatsoever. Inside, however, my heart was thumping a mile a minute and I was as furious as I had been in a long time.

When I climbed into the waiting cab, Casey took one look at my face and with typical Irish intuition, bit off the start of the question he had been about to ask.

Beautiful on the outside he might be, I thought on the ride home, still fuming over the conversation, but Mr. Pandora had secrets that made him—at least in my eyes—as repulsive as any monster. I understood exactly what he had meant by the words "that trade," and I was very afraid for my little Mae Tao.

Chapter Three

M y temper had cooled by the time Ruth greeted me at her front door, and when she asked, "Well?" expectantly, I was able to respond calmly.

"No luck, I'm afraid. Mr. Pandora said he carried freight, not people, and I must have been mistaken."

"Well, there you are, then," Ruth responded cheerfully. "Martin was right. You probably saw one of the locals who bore a resemblance to your Mae Tao."

"Perhaps," I agreed vaguely and moved the conversation onto safer ground. "Are you still up to an afternoon of shopping?"

"Are my eyes still blue?" my sister retorted, and we shared a laugh before she went to find her purse and gloves. The Hudson sisters, as different as night and day in some areas, had always shared a mutual fondness for pretty fabric and big hats.

I intended to find Mae Tao, regardless of any opposition, but I had no idea how or to whom to turn. Ruth's earlier observation that I had been in California for only a few hours was obviously correct and I knew it would take time to put together a plan, so I pushed my nagging worry for the little Chinese girl into a back corner of my mind and spent the afternoon among the merchants of San Francisco.

Without ever discussing the matter between us, my jaunt to the Pandora Transport Company didn't come up in either Ruth's or my conversation with Martin that evening. He arrived home in time for a late supper, told us about his day, and asked about ours. When we mentioned our time spent looking at fabric and dress patterns, he smiled.

"You should each get something new. Mr. Gallagher has asked me to be part of the bank's presence at the city's summer cotillion, and he specifically asked me to bring Dinah along. She seems to have taken on celebrity status."

Ruth flushed at the implied question mark at the end of Martin's sentence and quickly admitted, "I saw Mrs. Gallagher about a week ago when I was shopping and told her about Dinah's visit. I'm not going to apologize for being proud of my sister, Martin. Dinah endured God only knows what horrors and emerged as a heroine in my eyes."

"Ruth! What have you been telling people? I'm no heroine!" She clearly heard the horror in my tone but refused to be cowed.

"That's not what Father's letter said, or the German ambassador's poor wife, who told a local newspaper how brave and kind you were to her when her husband was murdered, or the wounded soldiers, who recounted how you nursed them through their injuries. It's noble of you to be so modest, Dinah, but I want people to know about my brave sister."

I sat speechless. I knew that I was as far from brave as it was possible to be, that actions arising from restless, self-centered impatience and anger bore only a superficial similarity to courage. I also knew in my heart of hearts that the times I acted fearlessly had occurred because I was simply too foolish and pig-headed to realize I should have been scared witless. I recalled a few of those times with shame and remembered many more instances of terrified, whimpering immobility. Heroes were the men on the walls of the compound, men that expected death from a sniper's bullet any moment yet rose to their shift and did their duty without complaint. Mae Tao's mother was a true heroine, creeping through a dangerous city to find food to cook for us and then returning to the compound's kitchen with an apology for the simplicity of the fare. My bad temper should never, never be compared to such legitimate bravery.

"Anyway," Ruth hurried on with her explanation to Martin, ignoring the look on my face, "Mrs. Gallagher expressed an interest in meeting Dinah, so I'm sure she shared our conversation with her husband and that's why he invited Dinah specifically." To me, she added, "In previous years, the papers have described the cotillion with a string of glamorous adjectives, and I've never seen the Grand Ballroom of the Palace Hotel so I can hardly wait to get inside and absorb its magnificence for myself. Anyone who's anyone from San Francisco society attends—the Floods and the Crockers and the Calhouns—just everyone and now we are to be guests, too! It's the invitation of a lifetime! Martin, you've made your wife a very happy woman! Thank you thank you thank you!"

She hopped up from her chair to give her husband a quick kiss on the cheek and I saw how pleased he was that Ruth was pleased. The look of devotion I caught on his face made me consider the occasion— and Martin, for that matter—more charitably. I hadn't the heart to dim the happy glow on my sister's face, although privately I told myself I would immediately set anybody straight who tried to give me hero status, Gallaghers, Floods, Crockers, and Calhouns included.

In an inexplicable and totally unexpected way, I settled into life in San Francisco as if I'd been born there. Something about the city spoke to me: the extraordinary beauty of the surrounding waters, the early morning fog that enveloped the city in mystery until burned off by the sun, the challenging hills, the contagious energy that seemed to run through the city's business district like an electrical current. Sometimes Ruth and I toured the city together, enjoying all its progressive grandeur, admiring the Ferry Building with its four great clock faces and the gorgeous façade of the Palace Hotel, the largest hotel in the world.

At other times, when Ruth was too indisposed to accompany me, I thought nothing of cheerfully going off on my own, and Martin, despite his finely developed sense of propriety, saw no problem with my doing so. In those days, San Francisco held the allure of a lover and somehow Martin, even more than Ruth, understood the city's appeal.

I was thrilled by Golden Gate Park and spent hours there enjoying the delightful children's playground, the Conservatory with its splendid glass dome and landscaped flower beds, the new de Young Museum, and wandering the acres of the Japanese Tea Garden.

Every morning I rose anticipating a new adventure and was never disappointed. Days passed and—to my shame, my everlasting shame—the memory of little Mae Tao, fresh off the number two Pandora steamer and turning plaintively to look at me over her shoulder as she was led away, grew fainter and fainter. The more I settled into life with Ruth and Martin and the more time I spent discovering the spectacle that was San Francisco in 1901, the more my original concern for the young Chinese girl faded.

To this day, I make no excuse for my self-absorbed conduct. I carry the memory as a burden of conscience, one of many. I always will. And who knows how my life would have been different, how my story would have progressed—or whether there would have been a story at all—if I hadn't felt duty-bound to accompany my sister to a meeting of The Presbyterian Woman's Occidental Board of Foreign Missions?

When Ruth first told me that the ladies wanted to meet me, I gave her a searching look before asking suspiciously, "You haven't painted me in heroic colors, have you, Ruth? They understand I'm just an ordinary flesh-and-blood woman, I hope."

"They understand that you are my sister and Dr. Hudson's daughter. No more and no less."

"I won't have to give a speech or anything, will I?" I persisted. "I really have no gift for extemporaneous speaking, and I have no words prepared or practiced."

"You will have to be pleasant," Ruth answered, a rare touch of asperity in her voice, "and I imagine forcing yourself to be so will take all the preparation and practice time you have to spare. I assure you no one will ask for anything more."

My sister's surprisingly censorious response made me feel, however fleetingly, ashamed of my lack of evangelical fervor. In some totally unanticipated way it was as if my first weeks in San Francisco had scoured my mind clean of the recollection of that eight-week siege of Pekin. The vivid sights, sounds, and smells of last year's summer had faded, and bad dreams rarely surfaced; Johanna's face was distant and my father's voice almost stilled. I felt as if I had been reborn into the exciting energy of San Francisco and reveled in the freedom from memory.

Thinking about Ruth's words and tone later that day, I realized I'd allowed—willed?—the memory of Mae Tao's last, beseeching look to dim against the brilliance of San Francisco and a multitude of self-serving sensations and interests. With the wincing sensitivity of conscience, I knew that much of my resistance to accompanying Ruth to the meeting of the Board of Foreign Missions had to do with my reluctance to be once more caught up in a cause of good works. I understood on a purely intuitive level that attending the meeting had the potential to change my current priorities and I resisted any change to my activities. I liked starting the day with only my own entertainment in mind. I enjoyed planning my pleasures without a by-your-leave to anyone, Martin off to his job right after breakfast and my sister often sequestered and indisposed, apologizing for her lack of involvement in my visit because of the physical symptoms of her pregnancy. Ruth didn't realize how being left on my own invigorated me. For most of my life I had been my father's encouragement, my siblings' support, and for the young Chinese girls of our mission school an example of the correct mix of female virtues to which they should aspire. I had been stoic in danger, cheerful under the threat of imminent death, and brave for the sake of those around me, including Johanna. I had done all that and been all that with little effort and less thought. Such conduct was bred into me and I would have been more likely to walk naked through the streets of Pekin than fail in the duties and responsibilities for which I had been trained all my life.

My emotions in the early weeks of my California visit, especially feeling freed from a lifelong responsibility for other people, went straight to my head. Knowing no burden but my own entertainment was as intoxicating as alcohol. But, of course, such self-indulgence could not, should not last. It's true that I bloomed late, but inevitably the bud opened completely and the blossoming was finished. Whether

I liked it or not, each of my parents came from a long line of reformers and the converged bloodlines must ultimately bleed through. In my case, sooner rather than later. The first time I heard Miss Donaldina Cameron speak— in fact, at that very moment—I rediscovered the Dinah Hudson I had tried to leave behind in China, and from that day forward I never sought to be anyone else. Some things were just meant to be.

When Miss Cameron rose to address the group of assembled church women later that week, I settled respectfully into my chair and cast a surreptitious glance at the grandfather clock in the corner, never expecting that what I was about to hear would change the course of my life forever. She was an attractive woman in her early thirties and except for the traditional Chinese *sahn* of blue silk that she wore looked exactly the part of a respectable Presbyterian woman, displaying nothing of the reformer about her. Her presence was a welcome addition to the afternoon: brown eyes alight with intelligence, thick bronze hair already showing silver, and a direct way of speaking that I heard with relief. At least this final presentation of the afternoon, I thought with the self-absorption that had engulfed me over the past few weeks, would not be numbingly boring and then realized from Miss Cameron's first words that I would have to rework my opinion of this woman completely and immediately. The words *boring* and *Miss Cameron* could, should never be used in the same sentence.

The entire audience sat spellbound by the story she recounted: of a note from a desperate young Chinese girl slipped into her hand, of an afternoon foray into a narrow alley in one of Chinatown's most dissolute areas, of a policeman breaking through the door with an ax and the subsequent wild chase through low hallways until, from behind a stack of wooden boxes, a child's white hand appeared waving desperately for attention as her captors disappeared into subterranean tunnels that honeycombed the entire Chinese region of the city.

"Ten years old," Miss Cameron stated firmly, "and destined for a life of prostitution. Shipped to our shores specifically for slavery and because of it marked for an early death from illness and abuse."

We were all sitting upright by then, my casual slouch having disappeared two minutes into the tale. How could I have labeled this woman as a typical do-gooder, holding church membership because it was expected of her, because her mother had done so and her mother before her? This Donaldina Cameron cared about people, about the lives and the futures of the girls of whom she spoke. The vehemence in her voice, the unflinching details of her story, the way she spoke of things that were usually relegated to whispers and shadows displayed an extraordinary woman. I knew from that moment that she would have a role in my life and the sudden burst of energy I felt at the prospect had nothing to do with streetcars and skyscrapers and everything to do with the passion of a cause. My parents' daughter, after all.

When Miss Cameron finished her talk—concluding with a plea for financial assistance for the Mission Home for Oriental girls, which she called "920" because it was located at 920 Sacramento Street—the room remained strangely still. Then, her hearers once more back in the present, a quiet wave of applause spread throughout the audience. Nothing as grand or enthusiastic as she deserved, I thought indignantly and rose with haste, ignoring Ruth's hand on my arm, to shoulder my way to the place where Miss Cameron stood.

"Thank you." I spoke without introduction or preamble. "Thank you for what you do. I can see that it is honorable work and I want to help," sharing my admiration in the sing-song cadences of fluent Mandarin.

At my words, Miss Cameron turned to face me, giving me her full attention for several seconds before she spoke. "Miss Hudson, isn't it? How do you do? I arrived at the very end of your introduction to the group and heard only your name, but I can tell from your excellent intonation that you have spent a great deal of time in China. Unfortunately, I am completely lacking in musical talents so no matter how I try, I cannot master any of the Chinese dialects. We must converse in English, I'm afraid." Her voice possessed a slight Scotch burr—*cannot* become *canna* and the g almost absent from the word *lacking*—that possessed a music all its own.

I understood her comment about speaking Chinese. Because I possessed musical talent, learning the language had been much easier for me than my brother, who couldn't carry a tune in a bucket. Our Chinese friends were always too kind to do anything but wince at David's attempt at speaking their native tongue. He couldn't help but notice their pained reaction to his attempts at conversation, but he accepted my superior language skills with good grace and humor. In fact, I had often heard the same wry, self-deprecating tone in my brother's voice that I heard in Donaldina Cameron's, which made me like her even more. I smiled and repeated my words in English.

"Honorable," she repeated, giving the word deliberate thought. "Yes, the work at 920 is honorable but I seldom think of it in philosophical terms because what we do is so necessary, so urgent and immediate that I haven't time for abstract reflection. Miss Hudson, even with my superficial understanding of Chinese, I can tell you speak the language very, very well. What are you doing for the next several weeks?" Her abrupt change of tone and her question caught me by surprise.

"I'm visiting my sister, Ruth Shandling, until her first child is born, and I have nothing planned except to be available if she needs me." I recalled all the mornings I had without conscience left my wan and ill sister behind at home as I explored San Francisco. My words to Miss Cameron possessed more good intentions than truth. "Why? Is there some service I can provide for you? I'd be honored to help you in any way I can."

"My interpreter, Yuen Qui, is ill and needs several weeks to regain her strength, and while there are others of my girls that I could use in that capacity, I hate to take them from their work and studies. I could use someone with your knowledge of both Chinese and English to assist in several areas. It would be eight weeks at most, I imagine, and not constant. I might need you to spend some nights at 920, however, if you or your sister wouldn't object to your sleeping away from home now and then." She gave me another long, contemplative look. "I think you have the character for the work—or am I mistaken?"

Ruth, who had come to stand beside me, placed her hand on my arm and stated proudly, "Dinah isn't afraid of anything, Miss Cameron. Last year she spent fifty-five days in Pekin under siege from the Boxers, and I don't believe she turned a hair."

"That's not exactly true," I interjected hastily, "but my sister's point that I'm not easily cowed is true. My father once said that I lacked the necessary imagination to be afraid, and I fear he was right." Miss Cameron laughed.

"I don't need imagination, only a good ear for the Chinese language and an unapologetic temperament. I'm already late for another meeting, but do you think you could find the time to stop by 920 tomorrow?" She replied to my nod. "Good. Come sometime in the morning so you can visit the classes and plan to have lunch with me and my girls." To Ruth, she added, "You're welcome to accompany your sister, of course, Mrs. Shandling. We enjoy company." Miss Cameron looked across the room at a woman who stood by the door beckoning with a rather imperious wave. "I must go. It never does to be late when the subject is finances."

Later, going home, Ruth asked, "Dinah, are you sure you know what you're getting yourself into? Miss Cameron's work sounded dark and dangerous to me. I doubt if you've ever been exposed to what she and her girls have experienced."

"You and I lived in the same house in the same city for twelve years, Ruth. Are you telling me that you never noticed when one of our girls disappeared, that you never wondered what happened to her?"

"Of course, I noticed, but I never thought—"

"You never thought she disappeared because her father sold her into servitude or prostitution?"

"How could I ever have imagined something like that?" Ruth paused, then added on a less defensive note, "I never really considered it. Did you know about—?"

"Yes," I replied tersely. "I may not have had much imagination, but I had an awful lot of curiosity. Father had to explain the situation to me, what it meant for a daughter to be sold by her father and why a father would do such a reprehensible thing. The knowledge helped me view the importance of our mission and our school in a different way. If we could keep the girls under our watchful eyes until they were grown and if the girls received a basic education in domestic and academic skills, they could find work on their own. They wouldn't be at the mercy of a society that considered them expendable and valued them only as human currency."

"I didn't know," my sister responded sadly. "I'm sorry. I should have been more like you." I smiled at her, recognizing the sincere regret in her voice.

"One of me is plenty, Ruthie. You have never been able to conceive of anyone or anything as wicked, and that's not a bad thing. I'm sure such optimistic innocence is one of the many reasons Father protected you and Martin fell in love with you."

"Optimistic innocence," Ruth repeated softly, her tone giving the impression that the idea was new and not entirely welcome. She remained reflective and quiet the rest of the way home.

"I can't go with you," my sister told me the next morning when I appeared at breakfast ready for my visit to 920. "I want to, but I feel awful. I've been told that in another week or two this misery will pass, but until then I'm afraid I'm not able to be much company for you."

Ruth sat down at the breakfast table, took one look at the eggs and ham I'd set before her, turned an alarming shade of ecru, and disappeared quickly from the room.

Martin followed his wife out but rejoined me not long after saying, "I don't think Ruth is quite in the mood for breakfast this morning. Will it be like this until the baby's born?" The anxiety I heard in his voice made me feel unusually sympathetic toward him.

"Not typically. Just the first three months, I'm told. I'll take her some dry toast and hot tea when she can consider food rationally." He looked relieved and, to make conversation, I continued, "How are you enjoying your new promotion?" His expression took on a vague smugness that immediately erased all the good humor I felt for him and made me wish I hadn't asked.

"It's a lot more work, of course, and I'm responsible for the bank's clerical staff, that they get to work on time and carry out their duties properly, but Mr. Gallagher stopped by last week to tell me that he's pleased with everything I'm doing. He repeated that this position is a step on the way to bank manager. I have to believe that Ralph Gallagher asking us to join him and his wife as their guests at the city's summer cotillion is his way of moving me up the ranks."

"Provided I don't eat peas with my knife or talk about the benefits of labor unions," I commented dryly.

Martin narrowed his eyes at me, but he was growing used to my humor and only rejoined, "Yes, Dinah. I'd appreciate it if you would keep your preference for labor unions to yourself, at least while we're sitting at the table with the Gallaghers. The city's agitated enough about the topic without you stirring the pot."

I gave him a quick grin. "Of course, Martin. I wouldn't want to cause Ruth any more indigestion than she already has." My brother-in-law had enough good nature to grin in return.

Sacramento Street, as I later learned, had already gained the nickname "China Street" in honor of the red-brick building that sat innocently behind the numbers 920. Eyeing it from the curb, I thought it looked innocuous enough, a large, unimaginative, plain brick building of five stories, arched windows on each side of a dark front doorway, the words "Occidental Board of Foreign Missions" etched in stone over the door, and its only menacing feature the heavy bars that covered the windows.

My knock was answered by a petite Chinese girl with a radiant smile. The sight of her friendly face sent a pang of guilt straight to my heart with the piercing sharpness of an arrow. Her facial features resembled Mae Tao's and I knew from Miss Cameron's recent speech that while I had been enjoying myself these past few weeks, it was unlikely that poor little Mae Tao had been doing the same.

Miss Cameron greeted me with what appeared to be a bottomless reservoir of energy and good humor. Did she never grow discouraged? Was she always as fearless as she seemed? If appearances were any measure, the Mission Board could not have found anyone better suited for this work than the woman who stood before me, hand outstretched.

"Miss Hudson, I am so pleased you were able to visit us. Your sister—?"

"Is unfortunately indisposed this morning. Very indisposed, in fact." I gave a small shrug to express the helplessness of Ruth's condition, and Miss Cameron smiled her understanding.

"Well, we're glad you were able to leave her long enough to visit 920. Did you meet Lu Chu?" She motioned toward the girl who had ushered me into the house. "Our housekeeper, Miss Thompson, is away for the morning so Lu Chu has kindly taken on her duties."

"Hello, Lu Chu," I said in Chinese. "Your gracious welcome honored me." The girl's eyes widened at my words and she turned to look at Miss Cameron in surprise.

"Our guest speaks my language as if she were one of my sisters, Lo Mo, but she looks like you. How is this?" The girl spoke in soft, accented English.

"Miss Hudson has spent a great deal of her life in China, Lu Chu, and her ear for the language is much more exact than mine. Your Lo Mo would do well to learn from Miss Hudson."

"Oh no." The child's response was immediate and heartfelt. "No one is as good and wise as you." Then, fearing she had insulted me, she added, "I mean no disrespect to you, of course, Miss Hudson, but it is to Lo Mo that we owe our safety and our freedom."

"I understand perfectly and I completely agree. Your mother is indeed good and wise—but not so old, I think." I looked at Miss Cameron with a slight smile. "How did you come by the name Lo Mo—'old mother'? I can hear the affection in the words, but I would have thought Mo Chun a more apt name. Lo Mo is usually reserved for someone several years your senior—or is it just that to these young girls anyone older than twenty seems old?"

"When one of my daughters, Leung T'sun Tai, first called me Lo Mo, she was so very young that I'm sure I must have seemed ancient to her, though it's true I wasn't much older than eighteen at the time. For some reason the name stuck. I don't mind. I agree that being called Mo Chun would credit me with more dignity, but frankly sometimes I feel like a very old mother so Lo Mo is as apt as anything else."

For just a moment, I caught weariness and a touch of anxiety in her tone that answered my earlier musings. Donaldina Cameron was human and not as unfamiliar with discouragement and fear as I had originally thought. The name Lo Mo might fit her more than I realized.

"Now, Miss Hudson, let me show you around. Lu Chu, run ahead and tell the girls to have everything ship-shape for our visitor. We want her to be so impressed that she will be willing to stay with us for a time and fill in for Yuen Qui until she regains her health."

The little girl gave a blindingly beautiful smile and hurried away while Miss Cameron and I proceeded to explore the first floor at a slower pace. When I finally made it to the classrooms upstairs and to the sleeping rooms even farther up, Lu Chu had followed through on her assignment well. All the rooms were neat, the girls even neater. Most were in Chinese costume although a few wore skirts and shirt-waists, and all sat with their hands folded politely on their desktops, beaming a welcome from scrubbed faces. From the friendly sparkle of their black eyes, I would never have guessed that many had endured degradation and abuse on an unbelievably inhuman scale.

Later, Miss Cameron and I sat in the parlor, a tray of freshly brewed tea, cream, and sugar between us.

"So what are your impressions, Miss Hudson?" Miss Cameron eyed me over the rim of her teacup, waiting for my response.

"I sense," I answered slowly, "happiness in this house, and safety, and contentment. Yet on the faces of some of the girls, and truthfully, sometimes in your voice, too, I can see and hear that struggle and grief also inhabit this place." I set my cup down and leaned forward. "If I can do anything, anything at all, to increase the joy and diminish the pain, then I am at your disposal. Only I have an obligation to my sister, and I must be faithful to that, too. If you believe there is a way I can balance the two responsibilities, then I would love to be part of your efforts, even temporarily."

"As one of five Cameron sisters myself, I understand completely your duty to Mrs. Shandling and I guarantee not to abuse the time you volunteer at 920. I have other girls who can interpret if you are not available." She was going to say more but our conversation was interrupted by loud voices in the hallway just outside the parlor where we sat.

A woman's voice—an old woman, if I had to guess—cried in broken English, "No. Must come now. Now. Girl die." Then, slipping into Chinese, she added, "She will die anyway, but I won't have her spirit haunting me."

I glanced quickly at Miss Cameron and saw her lips thin and the smile leave her eyes as she whirled away from me and stepped quickly into the hallway. I followed her.

Standing just inside the front door was an old, bent Chinese woman. She tried to straighten as Miss Cameron approached but her back's deformity would allow her to do so only in a limited capacity. She was able to raise her head, however, and did so with a regal gesture that compensated for her lack of stature. The old woman spoke in a rapid, sing-song voice as she thrust a small white cloth toward Miss Cameron.

Miss Cameron turned toward me to ask, "I think I understood what she said but can you—?"

"Of course. She said the cloth is from a girl held in a gambling house on the corner of Tuck Wo Gai and Wa Sheng Dun Gaiby and that the girl needs help. The girl is ill. She sickens for home but they will not release her. They beat her instead. This woman says she has heard that the people in this house will help poor girls. She says we are to show the girl the cloth so she will know we have come to help."

Miss Cameron took the cloth. "Tell her thank you. Tell her we will do all we can. And ask her, Miss Hudson, if there is anything we can do for her since she is here."

The woman shook her head proudly in answer to the last question before saying, "I must go. If I am gone too long, they will suspect something."

I caught the fear in her tone and nodded. "Then, go. But first tell us this girl's name." The old woman shrugged off my request.

"I don't know her name. When the girls come into the house, they lose everything." Then she slipped out the front door with an awkward, unsteady step that I recognized as a sign of the ancient, vile practice of foot binding. The woman's matter-of-fact response chilled me. If even her name was taken from her, what was left for this poor, homesick, captive girl?

Miss Cameron dispatched a message to the police and asked me if I was able to stay into the early afternoon. "You will get a personal taste of our work at 920 if you can stay, Miss Hudson. You might as well see if it suits you."

"I'd love to stay," I replied, "and please call me Dinah."

"I'd return the offer, but Donaldina is a mouthful," Miss Cameron responded with a smile. "My friends call me Dolly."

I felt honored at the invitation but thought I could never call her by that casual nickname. Our ages were not that many years apart but something inherently grand about the woman made me believe she would always be Miss Cameron to me.

The message the police quickly sent by return hand assured us that two officers would be waiting for us at the corner the old woman had designated. Once she read the note, Miss Cameron calmly pinned on her hat, threw a lightweight cloak over her shoulders, and after asking Lu Chu to have a room and bed ready for a new guest, held open the door. I felt the adventure of the moment blended with a twinge of apprehension, but Miss Cameron looked neither excited nor afraid, only resolute and sad, determined to make this journey a thousand times if she must but still wishing with all her heart it wasn't necessary to do so.

Two men, both in plain clothes, waited for us at the rendezvous corner. The older of the two motioned us into the alley behind the buildings before asking in a low voice, "What have you got, Dolly?"

"A girl purported to be in old Wing's establishment. We've never been successful there before, Jesse, but maybe today's the day. This is Dinah Hudson, by the way, who speaks the language about as perfectly as a *fahn quai* can."

"Where's Yuen Qui?"

"Ill. I thought it was plague at first, but the doctor says not. He's ordered her off her feet for at least six weeks, and Miss Hudson has volunteered to fill in until Yuen's back to health." Miss Cameron introduced me properly to Sergeant Jesse Cook and after looking over his shoulder added, "Your companion is new, too."

"Dan's been pulled off the Chinatown Squad for a while and assigned to a problem on the wharf, so I've brought along young Colin O'Connor."

"Italian, then," Donaldina commented with a straight face, and we all smiled. Despite his name, I looked more Irish than Colin O'Connor, whose fair hair belied his green eyes and gave him a Teutonic look.

O'Connor caught my look and interpreted it correctly. Grinning, he explained, "My mother was from Berlin. Poor *da* never forgave her for bequeathing me this hair." Colin O'Connor looked to be around my age, a tall, well-built man whose suit coat seemed a little small, pulling as it did across his broad shoulders. A boxer, I guessed from his big hands, or a wrestler. A good man to have beside you in a fight and even more comforting because of the small ax he carried in one hand.

"I see you have a search warrant, Jesse, and we're already more conspicuous than we should be. Any longer and we might as well go home without even trying." Donaldina moved past the older policeman farther into the alley. "Show Mr. O'Connor the door that needs his attention."

After that, there was no more time for conversational speech for quite a while. Following a few powerful blows from O'Connor's ax, Donaldina was able to push through into a dark hallway with me on her heels.

"We are looking for a girl," I called in Chinese. "A young girl who may be ill. Here is your flag, child. Come out. Come out."

Several doors on each side of the hallway stood partially ajar, and O'Connor shoved them fully open with such force that some of the men that had been peering through the cracks jumped backwards with loud cries. One or two of the occupants ran shouting into the hall ahead of us and disappeared through other doors. The confusion, the hurrying shadowy bodies, and the racket of raised voices and crashing doors made the scene chaotic.

Donaldina held the white kerchief in front of her as she hurried into each room to examine its interior and contents.

"Nothing!" she cried with keen disappointment, "but I know she's here. I can see it on the men's faces. Where is that rascal Wing?"

I stood looking around the dim interior of a room crammed with crates and boxes as Miss Cameron conversed with Sergeant Cook in the hallway. I felt the same sharp disappointment I heard in her voice and was just about to join her in the hallway when a wrinkled mat caught my eye. To this day I don't know why I looked twice at a simple woven mat, dirtied with age and use. Somehow it seemed out of place, was all. Why would anyone place a mat in the middle of the rough, wooden floor of a room used to store old crates and barrels? The mat struck enough of a discordant note that I took my booted foot and pushed it to the side, exposing a trapdoor in the floor. I understood exactly what the discovery might mean and hurriedly crouched down to grab hold of the small rawhide pull attached to one of the boards. I could raise the floor board part of the way but hadn't the muscle to flip it completely open.

"In here," I cried, rising to go to the doorway to the hall where my three companions now stood. "I think I've found something."

It took Colin O'Connor only one strong jerk to open the trapdoor, and when he would have stepped down onto the ladder that was propped against the wall just inside the opening, I grabbed hold of his arm.

"No, you can't go!"

He looked at me in astonishment. "I'm safe enough. You needn't worry about me."

"Oh for heaven's sake,"—I didn't bother to hide my impatience— "why would I worry about a big, strong man like you? It's the child. If she's down there, what will she think when she sees you coming toward her? She'll be scared out of her wits. The rescue will be more frightening than the captivity. I'll go." Without waiting for response or permission, I tucked the white cloth we were to use for identification into my sleeve and sat at the edge of the opening, carefully placing one foot and then the other onto the top rung of the ladder. Then I stood upright, stepped down two rungs, slowly turned around and began to descend the ladder, grasping the wooden edge of floor for balance until I had descended too far into the darkness to use the floor as anchor any longer.

"I may not have a lot of sense, but I'm guessing you'll need this." At the last minute, O'Connor handed me a lantern, making the descent more of a challenge because I had to clasp it while also clinging to the ladder with both hands.

I was glad I had the light once I reached the bottom, however, because the space was black as pitch and cramped, the ceiling so low that I could not stand upright. At first, I felt a desolate disappointment because the room—if it could be called that—appeared to be empty, but then in the far corner I detected some kind of movement that drew me closer. What at first seemed nothing more substantial than a pile of old rags turned out to be a child, an emaciated, unconscious child whose only signs of life were fluttering eyelids and the shallow rise and fall of her bony chest.

"Dear little bird," I said softly, tenderly in Chinese, in case despite her apparent insensibility the child could hear me, "I am Qing and I have come to help you. All will be well now. Qing is here."

With the lantern swinging from my forearm, I picked up the girl's slight, featherweight form and slowly, awkwardly climbed the ladder until I was high enough to hand her body into Jesse Cook's waiting arms. When Cook stepped back, I heard him say something to Donaldina before Colin O'Connor reached down one large hand to me.

"Here. Let me help you." I didn't hesitate but reached up a welcome hand in return, allowing him to steady me until I once more stood above ground.

"Thank you," I told him as I reached down to brush the dirt and cobwebs from my skirt.

"My pleasure." Something unexpectedly warm in his response made me look over at him quickly. I couldn't read the emotion in his eyes and thought he might still be smarting from my earlier dismissive words.

"Mr. O'Connor, the tone I used with you earlier may have seemed a little abrupt——" I began, but he interrupted with a grin that suddenly made him look as Irish as a leprechaun.

"Miss Hudson, if your tone was abrupt—and, mind you, I'm not saying it was—I have no doubt I deserved the rebuke. Deserved it wholeheartedly and was honored to receive it from so estimable a young woman as yourself." For just a moment I found the man— his smooth baritone voice tinged with a rolling brogue, his handsome face, the admiration in his eyes—completely charming and stood there speechless until Donaldina, holding the Chinese girl, spoke from the doorway.

"Let's go, Dinah. Jesse will deal with Wing Chee, though no doubt the man will plead complete ignorance of how this child came to be lying under the floorboards of his warehouse. He's a slippery devil with a tong in each pocket." At her words, I forgot about the attractive young policeman next to me and went forward to take the unconscious child from Miss Cameron's arms.

"Let me carry her while you lead the way home."

Looking at the girl's colorless face, I admitted to myself that in a small part of my mind I had hoped this rescued child would—in an extraordinary, miraculous way—be my abandoned Mae Tao. But, of course, she was not. In real life, conscience is never mollified so neatly. Still, this was one less abused child, I thought, so I must be one child closer to finding Mae Tao. For once, I was happy that I did not have enough imagination to feel either discouraged or hopeless about the task I had set for myself.

Chapter Four

Once back at 920, I placed the rescued girl's unconscious form into the hands of a young, round-faced Chinese woman, who had greeted us quietly in the hallway with a demeanor that indicated she had been waiting for us. She reached out her plump arms without being asked, appearing neither surprised nor dismayed at the slight burden I handed her.

"We heard you were successful and already sent for the doctor," she explained to Miss Cameron.

Her words made me realize that information must travel as quickly among the Chinese in San Francisco as it had in our Chinese mission, where we had often witnessed a remarkable and covert ability for disseminating news among our Chinese congregation and community. How even the most private details of a quiet conversation could spread with such speed I never understood, but spread they did.

"Has this little one a name?" the young woman asked.

"I'm sure she does, but we will have to wait to find out what it is. Have Cook warm some broth and hot tea. The poor child is starving and needs nourishment." Miss Cameron was methodical and calm, obviously no stranger to such a situation.

"The tray was sent upstairs when you pushed open the front door, Lo Mo."

"Ah, Fei Yen, you are a treasure. You make my life much easier than I deserve."

Fei Yen's cheeks turned pink at the compliment but she did not respond, only continued up the stairs, the little girl's slight figure held gently against her breast.

To me Donaldina said, "You acquitted yourself admirably today, Dinah. I knew you had the temperament for this work. That necessary but undefined *something* shines from your eyes." I turned from watching Fei Yen climb the stairs, hardly hearing Donaldina's words.

"Will she live, do you think?"

In response, Miss Cameron placed a hand briefly on my shoulder. "I don't know, but she has a better chance of surviving here than in a cave under the floorboards of a gambling den. Be careful, Dinah. You must learn to be responsible only for what you can control and after that allow God to bear the weight and carry the burden. Otherwise, the work will crush you, and you will not survive in soul or body."

I gave her my attention then, catching something in her voice that spoke of past pain and she looked back at me with a direct, almost piercing, look. She did not continue with any additional details, however. Instead, she smiled and turned away, removing her hat as she spoke.

"Perhaps the lack of imagination in your character that your father once pointed out will be a blessing for you and protect you from the effects of mental exhaustion and nightmares. You lived through the siege of Pekin and don't appear any the worse because of that experience."

"I'm not completely immune to troubled emotions or bad dreams,"—no additional details from me either—"but I have a strong practical streak that generally keeps me from squandering time on useless speculation."

"A trait that will serve you well at 920." Miss Cameron's voice was again brisk and businesslike, the earlier telltale quiver of emotion I thought I had detected so completely gone I may have imagined it. "Would you like tea?"

Before I had a chance to answer, we both heard the heavy sound of the knocker against the wooden front door.

"That's Dr. Parker, I'm sure, and I want to spend some time with him. If you'd like tea, Dinah, ask for it in the kitchen and someone will be happy to get you a hot cup. I'm sure you could use it."

"Thank you, but I have to get home." I had just caught sight of the big clock in the hallway. "I had no idea it was so late." The knocker sounded again and I concluded quickly, "May I return tomorrow to see how the child is progressing?"

Donaldina spoke over her shoulder as she opened the door to the bearded man waiting on the step. "Yes, of course. Come anytime. You're always welcome. Besides, we need to talk further about your role here at 920 and your schedule." Then to the newcomer, "Dr. Parker, thank you for coming. She's upstairs."

As Donaldina led the man upstairs, I slipped out the front door, pulling it shut behind me and taking a deep breath as I did so. The past hours had gone by so quickly and the activity had been so constant and frenzied that I felt I must have stepped into another world when I stepped over the threshold of 920 that morning. With the familiar San Francisco sunshine on my shoulders, I needed to take a moment to re-gain my footing in the real world. *My* real world anyway, I thought, and knew I would no longer take the routine of my new life in California for granted.

When the Marines had marched into Pekin last August, rescuing those of us trapped there and scattering the Boxers at whose hands we had expected to die, I had promised myself that I would never assume a tomorrow. I would appreciate the present and the people around me. I would remember that I was only one small person in a very big world and that every day was a gift to be unwrapped and shared. Somewhere along the way, however, I had slipped back into the old, universal, and human habit of considering myself the center of the universe with my world the only real world and thus by subtle implication more impor-tant than anyone else's. But that sick little girl's world had been a pile of dirty cloths in a dark crawlspace so cramped I could not stand up-right, and Miss Cameron's world was a house full of girls who needed continual encouragement and affection if they were to overcome a past darker than anything I could consider without shuddering. This morn-ing had once more reminded me that we were all bound together by the fragile threads of humanity and mortality.

Deep in thought, I stepped into the street without looking and immediately jumped back, the driver of a heavy, horse-drawn cart shouting something rude at me as he narrowly missed knocking me over. The incident made me laugh out loud. Wouldn't that have been an ironic demise, knocked into the afterlife because I was meditating on mortality? I should be grateful I didn't often spend time in deep contemplation because if it were a regular pastime of mine, I'd very likely be dead already.

My sister waited on the front porch when I arrived home and wasted no time speaking her concern. "Dinah, where have you been? Do you know what time it is? I didn't know if I should contact Martin or Miss Cameron or the police."

Ruth's voice was sharp with worry and thinking that such anxiety couldn't be good for a woman in her condition, I put an arm around her waist and moved her inside, telling my story as I did so. By the time we reached the parlor, I had her full attention and she listened without interruption, speaking only when I had finished.

"Poor child. That man Wing must be a monster. How did you ever have the nerve to climb down into that dark space? I wouldn't have been able to."

"Of course, you would have. Remember the time we played hide and seek and you fooled us all by squeezing yourself into a barrel?"

"Yes, I remember, which accounts for my inability to tolerate small spaces to this day. You don't give yourself enough credit, Dinah."

"And you give me too much. Miss Cameron was in the hallway and I certainly wasn't going to let that giant of a policeman be the first person the little girl saw. I was the sensible choice."

Ruth made a small *hmph* sound that signified her disagreement but said only, "Are you thirsty? I have fresh lemonade and warm bread, too, if you're hungry."

"I'm starved," I admitted, following her into the kitchen.

"Apparently rescuing children from dire circumstances stirs up an appetite." I caught and returned the grin that accompanied my sister's words.

"Apparently, because I'm hungry enough to eat an entire cow. I'll try to last until Martin comes home for supper, though."

"Considering how late it is, you won't have to wait all that long." The kitchen held the unmistakable aroma of freshly baked bread, which Ruth pulled out of the breadbox and cut with a flourish. "Hopefully, this will tide you over for a while."

"What a little homemaker you've become, Sister."

"I must take after Mother because I cook when I'm worried. I remember the magnificent meals she would serve up anytime Father was away on uncertain business or when one of us was ill or in trouble."

I slathered butter on the bread and spooned on enough cherry jam to satisfy an entire Marine battalion. "If that's the case, Ruthie, I'll have to worry you more often. This is delicious." My sister smiled at the compliment and cut me another slice of bread.

Wednesday afternoon a tall woman with a kind face opened the door of 920 to my knock and greeted me without introduction. "Welcome, Miss Hudson. I was told to expect you. I'm Frances Thompson, by the way. Please follow me."

I walked up two flights of steps and entered the infirmary where the little girl from yesterday's rescue lay quietly. "She's very still. Is she—?"

I couldn't finish the question, and Miss Thompson answered quickly, "She awoke this morning and ate again. The doctor said he believes that with nourishment and rest she will recover completely." As I approached the child's cot, Miss Thompson explained, "Dolly is away right now, but she told me to expect you and to bring you up here as soon as you arrived, that you would want to know about the girl's progress."

"Miss Cameron was exactly right." I leaned down to place a hand on the little girl's forehead. "Do we know her name?" At my touch, the child opened dark eyes rimmed with long, black lashes and stared right at me. "It's all right," I told her quickly in Chinese. "You're safe now. No one will hurt you here."

The child continued to study me. Then, as if she had finally placed my face or perhaps my voice, she smiled and spoke so quietly I could hardly hear her. I bent closer and caught her words, "Thank you, Qing."

"What is your name?" I asked, and she smiled again.

"I am Suey Wah. You must have known that because I remember you called me your little bird. Only a very wise woman could know me even when I could not speak. You are Qing. I remember that, too. I have been waiting for you."

"Have you?" I straightened, smiling down at her bright gaze. "Only a very wise child could know I would be here before I ever arrived. How do you feel?"

"Hungry." She looked suddenly shy. "If it is not too bold to say so."

"It is not bold at all, just sensible." I turned toward Frances Thompson. "Our new friend is called Suey Wah, and she says she is hungry."

"Good. I'll leave you alone with her and arrange for something to be brought up right away," adding, "Please let her know that she may be disappointed because it will be very light fare. We've seen it before that a starved child's eyes are bigger than her stomach."

Soon after Frances Thompson left, Fei Yen entered with a tray that she set next to the child's bed. "I am told you are Suey Wah. I am Fei Yen. You are safe here because a kind father watches over this house. I and many other girls live here under the care of the great Lo Mo.

"Is Lo Mo the kind-faced woman who sat by my bed this morning?" Suey Wah asked.

"Yes," answered Fei Yen. "She is our mother."

"Then who is Qing?"

"Qing?" Fei Yen repeated the name with bewilderment. "We have no Qing here." The child brought out one thin arm from under her blanket and pointed at me. "This is Qing," she announced firmly.

"I was called Qing from early years," I explained quickly to Fei Yen. "An old man in our village gave me the name. I don't know why."

"Don't you? Well, I think it was a good choice for more than one reason." Fei Yen smiled at me, then turned to take a cloth napkin from the tray.

"I'll go now," I disengaged my hand from Suey Wah's surprisingly strong grasp, "and come again tomorrow. I know you will do as you are directed—eat and sleep and grow stronger."

"If that is your wish, Qing." The contented trust in the girl's voice humbled me.

"Yes, my dear little bird, that is my wish. Now let Fei Yen give you something to make your stomach stop growling. I believe you must have swallowed a dragon to make such a noise." Her little face creased into a broad smile at my weak attempt at humor.

"Good-bye, Qing."

"Good-bye, Suey Wah."

The formalities concluded, she pushed herself into a sitting position and reached for the bread even before Fei Yen could rearrange the child's pillow against her back and settle the tray in place on her lap.

"She's a tough little bird," I said in English.

"We are all tough little birds here," Fei Yen responded in English, standing and looking over at me, "and smart enough to recognize a safe nest when we see one."

Fei Yen's words made me realize that both she and the dainty Lu Chu I'd met yesterday had probably been in a similar situation to the little bird now happily slurping down broth. I felt humbled again because had I come from such a dreadful past, I doubted if I would carry myself with their same soft grace and gentleness.

"You'll let Miss Cameron know I was here," I said, stopping at the bedroom door.

"Of course, but she won't need to be told. When she left this morning, she told all of us, 'When Miss Hudson arrives, take her straight upstairs. She'll be worried about the child and won't want to spend time in conversation until she assures herself that the little girl is making progress.' She said when, not if, so she was quite certain of your arrival."

"Miss Cameron is very perceptive."

"Lo Mo understands people very well, but she seems to understand you especially well."

"Am I that easy to read?"

"When I look in your face, Miss Hudson, something of Lo Mo looks back at me. Perhaps that similarity allows her to apply the same insight to your nature that she applies to herself."

I accepted the words as a generous compliment and said so.

In return, Fei Yen dipped her head in a small bow. "The words were intended as a compliment, Miss Hudson," she agreed and turned back to Suey Wah.

Downstairs I said good-bye to Miss Thompson and the petite Lu Chu, who stood in the hallway next to the housekeeper.

"Miss Cameron will be sorry to have missed you today," Miss Thompson commented, "but I'm told we will see quite a lot of you over the next few weeks."

"I hope I can be of some small service." I pulled on my gloves and repeated my good-byes to both women.

I returned to 920 the next morning earlier than I had originally planned because at breakfast Ruth, with healthy color in her cheeks and sparkling eyes, announced that she felt wonderful and then asked if I could join her for a long-delayed shopping trip.

"Martin has promised both of us new gowns for the cotillion, and I know several establishments that carry the latest fabric and pattern books from New York. I can't wait to get started. I have an idea for you, Dinah, that will make you the new darling of San Francisco."

"I don't want to be the darling of San Francisco, Ruth," and then responded to the teasing look in my sister's eyes with a begrudging grin. "As you well know."

"Wouldn't you like to be someone's darling, though?"

"Only if I could be sure I'd be as happy as you and Martin." I sidestepped her leading question and continued, "I'm glad to see you feeling better and I don't want to waste the moment, but I would like to visit 920 and see how little Suey Wah is first. I'll go right now and promise I'll be back by lunch."

The distance between Grove and Sacramento Streets was not all that great and after two visits I had already become familiar enough with the route that I could take shortcuts that made the trip easier and quicker. I couldn't do anything about the hills, however, and when I arrived at 920, I was breathing heavily from the exertion of the incline.

A figure in uniform stood on the doorstep ahead of me, and I heard the heavy thud of his knock as I drew near. He must have heard my approach—no doubt my inelegant panting could be heard for miles—because he turned to face me, and I recognized the attractive face of Colin O'Connor, the young policeman from the Chinatown Squad.

"How do you do, Miss Hudson? You might not remember me. I'm—"

I stepped next to him and looked up at his face. "Of course, I remember you, Officer O'Connor, and pleased I am to see you." I slipped purposefully into an Irish inflection that caused him to smile broadly.

"You'll be making fun of my speech now, Miss."

I shook my head. "That was certainly not my intention, and I meant no offense."

"No offense taken." Before he could say more, Frances Thompson opened the door. She gave the two of us a look that while not exactly disapproving had a certain primness in it that bordered on the censorious.

"Hello, Miss Thompson. I'm afraid Officer O'Connor and I have accidentally descended on you at the same time," I explained hastily. "I've come to see Suey Wah."

"And Sgt. Cook asked me to check on the little girl we rescued on Washington Street and ask her a few questions."

At the officer's words, Miss Thompson's expression cleared. "Of course. I'll let Dolly know you're both here. Step inside, please, while I get her."

Colin O'Connor and I stood silently side by side until he finally asked, "Does she have a name then?"

"It's Miss Thompson."

"The child?" His incredulous tone made me laugh.

"Oh, of course, the child. Her name is Suey Wah."

"The words must mean something. From my short time on the Squad, it seems that most Chinese names have a meaning beyond the obvious."

"Suey Wah means water bird."

"Pretty. Like poetry."

"Most translations of Chinese names sound like poetry. The Chinese are a poetic, artistic people who appreciate beauty."

"You speak their language very well, Miss Hudson."

"I lived in China as the daughter of American missionaries for the last fifteen years."

"That would explain it then." We lapsed into silence again until Donaldina Cameron appeared.

"Dinah, I knew you'd be here, and whom have you brought with you?"

"Miss Hudson and I didn't come together," O'Connor explained quickly. "We just arrived at the same time. I'm Colin O'Connor. I was with Sergeant Cook on Washington Street the other day."

"Of course, now I remember." Miss Cameron put out her hand. "Forgive me, Officer O'Connor. My mind can retain only so much information before something drops out."

"I should have let you know to expect me, ma'am. Only like you guessed, when we confronted Wing Chee about the girl in his cellar, he acted so surprised you'd have thought we told him we found President McKinley there. I thought if the girl had survived and was able to talk, I'd ask her a few questions about how she got there."

"She has survived and she is able to talk, but don't expect too much, Officer O'Connor. She was very ill and starving for a long time and doesn't seem to recollect much about her experience. And the girls are often very reluctant to talk about what happened to them. The elements of shame and embarrassment limit their frankness. Still, you're welcome to try. I'd testify in court myself if I thought it would remove Wing Chee and that filthy den he operates from harming any more children. Come upstairs. The child has developed a strong affinity for Miss Hudson so if Dinah asks the questions on your behalf, Suey Wah may be more forthcoming in her responses."

"Hello, little bird," I said when I entered the room where Suey Wah recuperated. She apparently expected company, for she sat back against her pillow dressed in a clean cotton gown, her shining black hair pulled into two neat pigtails.

"Hello, Qing," the child answered shyly, her eyes suddenly lighting up. "Lo Mo said you would be here today, and I have been waiting for you."

"Do you understand any English, Suey Wah?" I asked.

"Only *stupid girl* and *quiet*."

"Then we will converse in your language," I said calmly, "because those are not words we will need to use. This is Officer O'Connor. He is one of the policemen who helped us find you." I added the last information because her eyes looked at the big man quickly and then furtively glanced away in a manner that indicated she was uneasy with his presence. "He would like to ask you some questions so he can find other girls and bring them to this safe nest. Don't be afraid."

Suey Wah raised her eyes to take a longer look at the policeman, examining him with a serious intensity that furrowed her forehead. "He is very big, Qing," she finally pronounced.

"Yes, he is."

"And very strong."

"Yes, he is strong, too."

"Is he your friend?"

I hesitated before responding, "I have only met him once, Suey Wah, so I cannot truthfully say he is my friend, but I believe he is here for good reasons and that he wishes to help other sick and frightened girls."

"He makes me think of other men who did not care whether the girls in their care were sick or frightened, but because *you* wish me to talk to him, Qing, I will." Having made her decision, Suey Wah settled herself more comfortably against the pillows and waited expectantly.

"What would you like to know?" I asked O'Connor. "She is willing to tell you whatever she remembers." Sitting next to the bed, I had to look up at him as he stood beside me, and I added, "I think you should sit down. She's already commented about how big and strong you are and standing up like that, you must seem like a giant to her."

Donaldina pushed a chair over to the officer, which he placed so close to mine that when he was seated our legs almost touched. Miss Cameron sat in a straight-backed chair positioned farther back and out of the way, an observer only, but I had no doubt her shrewd brown eyes would miss nothing of the exchange.

"Ask her how and when she got into San Francisco and how she came to be in Wing Chee's establishment. Ask her if she would recognize any of the people who were responsible for her imprisonment. Ask her what happened to her there."

Suey Wah's sad story came out in bits and pieces, a child betrayed more than once and bewildered by each betrayal. The youngest of seven children, she was the likely sacrifice when her father's crops failed.

"I was little and weak. My family was poor and we were all hungry. My father said I did not work hard enough to pay for the food I ate, and he could not keep me any longer. My mother cried and cried, but my father would not change his mind. He said one less mouth would mean more for the rest of them, and I was proud to do my duty for my family. I told my mother I was only a girl but I could do this brave thing. She was still very sad. I miss my mother."

I translated as dispassionately as I could, making a conscious decision from the start not to allow the girl's story to affect me in a visible way. The tale was not new to me, after all; I knew such things happened. Only it was different when I put this sweet little face into the story, more difficult to hear as her hand crept into mine for support during the telling.

O'Connor appeared surprised when I shared that the man who bought Suey Wah had told her father he would take her to the missionary school in Pekin because they were looking for kitchen servants there and were willing to pay for them.

"That's true," I explained. "We did buy children and at exorbitant, inflated prices. We feared what would happen to them if we didn't buy them. Most of the men who came knocking at the door were as unsavory as your Wing Chee."

But they never met the "Jesus women" from the missionary school, Suey Wah told me regretfully. They went on a boat, instead, many girls crowded into a small space, some of them sick.

"Two girls died of a fever on the same night. The man who ruled us on the boat, a man with straight dark hair, not bright hair like his "—she eyed Colin O'Connor speculatively—"wrapped them together in one cloth and dropped them into the sea. 'They will not be lonely now,' he told those of us who remained, but I think he was mocking us. Then he made us all disrobe to look at our bodies. He said he was looking for sickness, but when he saw one girl, a bigger girl, he took her away for a long time. When she came back, she was weeping. She bled in her private place. We were all afraid then." Suey Wah's hand tightened on mine.

I relayed only the key elements of her story in English to the listeners, but in Chinese I said, "Put that memory away, little bird. You do not have to be afraid any more. He was a very bad man, but there are no bad men here."

She looked at Officer O'Connor once more, then nodded as if assuring herself of his good intentions, and continued her story. When she and the remaining girls finally stepped off the boat, they must have been on the docks of San Francisco, but she could hardly have known that at the time. A man met the girls there and told them they had arrived in Gold Mountain, a rich and pleasant place, and that he had husbands for some and homes for others.

"We did not believe him," Suey Wah remarked simply. "We knew he was a bad man, too, like the others, but what could we do? We went with him. He brought us to a woman named Dow Pai Tai and she sold us to different places, some for house slaves and some to be daughters of joy. I did not see any of the girls again. I came to work in Wing Chee's kitchen, but I was little and weak, and I could not carry what I was told to carry. The master of the kitchen beat me. I was afraid all the time. An old woman in the kitchen told me about this place and about Lo Mo. She said the house was safe and the people kind. She promised to tell them to come and get me, but many days passed and no one came and I thought she forgot. I tried to do my work, Qing, even though I missed my mother and I wanted to go home, but the pots were very heavy. One night I dropped one and it broke and oh, oh, I was put into the hole!" Her voice shook at the memory and for a moment I rested my palm gently, wordlessly against her cheek for comfort. Suey Way heard what I did not say, smiled tremulously, and continued, "After a while, I knew I would die there. At first, I did not like the darkness so much, but I was very tired and I could sleep all I wanted. I thought about food for a long time, but after a while food no longer mattered. All I wanted to do was sleep. Until you came, Qing, and brought me into the light and then to this good place. And now I am here."

"Yes, little bird," I agreed, "you are here indeed, safe and sound." I turned to O'Connor. "What else do you want to know?"

I thought from the look on the policeman's face that he had been quite affected by her story, and he had to clear his throat twice before he spoke.

"Ask her if she knows the name of the man on the boat or if she heard the names of any of the men who were involved?"

But Suey Wah could not answer any of his questions, could only shake her head at every query, looking so sad at her inability to answer that I felt compelled to pat her arm and say, "It's all right, Suey Wah, that you do not know the answers to any of Officer O'Connor's questions. You have been very helpful." My words reassured her enough to allow her to smile.

"I will always be helpful for you, Qing. I will be your *mooie-jai* and do whatever you command." I stood to look down at her, her figure so slight that she hardly made a mound under the covers.

"I don't need a *mooie-jai*, little bird. You and I will be friends."

"Friends," she repeated happily. "That is a very good idea."

"Now it's time for this child to rest before lunch." Donaldina spoke briskly from the side of the room, and we all recognized the authority in her voice.

"Of course," O'Connor responded. He stood and said to me, "Tell her thank you for me. Tell her I think she is a brave girl and that I hope she feels better and stronger very soon."

I relayed his good wishes to Suey Wah and added some of my own, concluding with, "But now Lo Mo says you must sleep. I'll see you another day."

"Tomorrow?"

I hesitated. "Maybe tomorrow. I'll try, but I can't promise. Very soon, though."

"Tomorrow then," Suey Wah repeated with a contented smile, apparently not hearing my hesitation. Then I caught a twitch of her mouth and knew she had heard it quite clearly and was simply ignoring what she did not choose to hear.

Little minx, I thought affectionately as I left the room and knew I would be at 920 tomorrow regardless of any other plans I had for the day.

After saying goodbye to Donaldina, Colin O'Connor and I made the steep walk down Sacramento Street and stopped at the corner, each of us poised to go in a different direction.

"I don't think Suey Wah's information can have been much help to your investigation," I commented.

"Our best bet is to try to track down the steamer that carried her and the other girls," he began and catching the expression on my face quickly asked, "What is it?"

I had the sudden memory of the Pandora Steamer Two unloading its human cargo of Chinese girls and wondered if little Suey Wah could have been in the group of girls I saw on the wharf that day six weeks ago when Johanna and I had arrived in San Francisco, the group that had included Mae Tao. What were the chances that of all the Chinese girls in San Francisco, we would have rescued one who knew Mae Tao and might be able to help me find her? I shook my head at the idea. I believed God answered prayer—my being alive after the siege of Pekin was proof enough for me—but His answers were seldom so direct or obvious. Still, my father had always taught that life held no coincidence, that everything, no matter how insignificant, was part of a divine plan and an answer to someone's prayer, so perhaps I would discover a connection between Suey Wah and Mae Tao after all. When Colin O'Connor repeated my name, I realized I had been standing and staring off into space, a posture with which my family was familiar but which must have seemed like some kind of mental stupor to him.

"I'm sorry," I said. "I had a sudden thought."

"Is that what you call it, Miss Hudson? It seemed more like a vision to me."

"I don't have visions, and please call me Dinah." I almost told him about the Pandora Steamer and its huddle of little girls, but first I wanted to talk to Suey Wah again. My suspicions remained too speculative to be voiced.

"I will then, Dinah. Thank you. And I'm Colin to my friends. Well, I've friends that call me names other than Colin, but those would hardly be fitting for a refined lady like yourself to use." His irresistible grin accompanied the words.

"You'd probably be surprised at what I know and what I've heard," I responded, "but thank you for the compliment."

"This may seem presumptuous of me, but since we're standing here, I was wondering something."

"Yes?"

"I was wondering—you being new to the city and all—if you'd care to step out with me tomorrow, have a little lunch at the Poodle

Dog, and take a walk around Union Square. I know it's short notice, but I've got the day off, and I can't think of a better way to spend it than in your company."

"Are you sure you're only half Irish?" I asked, smiling up at him, enjoying the way the sun sparkled in his eyes. "You have the gift of charming speech, Officer O'Connor."

"Colin."

"You have the gift of charming speech, Colin."

"I don't deny it. But in this case I mean every word."

I knew I wasn't the refined lady he thought I was, but I found the idea of spending the day in this rugged Irishman's company to be a very attractive prospect. The last time I'd shared the company of a young man who admired me seemed a lifetime ago, a young Marine officer stationed in China who had monopolized me for several weeks before duty called him away. We'd written for a while following his departure, but with separation the interest faded on both our parts and then last summer I had ended up trapped in Pekin with other things on my mind, not the least being survival. I hadn't thought about that young Marine in quite a while but now wondered if he still served in the military, if he ever tried to find out what became of me, or if he had found another girl and never gave me a thought.

"I'd like that very much, Colin. Union Square is one place I haven't visited yet."

"Where are you staying?"

"I live with my sister and her husband on Grove Street, but why don't we plan to meet at 920? I'll need to spend some time with Miss Cameron first."

We agreed on a late morning hour, but before he stepped down the street, he turned back to me to say, "I was wondering something else, if it's not too bold."

"What?"

"What does Qing mean?" He stumbled over the name, which must be said properly as two syllables with appropriate emphasis.

"*Shee-ung*," I corrected with a smile. "Said one way it is the color for deep blue. Said another way and it means clear or pure. Many years ago I was given the name by one of the Chinese members of our congregation and it stuck."

"It's your eyes, of course," Colin observed simply. "Even I can figure that out." He smiled enigmatically when he spoke, making me wonder which meaning of the name he saw in my eyes. "I'll see you tomorrow then, Dinah." After he stepped away down the street, I took my standard shortcuts home.

When I mentioned Colin O'Connor to Ruth—doing so casually during our afternoon shopping trip—she ceased her scrutiny of a bolt of deep blue silk and stared at me.

"You met a young man who's taking you to lunch and with whom you will be spending the better part of a day and you're just now telling me? You're not supposed to make your sister wait for that kind of news. Really, Dinah, I don't recall you being this secretive before." Her muted outrage made me laugh.

"I am not secretive. I'm telling you now, aren't I? I could have slipped off tomorrow and left you in the dark about the whole thing. Maybe I put off telling you because I knew you would make exactly this kind of fuss about it. It's not a proposal, Ruthie, just an invitation to show me the city."

"But you like him?"

"I hardly know him."

"But you like what you know?"

"Yes."

"Is he handsome?"

"Yes. No. I mean not handsome in a storybook hero way, but he's tall and strong and he has very fine eyes. Very fine."

"He's Irish by the sound of it."

"Half. His mother's German."

"No surprise there. I believe half of San Francisco's police force and fire department are Irish. I don't suppose he's Protestant."

"Truthfully, Ruth, that subject never came up."

"Well, he might convert for you."

I could see her mental wheels turning and said sharply, "I'm having lunch with Colin O'Connor, not marrying him."

"Yet." When she spoke, I glared at her so long that she was forced to amend, "Or ever, perhaps. I know. Still——" She caught my eye and deliberately made a display of picking up the bolt of silk once more. "What about this color for your gown? It's almost a perfect match to your eyes."

My sister purposefully dropped the subject, but I didn't miss the calculating gleam that remained in her eyes for the rest of the afternoon. We might not have talked about Colin O'Connor, but he definitely accompanied us all the way home.

Martin joined us earlier than anticipated that evening, and after making the requisite admiring comments about the fabrics for Ruth's and my evening gowns sat down in the parlor after supper to read the paper—not surprisingly in Martin's case *The Chronicle*, an old-line publication of everything Republican and conservative. I had deduced early on that my brother-in-law did not have a progressive bone in his body.

Busy with kitchen clean-up duties, I was pleased to note that Ruth had drifted into the front parlor to spend time with her husband. Sometimes I worried about being an interloper in the marriage, although Ruth and Martin both assured me that had I not been visiting, Ruth would have been alone more often than not because of the demands of Martin's job so my presence was welcome and not intrusive at all. I thought that was likely true but still felt they might prefer some casual time together without me being part of the tableau or the conversation.

With the last dish dried, I took a final look at the kitchen to be sure it met Ruth's standards—I was content with a certain lazy order but not my sister, who liked everything in its place and refused to believe that a new baby would make a difference to her innate need for orderliness—when Martin appeared in the kitchen doorway.

An odd look on his face made me exclaim involuntarily, "Is something wrong? Is it Ruth?" He shook his head.

"No, nothing's wrong, but you have company in the parlor." Martin's expression indicated I'd become a stranger.

"Really? Someone from the home—from 920?"

"I don't think that's likely. He said his name is Mr. Pandora."

Now it was my turn to stare. "Jake Pandora?"

"He didn't give me a first name. Just Pandora. Would this be Mr. Pandora from the Pandora Transport Line?"

"Yes, I would imagine so."

"With whom you must have had some contact." Disapproval in his voice but no surprise.

"Martin, you needn't beat around the bush. Yes, I had contact with Mr. Pandora, and yes, I know you forbade me to visit his office, but I can't imagine it surprises you to know that I ignored you. I'm sorry, but Ruth will be the first to tell you that forbidding me to do something has the same effect on me that waving a red cloth has on a bull."

"Ruth doesn't have to tell me that, Dinah. I've known it for years. Shall I tell Mr. Pandora that you're available?"

"I'll tell him, thank you." My immediate thought was that he had come to share something about Mae Tao. "Is he in the parlor?"

"He's in the hallway. I wasn't sure about leaving him alone with Ruth. He has a look about him—"

"Yes, I know." I brushed past Martin and stepped out of the kitchen into the hallway, caught up once more in the absolute perfection of Jake Pandora's face as he raised his head to watch my approach. "Mr. Pandora, what a surprise," I told him, coming forward and extending my hand. "I never expected to see you again." He gave a wry twist to his mouth as he touched my hand briefly with his.

"I am well aware of that, Miss Hudson. You were very clear about your opinion of my morals at our last meeting, but as you can see, here I am." He looked briefly at the apron I still wore. "I've interrupted your supper."

"No, just supper clean-up. You've met my brother-in-law, Martin Shandling, but please meet my sister."

Pandora followed me into the front room and to me it seemed that the man suddenly felt awkward and out of place, desperately wishing himself anywhere but in the Shandling parlor on Grove Street. He was dressed much as he had been at our first meeting: dark trousers, dark collarless shirt, and dark jacket. Not that any of that mattered when you had the classical good looks of Greek statuary.

My sister did her best not to stare during the introduction and then we all four stood in a silent and uncertain circle until Jake Pandora addressed me brusquely.

"I'd like to follow up on our earlier conversation." He looked at Martin and Ruth deliberately before adding, "Privately."

Martin started to sputter something, but Ruth took his arm, saying sweetly, "Of course, Mr. Pandora," and pulled her husband from the room as he glared back at us.

"We'll be in the breakfast room if you need us, Dinah," concluding with a meaningful look at Pandora, "Very close. Right next door in the breakfast room." Apparently he thought I might have forgotten exactly where the breakfast room was located. When it was just the two of us, I sat down and motioned Pandora to do the same.

"You'll have to forgive him. Martin takes his duty as the male protector of the family very seriously."

"Clearly. Rest assured that your virtue is safe with me, Miss Hudson."

More's the pity, I surprised myself by thinking but said nothing, only waited expectantly for Pandora to speak. I knew from the odd look on his face that he had something he wanted to say, and that the words must come at his own pace and in his own time. I bit my lip to keep from blurting out the obvious question about Mae Tao and remained quiet.

"I was wrong." Whatever I expected to hear from the man, it was not an admission of error, no matter that his tone held little humility or apology. When I still did not speak, he continued, "After your visit, I thought it would be worth my while to check my facts. I figured you were just the kind of woman"—interfering busybody of a woman, he might as well have said—"to report the Pandora Two to the Port and Immigration authorities and not be quiet until you got someone to investigate. A bulldog of a woman who wouldn't let a subject drop until you got what you wanted."

"Thank you," I commented, keeping my tone purposefully mild but wanting to smack him. His tone left no doubt about his opinion of female bulldogs. Then one corner of his mouth twitched, and I realized he knew what I was thinking and was enjoying my reaction.

"I won't go into details, but I made my own inquiries and you were right. If you feel compelled to go to the immigration officials, feel free to do so. The Two brought in a load of Chinese girls in April and probably more on other occasions, all without my knowledge or approval."

I sat back in my chair and watched his face as he spoke, saw his chin lift as if he wanted to do battle with someone and caught the shadow of shame in his eyes as his gaze met mine directly. His regret and his grief—not too strong a word for what I read on his face—couldn't have been more obvious if he fell onto his knees and began to weep. Oddly, his words made me want to comfort him, to assure him that no great harm had been done and so give him back the defiant pride that I knew usually must characterize his demeanor. But, of course, I couldn't do that. Great harm had undoubtedly been done, and there was no way to ease the knowledge. I, who bore my own guilt for Mae Tao and for other trespasses equally as shameful, understood that truth only too well.

"I don't doubt that, Mr. Pandora, anymore than I doubt that you have taken the necessary measures to be certain the practice doesn't continue. Since you've conducted your own investigation, reporting the incident to immigration so many weeks after the fact seems redundant." This time it was his turn to search my face, looking, I believe, for mockery or disdain or disgust.

Finally he said, "Thank you," the words grudging but sincere. I couldn't decide if he was uncomfortable saying thank-you to a woman or simply unused to saying thank you in general. Either way, the words were a concession.

"In your inquiries, Mr. Pandora, were you able to track down the destination of the girls who arrived in April?"

"I'm working on it."

I thought of Suey Wah's wrenching story and wondered again if she might possibly have a connection with Mae Tao. "So am I," I told him. "Perhaps we should pool our knowledge and our resources."

I knew his first inclination was an emphatic *no* but perhaps past experience had taught him to think twice before dismissing me because he said instead, "All right. What and who do you know?"

When he spoke those words, Suey Wah's little face came clearly to mind, but I hesitated. This man was still a stranger and how did I know what his real motives were? I didn't think I had misread his apology, but I couldn't look into his head or heart and what if his motives had nothing to do with finding Mae Tao and everything to do with discovering who knew about his company's illegal trafficking in humans? I wouldn't reveal Suey Wah just yet, not until I had assured myself that Jake Pandora's intentions were honest and honorable.

"I have only a little information right now, but I think I may have discovered an eye witness to my missing girl's arrival. I'll know more by the weekend. What have you found out?"

He shrugged. "Not a lot yet, but like you I have some contacts I still need to talk to."

I almost laughed at his response because our mutual distrust was obvious in our carefully worded replies. For no reason I could name, I believe he realized the same and found a similar humor in each of us circling the other like two prizefighters just out of their corners.

"As I said, I'll know more by the weekend," I repeated. "How about you?"

"It's possible."

"Then what if we plan to meet at your office on Saturday and talk further then." He weighed the suggestion carefully before agreeing, looking for a veiled motive on my part or some undefined danger embedded in the plan.

I found his suspicious reluctance insulting and stood up abruptly, saying with poorly disguised annoyance, "One o'clock sharp on Saturday then, Mr. Pandora." He rose, too.

"Agreed, Miss Hudson."

We walked into the hallway and as I held the front door open for his departure admitted frankly, "I wouldn't have thought you had it in you to admit you were wrong. I hope you have no ulterior plan at work here."

He misread my words and meaning completely and responded with his own annoyance. "Your brother-in-law was close enough to rescue you if you were worried that I had designs on you. Just to set your mind at ease, I prefer brunettes."

I thought I was past blushing but felt a warmth in my cheeks that probably meant they were turning an obvious pink. I didn't know if the color signified embarrassment or anger.

I hope your investigative skills are sharper than your understanding of women, Mr. Pandora," I told him, recovering my equanimity and trying to imbue my words with a certain indifferent good humor. "I can't remember the last time I needed the protection of anyone or anything besides my own intelligence and wits."

I sensed that he had enjoyed making me uncomfortable, even for that brief moment, and the cynical humor in his dark brown eyes made me call his name as he stepped down onto the first porch step.

When he turned back to look at me, I said sweetly, "I appreciate your candor, Mr. Pandora, and I'd like to reciprocate. You should know that my preference is for fair-haired men in uniform." I paused, smiled, and added just before I closed the door, "Now you can set your mind at ease, too."

Martin frowned the rest of the evening, but I think it was Ruth's admiring comments about Jake Pandora that were the source of his irritation. My sister eventually noticed her husband's frown and went over to his chair to kiss him on the cheek.

"I was speaking only in general terms, darling," she told him. "Of course, no one can match either the strength of your character or your physique."

Martin brushed off her words with a sputter and a harrumph, but I noticed he regained his good humor after that and was good company for the rest of the evening.

The next morning Donaldina and I discussed how and when I could best assist the work at 920. She wanted to offer me some slight remuneration, but I couldn't take it as much as I would have appreciated having a little more pin money.

"I want to do this, Donaldina, and I don't want to be paid for my time."

"Are you sure? The Board already agreed to budget extra funds for your help. Don't allow any residual guilt you might feel force you into an arrangement that you will eventually regret and resent. I intend to hold you to your promises."

That morning I had shared with Miss Cameron my failure to follow up on Mae Tao's whereabouts and had admitted to her, my voice cracking, that I had no excuse for my lack of concern except my own desire for enjoyment. Donaldina had not judged or condemned me, but the steel I heard in her voice at the conclusion of our meeting made me realize that my story had generated in her a vague unvoiced doubt about my dependability and intentions. As unarticulated as her disquiet was and as much as she attempted to keep her tone level, I heard an unmistakable wavering of belief in my character as she spoke. I knew that the responsibility she carried for 920 and its inhabitants justified her concern, but the uncertainty I heard in her voice shamed and hurt me.

"I expect to be held to my promises," I replied. "I don't make them lightly." My words made her smile.

"You needn't take that tone with me, Dinah."

"What tone?"

"The one that dares me to challenge you, the same tone you probably used to hold the Boxers at bay for eight weeks." She stood up. "I believe our expectations are in complete harmony and that pleases me. We will see you next Monday morning and every Monday and Tuesday for at least the next six weeks. Beyond that, we will make additional arrangements for your services on a weekly basis, understanding that your sister's health may necessitate changes." She put out her hand. "It's a deal, Dinah. Men make them on a handshake. Why shouldn't women do the same?"

"Why, indeed?" I rose and grasped her hand in mine. "It's a deal, Dolly. You may rely on me." She understood the depth of meaning behind my words.

"I know," she answered simply, and the renewed confidence I heard in her few words warmed my heart.

Following our meeting, I went upstairs to find Suey Wah and nearly gasped when I entered the sickroom where I had last seen her. She was standing up fully dressed before Fei Yen, who was seated on a chair muttering and tugging at one of the sleeves of the child's plain shirtwaist.

"Suey Wah!" I cried. "Look at my little bird! Are you strong enough to be out of bed?"

"Oh yes," she responded, suddenly shy in my presence. "I am a very strong girl. Fei Yen and I wished to surprise you by coming down the stairs to you, but I fear my small arms have displeased Fei Yen because they do not fit this fine garment."

Clearly, the shirtwaist sleeves were much too long and Fei Yen, struggling to roll them up Suey Wah's thin arms in neat turns, finally gave up on the task, saying to me, "It is time for Suey Wah to join the other girls in chores and lessons, Miss Hudson. Lo Mo feels that the community is the greatest aid in the girls' return to good health. And Suey Wah must learn English. She is in America now. The doctor said being up would not harm her, only she must continue to rest every afternoon until she has fully regained her strength. Bah!" With the last impatient word directed to the stubborn sleeves, Fei Yen stood and put her hands on Suey Wah's shoulders, turning her to face me. "Your little bird heard you were here and wished to surprise you, and we would have done so, too, except for these large sleeves. Why is all this material necessary?"

Because I often asked myself that same question whenever I tried to fasten the many buttons at the bottom of flowing mutton-leg sleeves, I answered sympathetically, "I have no idea other than the fickle whim of fashion." I crouched down in front of Suey Wah and rolled up her sleeves with a quick and practiced hand. Leaning back on my heels, I smiled. "There. Will that do?"

Suey Wah held out her arms in front of her and eyed my handiwork. "Oh, yes, Qing. Thank you."

The appearance of her thin wrists that stuck out like two brittle sticks below the rolled-up sleeves touched me, and I moved quickly to take a seat on the edge of Suey Wah's bed, hoping the sudden activity would hide the emotion I felt.

"Suey Wah, I would like to ask you some questions." When Fei Yen would have left the room, I stopped her. "No, please stay if you can spare the time, Fei Yen. If Suey Wah cannot help me, maybe you would be willing to ask some of the other girls if they have the information I seek." To Suey Wah I said, "Suey Wah, I seek a little girl like you. I knew her in China for many years and her mother before her, and recently I believe I saw her on a dock in this same city to which you were brought. I fear for her. I fear she has been treated as cruelly as you, only—"

"Only no kind Qing has come to rescue her. Poor girl." Suey Wah's eyes, dark and yet bright in the beautiful way of the Chinese, looked at me sadly. "I will help you if I can, Qing," she reached out one small finger to my cheek, "but why do my words make you weep?"

Why, indeed, I asked myself, and did not try to explain.

When I said Mae Tao's name, I watched Suey Wah's face carefully, trying to catch even a glimmer of recognition. "She is small in stature like you," I continued, still hopeful, "but with a round little face and two rosy cheeks, plump like a pigeon. And she was not shy, Suey Wah, she was a bold, talkative little girl. Full of advice. Very sure of herself. Does she sound familiar to you?" Suey Wah's forehead wrinkled in concentration.

"At first it was hard for me to remember the trip across the ocean, Qing, but now I see things in my mind more clearly, like the boat and the men on the boat." Her voice faltered before continuing. "There was a girl among us as you describe. She liked to talk. Oh, she talked a great deal and she was very brave and she said she was going straight back to China as soon as she got off the boat. She said her mother would miss her. But I do not remember her name." She looked at me in apology. "I am very sorry, Qing. Perhaps her name was Mae Tao, but I cannot say. Somehow the name sounds familiar, but I can't say for sure. Many girls were on the boat all together and we were not allowed to talk very much. Then, after the two girls died, we became very quiet and spoke only in whispers so the men would not hear us. It was dark where we were kept, too, and after a while we thought only about food and light and being free from the boat."

"Did a man meet you on the dock when you got off the boat?"

"More than one man. We were separated and each man took some of the girls. The man who took me told us to hold hands and follow him. The brave girl I told you about was with me and I remember that when she tried to look around, he scolded us all. He was very fierce. We held onto each other and he led us to the house of that woman Dow Pai Tai. Oh, she was a very bad woman, Qing. Very bad. She made some of the girls cry."

"Did you see what happened to any of the other girls, especially the girl who liked to talk? She sounds exactly like the Mae Tao I remember."

"A man took some of the littlest girls away from Dow Pai Tai. He bought me, too, and then sold me to Wing Chee. I can't be sure but he may have taken your Mae Tao and he may still have her. He was a turtle man, they said."

I repeated the phrase, then asked, "What is a turtle man?"

"He led a tong. I heard someone call him a black dragon." Without thinking, Suey Wah lowered her voice when she said the last words. For her, just the name of the tong held power and menace. "At Wing Chee's I heard about this tong. Very bad, very bad, Qing. You must stay away from the black dragons. They are fearsome. Even Wing Chee was afraid of them. The look on his face when he said their name was the look of death. You must stay away from that tong!"

I squeezed her hand in assurance. "I will certainly stay away from those bad men, Suey Wah." I noted the high color in her cheeks and decided she had had enough excitement for one day. Looking over at Fei Yen, I said, "Now I think Fei Yen wants to take you to your lessons. It's time for you to start learning English, and here is your first word. Friend." I said the word first in Chinese, then in English twice before I asked Suey Wah to repeat it. She could not quite wrap her tongue around the *fr* at the beginning of the word, but I complimented her anyway before repeating the sentence, "Miss Hudson and Suey Wah are friends."

From Suey Wah's attentive reaction, I thought she was a bright, obedient child, quick to learn and eager to please. I felt a proprietary satisfaction at the idea and as I watched her walk off with Fei Yen realized how quickly I had grown fond of the child. I would have to be careful of allowing such emotion to rule my work at 920, recalling the sound of past pain in Donaldina's voice when she advised me to be responsible for only what I could control. From an honest look at the depth of my emotional engagement with Suey Wah—and after only a few days—I better understood the pointed advice. A progression of Suey Wahs and the retelling of her tragic story day after day with only minor variations would certainly take a toll on one's mind, heart, and spirit.

I left 920 in the late morning, the sight of Colin O'Connor's tall figure waiting on the sidewalk outside making me feel as excited as a schoolgirl on an outing. He wasn't in uniform but wore a fawn-colored sport coat over matching trousers and an open-necked white shirt. Very man-about-town. I had picked practical clothes for the day, anticipating a bracing breeze, intermittent June sunshine, and a great deal of walking, so my light blue shirtwaist and split walking skirt were unimpressive. At the last minute, however, Ruth had volunteered one of her most fetching hats, a small-brimmed, flat-crowned straw confection trimmed with feathers and ribbon. If Colin O'Connor and I had been contestants for a sartorial prize, he would certainly have won—I'd never had the opportunity to develop much of a fashion sense, although the sight of Colin O'Connor lounging against the corner of the building watching me approach made me suddenly wish I'd paid more attention to my appearance that morning—but at least I had Ruth's hat for confidence. My sister's contribution to the day was just the right touch, perky and pretty and feminine, its ribbon of deep blue a perfect match for the color my eyes took on in the sunshine. Until I developed my own sense of style, I was fortunate to have Ruth to dress me to advantage.

Colin straightened when I gave a little wave of my hand and called, "Hello. I wondered if we'd find each other."

"How could a man miss a girl like you?" he asked rhetorically in return and the admiring look in his eyes made me smile. "You look like those girls in the magazines."

"What girls?"

"Those Gibson girls they're called. The all-American girl." He turned, obviously intending me to walk beside him.

I fell into step next to him, saying with a laugh, "I think there's probably some irony in your saying that to someone who spent more than half her life in China, but thank you." I changed the subject on purpose. "What's the plan for the day?"

"We'll take the cable car to Union Square and enjoy the sights. Then I'm taking you to the Poodle Dog for some of the best beef you're ever going to have. Then I'll make sure you get home. I found out I'm on the beat tonight so we'll have to cut the day shorter than I wanted." He didn't sound happy about that fact, but when I tried to commiserate, he shrugged. "Two officers were injured in a brawl on Morton Street last night, and I have to fill in."

"I don't know where Morton Street is."

He gave me a sidelong look before commenting, "I'd think twice about a nice girl like you if you did."

"Oh, that kind of street."

"Yes, that kind of street. There's always trouble there for one reason or another." We walked a block north to Clay Street and stopped on the corner. "We'll soon be riding the very first cable car in the world, Dinah. Andrew Hallidie had it installed in 1873." The pride I heard in Colin's voice when he spoke about the cable car was repeated several times over the next few hours. Obviously, he knew a great deal about the history of San Francisco, but more than knowledge, I detected love for the city in his voice.

As we sat on the edge of the recently unveiled Donahue Memorial Fountain, the sun turning the fountain's water into tiny rainbows and glinting off the backs of the statue's huge bronze workmen, I asked, "You really love San Francisco, don't you?"

My question seemed to startle him. "Love it? Well, I've never thought of it that way before, but I suppose I do. I've never known anything else. My parents met here and married here and raised me and my brothers here. And my mother and da are both buried here, too. I suppose it's home."

"Do you live with your brothers?"

"No. There are three of us O'Connor brothers, but I'm the only one that stayed around. Sean went north to Alaska to look for gold and young Jamie had a hankering to see Mexico."

"Are you all by yourself, then, Colin?"

"I was 'til I joined the police. Now I've got a lot of brothers."

I caught the same proprietary tone in his comment about the police that I heard when he talked about the city and read him as a proud man of strong loyalties. I liked him the better for it.

Later, talking comfortably over lunch at the Poodle Dog, Colin asked, "So what do you think?"

"Of what?"

"Of the sights. Of the sandwich. Of me. You pick."

"Oh, I think the sights are splendid, the beef is as tender as you promised, and you are an excellent companion." I could tell my response pleased him.

"I'm not always going to walk a beat and live in a two-room flat at the top of Telegraph Hill, Dinah." He leaned across the table toward me, his green eyes serious. "I have plans for the future. There's a lot of money in this city and a lot of successful men. I plan to be one of them someday. San Francisco is a kind mistress for the Irish, begging your pardon for the comparison." I was intrigued by the confident ambition I heard in his voice.

"What exactly do you want out of life, Colin?"

He sat back in his chair not smiling. "Everything. I want everything."

"But who could possibly have everything?"

"Charles Crocker, James Phelan, William Tevis, Claus Spreckels—do you want me to go on?"

"No. I get your point. Well, good luck to you. I hope you get what you're looking for."

"I'd rather get what I'm looking *at*," he replied, meeting my look with an intent one of his own before relaxing with a smile. "A beautiful and intelligent woman like yourself deserves to be a rich man's wife."

"I'm not sure the life of a rich man's wife is everything it's purported to be," I responded thoughtfully, ignoring the compliment, "but I can't speak from experience. Although now that I think about it, I suppose our Chinese communicants must have considered our family to be rich as Croesus. Perhaps it's all a matter of perspective. Perhaps my sister's house on Grove Street is a mansion compared to a ten by ten hut with a dirt floor and a leaky roof."

"I haven't seen your sister's house, but a mansion is a mansion, Dinah. Next time we're out together, I'll take you around Nob Hill. Then you'll know what I'm talking about."

I liked the thought of spending further time with Colin O'Connor more than I was prepared to admit aloud. Like any woman of flesh and blood, the idea of a gentleman admirer held definite appeal, an appeal enhanced by the unambiguous approval I saw on Colin's face whenever he looked at me. The knowledge that he enjoyed my company gave our time together a certain energy that I found exciting.

"I haven't seen Nob Hill, so I'll look forward to a visit. My sister told me all about the mansions there, with horse stables bigger than her house and rooms encrusted with gems and marble brought over from Italy. It all sounds like the stuff of daydreams."

"Oh, it's true all right. You'll see." He stood. "Sad to say, I have to get you home now, but you'll see, Dinah. I promise." He infused the last two words with more than a guarantee for a second sightseeing trip, promising me something that he did not detail further and that I did not pursue.

Let events take their natural course, I told myself, and we'll see what happens. I could have warned him that it was never a good idea for a man to be too confident of my interest or his ability to engage it. I had been raised to be an independent woman, and I never appreciated an overt attack on that independence. I held it too dear and like virginity, I believed that once independence was lost, it was impossible to regain. That was something Colin O'Connor could learn about me over time, however, and I imagined the learning could be quite enjoyable for both of us.

Colin left me at the front door so my sister did not get the chance to meet him, but she listened with interest to my description of the day and with even more interest to my description of Colin.

"A touch of Irish brogue combined with a boxer's physique sounds like an attractive combination. And he helped save that little girl, you said, Dinah, so there must be a kind heart behind his green eyes."

"I don't know him well enough to say that's true, Ruth, but I'd like to think so. He was certainly touched by Suey Wah's story."

Ruth heard something in my voice that made her turn away from the stove to face me and ask, "Don't you like this Colin O'Connor?"

"I like him very much."

"Ah, so that's the problem."

"What's the problem?"

"You've always been like that, Dinah, cautious with yourself. I think you're afraid of trusting too much, but I can't for the life of me imagine why that should be. You've always been able to choose from an abundance of suitors and a line of admirers." She stopped in arrested thought. "You didn't have a secret heartbreak you're not telling me about, did you?"

"No, nothing like that, but I do like being sure about people before I entrust them with my confidence, and being sure about someone takes time."

"Not as much time as you think when you find the right person."

"But how do you know it's the right person? That's the problem I always run into, and I can't afford to make the wrong choice."

Poor Ruth. She started more than one sentence to explain the mysteries of love before finally giving up, saying simply, "You just know." At my skeptical stare, she added, "You'll find out someday. You just know."

It was the answer she always fell back on, and I was still waiting for something in my own life to substantiate it. Maybe, I thought, hopeful despite myself, Colin O'Connor would be the man to prove her point.

Chapter Five

On Saturday I expected to make the same trip to the Broadway Dock I'd made several weeks earlier when I had used my first full day in San Francisco to confront Jake Pandora. Surprisingly, Ruth felt quite comfortable with my visit to the Pandora Transport Company and didn't spend any time trying to talk me out of the excursion.

"You're dressed quite nicely today," she observed, examining my walking dress with an approving eye. "That lace jabot at the neck is a nice touch, and I've always thought there was something almost flirtatious about a flounce at the bottom of a skirt. And have you done something different with your hair? How unusual for you to spend so much time on your appearance! This meeting with Mr. Pandora must be very important."

I ignored her wide-eyed, too-innocent look and turned to face the hallway mirror in order to pin on my hat.

"I'd go with you," Ruth continued more seriously, realizing I wasn't going to respond to her teasing, "but if I want to get our cotillion gowns finished in time, I need to spend the day sewing."

I felt guilty that she should be slaving over my dress as well as hers, but when I told her so, she waved away my words.

"You know I've always enjoyed sewing, and the patterns I bought make it easier than ever to enjoy the latest styles. Wait until you see the finished products, Dinah. You'll be amazed." The look of pleasure on her face made me give her a quick, spontaneous kiss on the cheek.

"Don't spend too much time on mine," I cautioned. "After all, I'm just a visitor in San Francisco. These are Martin's and your associates, not mine."

"Hm-m-m. Well, that's true, I suppose, but every single gentleman who's anyone in the city will be there, and I intend to show you off to advantage. My expanding waistline will give me away immediately as a mundane wife aspiring to motherhood. On the other hand, I imagine many people will want to meet the beautiful and brave Dinah Hudson, and I want you to look the part. You never know who might fall immediately and desperately in love with you."

I was about to speak an unladylike retort when someone knocked on the front door. I opened it to a vaguely familiar face that took me a moment to place. "Casey!" I cried finally, then added with less confidence, "It is Casey, isn't it?"

He removed his cap to show a balding pate and grinned at me. "'Tis Casey indeed, Miss. I've got orders to pick you up and deliver you to Jake."

"Oh." I stared at him. "Well, that's certainly thoughtful of Mr. Pandora, but he might have asked first. I'm quite capable of arranging my own transportation."

"No doubt about that, Miss. Only now that I'm here, it would be a sad waste of time and effort if you didn't take advantage of the offer of my cab. Fare's all paid for, too. You can just enjoy the ride."

Behind me, Ruth pushed a short jacket at me, saying, "He's right, Dinah. Go on. Isn't that thoughtful of Mr. Pandora?"

I made a sound that bordered on a snort and grumbled, "More a guilty conscience than thoughtfulness, I'd say," and then felt guilty myself because I knew I hadn't misread the sincere regret in Jake Pandora's eyes when he had admitted his mistake about Mae Tao. I had my own remorseful conscience, besides, and added more charitably, "I suppose it is thoughtful, though I still wish he'd have shared his intention with me. What if I'd already left for the Dock? I'm not completely incapable of independent thought and action."

Ruth patted me on the shoulder as she pushed me through the front door. "Of course, you're not," she agreed soothingly. In her voice I heard how my sister would one day sound when dealing with a pouting child. "No one is doubting your abilities, Dinah. Not me. Not the gentleman who's driving the cab. And I'm sure not Mr.

Pandora, either." She gave a final pat to my shoulder. "Martin is coming home for a late lunch today so try to be back in time to eat with us. Good-bye." With that, Ruth stepped back inside the house and firmly shut the door.

Casey—apparently a man with a natural savvy about women's moods—wordlessly helped me into the cab before taking his own seat. That trip I didn't spend as much time as usual admiring the thriving streets of downtown San Francisco or absorbing its boisterous energy. Instead, I was considering what I could—or should—tell Jake Pandora. Should I share my speculation that Mae Tao and Suey Wah had arrived together? I could not be absolutely sure, and yet I felt an almost unnerving certainty that it was so.

When we arrived at the base of the steep alley where the Pandora Transport Company was located, Casey offered me a hand down. "I'll be right here, Miss, waiting for you, so take as long as you need."

"I'm Dinah, Casey, not Miss, and thank you."

"You can thank Jake. His idea, not mine. I'm getting my regular fare, and if I know anything about Jake Pandora, a generous tip besides. Not that I don't enjoy carrying you around San Francisco, of course. "

"I can see that the pleasure of my company and a generous tip would be about as much excitement as a man could stand," I remarked dryly, picking up my skirts and beginning the climb up the alley. Behind me I heard Casey chuckle.

Jake Pandora stood in the transport company doorway waiting for me. He looked cool and relaxed—or he may only have seemed so by comparison with me. The exertion of the climb combined with the constricting corset I'd donned that morning for no reason except vanity made me pant indelicately, and the Bay breeze and damp morning fog had loosened tendrils of my hair, which had been pinned into a becoming coiffure when I had left the house earlier. In exasperation, I pushed the loose curls behind my ears and unwittingly knocked my hat crooked in doing so. All this Jake Pandora observed steadily and without a word until I stood in front of him.

Then, with a perfectly expressionless voice, he commented, "Next time Casey can deliver you right to the door." I hesitated for just a moment, knowing an implied insult when I heard one, but couldn't help myself. I laughed out loud.

"I found my sea legs easily enough, but the hills of San Francisco are more of a challenge than the entire Pacific Ocean."

"Maybe you need to get out and about more."

"Maybe I need to stop being so vain and get rid of the confounded corset." I spoke without thinking and looked at him quickly to see his reaction. Corsets were not usually part of public conversation.

"That seems a sensible idea to me, Miss Hudson, but not right here and now, if you don't mind." He moved to the side and I entered the storefront.

"Rest assured, Mr. Pandora, that when I do break loose from the constrictions of polite society, I will do so as far from you as possible so as not to offend your delicate sensibilities." I could tell he wanted very badly to smile, and for a moment he looked as young and natural as I'd ever seen him.

Perhaps somehow able to read my thoughts on my face and unhappy at being considered normal, he scowled and abruptly asked, "So what kind of information do you have for me?"

Since I had intended to steer the conversation, I was annoyed that he had initiated the topic and responded cautiously, "I'm fairly certain I've located one of the girls who came over on the Pandora Two. Because she was mistreated, however, she's been very ill and her memory is shaky at best. I think with time she may be able to tell me more about the men who made the arrangements for the girls and the ones who met the ship. There's a man named Wing Chee and a woman called Dow Pai Tai involved, but they don't appear to be the instigators of this trade in children. Apparently they take possession of the girls and then pass them along to others for a price."

"You're right. Old Wing and the madam Dow Pai Tai are not the instigators. I'm sure they earn a tidy profit from the enterprise, but the men who had the idea to start with, who fund the ventures, and who are making a fortune from female slaves aren't Chinese. They're among the cream of San Francisco society, and they work very hard to keep their identities hidden."

"How do you know that?" I tried not to sound skeptical or shocked that people my brother-in-law admired or to whom my sister had introduced me might be responsible for buying and selling little girls, but I found the idea almost too incredible to believe.

"I had a talk with Ivan Fletcher."

"Fletcher?"

"The pilot of the Pandora Two—or I should say the former pilot."

"And this Ivan Fletcher is credible?"

"He was at the time." Something in Pandora's tone made me give his face a closer inspection.

"Ah, I see. That would account for the fading bruises along your cheekbones."

"Yes," he responded. "That would. I persuaded Fletcher that I was serious about my questions, and he should be just as serious about his answers." I recalled the mocking expression in the eyes of the man I'd spoken to on the dock the day I arrived. Ivan Fletcher, I was sure, and a man who would certainly need to be persuaded to remove the smirk from his face and the swagger from his walk.

"Good for you. Was he able to name names?"

"Only old Wing Chee."

"And what did old Wing Chee have to say? I'm sure your investigation didn't stop with Mr. Fletcher."

"I've known Wing Chee as long as I've been in California and whenever he's called to account, he slips into speaking Chinese and acting all ignorant and innocent about what's going on in his own house. He's a wily old bastard." Pandora flushed slightly and started to apologize.

"I've heard much worse, Mr. Pandora, and it will slow matters up considerably if you feel obligated to apologize every time you slip into the language of the docks. I'll keep talking about corsets and you can keep talking about bastards and we'll both be happy. I speak and understand Chinese fluently. Why don't you take me along with you for a visit to Wing Chee next time?"

"I don't think it's a place where you'd be comfortable."

I recalled a dark subterranean cavern under a wooden floor in Wing Chee's warehouse and a girl so ill and emaciated I at first mistook her for a pile of rags. "Then you've made a mistake in judgment, Mr. Pandora." My tone implied *another* mistake in judgment, but I refrained from saying so aloud. "You really should stop making assumptions about me. I visited his establishment once already but did not have the opportunity to meet Mr. Wing Chee personally at the time. I'm thrilled that I might be able to correct that omission, and I assure you I'll be perfectly comfortable. You tell me where and when and I'll be there. Is that the best way to find out who's profiting from the import of Chinese girls?"

"I don't know if it's the best way, but it's one way. Think of it as a puzzle, Miss Hudson. Slip one piece into place and it leads to another and then to another and pretty soon you have the whole picture."

"Well," I volunteered thoughtfully, "In a few weeks, my sister is making me rub elbows with the cream of San Francisco society at something called the summer cotillion, so I'll pay attention to what I see and hear there. I know wicked men don't wear the word *villain* embroidered on their cuffs, but champagne sometimes makes interesting conversation." I paused a moment, then asked bluntly, "I know why this matters to me, but why do you continue to care about this so-called puzzle? I told you I wouldn't report your transport line to the authorities, and I meant it. You're free and clear. Why are you staying involved?"

"Someday the Pandora name will be a household word because I intend for my steamship line to grow as San Francisco grows. What my children will inherit will be a successful and profitable business without the shadow of human slavery as part of their inheritance."

His words held a simple sincerity I didn't doubt, but I found my-self distracted by the inheritance part of his little speech. Somehow I hadn't pictured Jake Pandora married, let alone a father. The idea surprised me with a quick pang of disappointment.

"I see." I couldn't help myself. "How many children do you have?"

"None that I know of. Yet."

"Then your planning for the future is certainly admirable. What's our next step?"

"I'd like to talk to that little girl you mentioned. What's her name and where is she?"

"Suey Wah." I answered without thinking and stopped abruptly at the words. For no reason I could explain, I was suddenly reluc-tant to say more. What did I really know about this man? He said the right things, but what if he had motives of which I was completely un-aware? What if he were not as ignorant of the human cargo aboard the Pandora Two as he pretended to be? What if my saying her name had already endangered Suey Wah? I could have kicked myself for speaking thoughtlessly.

Jake Pandora did not say a word as all these thoughts ran through my head, and after a long pause, he commented, "I see. Well, I sup-pose there's no reason you should trust me, but I'm disappointed, Miss Hudson. I thought you were a woman unafraid of risk."

"I am when it comes to my own well being," I replied, scrambling for a response, "but not when it comes to others' safety, especially children." I refused to give the man the satisfaction of knowing that his apparent ability to read my mind had completely disconcerted me.

"A fearless woman then." The anger I felt at Pandora's offhand comment was totally out of proportion to his light words and slight touch of scornful disdain, and I believe my fierce and heated response surprised him. I know it surprised me.

"I never said I was fearless and I never will. I know better," Hearing the tremor in my voice, I took a breath. "I hardly know you, Mr. Pandora, so I think it's premature to have you meet my only witness.

Let's join forces against Wing Chee first and then we'll see. I should tell you I'm not always home and available. I'm doing some volunteer work."

"At the Mission Home for Oriental Girls on Sacramento Street. I know."

"How do you know?"

"I asked around," he replied. "How else would I have found that out? You're not a woman people forget." From his tone, I didn't mistake the comment for a compliment, and again I felt a vague uneasiness about what Pandora knew and how and why he knew it.

"So you must also know that I'm telling the unvarnished truth about my proficiency in the Chinese language. If for no other reason than your children's inheritance, you and I should visit Wing Chee together."

He shrugged and said, "All right. If you think you're up to it. I agree that I could use some assistance with the language. It will have to be a time when he doesn't expect us. I'll send word, either to your home or to the mission. I can figure out where to find you." Pandora eyed me. "In case you think you've put me in my place, you should know that spending time with a woman who doesn't trust me isn't an entirely new experience."

I smiled at that and picked up my skirts, preparing to make the less strenuous downhill walk to the bottom of the hill where I hoped Casey still waited with his cab. If Pandora's words *I can figure out where to find you* caused a tiny shiver, I didn't let it show.

"I don't doubt that at all, Mr. Pandora. Not at all," I said and stepped past him into the street. "In fact, I suspect it's more the rule than the exception. You let me know when we can surprise Wing Chee. I'll wait to hear." I looked back, but he had disappeared into the storefront's dim interior. I thought he might already be regretting our loose partnership, but I had no intention of allowing Jake Pandora to wiggle out of this arrangement. The idea that some of the city's palatial mansions Colin O'Connor so admired might have been built on the thin, pale bodies of little girls made me so furious I believed I could tear the buildings down with my bare hands. Since that seemed an unlikely possibility, however, I would be just as content with exposing the unscrupulous means that had been used to afford those grand houses. Let the bricks fall where they may.

I had promised Donaldina Cameron that I would be at her disposal for the next several weeks and she was pragmatic enough to hold me to my words without apology. Mondays and Tuesdays I was kept busy with Mission activities and the days always sped by. I spent additional afternoons at 920, too, and sometimes accompanied Miss Cameron to meetings with lawyers and city officials. Jake Pandora's words colored every introduction, however, and I never met a man, no matter how prestigious or educated, that I didn't wonder if he were involved in the slave trade of children. I had lost a measure of innocence and was glad of it. Naiveté had no place in opium dens and brothels.

Rescue requests like the one on which I had discovered Suey Wah were rarer than I had originally thought, and when I expressed my disappointment to Frances Thompson, she responded, "Dolly and I were just breathing a sigh of relief at the quiet, which probably means we'll soon be in for a rush of activity. That's usually how it works. Don't get too complacent, Dinah."

She was right, but the prophesied activity wasn't what I had expected. One afternoon, I was left in charge while Miss Cameron visited an influential judge and Frances Thompson slipped out to pick up a few kitchen commodities at a local shop. It was the first time I was solely responsible for the house and its inhabitants, and my concern must have shown because Frances stopped pulling on her gloves long enough to pat me on the shoulder.

"It's the middle of a bright Wednesday afternoon, Dinah. Don't look so worried. How many days did you survive the siege of Pekin?"

"It's not the same thing."

"My point exactly. I'm taking Fei Yen with me, but Lu Chu will know what to do if you have any questions. Don't let her frail looks deceive you. She's a sturdy helper to everyone in the house. Dolly counts on her and so do I, so I'm leaving you in her capable hands, not the other way around." She smiled at her little joke as she departed.

While the older girls worked at their domestic chores upstairs, practicing their small stitches on torn bed linen or trying their hands at knitting, Lu Chu taught an English lesson to a handful of younger children, including Suey Wah, around a table in the first floor classroom. I seemed, in fact, superfluous to the operation of the house. So much for the heavy mantle of responsibility, I thought, at exactly the moment I heard the thud of the knocker on the front door.

"I'll get it," I called, conscious of a little thudding of my own in the general area of my heart. What if this were a request for a rescue? Should I go alone? Should I leave the girls on their own? Should I contact Jesse Cook and how did I reach the sergeant? All my questions were unnecessary, however, because I wasn't being summoned to a rescue. Instead, I opened the door to face a rotund Chinese man and a pale, thin, bearded man dressed in a black suit and hat that gave him the look of an undertaker, although I soon discovered there was nothing gentle or solicitous in the bearded man's character. In one hand he held an envelope that he waved in front of my face like a fan.

"Miss Donaldina Cameron?"

I took both men in an instant dislike and replied, "Miss Cameron is away," planting myself firmly in the doorway and resisting the impulse to shut the door in their faces. I could tell from the triumphant expression that crossed their faces at the news of Donaldina's absence that they were not there for any good cause.

"My name is Quentin Farmer, attorney at law, and I represent Mr. Lin Chanyu here. May we come in?"

"You've caught us at an inconvenient time, I'm afraid. Perhaps you could come back when—"

"Miss—what did you say your name was?"

"I didn't say, but it's Dinah Hudson."

"Well, Miss Hudson, we're here on important legal business that involves one of the girls in this house, a girl kidnapped from her legal guardian, Mr. Chanyu here, and I have in my hand a court order that commands you to turn that girl over to Mr. Chanyu immediately."

Looking at the man's smirking face, I thought that I would rather cut off a finger than turn any of the inhabitants of 920 over to him or his equally disreputable companion, but at the same time, I didn't want to be the cause of a legal scandal involving the mission. With a reluctance I tried to hide, I ushered the men inside and into the small waiting room immediately off the foyer. Taking the envelope from the lawyer's hand, I slid out the papers, read the name printed in the heading, and gave a quick cough to cover my gasp.

"Why do you believe this Suey Wah is here at 920?" I asked in a purposely expressionless tone.

I saw a quick glance pass between the two men before Farmer answered, "Mr. Chanyu heard from some of his relatives in Chinatown that his fiancée had been taken away by a white woman and was being held against her will, kept from her loving husband-to-be."

I eyed the Chinese man with disdain. If he was a loving husband-to-be, then I was the recently deceased Queen of England, and legal scandal or not, I was not about to turn my Suey Wah over to this pair of scoundrels.

"I'm new here, Mr. Farmer, so I'll have to see if we have a resident by the name of—" I pretended to glance again at the document I was holding "—Suey Wah. Please have a seat while I check." Quentin Farmer did not sit down.

Instead, he reached and took the paper from my hand, speaking sternly as he did so. "Don't try any tricks, Miss Hudson. I've been here before, and I know what this place is capable of. Turn over Suey Wah without delay or I will summon the two policemen I left waiting outside to conduct a legal search for the girl. When they find her—and they will find her, Miss Hudson—I will have them arrest you for being in contempt of a court order. I can tell you that a refined woman like yourself would not enjoy spending time in jail. I won't enumerate the unsavory details out of respect, but it's hardly a place for ladies."

I wanted to tell this insufferable man that I'd spent several weeks of a summer as hot as Hades surrounded by an army of fanatical Chinese soldiers who shrieked the unrepeatable details of what they planned to do with all foreigners once they got their hands on them. I did not change clothes for over five weeks straight, and I ate roasted rodents with lip-smacking delight. Compared to that experience, the possibility of spending time in a California jail was no more intimidating than breaking a fingernail. I didn't say any of that, of course. Instead, I tried to look appropriately cowed as I exited the room.

"Lu Chu." I pulled the girl aside from her classroom lessons and told her about the men in the hallway waiting room.

"They have tried this before, those wicked men." For a moment Lu Chu's delicate face took on the look of a gorgon, and I saw what Frances Thompson had meant about the girl being both sturdy and capable. An understatement, really.

"I had a very bad feeling about them from the start," I replied, "but the document seems legitimate enough, and I have no doubt we'll have policemen in here in a moment. That Farmer isn't about to give me time to hide Suey Wah. Suey Wah, come with me."

My little friend, who had been sitting at the table with the other girls, came to me at once and put her hand in mine trustingly. I pulled her out of the room and into the kitchen. Desperately looking for a hiding place, I saw the big sacks of rice in the pantry at the same time I heard men's voices at the front door.

"Crawl under the shelf behind those sacks," I directed, "and be very small and quiet. Do not show yourself, even if someone calls your name. I will come and get you when the time is right. Trust me, Suey Wah."

She smiled, said quietly in Chinese, "I know how to be very small and quiet, Qing," and quickly disappeared into the pantry. I pulled its door shut, then went out the rear door of the kitchen and up the back steps to the second floor. I quickly crossed the second floor hallway and descended the front staircase to the foyer where two police officers with passive expressions stood listening to Quentin Farmer order them to search the house for a Chinese girl named Suey Wah.

"There is no Suey Wah here," I told the men indignantly as I descended the steps. "How dare you intrude like this!"

"Of course, she's here," Farmer told the officers, ignoring my protests.

One of the policemen asked sensibly, "What does she look like?" which caused Farmer to hesitate. He turned to Lin Chanyu with a questioning look. When the Chinese man shrugged his ignorance, Farmer sputtered, "She's little. She's Chinese. Find her."

The two policemen looked at each other with what appeared to be weary resignation before one of them turned toward me to say with apology, "We're sorry about this, Miss, but his paperwork is in order."

"Of course, my paperwork is in order. I'm an attorney." Farmer eyed me with dislike as I stood on the steps. "Try upstairs first. I'll bet she was up there trying to hide the girl under a bed." As the men tramped upstairs, I was grateful my ruse was at least initially successful. By coming down the front stairs, Farmer had assumed I'd been on one of the floors above. Perhaps by the time they made it down to the kitchen, they would all have tired of the search.

Despite the seriousness of the situation, I had a hard time not snickering at the look on Quentin Farmer's face when he stepped into the large room where the older girls sat at long tables sewing. For the first time it dawned on him that finding one single Chinese girl among a bevy of Chinese girls might prove more difficult than he had first thought, especially when he hadn't the slightest idea what his quarry looked like.

All four men entered the room and stopped abruptly, the police officers turning toward Farmer and asking, "Do you see her here?"

"I don't know," Farmer sputtered. "She's not my bride-to-be. What do you say, Chanyu? Is she here?"

The fat man stepped up to the table and in Chinese asked the first seated child, "What is your name, girl?"

She turned to look at me and when I nodded my permission, she quietly responded, "Xin Tu."

"And is one of your friends here named Suey Wah?"

"I know of no Suey Wah here," the girl answered.

"What did she say?" Farmer asked, obviously irritated that he could not follow the conversation.

I interrupted Lin Chanyu's halting reply. "She said she knows of no Suey Wah here, a fact I shared with you earlier, as you'll recall." I turned toward the two policemen standing to the side. "Really, officers, isn't this a fool's errand? There's no Suey Wah here, and all you're doing is frightening these girls, who have already had more than enough fear in their young lives."

The older of the two replied, "We're sorry, Miss, but we have to uphold the law. We'll just take a look around, and then we'll be gone."

In the meanwhile Chanyu had made his way around the table and returned to say to Farmer, "None of these girls is the one we're looking for."

"I know there are more girls somewhere." Farmer glared at me. "Don't try to hide it."

The policemen had exited, and I could hear their heavy steps in the hallway as they went from room to room on the floor.

"I'm not trying to hide anything." I glared back at him. "Our very young girls are at their lessons in the downstairs classroom. Is Mr. Chanyu planning to wed a child?"

"It is our custom—" Chanyu began, and I interrupted sharply, "You don't need to tell me about your customs, you old fraud. I know more about them than you do about this girl you're seeking, I can tell you that."

Farmer, who had apparently taken me into the same dislike I felt for him scolded, "Your tone is offensive, Miss Hudson."

"You are offensive, Mr. Farmer," I retorted and flounced out of the room in time to collide with the two policemen, as they returned.

"We'll take a look at the floors above, Miss, and then meet you downstairs."

As the officers went up the next flight of stairs, Farmer and Chanyu followed me down the steps to the front foyer. Farmer turned in the direction of the downstairs classroom with a speculative look in his eyes.

"We'll take a look at these young girls of yours now, Miss Hudson," and without asking permission, he and Chanyu pushed past me into the room where the little girls sat in subdued quiet. The older girls upstairs had seemed calm about the appearance of hostile strangers in their midst, but the little ones on their floor cushions were not as unaffected. The sight of their pale faces and wide eyes churned up both anger and fear inside me.

"There is nothing to be afraid of," I told them in Chinese. "These men seek a girl named Suey Wah, and I know none of you in this room is so named. Each of you say your name out loud for our visitors to hear."

The girls did so, one after the other, and when they were done, Chanyu asked, "And do any of you know of a girl named Suey Wah?"

I held my breath and then in a beautiful chorus of complete and wholehearted deceit, all the girls slowly shook their heads no, their response so unison in timing and motion that Farmer turned to look at me with suspicion, certain I must have somehow cued them to answer.

Before he could accuse me of anything, however, one of the policemen stepped inside the room long enough to say to the lawyer, "Nothing upstairs. I take it the girl you're looking for isn't in here either so we'll just take a look in the back of the house and then we'll be done." His tone clearly communicated his impatience with what he and his partner considered a waste of time and without the words being spoken, also told Quentin Farmer, Esquire, that they held him personally responsible for so pointless a pastime.

I had felt reasonably confident up until the moment I heard the officers step into the kitchen, but until they reappeared empty-handed, my stomach stayed in my throat and I found it strangely difficult to breathe. I couldn't get the vision of a small girl with two black braids and a smile that could break your heart out of my head.

"It's our official opinion that the girl you're seeking is not at 920 Sacramento Street," the older policemen stated firmly. "And now we'll be on our way. You'd better get your facts straight next time, Farmer. We don't appreciate wasting our time on a wild goose chase." They nodded at me before departing.

Farmer and Chanyu departed, too, but not without the attorney threatening, "This is not the last you'll hear of this, Miss Hudson. We will be back as often as it takes to find this girl, and you should keep in mind that kidnapping is a serious charge, which I will personally prosecute to the fullest extent of the law."

"Go away, Mr. Farmer, or I'll call those two officers back and have you arrested for trespassing. From the looks on their faces, I would guess they'd be more than happy to oblige. Take Mr. Chanyu and go back to whatever disreputable hole the two of you crawled from." I walked past them and held open the front door, repeating, "Go away, Mr. Farmer."

The two men did leave, albeit unhappily, and when I turned from closing the door behind them, I found myself being stared at from two directions, the older girls crowded onto the landing of the stairs and the younger girls stealthily peering from the doorway of the downstairs classroom.

"Everything is fine," I told them with a brisk confidence that fooled no one. "Lu Chu, please resume your lessons and girls,—" I looked toward the top of the front stairs—"please finish your sewing projects." Then with a grin I said in Chinese, "You were all superb, ladies. You acquitted yourselves as the brave girls I know you to be. Miss Cameron will be very proud of you." My words caused a babble of chatter and giggles to break out as I headed down the hallway toward the kitchen pantry where another brave girl waited quietly and patiently.

Later in the day when Donaldina returned home, I shared all the details of the incident and after listening wordlessly to my narration, Miss Cameron asked the questions I had been thinking all afternoon.

"How did Farmer learn about a girl named Suey Wah, Dinah, and how did he know she was here? And why is anyone interested in her at all?" We sat over tea in Miss Cameron's office and I leaned toward her, my elbows balanced on my knees and both hands clutching my teacup so firmly I risked breaking the fragile china.

"That's been troubling me, too. I've thought about it all afternoon. Suey Wah had been sick for some time before we found her, and I doubt if she was able to articulate her name for several days before the rescue. She hasn't been out of the house since she arrived. Could any of the girls have shared the news that 920 had a new resident named Suey Wah?"

"No, they haven't had an occasion to do so, and who would they have told? Besides, they know better. These are girls who understand only too well the dangers of talking too much. It isn't that using the law to try to reclaim a girl is a new ploy, Dinah. There are a few judges and attorneys who will—to their shame—sign anything for the right price. They don't see anything wrong with doing so, and they don't care that they've allowed those who traffic in human beings to take one of our girls back to the degrading life she fled. You have to understand that to the men who engage in these activities, each girl represents hundreds and hundreds of dollars spent to purchase her and transport her to California. If they lose her, they also lose all that money, so, of course, they'll do anything to get their hands on her again."

"Lu Chu told me you once followed a snatched girl with such stubbornness that you ended up spending the night in jail."

"That's true, I did, and the publicity of my incarceration worked in our favor for quite a while. It's been wonderfully quiet for months. Which makes me think there must be something especially urgent connected to our Suey Wah. What is there about the child that would motivate old Judge Mackiver to abandon his cigars and whiskey long enough to sign the order Farmer showed you?"

"Something she knows?" I suggested, thinking about Suey Wah's history.

"Or some*one* she knows."

"But who?"

"I don't know, and I doubt if Suey Wah knows. But someone is nervous enough to make sure the child doesn't have the opportunity to let slip any information that might mean something to me or you or the authorities, even if it means nothing to her."

"Farmer said he'd be back."

Although in different words, Miss Cameron repeated the same grim information Jake Pandora had shared. "Trading in Chinese girls is a very profitable enterprise, Dinah, and I know it's not funded by the likes of Wing Chee and Dow Pai Tai. I'm sure miscreants like those two get a cut of the profits, but people much higher up are making huge sums of money. If Suey Wah knows anything about any of the investors involved in the slave enterprise, she is at serious risk. The men I'm talking about cannot afford to have their prestige and social positions compromised by their illegal activities becoming public knowledge."

"But she doesn't know anything!" I protested. Miss Cameron's words were conjuring up all kinds of frightening pictures involving little Suey Wah.

"They don't know that, any more than we know if she will some-day recall a name or a face or a meaningful snatch of conversation."

"Suey Wah isn't safe, is she? They'll come back for her, and there are just so many times they'll overlook her behind the rice sacks." We sat in silence, contemplating our alternatives, until I said, "She should come home with me." It suddenly made such good sense that I re-peated the words, adding, "We can smuggle her to my sister's house this evening. It's a big house and there's plenty of room for her. Ruth will support me and Martin will do whatever Ruth asks. I know you want her to continue her English lessons and I can do that and Ruth can teach Suey Wah all the domestic chores she would have learned here. My sister is a wonderful seamstress and a great cook. No one will think of searching for Suey Wah in my sister's house, and I'll be able to keep her under my watchful eye. What do you think?" Donaldina listened to me soberly before allowing a humorless smile to appear.

"I think it's the best alternative for the time being, Dinah, but don't get too used to Suey Wah being in your home. She will be safer away from San Francisco entirely, but until I've worked that out, your idea has merit. First, find out from your sister if she'll allow it and then we can make the transfer. I've never placed any of my girls under another's care and doing so will take some adjustment on my part."

"I'll take good care of her." Donaldina stood and I did the same.

"I know you will. In fact, I'm sure of it. If I weren't, we wouldn't be having this conversation." We walked together into the hallway. "You acquitted yourself well today, Dinah. Thank you."

The warmth of Miss Cameron's rare compliment carried me much of the way home, and it wasn't until I was climbing Ruth's front steps that I had a thought that made me stop abruptly, breathless with alarm and shock.

"How did Farmer know about a girl named Suey Wah, Dinah, and how did he know she was here?" Donaldina had asked, and at the time I believed she was right to say that no one at 920 would have mentioned Suey Wah's presence there. I had forgotten about my trip to the Pandora Transport Company, however, forgotten that I had recently blurted out the child's name to Jake Pandora, which meant he could certainly have assumed her presence at 920. Of everyone involved thus far, he had the most personal interest in what the child had seen and heard because Suey Wah may well have arrived in San Francisco aboard one of his vessels. My heart pounded uncomfortably in my chest. Was Jake Pandora behind the day's menacing visit and the threat to Suey Wah? And even worse, was it my fault that it had happened?

I didn't want to think that Pandora would harm a child but was honest enough with myself to confess that my reluctance could have more to do with my pride than with his innocence. I didn't want to admit that he had tricked me with his handsome face and a false penitence in his dark eyes. No one likes to be played for a fool, but I feared I had allowed Jake Pandora to do just that, and it wasn't just a loss of dignity or reputation that made me want to weep from remorse and dread. My brash confidence, my need to flaunt my independence might have endangered a girl's life, and I knew I would bear some of the responsibility if anything happened to Suey Wah. I owed it to her and to my own peace of mind to discover the identities of the degenerates involved in her ordeal. If Jake Pandora were one of them, God might have mercy on him, but there was no way I intended to offer a similar consideration.

Chapter Six

When I broached the subject of Suey Wah staying on Grove Street for a time, my sister gave her immediate and unequivocal approval. I had told her about Quentin Farmer's visit and how he tried to convince me that his ageing partner in crime was engaged to marry the child. Their shameless and perverted announcement so outraged Ruth that her face turned the color of strawberry preserves.

"That man actually told you he planned to marry a child?! I don't believe it, Dinah! That's disgusting."

"The old reprobate tried to convince me that it was nothing extraordinary. Anyway, Ruthie, it was only a ploy. Someone must have heard that we rescued an unattached Chinese girl and decided there was money to be made by selling her. Again."

"Do you think it was that Wing Chee you mentioned?"

"I don't know," I replied but knew that I would have to look higher than Wing Chee for whoever had sent Farmer to 920's front door. I didn't, however, have the heart to share that disillusioning knowledge with Ruth, whose sunny good nature and kind disposition wanted only to see the best in people. One disenchanted Hudson sister was enough for the time being.

"She can stay in the room we've chosen for the nursery," Ruth enthused. "It's just sitting there empty, and it's exactly the right size for a little girl."

Martin, as I expected, showed none of his wife's enthusiasm for adding a temporary houseguest. Arriving home unexpectedly early that day, he listened without comment to Ruth's story and sent a disapproving glance my way before replying.

"My dear, your generous heart is a credit to you, but you're not in a condition to take on the responsibility of another houseguest—and a stranger and a foreigner at that! You don't need any more burdens at this time in your life. You need to be resting and gathering your strength."To me, Martin added, "I know you mean well, Dinah, but try to think of your sister instead of yourself for a change."

He was truly annoyed with me, I judged dispassionately, and wondered why his reaction seemed so out of proportion to the request. Martin seemed to have recovered from the recent stock market crisis that had generated national panic and briefly endangered the bank where he worked. For a few days he had looked as if he carried the weight of the world on his shoulders. Ruth, feeling her husband's tension, had worn a similar expression. Then one evening Martin came home with a bunch of fresh flowers in hand for his wife and the relieved announcement that however he did it, Mr. Gallagher had restored the bank's solvency and all was secure. Thus, I couldn't blame Martin's work for his resistant mood.

I wondered briefly if despite his protestations, Martin resented my presence in the house more than he was willing to admit and simply couldn't tolerate the idea of another human being crowding into his comfortable life. Or—the more chilling thought came suddenly to mind—perhaps Martin Shandling, rising young banker and eager newcomer to San Francisco's glamorous social life, knew more about the trade in Chinese girls than he let on and did not want that dark world brought so close to his wife and his home. Looking at his clear, handsome face and seeing him standing before me, the very personification of propriety and rectitude, the furtive idea seemed impossibly ludicrous, and yet Martin certainly could be involved in the illegal, immoral business. Anyone could be, even my sister's dearly loved husband—but oh, I hoped not! I sincerely hoped not. Wouldn't Ruth know if the man lying next to her at night had the heart and the conscience of a devil?

My sister replied to her husband's rebuke in a voice I had never heard from her before, not even when speaking to me and goodness knows she had had plenty of justified opportunity to quell me with icy tones over the years. Apparently Martin had never been on the receiving end of Ruth's chilly disapproval because he stared at her as if she'd transformed into a stranger before his eyes.

"You need not speak to Dinah as if I am some spineless, weak woman she can manipulate with a sensational story and a few well-placed emotional phrases. My sister is a credit to our family, but she is not the only Hudson daughter prepared to do the duty laid on her by her Creator and her parents. This is a child, Martin, a child, and we are not talking about her taking up residence in our home until she dies of old age. It is only for a few weeks, Dinah said, and it is the least we can do. We live very well, but we have not been given this vast array of material blessings to hoard for our own pleasure. I intend to read in the front parlor for a while and will be happy to talk with you further once you have had time to reconsider your decision."

My sister did not flounce out of the room as I surely would have, but her dignified departure was all the more effective because of her calm and unhurried exit. Silently, Martin and I looked at each other, our eyes undoubtedly holding the same startled expression we would have assumed had we just seen a genie appear from a bottle or a dearly loved kitten suddenly swell into a tiger. I swallowed the words I had been about to say and retreated to the kitchen, leaving poor Martin to decide his next action. When he approached me later to say stiffly that he agreed with Ruth that the small nursery would be suitable for Suey Wah's stay, I swallowed my words once again and contented myself with a meek, "Thank you, Martin. I'll let Miss Cameron know," careful not to let one shred of triumph creep into my voice or expression.

I returned to 920 immediately after supper to discuss Suey Wah's transfer. The clandestine plan we agreed upon would have seemed extreme, almost laughable, if we had not believed the stakes were so high.

"We may be watched," Miss Cameron commented placidly. For her, evidently, the idea that villains spied on the house was completely reasonable and unremarkable. "When you leave tonight, you will leave alone. Tomorrow morning I will depart 920 dressed in my most voluminous cape—as you've discovered, our mornings can be un-comfortably cool until the fog burns off—and I will have our driver take a roundabout trip to Grove Street. Expect me by eight o'clock. I have several appointments tomorrow and will not be able to stay long. Just long enough to leave Suey Wah in your capable hands." In an unexpectedly physical gesture, she placed both hands on my shoul-ders before concluding, "Do your best not to grow too attached to the child, Dinah. I have contacts in San Rafael that can guarantee Suey Wah a safe haven, and I intend to move her there as quickly as possible." She paused. "I must put her welfare above everything else."

"I understand," I replied with hesitation, "and I wouldn't have it otherwise, but I can't help being fond of her and I'll grieve when she leaves, even as I pack her bag and send her away. I, too, want to be sure the child is safe and happy." I said good-night and walked quickly home to let Martin and Ruth know that Suey Wah would be arriving in the morning and her stay, although brief, needed to remain completely confidential.

The two of them sat contentedly in the parlor, Martin enjoy-ing a rare pipe and Ruth knitting the tiniest cap I'd ever seen. The atmosphere of the room fairly pulsated with harmony and concord. They've made up, I thought to myself, watching Ruth's face beam at the news of Suey Wah's pending arrival and Martin sneak a look at his wife's expression with a touch of relief. His glance was so affectionate that my former thoughts about his duplicity in the slave trade seemed even more ridiculous than before. No one who gazed at his wife with such an infatuated expression could possibly be involved in so dark an activity as human smuggling. And then, ever practical, I told myself that whether I misread Martin's character or not, Suey Wah would be safe in his house. He would not want to bring danger close to Ruth anymore than he would want to draw attention to any involvement in illegal activities. Suey Wah could be sure of a safe haven on Grove Street, however long her stay.

Suey Wah charmed my sister from the moment the child walked

through the front door—safely camouflaged by Miss Cameron's flowing cloak—and that evening ingratiated herself with Martin by an instinctive respectful gratitude that he could not resist. I watched the girl's face carefully when Martin first spoke to her, looking for recognition of any kind in her expression, but she met his gaze openly with a shy smile and not a flicker of fear or hesitation. I was certain she had never heard Martin's voice or seen his face or figure before and felt a wave of overwhelming relief at her lack of identification. He might still be involved in illegal enterprises, of course, anyone could be, but Suey Wah's easy acceptance of Martin made me so cordial toward him that more than once I caught him watching me with an expression that mixed equal parts of gratification, bewilderment, and suspicion.

Not long after Suey Wah's arrival, I left the little girl carefully sewing stitches on a piece of practice fabric as Ruth worked on her dress for the summer cotillion. My own gown was complete and draped gently over the back of a chair in my room. I had stopped in the doorway to watch the two work, both figures intent on their tasks, diligent and—incomprehensibly to me—apparently happy to be sewing. My patience with tiny stitches and perfect seams was lamentably lacking. Ruth recognized my presence, looked up, and smiled.

"So you're off. Well, have a good time."

"I should stay home with you," I said, overcome with guilt. "I don't mind. I'll just send word to—"

"Nonsense, Dinah. I find sewing to be relaxing and enjoyable. If you stay and attempt the same task, you'll soon be sighing and pacing and grumbling and that would certainly ruin my pleasure. You've brought me good company with Suey Wah, and we're both quite content. By the way, you look very lovely today, Dinah. Now please go away." Ruth spoke the last words with another smile and in rusty Chinese said to her companion, "Dinah is going to spend the afternoon with a gentleman friend."

A flicker of alarm touched Suey Wah's face as she asked, "You will be careful, Qing, won't you?"

"Let's try English," I suggested gently before continuing slowly, "I will be very careful, little bird. You met the big policeman, the one who helped in your rescue. Officer O'Connor is a strong protector."

"Yes," but she did not look entirely convinced.

Ruth, noticing the worry on the child's face, leaned forward to point at the cloth and say in careful English, "These are very good stitches, Suey Wah. Very good. But the line seems crooked to me. Do you think so?"

Distracted, Suey Wah took time to process the English before peering at the cloth and replying, "Yes, I see. I will try again. I'm sorry."

Ruth inadvertently slipped into Chinese, "There's no need to be sorry. You already have a finer stitch than my sister and she never apologizes."

I could tell Suey Wah intended to rise to my defense until she saw the twinkle in Ruth's eyes. Realizing my sister was teasing, Suey Wah turned back to her cloth with a quiet comment. "Qing does most things so well that she probably has not had much practice at apologizing."

"In English," I reminded the girl, then grinned at my sister, adding, "At least someone appreciates my sterling qualities," before I departed.

Colin O'Connor had recently stopped by 920 to tell me he had another free day and ask if I was ready for my tour of Nob Hill. I was curious about the mansions there and just as happy to spend more time in the Irishman's company.

We had arranged to meet on a corner by the mission, a fact that annoyed Ruth enough to make her inquire sharply, "You're not ashamed of us, are you, Dinah? Or of him? I think it's time I met this young man of yours."

"I am not ashamed of either of you," I answered meekly.

"Then next time he can meet you here at your home like any respectable gentleman caller. The idea of the two of you meeting on a street corner! I won't embarrass you by telling you how that appears."

"Ruth!"

"I am not entirely the optimistic innocent you think," she retorted. "I understand more things than you give me credit for, so tell Mr. O'Connor that next time he is expected to make an appearance on Grove Street because your sister desires to meet him."

"If there is a next time."

Ruth gave a dismissive shake of her head at my words. "Of course, there will be a next time. Even without seeing him, I can tell the man's smitten. I'm not quite sure about you, but there are signs that you may be returning his favor. Just don't say or do anything rash until you've had a chance to meet more of the city's eligible bachelors. I would like to see you do better than a policeman on the beat."

"It's honest, respectable work!" I defended, adding, "and Colin doesn't intend to be a foot policeman forever."

"No?"

"No. He's very ambitious."

"Well, ambition is sometimes good and sometimes bad. I definitely need to meet this Mr. Colin O'Connor."

I gave a brief thought to Colin's ambition when he saw me approaching and turned to greet me, and then spent more time thinking about his smile, his green eyes, and the appeal of broad shoulders that tapered to a slim waist. He wore dark blue trousers with a light blue shirt under a coat of subdued summer plaid that strained slightly across his muscled back. Very man about town with a touch of warrior just below the surface. An appealing combination. The afternoon seemed to brighten considerably when I saw the unabashed admiration in Colin's eyes as he greeted me, although the sun didn't change intensity or position. My sister might be right about my favoring him, I thought, and considered the idea objectively. Colin O'Connor did not have Jake Pandora's physical beauty, but men shouldn't be so handsome they took your breath away. They should look exactly like this ruggedly masculine policeman.

"You're looking very fine today, Dinah. Very fine. Not like a visitor to Nob Hill but like someone that belongs there." His words and tone made me feel suddenly, ridiculously happy and promised a wonderful afternoon.

We rode a cable car part of the way to Nob Hill but disembarked before any mansion was in sight. When Colin led me toward an elegant horse-drawn carriage waiting at a corner, I exclaimed, "Is he waiting for us? What a treat!"

"Leo owes me a favor," Colin explained, gesturing toward the driver and trying to hide his pleasure at my words. "He's agreed to take us on a slow tour of the Hill." My escort assisted me into the cab and then hopped in to sit next to me. I was very conscious of his proximity and the attractive masculine smell of tobacco mixed with something faintly spicy that I guessed he used on his face after shaving. When Leo started the carriage, the jerk of movement caused me to fall against Colin, and he responded to the unexpected contact by kissing me.

I found the experience so pleasant that I participated without reserve before regretfully drawing back to say with a smile, "I think we should concentrate on the scenery."

"I am," he replied with no reciprocal smile but shifted away and leaned across me toward the window to point and say in a casual and less intense voice, "The Floods live there and Huntington next to them. Didn't I tell you the nobs live different from everyone else?"

"You did," I answered, doing my best to forget about the kiss and match his easy tone, "but different hardly covers it. Look at that front staircase!" After that I turned into a true tourist, awed by the sight of so much splendor and gawking at homes in the same way I might view animals in a special zoo created for my entertainment.

As Colin related the extraordinary tale of the Crockers' "spite fence," a barrier Mr. Crocker had erected to punish a stubborn neighbor who would not sell his property to him, I glanced out the window of the creeping cab and caught my breath.

"Who lives there?" I asked.

Colin heard my mild gasp of surprise, followed my pointing finger, and looked at the imposing red-brick residence with distinctive double towers, each with its own small widow's walk and intricate black wrought-iron railing.

"I don't know. It's new. You can tell that by the brick. Maybe it's vacant or up for sale."

"No. That man on the walk just exited the front door."

"Did he?" Colin, after giving me a curious look, leaned farther across me to try to get a better glimpse of the man walking briskly away from the mansion, but by then all he could see was the diminishing, dark-coated back of Jake Pandora. I, on the other hand, had seen Pandora full-faced as the front door closed behind him and he stepped down to the walk from the imposing porch.

Why would Jake Pandora be on Nob Hill, I asked myself, and immediately answered my suspicion with another, more reasonable question. Why shouldn't he be here? He was a businessman, after all, and might have trade with any of the men who lived in the area. He'd hardly expect Nob Hill nabobs to make an appearance in the narrow alley behind the lowly Broadway Dock. Of course, Jake Pandora would come to them and not the other way around, but for reasons I couldn't explain, the sighting left me uneasy.

"Did you know that man?" I had almost forgotten about Colin O'Connor, and his voice so close to my cheek startled me.

"I'm not entirely sure, but I think so. Someone I met my first day in town."

"From the expression on your face he must have made an impression."

I remembered my first look at Jake Pandora as he stood in the doorway of the Pandora Transport Office with the sun behind him giving his perfect face the look of an illumined Greek god. "I suppose he did."

"I don't think I like that," Colin murmured and kissed me again, this time reaching for me and pulling me into a much more intimate embrace. "I don't think I want any man but me to leave an impression on you," he whispered, reaching up to wrap a finger around a curl that had escaped from my hat.

I was the one to push away finally, saying in a creditably calm voice, "You are definitely leaving an impression, Colin."

"An unforgettable one, I hope, at least as unforgettable as that man you saw, whoever he was. I'm not afraid of competition, Dinah. I can hold my own."

I never imagined otherwise," I responded calmly, "but I hardly know you well enough to speak with any authority on the subject." I turned toward Colin with what I hoped was an enigmatic smile but appreciating without any ambiguity the faint, burnished blonde stubble on his cheeks, the masculine, sun-browned complexion, his eyes that showed more hazel than green in the interior of the cab, and his wide mouth that had proved both skillful and satisfying.

Colin tried to read my meaning in my face—was it invitation? regret? relief?—and then gave up with a good-natured shrug. "I don't always understand you, Dinah, and I believe that's the way you want it."

"A woman likes to think she carries a certain mystery about her, Colin. Don't hold my feminine weakness against me."

He gave a short laugh. "Much as I might enjoy the discovery, I've not found one weak thing about you. I realized the kind of woman you were the moment you pushed me to the side with a scold and climbed down into Wing Chee's cellar. But don't ever apologize for it. I've discovered a preference for strong-minded women and believe it will be a moment to savor when they finally do capitulate."

I decided Colin O'Connor had grown just a trifle too sure of himself—that would teach me to enjoy kissing so much—and I sat back against the seat, making a minor fuss of smoothing my skirts and settling my hat before saying sweetly, "*If* they finally capitulate, Colin. It never does for a man to be too sure of himself."

Unabashed, he settled himself just as comfortably next to me. "That's how a man wins, Dinah, by knowing what he wants and doing whatever it takes to get it. He can't hesitate and there's no room for doubt. How do you think these mansions on Nob Hill got built?"

I recalled the oppressive atmosphere of Wing Chee's establishment and Suey Wah's terrible story on board the Pandora Two. At least one—possibly more—of those grand homes had been built on the suffering of children. I didn't speak my thoughts, however, only commented, "However these mansions got built, they certainly are magnificent."

Colin, taking a cue from my tone and expression, stuck his head out the window to call to the driver, "We're done here, Leo. Turn us around and take us to the Poodle Dog. We've worked up an appetite."

At home that evening, I realized how easily and how seamlessly Suey Wah had infiltrated our lives. She was the quietest child I had ever known, whether seated at the table or perched on the sofa by the fire. She missed nothing, however, always watchful with an endearing eagerness to do whatever she was asked.

At meals, Suey Wah observed my sister with particular care and hopped quickly to her feet whenever Ruth indicated she was going to rise from her chair to carry off a dish from the table or bring something from the kitchen.

"Please let me be your legs, Mrs. Ruth," Suey Wah would plead quietly and convincingly. Didn't we realize, her tone said, that running errands for Ruth was the highest honor to which one could aspire?

At first, Ruth seemed uncomfortable with the attention, but it so obviously pleased the little girl when she was allowed to help that my sister soon learned to take advantage of the extra set of arms and legs. I knew Suey Wah's behavior pleased Martin but didn't realize how fond he had become of the child until one evening after supper as he stood in the parlor doorway observing Suey Wah seated primly on a hassock next to Ruth's chair with her eyes fixed on Ruth's knitting needles.

"Doesn't she ever giggle," Martin asked me in a low voice, "or run in the hallway or play with dolls or beg to go to the park?"

"I assume you're inquiring about Suey Wah and not Ruth," I remarked and when Martin did not smile at my little joke continued, "She's a little girl who's seen terrible things, Martin. Sold by her father, then a victim of abuse and squalor, used to beatings and darkness and the very real threat of death. I imagine that right now she is just fearful that this life, which must seem like heaven to her, will be snatched away from her and she is being very, very careful to do everything right." For the first time I noticed that Martin had something tucked under his arm. "What have you got there?"

"A checkerboard. A child should play games once in a while, and this is all we've got in the house."

I eyed him with unexpected but sincere affection and stepped to the side before saying, "You are absolutely right, Martin, and checkers is just the thing. It will help with her English, too."

When he approached Suey Wah and began to speak to her, Ruth met my glance across the room, smiling in a way I recalled from an illustration of the Cheshire-Cat in my childhood copy of *Alice's Adventures in Wonderland*. I was right all the while, my sister's expression said, and then she turned to join in the conversation with Suey Wah and her husband.

Do your best not to grow too attached to the child, Miss Cameron had warned, and we had done our best, only our best wasn't good enough. Even after a few days it would be very difficult to say good-bye to the little girl with the shy smile and sparkling black eyes. If Suey Wah stayed much longer, saying good-bye would be impossible for all of us.

Later in the week, I received a hasty message from 920, asking me to accompany Miss Cameron on a rescue. I immediately hurried to the mission, bursting through the front door and nearly colliding with Frances Thompson, who took in my disheveled appearance with one glace and pointed down the hall.

"She's waiting for you in her office."

Miss Cameron showed me the anonymous note she had received, written in English in big, black letters: "Help me. In very bad place. Help me home. Or I die."

"But where—"

"One of Woon Ho's young residents delivered it. 'Not for me,' she said, to be sure I understood she had no desire to be rescued, 'but for

Chu Hua. She will not last. Too weak. Too afraid.'" At my uncompre-
hending look, Donaldina explained, "Woon Ho runs a high class parlor
house, Dinah. There are no little girls there, and we never have success
convincing the inhabitants to leave their lives and come to 920."

"Why not?"

"You'll see when we get there, but the girls are waited on and live in
relative splendor. They cannot imagine why they should trade beautiful
clothes and plenty to eat and days free to sleep in luxury for the cotton
dresses and daily chores we offer at 920. The men who frequent Woon
Ho's establishment are mostly well-to-do Chinese and the girls, poor
things, imagine they will be young and—more importantly—healthy
forever. They don't understand how quickly youth disappears in their
line of work, and then there's disease. The girls are examined daily and as
soon as anyone shows any symptoms of ailment or pregnancy, she disappears. Of course, they all think it won't happen to them and of course, it
will." I followed her into the hallway as she murmured, "But when we're
asked, we go. Maybe this will be our first success."

I recognized Sgt. Jesse Cook waiting for us on DuPont Street and
felt my pulse quicken as I looked around for Colin. He was absent,
however, replaced by a man introduced as Detective Dan O'Brien.

"You know we've never had luck with this kind of visit, Dolly,"
Sgt. Cook said.

"I know, Jesse, but I can't ignore this." Miss Cameron handed over
the crude note she had received.

"There's something not right," the sergeant observed, frowning
over the paper, then repeated, "It doesn't feel right."

"I agree. If you'd rather Dinah and I go in on our own, I'd understand." Jesse Cook handed the paper back to Donaldina, who folded it
carefully and thrust it into a pocket.

"No, Dolly, I wouldn't do that to you. Besides, Dan said he was
feeling the luck of the Irish today. Didn't you, Dan? Let's go see if we
can find this Chu Hua of yours. I'd give a week's pay to shut Woon Ho
down. Maybe Dan's right and this will turn out to be our lucky day."

Miss Cameron's and Sgt. Cook's instincts, however, were correct from the start. The two policemen shouldered through the front door and when an old woman confronted them in the hallway, they demanded that she present Chu Hua.

She gave an exaggerated shrug and responded in Chinese, "There is no one here by that name." When I translated her words, she shot me a dark, appraising look that was devoid of surprise or panic or fear. She knew we were coming, I thought, and better understood Miss Cameron's and Sgt. Cook's misgivings. I could tell from the woman's glance that something was definitely "not right."

"We'll see for ourselves, Woon Ho," Cook answered tersely. "Where are your girls?"

"Gathered in the front parlor, Sergeant. Come this way." Donaldina shared another puzzled look with the policeman, and we all followed the old woman down the hall where Woon Ho threw open the doors to a room.

I saw what Miss Cameron had meant about the luxury of the surroundings. This was nothing like the dank, rough interior of Wing Chee's establishment, and the room's inhabitants bore no resemblance whatsoever to Suey Wah's emaciated, mistreated body. The walls were covered in sumptuous red silk and the young women seated on cushioned teak couches looked unalarmed and contented, their eyes clear, their complexions fashionably pale from rice powder, and their gleaming black hair perfumed and coiled. When we entered, all faces turned toward us.

"We are looking for Chu Hua," I announced. When no one responded, I added, "If you know where Chu Hua is, please tell us so we can help her, and if you would like to leave this place, you may come with us, too. No one will stop you."

"These girls do not wish to leave," Woon Ho said, smiling in a way I'm sure she thought made her appear fond of the room's inhabitants but only succeeded in giving her the appearance of an old, thin she-wolf. "They are happy here. Their parents sent them to me so I could find husbands for them, respectable husbands from honorable families. I take good care of these girls."

"What nonsense you talk, old woman," I said, purposefully disrespectful, hoping to discredit Woon Ho in front of her charges so they might feel more willing to confront her. "We know why these girls are here." I turned my back to Woon Ho and spoke directly to those seated around the room. "This is not a good way to live. You will not have long life. Koon Yum cannot help you here. Her mercy cannot reach you here. You are abandoned. Come away with us to a house where you can be safe and healthy. Come." But I could tell my appeal had no effect on my hearers. The faces looking back at me held dark, expressionless eyes. Two girls shook their heads in disbelief at my preposterous invitation. The others maintained still, almost indolent, postures.

"The prostituting of children is against the law," Jesse Cook told Woon Ho sternly, and she repeated her shrug in a way that made my palms itch to slap her.

"So I am told, but what has that to do with me? These are virtuous girls, who trust me to find them virtuous husbands." Then, slyly, "Virtuous *Chinese* husbands. I must look among the Chinese because I fear I would not be successful finding virtue among other men living in San Francisco."

"Watch your tongue, old woman," I snapped without thinking. "You are not indestructible."

She turned to face me and gave me a long, leisurely, very disparaging look before answering, "I have heard of you, I think. The red-haired woman who speaks our language with a sharp tongue. Be careful it does not get pulled out by the roots." I didn't know if she meant my hair or my tongue.

Donaldina, wordlessly following the exchange, finally spoke. "Come along, Dinah. We can accomplish nothing here. We were expected, I think." Without another word she turned and exited the door we had entered. I followed her and the two policemen came after me. Once outside, we stopped to face each other.

"I don't mind saying that that visit puzzles me, Dolly. Puzzles me a lot. What do you think was going on there?"

"I don't know, but I feel a sudden urge to get back to 920 as quickly as possible. Thank you, Jesse. I'm sorry for the wasted time." Donaldina's disquiet showed in her face as she headed toward a waiting cab. As I followed her, I heard someone call, "Miss Hudson!" and turned, thinking it was either Sgt. Cook or Dan O'Brien with a last minute comment. To my complete surprise, Jake Pandora walked quickly toward me.

"You said you wanted to accompany me when I next visited Wing Chee," he explained without preamble, "and now is the perfect time."

"Hello to you, too," I said dryly. "Why now?" Behind me Donaldina called my name and I went over to the cab to explain, "Apparently I'm needed here, Miss Cameron. I'll return to 920 as quickly as I can, but I have something urgent to do first." She looked past me to observe Jake Pandora's clearly impatient figure.

"All right, but be careful. Something's afoot, and I'm very uneasy about what just transpired. We'll talk when you get back." She drove away as I walked back to Pandora and picked up the conversation.

"Why now?" I repeated.

"Your little visit to Woon Ho's here is already knowledge throughout Chinatown, and I have no doubt that Wing Chee thinks he's safe for the time being, that you've spent all the time you're prepared to spend chasing villains today. I want to catch him with his guard down. This way."

For the first time, I noticed Casey and his cab waiting at the curb and threw him a wave before climbing into the carriage behind Jake Pandora.

"You think we have the element of surprise," I observed, "but I've found it very hard to surprise anyone in the Chinese community, whatever side of the ocean you're on."

"It's worth a try."

"Yes, Mr. Pandora, it's worth a try." I recalled when I'd last seen him and wanted to ask why he had been on Nob Hill and whom he had been visiting there but decided that would be unwise for the present and contented myself instead with, "Have you found out anything new about who used your vessels to smuggle Chinese girls into the city?"

"No, but maybe I can convince old Wing that it's worth his while not to keep so many secrets."

"The Chinese keep secrets well, Mr. Pandora."

"Unlike women." My puzzled glance caught a small grin on Pandora's face. "Women like to talk too much." With a sinking feeling in my stomach I wondered if he were slyly taunting me that he had found out Suey Wah's name because I had foolishly let it drop during a conversation. Was Jake Pandora capable of such deep and calculating deception? We shared a queer, silent, strained moment as I tried to determine what kind of man sat across from me.

"What is it?" he asked finally, all traces of humor and teasing gone. The moment passed and I settled back against the cushion.

"It's nothing," I responded. I think he wanted to say more but thought better of the impulse. We traveled the rest of the way in silence.

I didn't recognize Wing Chee's establishment but read his name in the Chinese characters painted on the sign over the door. Pandora didn't knock, just pushed the door open and stepped inside, I following on his heels. We passed several rooms filled with men oblivious to our presence because they were bent over tables covered with what looked like small tickets made of thin paper. Their concentrated attention had the universal look of gambling about it. Over everything hung a pall of smoke and a sickeningly sweet smell I didn't recognize. Too busy peering into the rooms we passed, I bumped ungracefully into Pandora's back as he halted abruptly.

The man who had stepped in front of him and caused the sudden stop asked, "What do you want?" I translated the brief question.

"Tell him I want to talk to Wing Chee. Tell him he's an old friend of mine."

As I spoke, the young Chinese man looked at me with a flicker of something—curiosity, perhaps?—briefly kindling in his eyes.

"He doesn't believe you," I told Pandora, then directed the man, "Go tell your master his betters are here, and it would be to his advantage to hear what we have to say."

The man spoke one clipped word that indicated without misunderstanding that he did not think we were anyone's betters before he disappeared into a room at the end of the long hall.

"You don't have to translate that," Jake Pandora told me. "It's a universal phrase." His tone made me laugh despite our serious purpose.

"Good. I'm not sure I could say the words out loud in English."

"No false feminine modesty, please. I thought the language of the docks didn't bother you."

"For the most part that's true, but it doesn't mean I enjoy throwing around coarse obscenities. I'm as morally pedestrian as any other woman, Mr. Pandora, and at the mercy of the same strictures of society."

"I'm disappointed to hear that, Miss Hudson, because despite myself I've begun to hold you to a standard of intelligence higher than that of most other women I know."

Curious to know if he was serious or teasing, I would have responded to his remark, but the quick clip of soft soles against the wooden floor interrupted our discussion. The man approaching us must be Wing Chee, I thought, and was surprised that he looked so ordinary. I may not have expected horns and a tail, but I certainly didn't anticipate that he would have such a conventional face, genial smile, and eyes that beamed a welcome that seemed to indicate we were exactly the people he had hoped to meet in this very hallway. How could evil appear so ordinary? I had to adjust all my expectations.

When he stood before us, Wing Chee bowed respectfully, both palms tented under his chin. "Mr. Pandora, what a pleasant surprise to see you again." He said the words of greeting in halting English before lapsing into quick Chinese, the gist of his meaning being that he had thought all their business had been handled at their last meeting and confessing that he could not think of one solitary reason that Jake Pandora would visit his humble establishment again. He spoke too quickly and then stood waiting. The man knows that Jake's Chinese is rudimentary at best, I thought with a flash of understanding, and he's mocking him. Somehow, with nothing to support my conclusion, I was absolutely certain that Wing Chee could speak and understand English very well, certainly much better than his first faltering sentence indicated.

With Jake looking at me, impatiently waiting for me to tell him what the man had said, I addressed Wing Chee in his own language. "You are pitifully unconvincing, sir. Despite your little amusement at our expense, I know you speak English very well, as well as I speak your language. We will talk privately, immediately, and in English, and we will include Mr. Pandora in the conversation." To Jake I said, "Mr. Wing Chee has had a sudden epiphany of language. A miracle almost. He is now quite conversant in English." I concluded with a mocking disdain Wing Chee could not miss, "To think that so lowly and ignorant a man would believe he could fool us!" Chinese men were proud and very conscious of their own dignity, and I wanted to be certain this man understood that we—and especially I, a woman!—found him laughable and weak. That a lowly female had the temerity to ridicule him before another man would be deeply offensive, no matter if the audience was friend or stranger. The man's expression did not change, but despite the satisfaction I'd felt on Suey Wah's behalf, I wondered if I'd just made both a mistake and an enemy. Wing Chee nodded briefly and turned, indicating that we were to follow him into the room at the end of the hallway where the first man had earlier disappeared. The lion's den, I thought, and felt a moment of doubt, even fear, a moment so strong that I stood frozen to the floor. A surge of memories rushed over me and the familiar feeling of being terrified to the point of immobility threatened to overwhelm me.

Then Jake Pandora murmured, "I've got your back, Miss Hudson," and I felt a quick confidence. A completely unsupported confidence built on nothing except the cool self-assurance, the challenge, and the hint of respect I heard in Pandora's voice. Yet his words combined with a mental picture of the little face of Suey Wah restored my balance, and without further hesitation I entered the room behind Wing Chee.

Chapter Seven

P andora did not wait for the door to close behind us before he addressed Wing Chee curtly. "Money has passed hands between you and a man named Ivan Fletcher. Who provided you the cash?"

"The Chinese prefer a less blunt approach to important dialogue," I murmured to Pandora. He did not look at me but kept his gaze fastened on Wing Chee's face.

"No doubt, but I'm not Chinese. We Greeks are more direct." To Wing Chee he added, "From the amount of money that's been supplied over the past months, I know you must have a backer."

The Chinese man gave a typical shrug to indicate his unconcern. "I am not without resources, but even if what you say is true, why is it any concern of yours?" His English was impeccable.

"You made the mistake of using my steamers in your illegal dealings." Pandora's voice held an edge of fury that none of us missed, especially the man standing in the room's far corner, the man we had met upon arrival. I saw him stiffen and take a step forward. Wing Chee's bodyguard, no doubt, and quite prepared to ensure his master's safety, whatever it took. Apparently Pandora didn't miss the man's movement, either, because he softened his tone before continuing.

"Like you, I have a certain pride in my name. If you tell me who is behind the trade in Chinese girls, I'll do my best to keep you and your establishment out of the discussion when I bring the matter to the attention of the immigration authorities. I don't think you want the federal government investigating any of your enterprises, do you? They have little patience with anyone who violates the Exclusion Laws."

Wing Chee recognized the offer for the olive branch it was and replied carefully, "As I told you before, Mr. Pandora, I run a legal business and have no reason to fear anyone's investigation."

"But such an investigation can be so inconvenient," I interjected, "and so messy. Federal officials in and out of the building; your books examined; your staff questioned again and again. That kind of presence makes customers very uncomfortable. And I understand an investigation can continue for years. Once your name is on someone's desk, I'm told it never goes away. Unless you cooperate, of course. The government has a long memory, both for its friends and its enemies." The look I saw in Wing Chee's black eyes made me realize how very much he disliked me.

"I have business partners in city government who would speak in my behalf." A hint there? I wondered.

Jake Pandora must have wondered the same. "Do you? In any specific area?"

"As a business man, I deal with a number of people for legitimate reasons. The Board of Supervisors, the mayor's office, law enforcement, city financial leaders. I cooperate with all of them." The finality of Wing Chee's tone told me we would get no more information from him, but Pandora must have missed the inflection.

"Be more specific. Your eastern inscrutability doesn't impress me. Give me a name."

Wing Chee hesitated and in the pause that followed, the man in the corner stepped closer to say, "No more talk."

I saw Wing Chee's face tighten at the words and a flicker of—if not fear, certainly uneasiness showed before he dropped his eyelids briefly. When he looked at us again, he showed no trace of emotion.

"Chong Lin is right. I have already given you more time that I had to give."

I took a closer look at Chong Lin. He wore traditional loose pants and a canvas jacket with black bands tied around both upper arms. The most noticeable feature about him was the way he had tied his queue up on the top of his head. Not a traditional way of wearing the braid and a practice with which I was unfamiliar. When I met the man's look, he did not drop his eyes, which would have been another traditional response, but instead stared at me with the same expressionless look I had just seen on Wing Chee's face. I had to adjust my opinion—this man was not Wing Chee's bodyguard or even his friend. Of the two of them, it was not Wing Chee who held the upper hand.

"You fear this turtle man and his black dragons," I said on impulse, guessing at Chong Lin's black armbands. I recalled the gang's name from Suey Wah's story and remembered that she had been sure the name frightened Wing Chee. "But you should also fear the Chinese Squad and the immigration authorities. They can hurt you, too, and we can make sure they do." From the slight twitch of Wing Chee's face, from the sudden widening of his eyes and the swift curtain of impenetrability he drew across his expression, I knew Suey Wah had been exactly right. The man was deathly afraid of the black dragons. I had the experience to recognize such a look of bone-deep terror and shivered at the sight, perhaps at the memory, too.

Jake Pandora must have felt my quiver because he put a hand on my arm, ostensibly to guide me toward the door but perhaps to steady me, too. He threw Chong Lin a casual, examining glance before we moved toward the door.

I resisted the pressure of Pandora's guiding hand long enough to say to Wing Chee, "I am looking for a girl. Her name is Mae Tao. She is about nine years old, short and plump, with round, pink cheeks. She loves to talk and tell jokes and was a bossy little thing already years ago. I know she arrived in San Francisco this spring aboard the Pandora Two. I will pay for information about her, pay even more for the child herself." I knew Wing Chee wanted to ask how much I was offering but was not going to do so with Chong Lin standing so close. I lowered my voice so only he could hear and said in Chinese, "Double her cost. No questions asked. No report about it to the officials. You have my word and you know where to find me."

"You stay with the old *fahn quai*."

I smiled. "Not so old but otherwise you have it right. Cross her and you will think you've crossed the devil."

Pandora gave my arm another inelegant pull and this time I obeyed, exiting into the hallway ahead of him, very conscious that as we departed he had "my back" as he'd put it earlier—in a literal sense walking directly behind me, his intention to shield me from the presence of Chong Lin, who followed us out of the room and walked a few paces after Pandora, a quiet and ominous shadow of dark intensity.

Neither Jake Pandora nor I spoke until we sat in Casey's cab and knew we were well on our way out of Chinatown. Then Pandora asked, "What exactly are the black dragons?"

"A tong, but that's all I know," I explained. "I was told Wing Chee was terrified of them and he was. Did you notice?"

"Yes." After another silence, Pandora said, "Casey's planning to drop you off at the mission, or did you want to go to Grove Street?"

This time his easy knowledge of my habitats didn't bother me at all. I knew I should still be suspicious of him, still wonder about his involvement with the illegal smuggling of humans and the threatening visit Quentin Farmer had made to 920, but I wasn't and I didn't. His recent actions and words to Wing Chee had seemed convincingly genuine. If Jake Pandora was involved in anything reprehensible—and I was sure he had been so in the past and might still be dabbling in something illegal—whatever he was guilty of was not buying and selling little girls for slavery and prostitution. I had detected a sincere disgust in his tone when he mentioned the practice and talked about Ivan Fletcher and his despicable actions. Even if I misread the depth of Pandora's aversion, I believed he would never have involved his own transport line in the practice. I wasn't entirely convinced Jake Pandora was an honorable man, but he was certainly a business man, shrewd and in his own way as ambitious as Colin O'Connor. He had a plan for the Pandora Transport Line, and he was not about to jeopardize his vision for the future, which as far as I could tell included a money-making enterprise emblazoned with his name on every vessel and a house full of children emblazoned with the same identification.

"920, please. What's our next step?"

"*My* next step is to go back to some of my contacts with the name black dragons." At my indignant look, Pandora said, "You may not realize it, but there was no guarantee we were going to get out of that place with our skin intact, and I'm not prepared to be responsible for your safety again."

"No one asked you to be responsible for me," I retorted, stung by the patronizing tone I heard. "I could have held my own without you being there. Probably could have done better. You'd still be letting Wing Chee prattle on to you in the deceptive babble he passed off as Chinese if I hadn't called his bluff, and I'm the one who knew about the black dragons. As far as I can tell, your contribution to this venture was woefully lacking."

He opened his mouth to respond with equal scorn but then surprised me by agreeing. "You're right. You were indispensable and I beg your pardon."

"That's all right, then," my words a churlish grumble before I caught his eye and suddenly felt laughter well to the surface. "What a bad-tempered team we make, Mr. Pandora!"

"You're absolutely right about that, too, and call me Jake. My father's been dead for years."

I didn't think to reciprocate a similar invitation because I was too busy wishing he hadn't agreed with me so readily or so earnestly, but I kept that thought to myself. I had stated the obvious and he had concurred. Progress of a sort, I supposed, and it would serve no purpose to stir the pot again. We might as well both bask in our feelings of superiority over the other. Besides, I found being in charity with Jake Pandora and his returning the feeling to be quite a pleasant sensation. Rare but undeniably pleasant. I wondered how long the time of grace would last.

"I'll be in touch," Pandora said as I stepped out of the cab after it came to a halt in front of 920.

Once on the ground, I rearranged my hat, said, "Sooner rather than later, please, or I'll go ahead on my own," and walked toward the mission's front door without looking back. I thought I heard him make a comment behind me but couldn't make out the words and didn't bother to ask him to repeat them. Why allow reality to intrude on our mutually charitable moods, however fleeting they might be?

Miss Cameron appeared to be waiting for me when I returned to 920 and her greeting held relief. "Dinah. Good. I was getting worried. I've received confirmation from a source I trust that the summons to Woon Ho's establishment was a ruse meant to draw both of us away from the mission."

"But why?"

"To allow Mr. Farmer and his accomplice Mr. Chanyu another opportunity to search for Suey Wah. Those two scoundrels appeared on the doorstep as soon as we were out of sight. They showed another warrant signed by Judge Mackiver and they were accompanied by police who were much less sympathetic than the previous searchers. Frances did her best, but she was unable to stop the men from threatening our girls with all sorts of dire consequences if they did not reveal Suey Wah's whereabouts. One or two of the little girls were still crying when I returned. Frightened to tears. The idea!" I had never seen Miss Cameron as angry as she was during the recounting of Quentin Farmer's return invasion. "For our lack of cooperation, Judge Mackiver has threatened a contempt order. That crook is an embarrassment to the city. I would love to see him disbarred completely. It's a wonder he can move about at all with his hand in so many people's pockets! It must be such an uncomfortable posture."

I listened until she ran out of words and then prompted, "But who——?"

"I don't know, but I've asked several of our staunchest Chinese supporters to help me find out what and who is behind this ruthless search for Suey Wah. How fortunate the child remains safely sheltered!" Her words took both our thoughts to the same place at the same time, and we stood simultaneously.

"I must get home!" I didn't need to explain any further; Donaldina nodded her understanding.

"If there has been any indication of trouble on Grove Street, Dinah, let me know at once. I have many connections and I've just begun to martial my forces."

I hurried home, my heart in my throat most of the way, and only when Ruth appeared from the kitchen in answer to my loud, urgent call did I begin to calm. Suey Wah, enveloped in an apron much too big for her, followed my sister out into the hallway, both their faces showing nothing but a natural combination of puzzlement and alarm at my rushed entry.

"Are you all right?" I demanded. "Has your afternoon been uneventful?"

"Except for Suey Wah's small mishap with the flour canister, it's been very uneventful, Dinah. What's wrong? You look as if you were chased by banshees."

I thought of Quentin Farmer's dark, foxlike face and the grim presence of Chong Lin that hinted at violence and danger. "I believe I would prefer banshees," I said quietly to myself before I turned to face the hallway mirror, pulled out my hatpins, and shook loose my hair. "There's nothing wrong. I don't know why I was worried. My sensitive feminine temperament, I suppose."

Ruth gave an unladylike snort. "That's rich, Dinah. Now come into the kitchen and see what Suey Wah and I have been up to. Do you recognize the smell of Mother's oatmeal cookies? We've had fun, haven't we, Suey Wah?"

Ruth disappeared into the kitchen as she spoke. The little girl eyed me soberly, her expression older than her years, then came and took my hand. Together we followed Ruth toward the heady smell of freshly baked cookies, each of us clutching the other's hand more tightly than was warranted, neither of us saying a word.

I saw Colin O'Connor twice that week. He arrived at Grove Street Sunday afternoon to escort me to a band concert put on by the Policemen's Brass Orchestra in Washington Square Park. He had smiled when I told him Ruth's directive to appear at Grove Street and meet my family.

"I don't blame your sister for giving me marching orders. She wants to be sure you're keeping time with someone respectable. I'll be there at two o'clock, and I won't be late." He wasn't, either, knocking on the front door promptly at two.

At his knock, Suey Wah, who had been working on her English in the parlor, scurried upstairs to her room. Without my having to tell her so directly, she understood that her stay with us was to be as much a secret as we could control, and she made it a point to stay out of sight whenever we had a guest. It wouldn't always have to be so, I told myself hopefully, but I was responsible for her safety now and if that meant her vanishing with every knock on the door, so be it.

Ruth invited Colin into the parlor for a brief inquisition and Martin wandered in, too. Before sitting down on a side chair, I sent Colin a sympathetic look. With her usual gracious subtlety, Ruth had directed him to the chair directly across from where she and Martin sat. Colin O'Connor might be a grown up man and a veteran policeman who had confronted any number of criminals, but I thought he might still feel a trifle nervous facing the Shandlings. I needn't have worried. Colin had an easy manner about him, much more Irish than German, complimentary to Ruth and respectful about Martin's position at the bank.

"My mother always wanted me to be a policeman," Colin told Ruth. "I can't say it was my first choice, but she liked the idea of law and order, and she felt the job offered security, too. I joined to please her and then found out that she was right, the work suited me. I like keeping the streets safe for respectable folks, and I like the steady work and income the job offers." That was a clever comment from a potential suitor, I thought to myself, and relaxed even more. Colin knew what he was about.

"You must be both good and practical, Mr. O'Connor. That's a rare combination," Ruth replied enigmatically. She had watched and listened to Colin with an inscrutable expression so I couldn't tell if he were passing inspection or not, but at those words she stood, adding briskly, "If we keep talking, you won't make the start of the concert. Martin, you should have reminded me how late it was getting."

Martin rose to the occasion, accepting his responsibility meekly. "Yes, dear. I was just about to say something."

We walked toward the hallway together when Colin glanced down at the corner table by the door and commented, "It looks like someone's been practicing his Chinese. Or is it his English?" In her haste, Suey Wah had left her pencil and tablet on the table.

"Dinah's been quizzing me," my sister supplied quickly, scooping up the tablet and holding it against her skirts. "I haven't had to speak the language for years, and she challenged me to improve my rusty skills. She lists Chinese words and sentences and I translate. She times me, too."

"Dinah's quite the taskmaster," Colin observed. He didn't sound convinced but wasn't going to ruin the good impression he hoped to make by pursuing the topic. Perhaps he saw the English words written in childish block letters and realized that no adult wrote them. I wished Ruth had let me give an explanation—I was a more accomplished liar than she would ever be—but I was proud of her efforts and not very worried about Colin's stumbling onto the truth. He had been in on the story of Suey Wah from the beginning. If I hadn't promised Donaldina to say nothing of the child's stay with us, I wouldn't have been at all uneasy talking it over with Colin O'Connor. Members of the Chinatown Squad were some of 920's strongest allies.

As we walked toward the park, Colin took my hand, a simple gesture that for some reason seemed so intimate that for a moment I felt almost shy with him. He didn't allow time for shyness, however.

Acting like it was the most natural thing in the world to stroll hand-in-hand, he asked, "Well, how do you think I did? I couldn't tell from your sister's expression."

"Ruth was somewhat less transparent than usual," I admitted, "but I'm sure you did fine. I thought you handled all her probing and not very subtle questions well."

"It's what you think that matters most to me," Colin said softly, "so I'll set my mind at ease."

"You do that," I agreed placidly. "I wouldn't want any undue worry to spoil the music for you."

The band could have used less enthusiasm and more practice, but I still enjoyed the day. Colin introduced me to several of his colleagues, who were also in the audience, and I could tell from his tone that he was proud to be seen with me. The kind of admiration I heard in Colin's voice when he said my name was good for a woman's self-respect and made me reach for his hand on the walk home.

"I liked your friends," I told him.

"I'll hear about it tomorrow, all sorts of questions about what a woman like you would see in man like me."

"Don't you let them say that!" I answered indignantly.

"I can't fault them very much because I agree with them, Dinah. The idea that Colin O'Connor would be walking along holding the hand of a woman like you seems as unbelievable to me as I've no doubt it does to them. You have a look about you, Dinah, and it's all the more noticeable because you don't realize it."

"What kind of look would that be?"

He stopped to put both hands on my shoulders and turn me to face him, then examined my face with an objective eye. "You look like a queen."

"A queen!" It was the last thing I expected him to say. "Have you ever seen a queen?"

"In books."

"'Me, too, and Queen Victoria, God rest her soul, looked like a plump gray-haired grandmother." He gave a shout of laughter and we started walking again.

"You don't look anything like a plump, gray-haired grandmother, Dinah. It's just that you carry yourself like I imagine a queen would, head high like you own the ground you're walking on. When the sun shines off your hair it shows more gold than red and almost looks like a crown. There's just something about you, something—" he paused searching for the right word—"regal, I guess it would be."

I felt enormously flattered. "Thank you, Colin. I don't remember that anyone has ever paid me such a generous compliment before."

"If you gave me the opportunity, I'd promise to do it every day." His words startled me, hinting at something that was too serious too soon, and I made it a point to laugh.

"That would go straight to my head and be bad for my character." Then I pointedly changed the subject. "What did you think about the orchestra's performance?"

I think he realized he might have made a tactical error with the earlier comment and being an intelligent man allowed me to divert the conversation to a more inconsequential topic. We talked about the orchestra and the music the rest of the way home.

At supper, Martin remarked that he had liked Colin and found him to be more respectable and more serious than he'd expected, concluding with, "You know how the Irish are."

I chose not to pursue the subject of the reputation of the Irish but turning to Ruth asked, "What did you think of Colin, Ruthie?"

"He's not what I expected at all," my sister answered thoughtfully. "Not at all."

"Since you didn't give me any hint about what you expected, how do I know if that's good or bad?"

"You don't know," Ruth stated. "I'm not sure I do, either. Sometimes, Dinah, you surprise me." I didn't know what to say to her unusually cryptic pronouncement, and even Martin stared at her with perplexity.

"Will you see him again?" she asked me.

"We're going to visit the Cliff House on Saturday."

"Twice in one week seems rather—" Ruth paused to find the proper word and finally continued with, "—exorbitant. You must like Mr. Colin O'Connor."

I shook my head at her, unable to read her tone. "I don't know what you're up to, Ruth, but yes, I do like him. I don't see what harm taking a sightseeing trip to the Cliff House can do."

Martin came to my rescue. "No harm at all, Dinah. The man's a policeman, Ruth. He'll take good care of her. And you might recall that you and I took a number of enjoyable trips to the Cliff House."

"Of course, I recall, dear. They were very enjoyable," Ruth responded with a small smile and the topic of Colin O'Connor apparently exhausted for the time being, she turned her attention back to the meal.

The following week at 920 passed uneventfully, no bad characters on the doorstep or panicky summons for assistance. I helped with English lessons but generally had time on my hands, a circumstance that didn't agree with me. Miss Cameron finally shooed me out the door early on Tuesday and I decided to make an unplanned—and on his part no doubt unexpected and unwelcome—visit to Jake Pandora at the Broadway Dock. *I'll be in touch* was a promise he hadn't kept and one I wasn't going to let him forget. If I found the man physically attractive and enjoyed the unstated challenge of his condescension, I was not prepared to admit that those factors had anything to do with the trip. Unfortunately, the steamship office was dark and uninhabited. I pushed open the unlocked door and stepped inside, called Pandora's name, and waited for a response. When none came, I stepped back into the street, pulled the door shut behind me, and gazed up at the curtained windows of the second story. As I watched, I noticed one curtain twitch and then saw a hand pull the curtain back farther to reveal the young face of a lovely, dark-haired woman. We stared at each other a long moment before she dropped the curtain. She had features similar to Pandora's, the same dark eyes and golden-olive skin of the Greeks, glowing complexions that implied their homeland's seductive sun-lit warmth and hinted that it permeated through their skin into the core of their being. She had carried a touch of his arrogance, too, I thought, and was embarrassed at my intrusive and unwarranted speculations. Jake Pandora lived above his office, apparently with that beautiful woman who might well be his wife. I couldn't have said why I had assumed the man was unmarried. Something about the tone of his answer to my question about children of his own—*None that I know of. Yet.*—had cast him as a bachelor in my eyes, but now with the memory of that beautiful face in my mind, I realized the answer could have been a husband's answer, just not a father's. Yet. I had jumped to that conclusion because I wanted him to be unmarried, I told myself honestly as I trudged back to my waiting cab. Jake Pandora was the most handsome man I'd ever seen, and I enjoyed sparring with him and showing him how smart and fearless I was, enjoyed showing off. How humbling self-knowledge can sometimes be!

Of course, maybe Jake Pandora and that young woman lived together but weren't married, a circumstance I knew occurred but one that people didn't talk about openly. In fact, except from the pulpit, fornication didn't come up very often in polite conversation. A very unfashionable topic for all its universality. More's the pity, I thought on the ride home, because maybe if we talked about it, we would have fewer brothels and parlor houses, fewer young women dead too young from syphilis and the effects of brutality, fewer men like Wing Chee and Ivan Fletcher and Quentin Farmer profiting from fornication.

Still considering the subject, I arrived home and once inside, stopped to unpin my hat and pull off my gloves. The sound of a child's giggle startled me and I looked to the side to see Ruth and Suey Wah watching me from the foot of the stairs.

"You were deep in thought," Ruth said, smiling. "A penny for them."

The question in my sister's voice invited sharing, but I didn't have either the courage or the heart to discuss what had occupied my mind the whole trip home. I doubted that even Ruth, to whom I was closer than any other person and who had been a married woman for three years, would welcome a conversation about the topic I had been mulling. So much in our lives was left unsaid and for the time being, at least, I should probably keep fornication on that list.

Chapter Eight

Saturday dawned warm and sunny and perfect for an outing to the famous Cliff House. Colin, understanding his duty as respectable suitor, knocked on the front door but did not accept Ruth's invitation to come inside for cake and lemonade.

"It was very smart of you not to step through the doorway," I complimented, patting Colin's arm as we walked to catch the cable car, which would connect to the train that would finally deposit us at the beach. "I believe Ruth wanted to continue quizzing you about your character, your prospects, and your intentions. We'd have been there all afternoon."

"That's what I thought," Colin agreed. "She had that look about her."

"What look?"

"The 'I-don't-know-if you-should-be-trusted-with-my-sister' look. I've encountered the sight before and believe me, 'tis a frightful thing for a man to face." He slid into an Irish brogue so thick I had to giggle.

"So exactly how often have you had to prove your worth to the families of young women with whom you want to spend time?"

"Ah, Dinah, if I thought you really were jealous for my company, I'd be as happy a man as ever there was, but you're only making conversation, and I don't believe I'll deign to answer."

Being the fickle woman I was, I didn't especially enjoy picturing another woman on Colin O'Connor's arm, but I certainly wasn't going to let him know that. As we waited for the car's passengers to get off so we could board, I smiled up at him and replied in a voice intended both to tease and to flirt, "That's perfectly understandable. We'll both agree to keep our secrets to ourselves."

In a few moments we settled next to each other, and Colin grabbed my arm to steady me as the car jerked into motion. The movement brought him closer to my side. "Exactly what secrets are you keeping, Dinah? Is there someone else, another man you're not telling me about?"

I looked at him quickly, surprised by a depth of feeling that startled me. He must have seen the surprise on my face because he let go of my arm instantly and moved slightly away from me. I heard true remorse in his voice.

"I'm sorry. I know you're not ready to talk about any kind of serious feelings. You've made that clear. But you should understand that not talking about something doesn't mean it doesn't exist. I'm a patient man, by and large, and I didn't mean to distress you, but don't treat how I feel lightly, Dinah. It's not right, and I wouldn't be a man to handle that well. I care too much."

His words made me regret that I'd responded to his feelings so playfully, but I was not going to allow myself to be drawn into a conversation I was not ready to have. "I'm not treating you lightly, Colin, and I'm not spending time with anyone else." Then to be sure he understood that I still valued my independence, I added calmly, "If that were any of your business, which I'm not convinced it is."

"That puts me in my place right proper," he replied pleasantly. "I understand. What do you know about the Cliff House?"

He had changed the tone and the topic of conversation as adroitly as I might have, and I appreciated the effort enough to let him do most of the talking for the rest of the trip.

My first sight of the famous San Francisco landmark was enough to stop me in my tracks. "It's a castle, Colin, not just a mansion! A castle! I've never seen anything like it! How did anyone ever have the money and the expertise to build something so grand in such an extraordinary location?"

"It is a sight," Colin agreed. We stood shoulder to shoulder staring at the enormous structure, several lower stories filled with rows of windows and topped by turrets and towers and more windows, eight stories in all to my count, all of them built to jut out over the Bay, suspended like a crown over the waters.

"Come on now," Colin urged, giving my arm a gentle pull, no repeat of the firmness I had felt in the cable car. "There's a lot to see, and I want to show it all to you. We've got a great day for it."

He was right. It was a great day, a perfect day, in fact, enough warm sunshine to keep the breeze off the ocean from being too cool but not so much that traipsing through the sand would work up any perspiration. The beach under the Cliff House was filled with families and couples and individuals enjoying the tang of seawater in the air and the sound of waves that held the comforting rhythms of a lullaby.

"I love the water," I said, taking his arm for support as we walked. "Thank you for bringing me here, Colin."

He smiled down at me. "Ah, Dinah, it's my pleasure to see the sun in those sapphire eyes of yours. Let's go inside. You won't believe the view of the coast you get from the windows."

We walked leisurely along the beach toward the looming mansion, making desultory conversation, both of us comfortable with the other and enjoying the indolence that seeped into our bones along with the warmth of the sun. Once inside we walked up two flights of steps, entered a large public room, and were lucky enough to find a table that faced the Bay. After he ordered lemonade, Colin set his bowler hat on the table and leaned forward to point toward the large window.

"See the sailboats?" he asked. "Now that's something I've never done."

"Me, either, but I believe I'd enjoy it. I love boats and looking out at a horizon that's nothing but sky and water."

"We'll have to go sailing sometime then. I've got a friend who can arrange it."

I didn't respond, only smiled my agreement. At that moment spending time with Colin O'Connor on land or sea was an enjoyable prospect, and I hoped he understood what I didn't voice. He did understand, I think, because as he continued to comment on the view, he rested his big hand lightly over mine on the table. I relaxed and did not pull away.

Talking in low voices as we enjoyed the window view of broad sky and an ocean that sparkled like blue diamonds in the sun, it took a moment for us to become aware of a figure standing next to our table. I thought at first it was the girl who'd brought our refreshments, but when I turned I was flabbergasted to see Jake Pandora beside me and on his arm the girl I'd glimpsed in the window over his office. Pandora was hatless, wearing black trousers and a pristine white shirt open at the collar. Casual. Very handsome. He couldn't help it, of course, with that face but I thought with an unashamed touch of cynicism that there must surely be a streak of vanity there. The man seemed to have developed a fashion sense usually credited to women because I couldn't believe he didn't realize that the neutral colors and plain clothes he selected emphasized his good looks.

"Miss Hudson." Jake Pandora flashed a brief, white smile. "I hear I missed you on your last visit. I'm sorry."

I felt Colin stir restlessly beside me and quickly introduced them. "Mr. Pandora, this is my friend, Colin O'Connor. Colin, this is Jake Pandora of the Pandora Transport Line. We are——" I hesitated, unsure how to explain our relationship.

"Business acquaintances," Pandora supplied easily. "Miss Hudson and I share some common business interests." He indicated the woman who stood quietly by his side. "Elena told me a woman had come by the office, and I recognized you from her description. Miss Hudson, this is my niece, Elena Pandora. Elena, please meet Miss Hudson."

Niece, I thought with continuing skepticism, hah! even as I smiled at the young woman. Close up she was younger than I'd first guessed. I doubted that she'd turned eighteen yet.

"How do you do, Miss Hudson?" She had a soft, accented voice and a shy smile. A very pretty girl with pretty manners.

"Hello, Miss Pandora. Now that you jog my memory, I do recall seeing someone in an upstairs window when I was there last. I hope my uninvited entrance didn't disturb you." To Pandora, I explained, "The door was open."

"It always is." He turned his attention to Colin, who had arisen and moved behind my chair to place one hand proprietarily on my shoulder. I resented the implication of the gesture but could not shake off his touch without causing a scene I didn't want to precipitate. I was practical enough to understand that Jake Pandora's presence would elicit a similar reaction from almost any man who was with a female of his choosing. Even Martin had stiffened with what seemed to be an immediate antagonism when Pandora had visited Grove Street, and he and Ruth were happily married and devoted to each other. Some sort of jungle law at work, I supposed, and nothing to be done about it. Colin was large and tempered and Irish with an inclination toward jealousy, and I understood that his unspoken staking of a claim on me was a very human—a very male—reaction. I didn't like it, but I allowed it.

"Mr. O'Connor," Jake said with a nod of his head and a small, small smile.

"Pandora," Colin replied, not bothering with a nod, a smile, or a *Mister*.

Neither man extended a hand, and I finally took it upon myself to break the silence. "How serendipitous to see you, Mr. Pandora. You'll contact me soon about our mutual enterprise, I hope."

"Oh, yes, I'll be in touch."

I turned to his niece. "I was happy to meet you, Miss Pandora. I hope you enjoy the day's outing. It's a perfect day for it, isn't it?" She smiled agreement, caught the dismissal in my tone, and stepped away quietly, pulling Jake Pandora with her. She whispered something against his cheek that made him scowl, but he recovered his usual sardonic expression, shrugged, and murmured something back to her that I also did not catch.

Before walking away, he spoke over his shoulder. "A pleasure as always, Miss Hudson," using the tone I was accustomed to, the tone that indicated a meaning exactly opposite of the words. I thoughtfully watched him and his companion exit the room. That exchange had had the feel of something more than the coincidental and unanticipated meeting of casual acquaintances, but what?

Colin, who had taken his seat again, said my name sharply and I turned to face him. "How do you know someone like Jake Pandora?"

With the memory of his uninvited hand on my shoulder, I answered tersely, "As I mentioned, we have some mutual business interests that have their origins in China." To change the subject, I deliberately turned to stare out the large window. "Look," I remarked, "isn't that a Naval vessel in the distance? Did I ever tell you that my brother was in the Navy?"

Colin could not ignore my questions without appearing rude and using his answers, I relentlessly drove the conversation onto other topics and kept it there the rest of the afternoon. After a while, Colin gave up trying to interject Jake Pandora's name into our talk, and his expression gradually returned to normal so that we were both able to spend the remainder of the day very enjoyably. We made our way home slowly, both of us, I think, regretting that the day had to end. Colin O'Connor could be very charming company and his obvious admiration made me feel attractive and special, which only increased his admiration. A pleasant spiral of emotions that, combined with the perfect weather and lure of the ocean, made me return his kiss more fervently than either of us expected.

We had been walking along the beach in the shade of the overhanging bluffs and he had stopped abruptly to pull me into his arms. I stiffened at first but then responded in a way that obviously pleased him. When we resumed our walk, Colin's satisfaction with my response showed on his face, and I could almost hear his thoughts. *So much for that Jake Pandora* his expression said. I enjoyed kissing in general and kissing Colin O'Connor in particular, but I was female and I wasn't dead so I couldn't help but wonder if kissing Jake Pandora would hold its own attraction. I imagined it would. At the unexpected recollection of his full-lipped, mobile mouth I felt myself blush and was glad for the shadow of the cliffs. I think Colin may have noticed my increased color, but the look on his face told me he attributed it to the effect of our recent kiss and I didn't—by look, tone, or gesture—indicate anything to the contrary.

That evening, after receiving a chaste kiss on the cheek from Colin as he delivered me to my front door, Ruth asked about the day and without knowing why I shared everything with her except the meeting with Pandora. Why I could tell her about kissing Colin O'Connor but couldn't mention a few spoken words with Jake Pandora I didn't know, but the fact was that the experience with Jake Pandora at Wing Chee's had somehow altered my feelings about the man. Until I knew why and how, I felt safer not talking about him at all. For a woman who'd always considered that she possessed a minimum of imagination and sensitivity, Pandora had begun to trigger a surprising reaction that involved both those emotions. I found the fact to be disconcerting even as it held a certain pleasant suspense. Kissing one man while thinking about another was just outrageous enough to make me ashamed of myself. Almost ashamed, anyway. When had I learned that particular deceit?

My sister said good-night at the door of my room, adding "You're leaving something out, aren't you?" Her comment surprised me with its perception and Ruth smiled, enjoying my surprise. "That's all right, Sister. I suspect you'll tell me when you're ready." Changing the subject, she added, "Suey Wah is such a delight, Dinah. I love having her with us. Do you think there's the slightest chance she could stay with us? I mean stay permanently. Martin's the one who brought up the idea. He's become as fond of her as I have. Will you talk to Miss Cameron about it?"

"Yes, but don't get too hopeful about the idea. Suey Wah is a special child, and I know Miss Cameron is arranging a place for her farther north and inland."

"But you'll talk to Miss Cameron about it anyway, won't you?" Ruth repeated insistently. "We'll sign papers or whatever it would take. Promise you'll mention the matter to her."

"I promise."

"That's all I ask. We'll leave the answer to God."

I didn't have the heart to try to dissuade Ruth from her idea of adopting Suey Wah, but I knew Donaldina felt strongly that moving Suey Wah out of the city was in the child's best interests, and I thought that when it came to Donaldina Cameron, even God might take a moment to ask her opinion first.

All next week Donaldina waited for the repercussions promised by Quentin Farmer's recent visit. She marshaled the support of prominent judges and merchants and clergymen, whose backing had helped in the past and whose loyalties were never questioned. She also advised the mission's Chinese supporters about the threatened legal action against 920 and asked them to prepare to speak on the mission's behalf if doing so would prove helpful. Most importantly, she mobilized the women of The Mission Board, whose contacts and influence —and husbands— permeated all aspects of respectable San Francisco society and life. Whether Donaldina's spirited and immediate actions were the reason or not, the week passed quietly with no more hostile visitors seeking a child named Suey Wah, no police tramping through the house, no warrant of contempt served or as far as we knew even pursued. Perhaps Judge Mackiver's more temperate colleagues made their opinions known, perhaps Quentin Farmer felt the cool breath of condemning public opinion against the back of his neck, but life at 920 settled back into its comfortable routine. Everyone, the girls included, gradually relaxed, so much so that I finally felt I could follow through with Ruth's request to ask Donaldina about Suey Wah's future.

"I'm not asking for me. It's for Ruth, and even more, it's for my brother-in-law Martin. They have taken that child into their hearts. Honestly, when I think of some of Martin's comments about the Chinese and how he resisted allowing Suey Wah into his home at all, the change is nothing short of a miracle. My sister is the kindest, most patient woman I know. She's going to make a wonderful mother and since she's going to be a mother anyway, why not mother two instead of one? I know you warned all of us not to get too attached to Suey, but we—they—have and the damage is done. The child couldn't ask for a happier, more loving home, and I know they'll make sure she has the same opportunities available to their own children. What could you find for Suey Wah that could possibly be more advantageous for her?"

"I can find a place where she will be safe, Dinah, something you cannot guarantee but should take into consideration. You know better than anyone the threatening activity Suey Wah's presence has gener-ated." I couldn't argue with her statement of the facts as we knew them at the time and I didn't try, but something in my expression made Donaldina concede, "I'll think about it, Dinah, if only to be sure I'm not overreacting to the situation."

I was content with her promise, thanked her, and that night told Ruth and Martin that there might be hope for Suey Wah's adoption into our family. "Miss Cameron is worried on Suey Wah's behalf," I explained. "She takes her responsibility for the girls very seriously and we can't fault her for that."

My sister stood to kiss me lightly on the cheek. "No one is fault-ing Miss Cameron for anything, Dinah. I know we all have the same objective, just different ways of reaching it. And thank you. You're my very favorite sister."

I laughed at that. "I'm your only sister, too, coincidentally, so I won't let your admiration go to my head. And shouldn't you be getting ready for bed? Women in your condition need their rest."

Ruth was so obviously blooming in health and spirits—and waist-line—that it was her turn to laugh. "Nonsense. I'm going to finish your gown tonight, which means only one more fitting, for which I know we are both grateful. I know you are many good things, but a good mannequin is not one of them. Come along and let's get it over with. In case you've forgotten, the cotillion is this weekend and unless you want to attend pinned instead of stitched, I need your complete cooperation tonight." To Martin, she added, "If you hear Dinah scream-ing, it will only be her impatient bad temper you hear. Just ignore her."

"No problem whatsoever," Martin said, reaching for his pipe, and I knew from his tone that the idea of ignoring me was something he contemplated with a certain degree of wistful anticipation. "I'm teaching Suey Wah chess. We'll stay out of your way, won't we, Suey Wah?"

The girl gave Martin a smile and I marveled at the affection I caught in the look they shared. For Suey Way, here was a man who held no fear or threat, only love and trust, and for Martin— well, the man who had once pronounced that "if you've seen one Celestial, you've seen them all," had discovered that individuality and character and personality were as conspicuous among the Chinese as they were among Californians. Progress on two fronts, I thought with satisfaction.

Ruth fussed over my dress for the rest of the evening, pinning and basting, repinning and basting until I truly did want to scream.

"There!" she exclaimed. "I'm done! Now stop all the wiggling and whining, Dinah. Have you always been this impatient?" Without waiting for an answer, she began to slide the dress down over my hips to the floor. "You're going to be the most beautiful woman there this Saturday. Mark my words. You will take people's breath away."

"I suppose you mean that as an encouragement, but I find the prospect of an evening gala unnerving and would prefer to blend in with the crowd."

"Would you say that if your Colin was going to be there?"

"He's not *my* Colin and yes, I think even then. I really don't want anyone to make a fuss over me, Ruthie. I'm not being falsely modest. I truly dread the idea of people treating me as if I'm something special or a heroine of any kind."

As Ruth handed me my robe, she observed, "You're serious about that, aren't you?"

"Very."

"But why? No one means any disrespect by the attention and what you endured really was extraordinary. It's natural for people to admire someone who was caught up in a difficult situation and somehow managed to acquit herself with faith and courage. Those are godly virtues.

There's nothing wrong with expressing—or accepting—admiration for commendable behavior."

I wanted to tell Ruth what those weeks trapped in Pekin had really been like, wanted to strip away the glamour and the exotic excitement that the newspapers had apparently attributed to the experience and explain why the idea of anyone holding me up for admiration was almost unbearable for me to contemplate, but I didn't have the way or the words to express myself.

After a silence, Ruth said gently, "I'll do my best to keep any attention to a minimum, Dinah, because I can see that the idea distresses you. I'm sorry I didn't know that before I commented about you to Mrs. Gallagher, but I'm afraid it's too late to change people's expectations now. Many of San Francisco's finest want to meet you, and you'll have to handle the attention in a mature and gracious way."

"I can't recall that anyone has ever put the words mature and gracious and my name all in the same sentence before," I muttered, "so I don't think your expectations are very reasonable." I caught her glance and despite my serious intention I started to laugh. "But I promise I'll do my best not to run shrieking from the room."

"That's the spirit," Ruth replied, laughing, too. "I knew I could count on my favorite sister."

The dresses my sister had worked on so hard for so many days were a credit both to her skill as a seamstress and to her unerring eye for style. She'd always had the flair, even as a little girl, and when we stood facing each other dressed in our cotillion finery we both had compliments for the other.

"You look wonderful," I told Ruth. "That pale rose is perfect with your complexion and the overskirt is perfect to hide your—" I stopped, deciding I had probably already gone too far for tact, but with her usual sunny disposition, Ruth just laughed.

"My expanding mid-section you mean? Yes, that was the intention, although now that I see it on, I realize the only way to hide this waistline would be to attend wrapped in a blanket. Unfortunately, Martin frowned at the idea, so this dress was the best I could do. Anyway, I don't mind if I look like an expectant mother. That's what I am, and I don't want people to think I'm anything but thrilled about it." In a rare moment of self-doubt, she added, "It is proper that I'm attending, isn't it, even in my rather advanced and obvious condition?"

"It's 1901, not 1801," I replied, "and good old Queen Victoria with all her notions about propriety is gone. Of course, you should attend. Don't be silly. And anyway, the way you've designed that dress, no one would guess a thing."

Ruth reached to rearrange the long rows of pearls draped around my neck. "Those are a nice touch, Dinah. I remember your eighteenth birthday when you received them. What do you think about your dress?" I turned to look at myself in the long mirror.

"I think you did a beautiful job, as usual, but I wonder if it suits me exactly."

"I knew you'd say that. You're a striking woman, Dinah, but in a unique way."

"Is that what they call damning with faint praise?"

"No, no, no. Look at you. You look exactly like the Gibson girl pictures in any of the magazines except you don't."

"That clears it up then. Thank you." Ruth gave another little laugh.

"I just mean—" Ruth paused for thought. "Your figure is wonderful, small in the right places and, well, not small, in the right places, and your face is attractive, but there's a character about it that makes it different, makes it better than beautiful. You look like a real woman, Dinah, not like someone's idealized picture despite the Gibson Girl similarities. Anyway, the dark blue satin is perfect for you."

"Don't you think it shows a little bit too much of me?" I stared in the mirror at the expanse of skin that I was not used to sharing with the public. "Shouldn't I have something on my shoulders and did you mean for these little pieces of whatever they are to drape along my arm like they do?"

"You'd never have gone out in public wearing the gown if I'd followed the pattern exactly. You look completely proper. Sort of."

"And if Father saw me wearing this, would he let me out in public?"

The question made my sister pause for a moment. When her mental justification was complete, she answered, "Father isn't here so you'll just have to trust my judgment. Now grab your wrap and meet us downstairs. Martin has been pacing impatiently by the front door for the last hour." I didn't miss the fact that Ruth never answered the original question.

I had viewed the Palace Hotel from the street on several occasions, but nothing prepared me for the spectacular and glamorous details of a close-up inspection. All of us, even Martin, held our collective breaths when the carriage Mr. Gallagher sent to claim us pulled off of New Montgomery Street and lined up behind at least ten other carriages waiting in the hotel's Grand Court to unload their passengers.

"It sits on over two acres," Martin whispered in an awed voice, "and the foundation walls are twelve feet thick. It's the largest hotel in the world."

When we stepped out of the carriage, we were greeted by music played by a small orchestra situated across from the hotel entrance. Two well-dressed men held open the doors and a third attaché ushered us forward with a courtly gesture.

"You're with the Gallagher party," he stated with an assurance that suggested someone had stamped the name on our foreheads without our knowledge. "Follow me, please. Mr. and Mrs. Gallagher are expecting you." Ruth took Martin's arm and with me following slightly behind, we moved through the spacious central court. I tried very hard to act like I belonged there, but it took all my will-power to keep from staring upward and open-mouthed at the six stories looming above us. The huge hall we entered was already filled with people, some standing engaged in conversation and others seated at tables. Large, marble double-pillars outlined the space and wall sconces threw light everywhere, reflecting off the china and glassware on the tables and twinkling from the abundance of jewels worn by the women that moved elegantly about the room. It seemed we had stepped into a sky full of rainbow-colored stars. The effect was dazzling, breath-taking.

"Ah, Shandling." A man separated himself from a group of men standing by one table and stepped toward us with his hand outstretched. "Good to see you."

"Hello, sir," Martin responded, taking the man's hand. Mr. Gallagher, I guessed from Martin's respectful tone and was eventually proved right. Ralph Gallagher. A sleek, dark, panther-like man, shorter and slimmer than Martin but somehow unquestionably more powerful. A man smooth in his speech and cool in his demeanor. He reached toward a woman and brought her forward to stand next to him.

"This is my wife, Irene," he told Martin. "I believe our wives have met."

"Yes, we know each other," Irene Gallagher said, as smooth and cool as her husband. Perversely, the characteristics I found tolerable, even evocative, in him seemed objectionable in her. I disliked Irene Gallagher immediately and through the evening nothing occurred to make me change my opinion, though I was honest enough to realize that my feelings may have reflected my general state of mind more than her character. The woman gave Ruth a cursory greeting and turned toward me, eyes alight.

"And this must be the brave Miss Hudson." At her words, Ruth threw me a quick, worried, pleading look.

"Yes, I'm Dinah Hudson," I replied with what I hoped was a pleasant smile. "How do you do, Mrs. Gallagher? I've heard so much about you from Ruth."

"Not nearly as much as I've heard about you. Such a brave young woman! So remarkable! I'm sure I'd never have comported myself with the same degree of courage and ingenuity. You were in the papers, you know."

So this is how it's going to be, I thought with a touch of despair, but answered easily, "No, I didn't know, but sideshow freaks and scoundrels make the papers, too, so I'm not sure I should be grateful for the attention."

Irene Gallagher gave me the same startled but appraising look she would have used if I'd suddenly begun to babble in tongues before she decided to laugh. "Well, your coverage was all good, believe me. Come and sit down and tell me all about it."

Not *all* about it, I thought, continuing my reactionary mental monologue, you don't want to know *all* about it. You would find the particulars both repulsive and monotonous and hardly appropriate for refined conversation around the dining table of a grand ballroom. The details would dim and disappoint the bright curiosity in your eyes, would make your silk shrivel and your feathers fade.

I sat down as bidden and at the last minute Ruth intervened herself between Mrs. Gallagher and me, taking the chair meant for me and nudging me gently to her other side. Irene Gallagher was not happy about the move but too well-bred to say anything. Under the table Ruth found my hand and gave it a hard squeeze; I don't think I ever loved my sister more than I did at that moment.

For all that intangible unpleasantness, the evening did not start out badly. Irene Gallagher was not the only person at our table, and the woman on my other side conversed comfortably about topics that had nothing to do with me personally. When I mentioned that I was assisting Donaldina Cameron, she asked for more information and listened intently.

In addition, the surroundings were beautiful, the meal delicious, and at the conclusion of the meal, the orchestra promised a professional level of music that I hadn't heard in a long time. Certainly nothing like the Policemen's Brass Orchestra, I thought with an inward smile, and prepared to enjoy myself. At the first song, I watched Martin lead a glowing Ruth to the dance floor and turned to find Ralph Gallagher beside me, his hand outstretched.

"May I have the honor, Miss Hudson?" he asked in a manner surprisingly old-fashioned for a modern-day man of commerce and industry.

I was flustered for a moment, forced myself not to look at his wife to see how she felt about an invitation which should properly have been hers, and finally stood. Frankly, I would have preferred the man clearing the dishes from our table to Ralph Gallagher, but I couldn't think of a way to refuse him for the first dance and then proceed to dance with other men later in the evening. Such behavior was not socially acceptable, and this was Martin's employer, besides.

"Of course. Thank you."

Ralph Gallagher danced well and possessed the ability to converse easily as he did so. I had not danced in a long time and confessed the fact to him as the music began.

"That's why men lead, Miss Hudson. To keep women moving in the right direction."

I wanted to bristle at the remark but contented myself with saying, "I have often wondered about that arrangement, Mr. Gallagher, and am relieved to have you provide so logical an explanation."

After a slight pause, my partner murmured, "I am not my wife, Miss Hudson. I know when I'm being mocked or patronized."

I looked at his face quickly, but he was smiling. More than smiling, I realized. Flirting. The man was flirting with me!

"I have not mocked your wife, and I am certainly not mocking you. Believe me, I haven't the social competence to do so with the subtlety with which you're trying to credit me. I promise that if I ever hold you up to ridicule, you'll be the first to know it."

He laughed at that but said no more, and we finished the dance without further talk. As we walked off the dance floor, we were stopped by a couple who said they wished to meet me, and they in turn were joined by another couple. After that a man I didn't recognize asked me for the next dance and for the next few hours the evening was a blur. In passing I met the infamous Judge Mackiver, who smelled like cigars and brandy and was intoxicated enough to leer in the general direction of my chest. I found him offensive and ridiculous and had to stop myself from scrubbing at the spot on my shoulder where his hand had brushed.

Mackiver introduced me to Abe Ruef, a prominent attorney

whose name was well known in the city and to Eugene Schmitz, a man rumored to have designs on the position of mayor. I knew better than to make hasty judgments but my instincts told me that Ruef and Schmitz and Mackiver were cut from the same cloth: all prominent and successful scoundrels. San Francisco seemed to have an over-abundance of such men.

Mayor Phelan also found his way to me through the crowd. He was a clear-eyed, bearded man of obvious intelligence and gracious speech. A natural politician, an Irishman, a gentleman, and as Ruth had pointed out to me hopefully, also a bachelor. I liked the mayor a great deal, enjoyed our dance and our conversation, and was flattered when he returned for a second dance. He asked me about my experiences of the Boxer Rebellion—nearly everyone did—but he seemed sensitive to the tone of my responses that indicated I did not wish to spend a great deal of time on that personal history. Unfortunately, not everyone was as perceptive or as kind as he.

Whenever I returned to our table, Irene Gallagher would drag over a new audience and introduce me as the "heroine of Pekin," pronouncing the words with the same dramatic relish she would have used if she were reading the cover of a particularly salacious romance novel. She treated me like a pet monkey capable of a string of clever tricks, and I found it increasingly difficult to be civil to the woman. When I overheard Ruth telling her that I was still bothered by unpleasant memories of the events of that summer and wanted to remain as anonymous as possible, I hoped that Mrs. Gallagher would understand the message Ruth intended by her murmured comment.

Mrs. Gallagher's only response, however, was to lean forward and ask in a voice that was not as low as she imagined, "What events exactly, Mrs. Shandling? There were always rumors that some of the white women fell into the hands of the Chinese barbarians and were treated quite shamefully." Her tone left no doubt about what she meant by *quite shamefully*. Raped, she might as well have said, her tone a mix of curiosity and horror and disgust. Her outrageous curiosity made me want to slap her hard and perhaps I would have, despite Ruth's best efforts to insert herself between us, except exactly at that moment Jake Pandora asked me for the next dance.

I had not seen him before that moment, but as I looked up at him, I wondered how I could possibly have missed him. If ever a man belonged in formal evening clothes, that man was Jake Pandora. The black coat and tails, the perfectly tailored waist coat and full trousers and pristine white shirt with gold buttons and black silk tie all complimented him, emphasized his lean waist and broadened his shoulders, made him astonishingly handsome. I wasn't the only one who thought so, either, because I watched several women on their way to the dance floor turn their heads to glance back at him as he stood next to my chair.

I gawked, swallowed, and blurted, "What in the world are you doing here?" Not, perhaps, the most sophisticated response I might have made, but I've never handled surprises well.

"Good evening to you, too, Miss Hudson. Is that a yes or a no to my offer?" I took his outstretched hand and allowed him to draw me to my feet.

"A yes."

"Good." I was still so amazed to see him that I could only stare, so that finally he murmured, "You may have noticed that there's a floor set a little closer to the orchestra and I believe people use that for dancing."

"Don't be so clever, Mr. Pandora." He continued to hold my hand as he led me away from the table, and we didn't speak again until we had joined the crowd of dancing couples. Then I said, "How did you ever wrangle an invitation to this evening?"

"It's all about who you know."

"And you know the right people?"

"I do."

"I don't know why I find that so hard to believe."

"I know why. Because I'm the son of Greek immigrants. Because my education was acquired on the docks. Because I live in rooms above my office instead of in a fine Nob Hill mansion. That's why. I pegged you as a snob the first time I saw you, and it appears I was right after all."

"Wrong yet again, Mr. Pandora." His words stung, but I wasn't about to admit it. "My opinion of you has much more to do with your bad manners than with your education or your parentage or your living quarters. All those things deal with the surface of a man, but bad manners reflect inner character. Besides, you must admit that we didn't get off to a very good start with that small matter of the Pandora Two between us. I admit to being far from perfect, but I am not a snob." He was silent a long time, long enough for the music to end and for both of us to begin a leisurely walk back to my table.

"No," he agreed, finally. "You're not. I am sometimes hasty in my assumptions, a fact you've probably noted." Another slight pause, then a thoughtful, "I don't know exactly what you are, Miss Hudson, but you are not a snob. I'll grant you that." As I sat down at our table, he bent forward and said in a voice so low only I could hear, "You ought to wear that color more often. It does remarkable things to your eyes." Without looking at me, he straightened and strolled leisurely away, women sending a variety of glances—all of them admiring, some of them speculative, and a few openly inviting—after him. The crowd parted for him as the Red Sea must once have split for Moses.

"Was that Mr. Pandora?" Ruth asked. "I didn't realize he would be here. I'm surprised."

"So am I," I replied. "Believe me, Ruthie, so am I."

I hadn't known what to expect from the evening and was relieved as the hours passed and questions about the Boxer Rebellion and my experiences under siege waned. Ruth was having a wonderful time—she always carried a radiance about her when she truly enjoyed herself—and because she was happy, so was Martin. I observed the two of them together with a touch of wistfulness. Ruth loved and was loved in return, and somehow that fact seemed to reduce life to its simplest, most gratifying perspective. My sister had always seen life in different terms and in different colors than I, had always sought out the good in people and situations and even as a child had attracted affection from the most unexpected characters. I wished I had her ability to see good and to be good but knew that was not the case and never would be, yet to see Ruth happy and smiling had the same energizing effect on me as a good tonic.

I didn't enjoy the evening simply because Ruth was happy, however. That would credit me with far too generous and altruistic motivations; vanity would be the more honest reason. Heroine status aside, I was a single woman complimented and admired and much in demand. I sat out dances only if I chose to do so and maintained a steady stream of partners made up, by and large, of pleasant, polished, engaging men. I had to laugh at my spoken intention to Jake Pandora to listen to the conversations in the hope of finding out more about the human smuggling trade. Even with the lavish flow of champagne, the people around me were much too practiced and urbane to say anything they didn't want repeated a hundred times over.

I had just returned from a trip to the Ladies' Lounge, still smiling at the mental picture of myself eavesdropping, when I was approached by a man and woman. I could tell, just by the apologetic way the woman met my gaze, that they were going to ask about China, and I steeled myself for the requisite questions and comments. They were both gray-haired, older than my father in appearance, and had an appealingly ordinary look about them. No diamond stick pin the size of a fireplace log in his lapel or enormous earrings dangling like chandeliers from her ears; both wore perfectly presentable evening dress but not to excess. I warmed to them as people I thought I would like.

"Miss Hudson?"

I put on my polite face, nodded, and waited.

"I'm Eleanor Thomas. This is my husband, Stanley. We heard that you were here tonight, and I realize it's hardly the time and place for such a discussion, but we were wondering when you were in Pekin during that terrible time if you had the opportunity to meet Captain Myers."

"Not really," I answered, surprised by the inquiry. "The captain led the troops that rescued us, but he was wounded himself and transported to the naval hospital in Yokohama. I recall that he was pointed out to me, but I'm afraid I wouldn't recognize him if he walked into the room right now. Is he related to you in some way?"

Eleanor Thomas's ageing face softened. "Not exactly, not the way you mean. Our grandson, Reese, served under him and admired him a great deal."

"I see," I said but didn't, not really. The conversation was headed in a direction I hadn't expected and didn't understand.

"My husband told me not to bother you; he told me it would serve no purpose, but I had to meet you. I wanted to see someone who had been part of the group rescued by Capt. Myers's Marines. I told Stanley it would make a difference, and I don't know how exactly but it has. You're so lovely and I can tell by your face, you're kind, too, and that helps me."

By then I was completely baffled. "Helps you," I repeated. "I'm sorry, but I don't understand."

She reached out to pat my arm before smiling gently and responding, "Of course, you don't, my dear. How could you? Stanley was right. I've made a mess of it, embarrassed you and myself, as well."

"You haven't embarrassed me at all, Mrs. Thomas. I just don't understand what I've done to help you."

"Our grandson, our son's only child, died with the Marines during the rescue, Miss Hudson. Only two men were lost in the attack, but one of them was our Reese and, of course, that makes the number *two* a very great number indeed." Her voice cracked and behind her Mr. Thomas rested a hand softly on her shoulder. "He was a fine young man, Miss Hudson, and he loved military service, was proud to do his duty, but we miss him terribly. His mother hasn't been outside her home since she received the news and our son—well, it was a terrible blow to him. A blow to all of us. I don't know if we'll ever recover. But seeing you here, so beautiful and alive helps me understand Reese's sacrifice."

She continued to speak, but my gaze was transfixed on her husband's face. For a brief moment, he looked so anguished at his wife's words, so completely desolate, that I moved forward instinctively to put my arms around him for comfort. Mrs. Thomas had learned to talk about her loss, but I thought this man had not and for whatever reason might never be able to. Of course, I could not embrace him, standing there as we were on the edge of the dance floor of the most lavish room in the largest hotel in the world, surrounded by San Francisco's most elite and influential citizens, but for the moment it was all I could think to do to alleviate the profound grief I saw on his face and the glaze of tears that made the older man's eyes sparkle in the lights.

"I am so sorry, Mr. and Mrs. Thomas, so very sorry for your loss. I wish it hadn't happened. I wish there had been another way." But I had longed for rescue at the time, I recalled, and not cared that more lives would be endangered, and when the Marines had marched into Pekin, I had cheered as loudly as everyone else with no thought for the soldiers who had fallen during the approach. Why in the great and divine theme of life had my continuing existence held more importance than the well-being of their beloved Reese? I didn't know what else to say to them, didn't know how to make sense of those violent days in Pekin and the death and grief and loss that had occurred on all sides of the conflict.

"Leave Miss Hudson to her dancing, Eleanor." To me Mr. Thomas gave a courtly bow, his look of terrible sadness and longing completely gone. Now he looked like what he was: a successful California business man of sound mind and good manners. He smiled at me. "You've been surrounded by men all night, young lady, with a line no doubt forming behind me as we speak, so thank you for your time. We appreciate it. Eleanor has spoken of nothing else since she heard that you were present this evening. I hope we haven't distressed you."

"No," I responded. The word came out a whisper, and I cleared my throat to repeat it. "No, not at all. How could you ever think that? I just wish——"

When I faltered Eleanor Thomas patted my arm again and said, "I know, I know" before turning to place her hand on her husband's sleeve and say brightly, "This is our dance, Stanley. You promised, remember?"

Even then, I think I would have recovered from that emotional meeting if immediately on the heels of the Thomases' departure I hadn't seen Irene Gallagher approaching and heard her say, "There's the brave girl now. You've been hiding from your admirers, Miss Hudson. Shame on you," everything about her false and condescending and as far from the genuine emotion of Eleanor and Stanley Thomas as it was possible to be.

I didn't bother to look at Mrs. Gallagher; I simply turned on my heel and rushed out of the room. The farther down the hall I got, the faster I hurried, until I was finally holding up my skirts practically to knee level and running. I might have had demons at my heels, which wasn't so very far from the truth.

When I finally stopped my mad rush, it was only because I was winded and literally gasping for breath. Corsets did not lend themselves to that kind of vigorous exertion. By then I was in another hallway, one dark and empty, and I peered through the closest doorway into what looked like some kind of intimate dining area before I stepped inside and sat down at a table there. The hallway's lights illuminated the area by the door where I sat, but the rest of the room was dark, lit faintly by moonlight that shone through the high row of windows along one wall. I had cut and run, I thought, and couldn't regret the action no matter what followed. I felt so sick of place and time and so tired of pretense and secrets that I wanted to be somewhere— anywhere—else. I couldn't make myself get up and go back. I just couldn't. I knew Ruth would miss me and I didn't know how I'd get home, but I was finished with the city's most glamorous fête and I wasn't going back. I'll just sit here, I told myself, just sit here for a while, and then I'll figure out what to do, but I'm not going back in there. I am not.

After a while, the light from the hallway was blocked by the figure of man standing in the doorway. He looked in, saw me—probably heard me still trying to catch my breath after my run, more likely—and came to pull out another chair at the table where I sat.

"May I join you?" asked Jake Pandora, and I wasn't even surprised to see him. Something was going on there, too, something to do with Jake Pandora and his presence in my life, no such thing as coincidence, and everything, no matter how insignificant, part of a divine plan and an answer to someone's prayer. I had to believe that when it came to the life and death of young Reese Thomas. Maybe it applied to Jake Pandora, too.

When I didn't speak, we sat quietly for what seemed like a long time until he reached out and gently placed his hand over mine. "Stop that, Dinah."

Without realizing it I had reached up and grasped the two long strands of pearls I wore, holding them in an unnatural posture, a hand on each side and with a death grip. I couldn't speak or move. I must be going insane, I thought in one clear part of my mind. Could it happen like this? One moment dancing and smiling and making social chatter and the next completely mad? My breathing had quieted but in direct proportion to my slowing heart my hands had begun, seemingly of their own volition, to clench the pearls I wore, clench and then briefly loosen their hold, clench again and loosen again, in a strange way mimicking the steady rhythm of my heart that I could hear beating in my ears.

Pandora's hand over mine was warm and firm, the hand of a working man, calluses on his palm and the skin of his fingers rough to the touch. Enormously comforting. The touch unnerved me to even more improbable and uncharacteristic behavior. I began to cry and jerked my hands free to try to wipe away the ever-increasing tears, an impossible task.

I sensed that my companion was as unnerved as I by my unexpected weeping and perhaps uncomfortable, and I tried to tell him to leave me alone, just go away so I could compose myself without anyone's attention, but all that came out of my mouth were unintelligible sounds, small trembling gasps and sobs I tried to stifle. After a moment of hesitation, he handed me a large handkerchief and went to stand in the doorway with his back to me. I was grateful that he hadn't attempted any awkward comfort, no arm around my shoulders, no soft "What's wrong?" or even worse, "It will be all right." What solace would words like that offer? Some things could never be made right. Reese Thomas would not appear on his mother's doorstep to lure her once more into the sunshine. The family would pick up the pieces and find a way to continue—as we had done when my brother Joe died—but the boy's death had wounded the Thomases in a way that would stay with them forever. And somehow I felt responsible.

"I hate all the fuss."

Pandora, recognizing intelligible speech, turned in the doorway to face me but didn't come any closer.

"I hate all the fuss," I repeated, "all that brave young woman nonsense, all the questions and the undisguised curiosity and acting as if any of it mattered to them. I hate it. I told Ruth I didn't want to come. I told her what it would be like. No one understands, not even Ruth."

"Understands what it was like in Pekin, you mean?"

"No," I retorted fiercely. "Understands about me."

"What is there to understand about you?"

Pandora's tone, conversational, unperturbed, remotely curious, and slightly amused steadied me. I began to calm, felt my irrational panic and that horrible combination of guilt and responsibility and dishonesty and shame begin to fade. My heartbeat slowed and my hands rested quietly in my lap.

"That I'm a coward and because I'm a coward, a man died." I apparently thought my words much more shocking than he did because he strolled back into the room, pulled out the chair across from me, straddled it, and rested his arms on the chair's back to look at me in the dim light.

"Really? That's not the picture you present to the world."

"I'm not just a coward, I'm a hypocrite, too. Everything about me is a façade."

"I see."

It was his attitude of casual indifference that caused me to spill the story I had never shared before. That's the only reason I can think of to explain why I told Jake Pandora, of all people, the shameful story of Alfred Betterman from London, England, the little man who died because of my cowardice and foolishness.

"No one was supposed to step outside the walls of the legation. It was an order we all knew and it was sternly repeated many times a day. The Boxers surrounded the little compound where we were holed up, and all the women and children were supposed to stay behind the walls of the British Embassy. But sometimes at night I would go to the edge of the embassy gardens for a little privacy and fresh air, and one night I thought I heard someone call for help. Honestly, I thought I heard someone. I had seen what the Boxers did to Chinese converts, and I knew that many of our own Chinese congregation had fled to Pekin from the countryside and were being flushed out of their city hiding places and murdered. I thought, what if it's someone I know calling for refuge. I was restless, besides. It was hot and late and I thought, what harm can it do? I'll just take a quick look in the park outside the legation, but all the time I knew I shouldn't do it, that I was just asking for trouble. Dear God, if I could just go back to that moment and make a different decision, I would. But I can't.

"I stepped outside the walls, hardly any distance at all, and he came after me. Corporal Alfred Betterman of the British Consulate force. He called, 'Come back, Miss. Come back right now,' and hurried up behind me. He saw the glint of the gun, I think. I don't know for sure, but I believe the moonlight reflected off the sniper's weapon and Corporal Betterman knew right away what it was. I saw the knowledge in his face, but I didn't see a bit of fear. Isn't that something? Someone was aiming a gun at us but he didn't seem a bit afraid. He stepped in front of me, grabbed my arm, and tried to pull me along, and that was when the sniper fired his first shot. It missed us, but I felt the bullet's breath by my cheek and I froze. I couldn't move, not one step. I was so frightened and all I could do was stand there. I couldn't think and I couldn't talk. I couldn't do anything but stand in the moonlight and invite the shooter to try again. Corporal Betterman could have run for safety, but he wouldn't leave me. I can still hear his voice, encouraging, urgent, 'Run, Miss! Come on now, run!' and when I finally did, I could hear him running behind me. Then I heard another shot, and he wasn't running any more. I looked back and he lay on the ground. That brave little man! He was dead before he fell."

"How do you know that?"

"Oh, I went back. I couldn't just leave him there. I crouched over him and his eyes were open, but there wasn't any life in them. I could tell. Do you understand what I mean?"

"Yes."

"Then more soldiers came toward us from the legation, two were firing their rifles to cover the others, I guess, and two more grabbed me and Corporal Betterman's body and dragged us both back into the compound. Thank God no one else was hurt. No one ever said a word of blame to me, either, but I wanted them to. I wanted someone to shout at me that I was a foolish, stupid woman and because of my cowardice a good man was dead! The ambassador told me that the only family Corporal Betterman had was the army, that it was his whole life and all he ever wanted, but I wonder if that's true. He was there from the beginning of the siege so we were together in close quarters for weeks, but I don't remember him and I never knew anything about him when he was alive, not what he liked or what annoyed him or made him laugh or lose his temper. I'm ashamed about that. It seems wrong, doesn't it? Death shouldn't be anonymous. I did what I knew I shouldn't do, and he paid for my disobedience. Because I was so frightened I couldn't move, he came back for me and because he came back for me, he died. That's why I hate all that brave heroine talk and all that nonsense about being fearless and cheerful in the face of danger. It's all a lie and I hate it."

After a moment, Jake Pandora said, "That explains it then."

Whatever I expected to hear, it was not words expressing the satisfaction of a riddle solved. Something a bit more sympathetic would have been nice, although I—and probably he—knew if he said anything that sounded like he was humoring me or speaking sympathetic words he thought I wanted to hear, I'd have bitten his head off.

"Explains what?" I finally had to ask, certain he waited for the question.

"The way you are. That need you have to make sure people know you aren't afraid. That prickly fearlessness. It's important to you that people see you as resolute and independent and able to go it alone, nothing tentative about Miss Dinah Hudson!"

I didn't have to mull over his comments; the moment he spoke the words, I knew them to be true and was humbled that what I'd held inside so deeply and so secretly had somehow still managed to seep out and reveal itself. At least to him.

"Don't be so clever, Mr. Pandora." I repeated my words from earlier in the evening but without the edge, too weary and wrung out from emotion and tears to keep up appearances any longer. "You're right, though. I've felt so ashamed for so many months. No culture values cowardice, you know, and I thought if people knew the truth about me, I wouldn't have any place to go."

I heard him take a quick breath and get up quickly to come and crouch in front of me. "Listen, " he told me, looking up into my face, "being afraid doesn't make a person a coward, it makes a person human. Just because you feel the need to prove your courage doesn't mean you don't possess it. You do. You have more nerve than many men I know."

Crouched as he was, we were close to eye level so I could watch his face as he spoke. A streak of moonlight came in through the row of windows and lit up a portion of his face, illuminated the trace of dark stubble just beginning to show on his cheeks, smoothed his perfect skin, and shadowed the contours of cheek and temple. Involuntarily I laid the palm of one hand against the side of his face, just to feel the skin, just to see if it was as cool and perfect as it looked, and I heard him take a second quick breath. At that moment everything about him was mesmerizing and so incredibly attractive that I would have done anything he asked. Anything. I was very tired but relieved, too, experiencing an unexpected and contrary exhilaration from my confession. Jake Pandora and I had shared something intimate. In a figurative sense, he had seen me naked and vulnerable, but the mental, more literal picture that came with the thought brought quick color to my face. Even in the dim room I know he saw my blush, and I believe could read how pliable I was at that particular moment, pliable and willing, because something in his own face changed. From the sudden tensing of his body I knew that I had become desirable to him in a very human way. He stood quickly and took both my hands in his to draw me to my feet so that we stood very close. In the stillness, I could hear his breathing, quick and shallow. He said my first name in a voice that didn't sound like him at all and would have kissed me, a kiss I would certainly have welcomed, returned, and pursued. I liked kissing, after all, and at that instant I more than liked Jake Pandora.

I will never know where that particular moment might have led because from the doorway Ruth said my name. I jumped away from Jake, Ruth's voice acting like a bee sting. Jake turned more slowly.

"Yes." My voice was only a whisper, too breathy and hardly audible. "Yes," I repeated more firmly.

With one glance Ruth took in the situation, at least the situation as she saw it. "What are you doing here, for heaven's sake?" She entered scolding, but when she got a clearer look at me, she whirled on Pandora. "What have you done to my sister to make her cry?" The protective outrage in her voice warmed me. Just then I had two champions, which were two more than I deserved.

"No, no, Ruthie. Jake found me this way. It's not what you think. I was upset."

"Upset about what?" Ruth's tone was mollified, but she still placed herself between me and Jake, her back to him in a dismissive way.

"Everything. Just everything. I met a couple whose grandson died during the Pekin rescue, and it affected me. And then Irene Gallagher kept going on and on as if she enjoyed making me uncomfortable, and I couldn't stand it anymore. I couldn't stand any of it. I'm sorry. Is Martin in trouble because of me?"

"Martin? Of course not. The men wandered away for cigars or something—I'm not exactly sure what men do when they wander off in a group—and that's when I looked for you. Some of the waiters remembered you running down the hallway. Like she was being chased by wild Indians is how they phrased it, and I just followed the trail of witnesses."

"I won't go back in there," I told her firmly. "I'm done for the night, but you should go back and enjoy the rest of the evening. Find your husband and enjoy a few more dances and another glass of punch." I took a breath before concluding with all the penitence I could muster, "I'm sorry, Ruthie. I wouldn't spoil your evening for the world. One of the attachés can arrange a cab for me, and I'll be fine once I'm home. Too much champagne, I think."

Pandora had stepped farther away from the two of us but still close enough to hear what was said. "I'll take your sister home, Mrs. Shandling." When Ruth turned to examine him with a skeptical expression, he gave a faint smile and added, "I give you my word that Miss Hudson would not be safer with a brother than she'll be with me."

I was sure that Jake Pandora's intentions had been anything but brotherly ten minutes earlier, and I think Ruth realized the same.

"I don't want you to worry, Ruth. I can go home by myself." My words had the opposite effect on my sister, however.

"That's not a good idea. I suppose Mr. Pandora will have to do, and we have his word, after all." Neither Jake nor I missed the faint trace of irony in her tone. She linked her arm with mine and we

walked together into the brightly lit hallway where Ruth shook her
head at the sight of me.

"You're a mess, Dinah. Look at your hair," but I heard affection and
loyalty in her tone that said she loved me, mess and all. She didn't say
another word to Jake, hardly acknowledged his presence except for a
quick nod of her head in his general direction before she left us.

Jake and I did not exchange any words until he summoned a cab
and the two of us were eventually settled inside. Then I felt obligated
to defend Ruth's brusqueness.

"My sister generally shows better manners. So do I, for that matter. The problem is that she doesn't trust you."

"Wise woman."

That's all we said on the trip to Grove Street. Pandora sat as far
away from me as he could get inside the cab, and except for a quick,
initial look at me as the cab pulled away, spent the remainder of the
trip with his arms folded against his chest and his head dropped. The
posture gave him the look of a sleepy but very handsome Buddha,
which made me smile to myself. I was tired, too—exhausted would
have been more accurate—but relaxed and oddly happy. I thought that
the man across from me had a great deal to do with how I felt but realized it wasn't the most advisable time for me to consider anything with
depth or objectivity. Still too shaky, inside and out.

The cabbie pulled up at the curb, and I started to push open
the door and step down, but Jake was already there with his hand
outstretched.

"You don't have to—" I started, but he interrupted with the tone
I'd come to expect from him.

"I know I don't. Allow me the opportunity to act the part of a gentleman one last time before I return to the docks from whence I came."
He was mocking himself this time, not me, and I didn't respond.

At the foot of the front porch steps I stopped and said involuntarily, "The front door's open!"

"It shouldn't be?"

"You must live in an interesting neighborhood if leaving the front door ajar when you leave is normal practice," I retorted. "Of course it shouldn't be open. When we left, the door was shut. Firmly shut. "

"And there's no one else here?"

Fortunately, I had delivered Suey Wah to Miss Cameron that afternoon for an overnight stay at 920 in our absence and knew the house had been left empty. I recalled Martin pulling the door closed behind him when we had departed for the Palace Hotel. In passing I thought that Pandora had asked an odd question for the occasion. What did he know or at least suspect?

"No," I finally answered. "No one. How odd." I turned to step onto the porch but was halted by his hand grasping my wrist.

"I'll go. You stay here." The idea that he thought I would do as he ordered was almost laughable.

"Of course, master," I replied and fell into step right behind him. I'm sure he wanted to say something quelling about my insubordination, but by then he had pushed open the front door and we both stepped into the hallway.

"We could stand here in the dark," I whispered, "or I could go and turn on the lights." Without waiting for his approval, I moved quickly to the oil light on the bureau in the hallway and then to the parlor electric lights Martin had had installed when he'd commissioned the house.

"Will you please try to stay close to me?" I couldn't miss the exasperation in Jake's tone. "At least let me make sure there's no one in the house before you assert your independence."

I had already noticed a few things that made me uneasy. "The closet door is open," I volunteered, "and I'm sure it was closed when we left. And the sofa is pulled away from the wall. We didn't leave it like that."

He and I moved from room to room as I mentioned all the small, subtle changes I noticed. Finally, the upstairs and downstairs inspected and as much put back to normal as I could manage, I stated the obvious.

"Someone was here while we were gone."

"Looking for something," he agreed. "Something small. Or some-one small."

"Oh, damn!" I said, realizing what his words meant and slipping into profanity, which I didn't recall doing even in the middle of a Boxer attack. I wasn't quite myself, I suppose, so it took me longer than it should have to work out why intruders had spent time in such a careful search of the house.

"What is it?" he asked.

For a moment I had the distinct feeling that Jake Pandora knew exactly what the trespassers had been looking for, knew but wanted me to say the words out loud anyway. Wanted me to trust him. He had to remember as clearly as I that not very long ago I'd been prepared to trust him with every part of me, would have been, however briefly, clay in his hands to touch and form and mold any way he chose. But this was different. This wasn't about me; it had to do with a little girl and regardless of what I wanted, I couldn't risk her. Dolly Cameron had made me promise complete confidentiality and I wouldn't betray her or Suey Wah.

"Burglars I suspect," I said lightly, "but nothing's missing, and they're obviously gone so you don't need to stay any longer. I'm safe. Thank you, though." Feeling awkward for a moment, I added, "For everything," and hoped he understood. He stepped closer and with one hand lightly fingered a loose curl that bounced annoyingly against my cheek.

"Your sister was right." This time when he waited for me to rise to his verbal bait, I didn't respond. He smiled, recognized my silence for the gesture it was, and concluded, "You are a mess."

Good, I thought, we're back to bad manners, but I felt a faint regret that was difficult to pin down. He didn't say good night, only asked when he reached the door, "Have you ever read a book called *The Red Badge of Courage?*" When I shook my head, he advised, "Read it. You'll understand why when you do." His concluding words advised me to lock the door behind him when he left. I didn't, however, because I knew I was safe. Whoever had been in the house had hoped to find Suey Wah, had left without their quarry, and would not be back any more that night.

I had so much to think about, so many emotions to untangle and sort through that I thought I would not be able to sleep, but I was wrong. I fell asleep as soon as I pulled up the covers and only awakened briefly when Ruth later pushed open the door of my bedroom to be sure I was home safe and sound. I thought she might want to discuss the evening in more detail and did not feel up to that kind of conversation, so I closed my eyes, prepared to feign slumber for as long as necessary, and then fell quickly, deeply, and dreamlessly back to sleep.

Chapter Nine

When I stepped into the breakfast room the next morning, I said involuntarily, "Ruthie! You look tired. Why don't you skip church this morning? God will understand."

"Understand what exactly? That I stayed out too late carousing and so cannot keep the Sabbath Day?" Her tone made my comment sound like a recommendation to kill the family cat.

"First, from someone who has spent a little time around sailors, let me assure you that dancing with your husband and drinking punch is not carousing. And you have to think about the baby."

My sister's face, even with smudged circles under the eyes and pale cheeks, got a set, stubborn look that told me I should concede defeat because she had made up her mind and would not change it, whatever sensible idea I put forward.

"Well, you can nap this afternoon, I suppose, while I go collect Suey Wah from 920."

Ruth accepted my compromise and asked hesitantly, "Dinah, when you got home last night, did everything seem all right to you here at the house?"

Because I had been expecting her to bring up my behavior of last night or my feelings about Jake Pandora, I heard Ruth's question with something close to relief because that was one thing I was prepared and able to discuss.

"Well, the front door was open."

"What?!"

"Yes, I thought it was strange, too, and I was glad Mr. Pandora was along because he went in first and checked out the house from top to bottom. Of course, the house was empty, and it didn't seem that anything was missing. Why?"

Ruth shrugged lightly. "Just a feeling I had, that's all. The sense that something was different. Do you think it was a burglar?"

"No. Nothing was stolen, was it? Maybe the front door just didn't latch properly. Or maybe"—I paused dramatically—"we have a ghost!" Ruth's skeptical response was what I hoped for and my ploy to steer the conversation away from last night seemed to work. Mention Jake Pandora casually, like he was no one special—which of course he wasn't, was he? *Was he?*—acknowledge the open door, and credit anything amiss that I might have neglected to return to normal to the presence of something unseen and slightly ridiculous. Burglars and ghosts. Perfect scapegoats.

We walked to the Old Presbyterian church, despite Martin's forceful intention to get a carriage for us. "You're tired, Ruth, and we can afford to hire a carriage. We could afford to own one, for that matter. It will take me just a minute to find one to hire. They're always waiting down at the corner. She shouldn't walk, don't you agree, Dinah?"

"Yes, Martin, I do. I agree completely and absolutely. However, I can tell from having been exposed to that particular look on my sister's face for many more years than you that you are wasting your breath about the carriage." To Ruth, I added, "I hope the fact that you're distressing the two people closest to you doesn't get in the way of your worship. I never realized that God intended the Sabbath Day to be a day of worry and discord, but it seems you know more about that than I and apparently more than the Almighty, too." I felt a twinge of guilt when my sarcasm made Ruth flush, but it had the desired effect.

"Perhaps we could take a carriage home," she offered. "There's usually a line of them lined up on the street after the service."

Martin flashed me a small, quick smile before answering, "That's a fair compromise. I'm sure we'll all welcome being off our feet by then."

For a while Ruth ignored me, still feeling the sting of my criticism, but she kept the upper hand, after all. As we settled ourselves in the pew, she leaned toward me to whisper, "Don't think your distraction

worked, Sister. Regardless of robbers and ghosts and naps and carriages, I'll still want to hear about your evening." As the organ sounded
the chords of the opening hymn, she smiled at me too sweetly and
opened her hymnal.

The promised discussion didn't occur until much later that evening,
Suey Wah retrieved and tucked away for the night, my sister back to her
usual bright self, and Martin quietly snoring in the parlor with his chin
fallen onto his chest. Ruth and I sat over tea at the kitchen table, and that
was all right because I thought I was ready to talk about most of what
had gone on the previous evening. Not everything, though. Not that rush
of feeling I'd had toward Jake Pandora, not the way his touch had turned
me briefly into a stranger, not what I now realized had been good, old-
fashioned lust. Not as old-fashioned as all that, I suppose, and definitely,
surprisingly good—but lust, just the same.

I stumbled when I tried to explain how talking to the Thomases
had made me feel and stumbled even more sharing the story of Alfred
Betterman, but somehow it seemed that relating the incident to Jake
Pandora had freed me from the terrible, secret burden of shame I'd
carried with me for so many months. A week ago, the idea of telling
Ruth about that night outside the legation hadn't been something I
could even consider. Now, although the telling still had an element of
awkwardness about it, I was able to clutch my teacup and softly reveal
all the fear and grief and responsibility of that dreadful time.

Ruth kept her gaze fixed on my face as I spoke and when I finished
reached across the table to take my hand. "You should have told me before," she said. "Why did you think you had to keep it all to yourself?"

"I didn't want to trouble you with the details, and I couldn't say
the words out loud, anyway. They wouldn't come."

"Until Jake Pandora—"

"No," I interrupted firmly. "He just happened to be there when the
words spilled out, but it wasn't his doing. It was the look on Stanley
Thomas's face and Irene Gallagher's constant harping and—more than
that. Just everything, Ruth."

"I know you didn't like Mrs. Gallagher, and I admit she takes some getting used to, but I find her such a sad woman that I can't hold her actions against her."

"Sad? Why would you say that?"

"I don't know, exactly, except that I don't think she and her husband are very close, even though he's given her every material thing a woman could want. You missed her talking about their brand new house on Nob Hill. The Gallaghers imported New England red brick and had it designed in a style Irene remembered from her childhood on the east coast. She was telling us how they added twin towers to the design along with matching observation decks, and how they brought a man all the way from Boston to create the design of the wrought-iron railings."

I had a sudden memory of sitting next to Colin and seeing Jake Pandora exit exactly that house on Nob Hill. I supposed it was possible that he had business dealings with Ralph Gallagher, but I tucked the knowledge away for later thought.

"That's interesting," I commented, returning to the conversation," but what does that have to do with your feeling sorry for Irene Gallagher? A custom-built new home in the city's most affluent neighborhood doesn't sound like a reason for sympathy."

"I know, but when she was talking about it, she kept asking her husband to elaborate on the details, and he was completely disinterested in everything she said, almost dismissive, and certainly bored with the topic. I was embarrassed for her, really, and felt so thankful for the life I had, a loving husband and a fine home and the baby—" Ruth's voice drifted off for a moment before concluding, "Of course, the Gallaghers have two sons, so Irene must know the joy of children, too, so I can't explain why I feel sorry for her, and I have to admit there were a few times last night that she was truly disagreeable."

"Thank you for that concession. You're a much better woman than I am, Ruth, because I found Mrs. Gallagher and several of her society friends to be disagreeable more often than just a few times."

"So you ran away."

"In the contrary way of life, I run when I shouldn't and can't run when I should. Yes, you're right. Last night I ran away. "

"And Jake Pandora found you."

"Somehow."

"I saw him leave the room abruptly. He's hard to miss, you know."

"Indeed." I didn't miss Ruth's slight flush and sighed. What would it be like to spend one's life with a man whom other women were always sighing over and ogling? Women were allowed that kind of attention but not men. Men should not be that beautiful.

"He must have seen you depart and followed you. How attentive of him! I didn't realize the two of you were that friendly." My sister imbued the word friendly with all sorts of connotations that I hastened to correct.

"We're not friendly, not the way you mean, and I don't know why he decided to follow me, if that's really what he did. I do know that once he found me, he wished he hadn't. Men are so helpless when it comes to tears, and I was certainly crying! He was trying to comfort me, I think, but didn't know what to do or how to do it."

"Ah." Ruth's single syllable conveyed an amused skepticism, but she decided to move on to other topics. "Now, tell me the truth about intruders in our home last night and don't bother talking about burglars or ghosts because they're both on the list of topics I don't believe."

"I think someone knew we were gone and expected to find if not Suey Wah herself, then at least something to prove she resided here."

Ruth was quiet a moment, digesting the information. "And did they find it, do you think?"

"Yes, I fear so," I replied, considering the small *sahn* I'd found wrinkled and disturbed in its bureau drawer and the child-sized slippers that had sat so prominently by the bedroom door.

"Oh, dear. Don't let Martin know or he'll make us take some kind of drastic action."

"I don't think it will be Martin's decision, Ruth. I have to tell

Donaldina tomorrow, and I know what she'll say. Her girls' safety is paramount to her, and she's already worried about Suey Wah and questioning her stay in San Francisco." I added gently, "I'm afraid you shouldn't expect the child to remain with us much longer."

My sister's disappointment showed in her expression, but she still responded firmly, "If Suey Wah will be safer elsewhere, then, of course, she must go. I understand completely. But the house will seem empty and lonely without her."

"Only for a few more weeks. Then you'll be busy with the baby and unable to recall that the house ever seemed empty."

"I suppose you're right." Ruth stood abruptly to gather our empty cups and saucers. "Now it's time for bed. I'm tired." As an afterthought she added, "I realize last night wasn't as enjoyable for you as I'd hoped, but did any of San Francisco's eligible bachelors catch your eye?" I banished the memory of Jake Pandora's cool skin under my fingertips.

"No. I'm sorry. You did your best, though, so don't blame yourself. I'm afraid you might be stuck with an old maid for a sister." Then I thought of Donaldina Cameron, single, too, but impassioned for a cause that altered and saved lives. Miss Cameron made more of a difference in the world than Irene Gallagher would ever make should she live to be a hundred. "Not that I'm ashamed of that, mind you, or think being single is a disease or a flaw to be fixed."

But Ruth wasn't listening. She had already reached the kitchen doorway and turned into the hall toward the stairs, but I could still hear her from where I sat.

"Old maid indeed," she said aloud, laughing a little as she spoke. "I'm pregnant, not blind and deaf. An old maid. That's rich." Laughing at me, I knew, but I didn't have the energy to defend myself. My sister wasn't the only one who was tired.

That night as I sat on the edge of the bed plaiting my hair, Suey Wah knocked timidly on my door. I looked up, saw her, and smiled an invitation.

"Come in, my little bird. I thought you were asleep."

"I was, but I was frightened by a dream." She looked frightened still, eyes too dark and wide and her complexion pale.

"Then come here." I held out my arms and when she came into my embrace, I could feel that she continued to tremble. "It was only a dream, little bird. You're safe here." Suey Wah climbed up on the bed next to me and snuggled against my side.

"I don't think I am safe here any more, Qing."

"Why not?" I turned to look down into her small face.

"I don't know. I feel it, though. And there was the dream."

"Can you tell me about it?"

Suey Wah frowned with concentration. "A big, shiny man was in my dream, and he was surrounded by stars."

"An angel, Suey Wah?"

She shook her head vigorously. "No, no, Qing. Not an angel. A bad man, I think, but now I cannot remember why I thought he was bad."

I stood and pulled back the covers as invitation. "Crawl in, little bird. You should sleep with me tonight. We'll be safe if we are together." Suey Wah obediently crawled under the covers, which I pulled up to her chin. I planted a quick kiss on her forehead, saying, "You know you may trust me to keep you safe, little bird."

"Oh, yes, Qing. We are friends, you said, and friends protect each other."

I turned off the bedroom lamp so the room was in darkness and before my own head reached the pillow, I could hear that the child's breathing had slowed and softened, indicating that she had already returned to sleep. I lay for a while staring into the dark room, said a prayer for Suey Wah and another for my lost Mae Tao, and then I, too, slept as soundly as the little girl beside me.

The next day when I shared my fears for Suey Wah with Miss Cameron, she said exactly what I had anticipated. "I arranged a safe place to send the child weeks ago, Dinah, but because you asked so convincingly to allow her to stay with you and your sister on Grove Street, I didn't pursue the matter. Now, however, I hope you understand that I can't risk Suey Wah's safety any longer. I know all of you will be disappointed, but the child needs to leave San Francisco. It's not safe for her here. I've had more than one source tell me about a white man willing to pay a generous reward for Suey Wah."

"Who?"

"No one is able to attach a name to the man, despite efforts to uncover his identity, and we need to accept the fact that we may never know. Frankly, I think that's because there is more than one man involved. I've long held the opinion that San Francisco is home to a clandestine network of smugglers far larger than we realize, a network made up of many men, some prominent and some not. I don't think it's as easy as identifying one chief criminal who's pulling the strings like a puppet master. As long as the Chinese Exclusion Act remains in place and Chinese women are not legally allowed into the country, men will continue to profit from importing them illegally and under the same deplorable conditions as Suey Wah described. Chinese men— and white men, too—will buy them for whatever purpose they choose and because no one acknowledges that the girls are in this country, no one will lift a finger to help them. It is outrageous but it's also life. Politicians with limited vision or narrow and self-serving interests often make laws that have unexpected and unfortunate consequences."

"Someday when women have the vote, we'll change that."

Donaldina raised one skeptical brow. "If I had the time, I'd debate whether we'll see the vote in my lifetime—see it ever, for that matter—but I have a meeting with the Mission Board this morning, so I'll spare you my opinion about the probability of women's suffrage. I'll reach my contacts this week and let you know about Suey Wah's departure as soon as I have specifics." She rested a hand briefly on my shoulder. "It's the right thing to do, Dinah. You know that."

Of course, I knew that, but the idea of sending Suey Wah away to strangers was difficult for me to consider, and over the next few days, as Ruth, Martin, I, and Suey Wah herself adjusted to the idea of the child's departure, a pall of sorts descended over the house on Grove

Street. Without speaking about it, Suey Wah appeared in my doorway each night and silently crawled into bed next to me.

The night before she was scheduled to leave, she did the same, but as we lay in the dark room, Suey Wah said quietly, "I am very sad to leave, Qing. Must I?"

"I'm afraid so, little bird. Lo Mo has found a safe nest for you, somewhere where the shiny man cannot find you and hurt you."

"I will return as soon as I can."

"I know, and we will always have a place ready for you."

"I will not get to see Mrs. Ruth's baby."

"We don't know that for sure. If we find the shiny man and put him in jail where he cannot hurt you, then you can come back to Grove Street and be the baby's sister."

Suey Wah gave a contented sigh, and reached for my hand under the covers. "A sister and a friend, Qing. Could it really be so? I left my sisters behind when my father sold me."

I gave her little hand a squeeze. "Yes, it could be so. We don't have to look alike or be born into the same family to be sisters and friends, you know."

"I know." Suey Wah's voice was faint and close to sleep. "I know it is the heart that matters." Her voice trailed off into sleep.

The heart indeed, I thought, blinking back tears, where Suey Wah would always have her own corner, even if I never saw her again.

Colin O'Connor stopped by 920 that same week to invite me to join him on an afternoon outing to Golden Gate Park.

"I'd love to go!" I exclaimed. "The park is one of my favorite places in the world!"

"I know. You told me. That's the reason I picked it."

I looked at his grinning face in puzzlement. "I don't remember that."

"Ah, mavourneen, there's not a thing about you I could ever forget. You mentioned your fondness for the park over lunch at the Poodle Dog the first day we ever stepped out together. You were just making conversation, I know, but I stored it away for future reference. It's my duty to make you happy, you know."

His smile and the open admiration in his eyes had the ability to do just that. Colin O'Connor was an uncomplicated pleasure in a world that had become complex and treacherous. I didn't know if what I felt for him was love in any conventional sense of the word, but I enjoyed his company, admired his appearance, and appreciated his devotion to his job. I felt he was a man of heartfelt vocation and because I saw villains without conscience or integrity around every corner, I clung to Colin's easy manner and clear green eyes with an enthusiasm that with hindsight I realize made him more certain of my regard for him than was truly warranted. He was very comfortable to be around, with none of those churning emotions in the pit of my stomach that Jake Pandora caused, and I was always very conscious of—and comforted by—the sense of Colin's masculine strength and determination to take care of me at all costs. He was ambitious but that couldn't be considered a fault. Men were supposed to be ambitious and especially men in 1901 San Francisco. Ambition was inhaled as an integral part of the air of the city. And because he was good looking in a traditional way, people were not always turning around to stare after Colin whenever we were out together in public. I found the effect Jake Pandora's appearance had on other women to be understandable but disconcerting and often annoying.

Colin and I spent part of the afternoon at the Spreckles Temple of Music, a huge conservatory opened just the year before. That afternoon stands out as one of the happiest times I had known since I'd first arrived in San Francisco. With my hand tucked under Colin's arm, we strolled and talked.

"Like we were married," Colin remarked lightly when I mentioned how much I was enjoying the afternoon, and I was so happy in the moment that I didn't say anything to correct or chide him. I felt in perfect charity with Colin O'Connor and hadn't the heart to speak anything discouraging. When the moment passed without my challenging his assumption, he broke into soft song, his breath against my cheek and his fine Irish tenor singing just to me:

Dear thoughts are in my mind / And my soul soars enchanted
As I hear the sweet lark sing / In the clear air of the day
For a tender beaming smile / To my hope has been granted
And tomorrow she shall hear / All my fond heart would say
I shall tell her all my love / All my soul's adoration
And I think she will hear / And will not say me nay
It is this that gives my soul / All its joyous elation
As I hear the sweet lark sing / In the clear air of the day.

For a burly and thoroughly masculine man, Colin O'Connor seemed sweet and endearing at that moment, and when he concluded his serenade with what he intended to be a chaste kiss on my cheek, I intentionally turned my head so it was my lips and not my cheek that received the kiss. Surprised, he stopped abruptly in the middle of the walkway.

"Lovely," I murmured, adding with a touch of mischievous brogue, "'Tis your father's voice you must have inherited." I smiled at Colin and tightened my hold on his arm as we resumed our walk.

I remember being happy that afternoon and thinking that perhaps this was what Ruth had meant so many weeks ago when I asked her about finding the right mate. I had been skeptical about the simplicity of her reply "you just know," but my contentment in Colin O'Connor's company that day suggested that maybe it truly was that simple.

On the morning Suey Wah was scheduled to leave, the unheard of happened— Martin left late for work. He purposefully stayed at home and waited on the porch with us for the cab. When the carriage stopped at the curb, he unclenched his fist and in a self-conscious gesture extended his palm toward Suey Wah. Martin's open hand revealed a slender chain from which dangled a small golden pendant in the shape of a bird. Suey Wah was so affected by his gift that at first she would not accept it.

"Oh no, no, no, Mr. Martin. I cannot take such a precious thing. It is too fine for me. Please do not make me take it."

"Nonsense. Here, Ruth, you fasten it. My hands are too big and clumsy."

Ruth latched the chain around Suey Wah's neck and then came to stand next to Martin, both of them looking at the girl mournfully. It was up to me to stay brisk and business-like or we'd all be crying like hungry babies.

"Very pretty," I said, taking Suey Wah's hand in one of mine and picking up the small valise containing her few belongings with the other. "Now come along, Suey Wah, or we'll miss the schooner Miss Cameron arranged to take you up the coast." I glared at my sister and brother-in-law. "Do not make this child—or me—weep. Suey Wah is headed for a wonderful place, a school for girls in a beautiful city filled with fruit and sunshine. She will be happy and healthy. Many girls have applied to enter this school, but very few are accepted. It's an honor that our Suey Wah is one of the select few. You should be happy for her."

"We're as happy for her as you are," Ruth sniffed in return and managed a smile as she and Martin stood in the front doorway watching us descend the porch. Suey Wah tried to wave and walk at the same time until we climbed into the cab that waited for us at the curb. I had hoped for Casey's familiar face, but the driver was a stranger.

"I do not like so many good-byes," Suey Wah said simply, and her words reminded me of Johanna standing by the railing of the *Solace* as we arrived in San Francisco last spring. "Life is just a series of good-byes," my companion had said at the time and I recognized the same tone in Suey Wah's plaintive comment that I'd heard in Johanna's voice. As response, I repeated the thought I'd expressed to Johanna then.

"I know, but don't give the good-byes so much attention that you miss the warmth of homecoming." I wanted to tell Suey Wah about the gradual healing I read in Johanna's letters, wanted the child to know that the pain of loss and the fear of change could and would eventually lessen, that even nightmares might disappear when life was filled with affection and acceptance and a sense of belonging. But that seemed too much information for such a little girl, so we sat quietly side by side in the cab as we headed toward our destination at the docks.

I suppose if Suey Wah hadn't lost her footing as she climbed out of the cab and fallen to one knee, I wouldn't have been so occupied dusting her off that I missed the unnatural atmosphere of the docks that day. But she did and I did and it was only after our cabbie had driven away that I looked around and felt the difference. Not the usual busy but cheerful hubbub of the docks that combined the calls and chatter of voices with the slap of water against the hulls. Not the usual bustle of people coming and going, either, but huddles of men talking in a steady, low murmur that I knew instinctively did not bode well. Still hoping for the best, I took Suey Wah's hand and walked quickly toward the docks on the other side of the street, watching the growing gathering of men out of the corner of my eye. From a distance I had already identified the yacht that Miss Cameron had arranged to take Suey Wah through the Golden Gate and north up the coast to Mission San Rafael. A woman named Sarah Fremont would be waiting onboard the vessel to accompany Suey Wah on the trip to the School of the Archangel, her new home.

"I know there are easier and more direct ways to get Suey Wah to San Rafael," Donaldina admitted, "but I thought the more obscure the better. Trains stop and go, and people are always getting on and off. I don't trust all that commotion. This way, once she's on board, the trip will be non-stop. She and Miss Fremont will be the only passengers on board so there's no chance of anything happening to the child."

"How did you arrange that?" I asked, impressed, and Donaldina smiled at my question.

"920 has a variety of benefactors, Dinah. This particular man owns canning factories as well as a very fine schooner. He was more than happy to provide safe passage when I approached him, and he's worked with us often enough to know not to ask who or why."

I could see the yacht from where I stood—its appearance noticeably different from all the other craft in view—but between us and the handsome vessel milled an expanse of angry men, some of them shaking fists and all of them loud. I was completely at a loss to explain what I saw and grabbed the arm of a passing man.

"What's happening?" I demanded.

"Strike, lady. And about time."

"But I need to—" I began, only to have him interrupt me and repeat the words as if I were a slow child.

"It's a dock strike, lady. We'll shut the waterfront down until we get what we're asking for." He took a closer look at me and added, not unkindly, "You don't belong here. There'll be trouble as soon as the Employers' Association gets wind of what's happening." He shook my hand loose from his arm and disappeared into a nearby crowd.

I was conscious of Suey Wah's quiet presence by my side, her hand trustingly resting in mine, and decided the man was right. We didn't belong there just then. The schooner beckoned in the distance, but it appeared that we had no way to reach it until the gathering throng of men dispersed. Behind me I heard shouts and turned to see a number of policemen advancing toward the strikers, wooden batons in their hands. Here was trouble for sure, I thought grimly, recognizing from past experience the looks on all the men's faces, dock workers and policemen alike, a universal, international, and distinctively male look that anticipated and welcomed the idea of a fight.

I tried to see if Colin was among the policemen but couldn't identify his fair hair under the sea of police hats. Then, because I knew I had to do something if Suey Wah and I didn't want to be caught right in the middle of what was clearly going to be a violent altercation, I took a firmer grasp on the child's hand, picked up the valise with the other and swung it forward with all my might to clear a path through the crowd that had begun to encroach on the place where the girl and I stood. I suppose it was astonishment at my presence as much as the threat of a small, worn valise that made men move aside, but whatever the reason, Suey Wah and I managed to return to the side of the street where we had first stepped down. We walked a few paces and stopped at the corner, looking over our shoulders at the noisy melee, which had begun in earnest. Men shouted, fists flew, and policemen's batons connected with surprisingly audible thuds. A concert of violence. I looked down at a wide-eyed Suey Wah, who had not said a word during our entire push through the crowd to cross the street. The raucous noise made any attempt at conversation useless, but I gave her as brave a smile as I could muster and she rewarded me with a very tiny one of her own. What did it say about both of us that we took bloody violence in our stride without any feelings of shock or outrage?

We walked quickly away, trying to put distance between us and the fighting, and stopped only when I recognized the alley we had just passed. I had climbed that narrow street a number of times to reach the office of the Pandora Transport Company. At the same time I recognized the alley, I also recognized one of the faces in the steadily growing crowd that continued to spread out behind us with no sign of diminished hostilities. The man I saw wasn't involved in fighting, however. Instead, he walked along the edge of the street with a furtive grace that allowed him to dodge all the groups of battling men. He was following someone, glancing toward the crowd, looking behind him, then shifting his attention to the side of the street where Suey Wah and I walked. For a moment all I could remember about the Chinese man was that I had met him somewhere sometime over the past several weeks. When I finally recalled the where, I felt a moment of complete and utter panic. His name was Chong Lin and I had seen him at Wing Chee's establishment. He had worn the same costume then, too— loose pants and a canvas jacket, black bands tied around both upper arms, and his braid tied to the top of his head. I had learned that such a man was called a highbinder and that his hairstyle advertised his vocation as a deadly assassin and member of one of several fierce Chinese tongs that battled each other for supremacy in Chinatown. As the tide of strikers and policemen continued to seep toward the corner where I stood with Suey Wah, I saw Chong Lin's gaze find us. I should have known all along that we were the object of the man's search, but I didn't make sense of what I saw until he abruptly stopped his forward pace, turned, and stepped into the path of the oncoming crowd in order to cross the street.

He's coming after us, I thought with certainty, and made the quick decision to turn up the alley toward the Pandora Transport Company, still firmly grasping Suey Wah's hand. The choice was the lesser of two evils: the ominous—and I was sure deadly—threat sidling carefully through the now-crowded street toward us or my doubts about Jake Pandora's sincerity. The decision was easy and quick. I would trust Jake Pandora for the time being and allow him to see Suey Wah. Doing so might take her into the lion's den, but I didn't know where else to go to escape Chong Lin's menace. At one time I had thought the violent crowd of men put us at the greater risk, but with the Chinese man's deliberate approach, I knew I was wrong. We had much more to fear from that one man than from a hundred striking dock workers. With Suey Wah beside me, we hurried up the steep alley toward the storefront office of the Pandora Transport Company. I didn't say a word and I never looked back. Suey Wah, sensing danger in my grasp and pace, somehow kept up with me.

Without bothering to knock at the closed entrance of the office—hadn't Pandora told me the door was always open?—I opened it, yanked Suey Wah inside, closed the door firmly behind me, and leaned my back against it.

The two men in the office stood wordlessly staring at us—Jake Pandora and the young man I'd seen in the office on my first visit there last spring, whose name I recalled as Eddie. Both men were obviously surprised at our abrupt entrance, but it seemed to me that Pandora's face held the remnants of other emotions that might have included anger and frustration. Something about his narrowed eyes and lips pressed thin made me think that I had interrupted a discussion that had not been pleasant for either of them. Still, I noted with resignation, even in annoyance and anger, it was impossible for Jake Pandora to be anything but classically handsome. Not even bad temper could mar the faultless lines of his face.

Recovered from his surprise, Pandora said without inflection, "Good morning, Miss Hudson." If he wondered what I was doing there and why I and a small Chinese girl had crashed into his office with a breathless haste that hinted we were pursued by devils, he didn't ask. He just greeted me by name and waited.

"Good morning, Mr. Pandora," I replied, still trying to catch my breath. "Suey Wah and I seem to have picked a bad day for a walk along the waterfront. There's fighting, you know."

"Yes, I know." Jake walked closer to me, made a more careful study of my face, and turned to say, "Take off for lunch, Eddie, and take a long time. We can pick up the conversation when you get back. I'm afraid nothing's going to change in the time you're gone."

"Yes, sir." Eddie started toward the door where I stood but had to stop because I stood like a wall between him and his exit.

"Sorry," I said, reluctantly moving aside and pulling Suey Wah closer to me as Eddie opened the door. I didn't look outside to see if our pursuer was in sight but did ask Eddie in a whisper, "Do you see anyone in the street outside?"

The young man didn't indicate that he thought my question at all extraordinary, only took a quick look and replied seriously before he exited, "No, ma'am. I'd guess everyone's down at the docks."

I pushed the door shut behind Eddie, but when I would have re-taken my door-blocking position, Pandora stepped forward and threw the latch on the door to lock it. At one time I might have found such an action threatening, but I knew that he had read my expression and in his own way was assuring me of safety. Something about his gesture caused a great swell of relief in the general area of my heart. I had been right not to fear him on behalf of Suey Wah and right to come to the Pandora office for protection. I couldn't have articulated why such a simple deed on his part would generate so emotional a response on mine. It just did.

"This is Suey Wah." I finally let loose of the girl enough for her to take a small step toward Jake. "Suey, this is Mr. Pandora. My friend, Mr. Pandora."

She tented both hands and bowed toward him, then raised her head to give him her charming smile. "How do you do, Mr. Pandora?" she said in careful English, not quite able to articulate all the consonants of his name. "Qing is my friend, too. Aren't we fortunate to have such a very fine friend?" Suey Wah's open little face smoothed away any residual bad temper that had darkened Pandora's expression. How could anyone be immune to the child?

"Yes, indeed. Very fortunate." He returned her smile before he raised his head to look at me with an expression that asked a question I had no trouble hearing even without words.

"Suey Wah, please go sit on the chair by the little table and wait for me while I talk privately to Mr. Pandora."

She started away obediently but Jake stopped her, saying, "Wait. I have a better idea." He went through a doorway in the back of the office and called, "Elena! Come down here, please."

I heard light footsteps on the stairs and Jake reappeared followed by the young woman I'd originally seen as a face in the window and had later been introduced to as his niece.

"You'll remember my niece, Elena. Elena, this is Miss Hudson."

I put out my hand toward her, saying, "How nice to see you again, Miss Pandora," ignoring the fact that the circumstances of this meeting were anything but nice.

She had Jake's white smile. "I remember you, Miss Hudson. You are too beautiful to forget." The honest admiration I heard in her voice made me flush with embarrassment.

Jake continued smoothly, "And this is Suey Wah, Miss Hudson's young friend, who, I think, could do with a glass of water. Would you take her upstairs and see that she has whatever she needs?" Suey Wah glanced my way to be sure I approved of our being separated.

That's a good idea," I agreed quietly. "We had a bit of a run up the hill and a glass of water would be welcome. I'll be right here with Mr. Pandora, Suey Wah." Elena reached for Suey Wah's hand, and the child hesitated only a moment before returning the grasp.

Very seriously Suey Wah asked, "You won't forget and leave without me, will you, Qing?"

Her simple question touched me enough that for a moment I thought I might cry. "I will never forget you, Suey Wah, and I would never abandon you. We're friends, are we not?"

She smiled at me happily, reassured, and disappeared with Elena into the back room where I heard Elena ask Suey Wah a quiet question as they ascended to the second floor.

"Now, Miss Hudson, dispel the mystery, please." Pandora folded his arms across his chest and waited. As an afterthought he added, "Sit down if you'd like."

I ignored the offer and told him step-by-step everything that had occurred from the moment Suey Wah and I had exited the cab until we appeared in the office of the Pandora Transport Company. Jake listened without interruption to my story. When I finally stopped talking, he was quiet himself for a moment. Wearied by the telling, I took him up on his earlier offer, sank into the nearest chair, and waited for his reaction.

Before speaking, Pandora unlocked the office door and stepped outside, closing the door carefully behind him. He was gone several minutes before he returned and picked up the conversation.

"There's no one, Chinese or otherwise, anywhere in the alley or in the general vicinity now. The place is like a cemetery. The strike must be keeping everyone busy at their own pastimes. Why would a high-binder be interested in the child?" As I had recounted the morning's adventures, I had wondered if what I related was all old news to him, and I was heartened by his question. If Pandora truly didn't understand why someone might be after Suey Wah, wouldn't that prove he wasn't involved in the smuggling trade?

I gave up trying to decipher his intention or my reaction and answered, "Because he knows that Suey Wah was smuggled into the city, probably on the Pandora Two along with Mae Tao, the girl I saw on the dock when I first came to San Francisco, the girl I approached you about."

"I remember." A certain dryness in his tone that I didn't pursue.

"If that's the case, then to have Suey Wah safe and protected at 920 could threaten the smugglers' anonymity. When these girls disappear into the vast Chinatown underground, there's no chance for them to identify anyone or share anything they might remember. They speak only Chinese and would not have the desire or the will or the knowledge to expose their kidnappers. But I took Suey Wah under my wing and taught her English, and by doing that I placed her in danger. If it turns out she saw someone or something she shouldn't have, her information could expose the whole disreputable organization."

"Can she identify someone?"

I hesitated a moment. Was there an ulterior motive to his question? Did he desire to know the answer for a purpose all his own?

"No," I finally replied. "At least, not that I know of. She's had a dream that seems to tie in to her experience and there's a man in the dream but he doesn't have a face or a name or a voice. He's just a figure, a shiny figure, she calls him. She doesn't know anything that could incriminate anyone."

Jake sat down across from me. "So why did you come here?"

"Your office was close and you once told me the door was always open." I glanced toward the latched lock with a smile. "But it doesn't look like that's always the case."

"It depends on what side of the door you're on, Miss Hudson."

"I see."

"I don't think you do, but explaining what I meant would take more time than we have right now. Do you still want to get Suey Wah onto that schooner?"

"Yes, but I don't see how—" He stood abruptly, nearly knocking over his chair in the process.

"We are not at the mercy of those damned strikers," but from his tone I thought he did not entirely believe the words himself.

"Will the strike hurt your business?"

"Not just hurt. Ruin. I make my business on the waterfront. The only thing that might help is if my crews realize they have as much to lose as I do. I'm not a member of the Employers' Association, and I pay my men a fair wage. Everyone knows that, just like they know that if I have to, I'll take a steamer at a time out by myself. I started as one man with one boat, and I can do it again."

I'd been right when I first arrived to think he was angry. Just talking about the strike made him angry again.

"Maybe it won't last very long."

"I take a financial loss every day the steamers are at dock. Eddie was going over the numbers with me." I heard the frustration in his voice.

"I'm sorry. I believe you about your own hired men, but you must realize that the desire to work only ten hours a day instead of twelve isn't unreasonable."

"It's different for my crews, Dinah. Sailors work a different way, full days and nights to carry the load, and then a fair amount of days and nights off until the next trip. I'm not unreasonable. I understand that some of them have wives and families." He shook his head in irritation. "Well, there's nothing to be done about the situation right now, and maybe the police will break the strike. Was your friend there?"

He asked the question so unexpectedly that at first I didn't have any idea what he was talking about and responded blankly, "What friend where?"

"The friend you were with at the Cliff House. The big man with fair hair."

I found his question more gratifying than suspicious and answered, "His name's Colin O'Connor and no, I didn't see him there today, but it's possible I missed him. The crowd of police I saw all looked the same behind their buttons and stars." Because his question lent itself nicely to one I was pondering, I commented, "Your niece is a lovely girl."

"Yes, she is. Takes after her mother not my brother, that's for sure, for which the girl should be grateful. Elena is here to marry the man her parents arranged to be her husband."

"Arranged?"

"A close friend of my father, a man named Stavros Gravari, came to America several years ago, settled in Santa Barbara, and started the successful Gravari Fishing Company. Many people in San Francisco would recognize the name. Stavros's oldest grandson is of marriageable age, and the family wanted a good Greek girl from the old country for him. With my father dead, Stavros approached my oldest brother, who talked to Elena about the idea. To his surprise she was willing to consider the match. Elena has a good head on her shoulders and an unexpected taste for adventure. She came into New York where she was met by my oldest sister, Aura, who lives with her family on the east coast. Aura put her on a train to St. Louis where another sister claimed her, and so it went until Elena ended up here in San Francisco, her last stop."

"You must have quite a few siblings."

"Six. All older."

"And all spread out, it sounds like."

"Elena inherited her beauty from my sister-in-law and an adventuresome streak from the Pandora side of her family. We like to be on the move."

"Is Elena's wedding date set?"

"It was set for September. Her husband-to-be and his father were supposed to arrive sometime next week to take her south to spend some time with their family before the wedding. For old-country Greeks, that's pretty progressive. Elena hasn't met her young man yet, but they've exchanged letters and pictures and probably some words that neither set of parents would approve of because my niece favors the young fellow more than I would have thought possible from polite correspondence. The two young people might think they know their own minds, but both families still have to approve the match and that's what Elena's impatient for. I hate to be the one to tell her that the strike will delay the meeting and probably the wedding."

"The Chinese arrange their daughters' marriages, too," I said thoughtfully. "I used to deplore the practice, but now I think it might have its place and purpose."

He gave a little grin at my words, apparently surprised. "I never thought to hear a woman like you say such a thing."

"Both my mother and my sister married for love," I told him, "and they were very happy with their choices, but marriage can be a burden."

"You surprise me again, Miss Hudson."

"Marriage holds more serious consequences for a woman than it does for a man," I explained, wishing I hadn't allowed the conversation to drift onto this topic but too far in not to finish the thought. "Until the laws change, wives remain little more than property. A woman needs to think the decision through because she's risking a great deal when she takes those vows, and I don't know how the laws will ever change when women can't vote."

"Maybe there are some men who see things the same way you do."

"Maybe," but my voice held a skepticism he didn't miss. "Anyway, I wish your Elena well. Right now I need to decide what to do with my Suey Wah."

"You want to put her on that schooner, don't you?"

"It's the right thing to do for her safety," I replied soberly. "I want Suey Wah to be out of harm's way, but it's hard to send her to strangers. We got used to having her around, and she was easy to love."

"That happens sometimes."

Something in his tone, something that hinted at meaning beyond the words, drew my gaze to his, and we stood staring at each other, neither of us smiling or speaking until we heard footsteps on the stairs that made me step back quickly and say, "Yes, I want to put her on that schooner."

"All right then." Pandora's tone was brisk. "I can help you with that."

I tried to hear or see something in him that hinted at deception or a wickedness below the surface, and not oblivious to my silent intent he added in a low voice, "I know you've had your doubts about me for a long time, Dinah, but you'll have to trust me. I wouldn't hurt the child—wouldn't hurt any child—and I wouldn't hurt you."

Behind me, Elena said, "Uncle Jacobi, Suey Wah told me there were men fighting on the docks. Did you know?"

Pandora waited a moment for a response from me, but when I said nothing, he shrugged and turned to his niece. "Yes, so Miss Hudson has been telling me." To Suey Wah, he said, "I understand there is a fine vessel waiting to take you to your own safe harbor." The metaphor escaped Suey Wah's literal turn of mind and seeing her puzzled expression, I translated Jake's comment into words the girl could understand.

"Yes," Suey Wah answered, "so Qing says and she is my friend who would not lie to me." Neither Jake nor I missed the slight tinge of sadness in her tone. "Qing says I will learn many things at my new school and one day I will be able to return to my friends, to Mrs. Ruth and Mr. Martin, to Lo Mo, and to my dear Qing. It will not be so very long, Qing says." Suey Wah paused before concluding, "But I believe it will seem very long to me."

"Sometimes we must do the hard thing," I said, refusing to be drawn into a discussion that promised more emotion than I was ready to handle. "Now say your thank you to Miss Elena. Mr. Pandora is going to get us to the yacht. We hope it's still there."

Suey Wah bowed her thanks and took my hand, asking as she did so, "But how will we get past all those angry men?" I led her into the street past Jake Pandora, who stood holding open the door.

"I have no idea, but Mr. Pandora says he knows a way," I paused before adding deliberately, "and I am sure we can trust him to get us to the schooner safely."

Jake Pandora did exactly as he promised. His knowledge of the back streets and alleys allowed us to take a circuitous but successful trip completely around the clashing strikers and policemen, although sounds of the conflict were always present. As Jake had noticed, other streets in the vicinity were empty of traffic and pedestrians and remained so as we moved north. Except for the increasingly distant shouts, we could have been the only people in the city.

When we finally stood on the dock that stretched out toward the schooner—the vessel still waited, thank God—I lifted a hand and waved the bright blue kerchief I'd been wearing as a sash around my waist in the general direction of the yacht. In almost immediate response, I saw a quick wave of red from the deck of the boat. Someone had been watching and waiting for us. A good sign. We had moved north of the chaos of the strike and our menacing shadow had disappeared, as well. It appeared we would have no interference when we transferred Suey Wah to the waiting vessel. A small boat was lowered from the yacht onto the water, and we watched its approach.

As we waited, I commented, "It's a beautiful yacht, isn't it? I'll bet it's a smooth ride. I love the freedom of being on the water."

When the small boat grew close enough, the man rowing stopped to throw some ropes toward us. Jake stepped up, caught them, and fastened them to an upright along the pier. He pulled the small boat closer as the man picked up the oars again, and when the rowboat finally knocked against the wharf, a woman hopped out, grabbing Jake's hand for support but so steady on her feet I thought she would have landed safely on the pier without his help. Smaller than I in both height and breadth, she still gave an impression of competence and energy and athletic strength.

"Miss Hudson, I'm Sarah Fremont. I'm honored to meet you." She had an infectious smile and a face that bubbled with good humor. "And is this Suey Wah?" At Suey Wah's shy nod, Miss Fremont said in perfect Chinese, "This is a great adventure, is it not, child? Were you very afraid?"

I could tell Suey Wah liked Miss Fremont instantly, felt a quick, ignoble pang of jealousy at the woman's perfect language skills and the responding interest I saw on Suey Wah's face, and was immediately ashamed of myself.

"I was not afraid at all. Qing said we would be safe and Mr. Pandora promised to take good care of us. *Is* this an adventure?"

"A very big one for such a little girl, but then I've heard it is not the first adventure you've had. Are you brave enough to come with me?" Miss Fremont held out her hand and after giving me a quick look, Suey Wah detached her hand from mine and placed it in Miss Fremont's.

"Yes. Qing says I am to go." Suey Wah looked from the woman to the yacht floating like a cork on the blue bay water. "Will it be a very long trip?"

"A snap. You'll see. And it's a wonderful boat with all kinds of treats on board. And then there is a school full of girls waiting to meet you. Oh, Suey Wah, we will have a wonderful time!" Sarah Fremont had an enthusiastic way of speaking that made a person excited just listening to her. She could have read the train schedule aloud and we'd still have felt like shouting "Yippee!"

Suey Wah turned her face toward me. "Good-bye, Qing. Will you come and see me?"

"I will. I promise."

"And will you let me know when Mrs. Ruth's baby is born so I may say a prayer for the little one?"

"Of course, I will."

"Then I suppose I am ready to go."

I leaned down, kissed her cheek, and whispered in her ear, "Be brave, little bird. This will be the best nest yet."

Without warning, Suey Wah wrenched her hand from Miss Fremont's grip and threw both her arms around my neck. "I will miss you very much, Qing."

I gently detached Suey Wah's arms from my neck. "And I will miss you, but Miss Fremont is waiting for you. Go on now."

Jake handed Miss Fremont into the small boat first, then lifted Suey Wah into Miss Fremont's waiting and capable arms. He and I stood shoulder to shoulder and watched them as they were rowed back to the yacht and were helped on board. I could see Suey Wah's little hand waving wildly from the deck and after a wave of my own, I turned resolutely away.

"I would appreciate it if you'd help me find a cabbie that will take me back to Grove Street," I said with as dispassionate a tone as I could summon.

"I can do that."

"And thank you. Thank you very much. I feel such relief knowing Suey Wah is out of harm's way."

"What about you?" As we retraced our steps, his casual question puzzled me.

"What about me?"

"Are you out of harm's way?"

"I was never in harm's way."

"Think, Miss Hudson, think. If someone thought the child knew dangerous information, and someone knew you spoke the language and had spent a great deal of time with the child, what natural assumption might that someone make?"

"Oh." I stopped so abruptly that Pandora bumped into me. I brushed off his muttered apology. "Oh, I see. But I don't know anything because Suey Wah didn't know anything."

"I believe that, but I'm not a man whose life could be ruined if he were connected in any way with smuggling Chinese girls into California, an action both illegal and immoral. You should probably watch your step."

I had not considered the idea that I might be in any danger until Jake Pandora put the thought into my head, and the notion made me bad-tempered. "I will, but I hate having to be circumspect." We started walking again.

"I have noticed that prudence does not come naturally to you."

"As much as humility comes naturally to you," I retorted as we began to climb a steep side alley.

"I am generally considered to be a good-natured man of acceptable modesty."

"Considered by whom? Strangers and foreigners?"

"By people who know me, Miss Hudson, people who don't always feel the need to contradict and be so damned right all the time."

I halted once more. We were on an incline and because I was walking ahead, when I turned to face him we were almost at eye level.

"Is that what you really think of me?" I demanded.

"What I think of you, Dinah, depends on the day I'm thinking it, and right now I think"—he smiled, put a palm to each side of my face, and kissed me squarely on the mouth—"I want to kiss you." He kissed me a second time before he put both hands on my shoulders and turned me away from him to face forward. "That happens sometimes on the rare off moments when I don't feel like throttling you. Turn right here." I turned, taking his direction and his kiss in stride.

"You are an exceptionally handsome man, Mr. Pandora, and probably used to women throwing themselves at you, but there's one thing you don't know about me." By then we were walking side by side and without missing a step he turned to glance at me.

"And what would that one thing be, Miss Hudson?"

"I never throw myself at men who are more beautiful than I am. It goes against the grain."

I could tell by his expression that my words startled him. He stopped briefly in his tracks, began to laugh in a way that despite my bold words I found incredibly attractive, and resumed his stride. There is something about humor in a man that overcomes a multitude of deficiencies, not that I saw all that many deficiencies in Jake Pandora at the time. He wiped the back of his hand across his eyes, which had teared up from laughter.

"Thank you, Miss Hudson. That's good to know. I'll keep it in mind. Take a left here, please. Casey sometimes uses this corner. There, I see him. He'll get you home safely."

"I thought you might be in the thick of things, Jake," Casey called from a distance. When he saw me, he doffed his cap. "And you here, too, Miss Hudson! That beats all. Not the place for a lady right now, I don't think."

With Suey Wah's departure still on my mind, I was tired and sad and

angry, yet in a strangely benevolent humor for all that. "You are absolutely correct, Casey, and I will be forever in your debt if you can get me
back to Grove Street without putting me in the middle of a street fight."

"I can do that easy enough. I know these streets better than Pandora
here, and he's a master of these docks." I didn't wait but climbed into his
cab without assistance.

"Thank you again," I said to Jake Pandora. "I'd have been lost without you today." I paused purposefully before adding, "I'm afraid that's as
complimentary as a woman who needs to be right all the time can get."

Pandora grinned at me. "I'm willing to accept whatever concessions
you can spare, Miss Hudson. By the way, I have some information you
might find interesting."

"What?"

"It's not the time or place to discuss that now," Pandora answered,
casting a quick look in Casey's direction. "As long as the dock workers
are on strike, I'll have time on my hands. If you're free Friday, I'll treat
you to lunch and some information that might come as a surprise."

"You're acting awfully coy, but all right, as long as I don't have to
dodge fist fights and street brawls."

"They didn't seem to bother you today."

"I've had more experience with that kind of thing than I care to
think about. Make no mistake, if I had my choice, I'd live a peaceful life."

Jake Pandora eyed me with speculation and a half-smile. "Would
you now? I wonder." Without giving me the opportunity to defend my
comment, he reverted to the topic of our Friday meeting. "Casey can
come round Grove Street and pick you up just before noon on Friday.
If it's not safe, he'll let you know." He tossed a coin to the man he'd just
volunteered and directed, "Get her home safe, Casey, and then come
tell me what you know about this damned strike."

Casey successfully completed the first part of his instructions and
left me at the curb on Grove Street, waved a perfunctory farewell, and
took off with his cab at a slow trot, presumably to conclude the second
part of Jake Pandora's request.

Chapter Ten

The dock strike quickly became the talk of the town. While Martin grumbled about the general unacceptability of strikes and the papers followed the strike's progress with bold headlines, Ruth and I tried to become accustomed to the house without Suey Wah's presence.

"She was so little and so quiet," Ruth remarked sadly. "It's hard to believe I could miss her as much as I do." I felt the same but did my best to bolster my sister's spirits.

"I know, but we'll see her again, and I was very impressed with Miss Fremont. I wouldn't have left Suey Wah with someone I thought was incompetent or unkind, Ruth. And—" I always concluded with the same reminder "—in just a few weeks your new arrival will keep you so busy you won't have time to miss Suey Wah."

My sister invariably reacted to that comment with a vague smile and the slightest pat to her stomach, assuring herself that a baby did indeed rest there. "I know. Mother's birthday was in September. Wouldn't it be nice if the baby came on that same day?"

"I think that will be entirely up to the baby."

Ruth sat down heavily, pulled her knitting into her lap, and then enjoined, "Now tell me again about how Mr. Pandora came to your rescue. I must say I never considered you to be a woman who needed to be rescued so frequently, Dinah." I looked at Ruth quickly enough to catch her small smile.

"I asked his help one time, Ruthie. That doesn't constitute frequent rescues."

"There was the night of the cotillion, too, don't forget."

"He was not rescuing me from anything that night."

"No. Now that you mention it, I agree that it did not look like he was preoccupied with rescuing you. Just the opposite, you might say." She smiled again. "He's certainly a handsome man." When I didn't respond, she raised her head from her knitting and looked at me with innocent eyes. "Don't you think so, Dinah?"

"He's handsome, all right."

"But maybe you prefer blonde, burly policemen."

"Maybe I do." I let her tease me for the remainder of the afternoon, but my meeting with Colin two days earlier had not gone well.

He had met me outside 920 Tuesday evening as I started on my way home from a disappointing day that had included spending the morning tracking down an ultimately false lead to Mae Tao, a futile search for a house slave who had sent a request for rescue, and the rare occurrence of a young woman resident that had run away from the mission to return to her life at a high-class brothel. We had followed that older girl there only to have her tell us she did not wish to be rescued, that she found her lessons tedious, her clothes plain, and her accommodations inadequate.

The girl's unwise choice hurt and surprised me but did not seem to have a similar effect on Miss Cameron, who looked at the girl squarely and said in passable Chinese, "The road you take determines your destination. If you change your mind, we will always have room for you."

"It happens, Dinah," Miss Cameron said later, "and I advise you to accept the fact and stop fuming about it. Making bad choices is universal and international and we can do nothing about it but be ready to pick up the pieces if we are asked to do so."

I knew she was right, but the three unsuccessful rescues put me in a sour mood for the walk home. I looked forward to a solitary trip in order to work through the unpleasantness of the day and prepare myself for the first afternoon returning home without Suey Wah's little figure waiting for me in the hallway. Because of my heavy thoughts, I viewed Colin O'Connor's approaching figure with less than wholehearted welcome.

He fell into step beside me, looked sideways at me as we walked, and was quiet for a while. Finally he commented, "'Twas a bad day you had then."

"Yes," I agreed without slowing my pace, "very bad."

"What can I do to make it better?"

"Nothing, unless you have a magic wand to wave and make young girls less foolish."

"Trouble with the little Suey Wah?"

"No, not Suey. She's well out of harm's way by now, thank God." I gave Colin a brief version of the day's disappointing events as we waited on the corner.

"You can't save people who don't want to be saved, Dinah. You're intelligent enough to recognize that. Most of those girls you worry so much about are happy to sell themselves. It's a better life than they'd have had otherwise."

I found his comments so extraordinarily ignorant that I rounded on him fiercely. "That's an offensive thing to say, Colin! You've spent time on Morton Street. Do those women look happy to you? Believe me, they're not seeing any benefit from their abused lives. It's men that profit from their bodies and then dispose of them without a second thought as soon as a woman dares to grow old or ill."

"I'm sorry. I only meant—"

"I know what you meant." I hurried across the street with Colin sprinting behind me to keep up.

"Dinah, don't take that tone with me."

I paused on the other side of the street to turn and glare up at him. "What tone would that be exactly?"

"That superior tone, like I'm too common or too uneducated to understand what you're saying. And don't turn your back on me when we're talking. I'd never do that to you. It's not respectful and I deserve better."

"Deserving doesn't come into it. If the idea of a woman with a temper, a will, and her own opinions bothers you, maybe you should find another woman to spend time with." When I whirled away and tried to take a step, Colin grasped my arm.

"I don't want another woman. I want you. Only you. Temper and will and opinions and all." He would have kissed me right there in the middle of that public walk, I think, except I backed away hastily.

"Let go of my arm, Colin. It's not the time or the place."

He released me immediately, apologizing a second time. "I'm sorry. I don't know how to talk to you when you're like this, Dinah. I don't know how to make you listen to me. I didn't mean what you thought I meant before. Sometimes you don't give a man a chance to defend himself."

"Men have lots of chances to defend themselves, Colin," I replied, but more gently. "To start with, the law defends them, and if they don't like the laws they can vote to change them."

"And is it my fault now that women don't have the vote?" The hint of despair I heard in his voice made me chuckle, my good humor slowly returning.

"No, my dear. I concede that the absence of universal suffrage is not your fault."

"Well, I'm glad I don't have to carry the blame for that, at least." He lifted my chin with his thumb and pretended to examine my face. "Looks to me like the storm clouds are disappearing and that might be a bit o' sunshine I see in your face."

I pulled away. "You may be right, Colin O'Connor, but if you plaster the Irish brogue too thick, I guarantee the sunshine won't stay. Now I have to get home. Ruth will be waiting supper."

"Dinah—" Something on his face or in his tone made my heart go out to him. Maybe just the way he stood there, his posture intangibly forlorn and his expression confused.

"Yes?"

"Don't treat me like I don't have feelings. I do, and they run deep."

The plain sincerity in his tone made me ashamed of my recent outburst. "I know you have feelings, Colin." We shared an awkward pause. I thought he waited for more from me, perhaps an expression of my own feelings or even an apology for my bad temper, but I had no intention of saying anything more on any subject.

At last, Colin asked, "Are you busy Friday? I've got the whole day off. I thought we could make another trip to Cliff House. Maybe take in the Sutro baths, if you've got a bathing costume."

The idea was appealing, but I answered with regret, "I'd love that, Colin, but I already have plans for the day. I'm sorry."

"Your sister?"

"No, not Ruth."

"With someone else then?" he persisted.

"Yes, with someone else," I admitted carefully. I didn't appreciate the reaction my words caused: the hurt I saw on his face and a level of suspicion he wasn't able to hide quickly enough.

"Do I have a rival for your affections, Dinah?"

The memory of Jake Pandora's kisses came unbidden to mind. Was he Colin's rival? Good looks aside, there was something about Pandora to which I was very attracted, an attraction that also held the hint of a feeling I'd once experienced caught in an undertow while bathing in a river. Inexorably drawn away from the safety and the familiarity of the shore into waters that held the potential for deadly disaster.

When I didn't answer, Colin said, "You owe me the truth, Dinah."

"I don't know if I owe you anything, Colin, but if I do, now is not the time to pay the debt."

"If you're spending time with that man, Pandora, you're making a serious mistake."

His assumption surprised, even shocked me, so that I replied sharply with the arrogance Colin disliked, "I don't see how that would be any of your business."

With cause for provocation, his measured reply was equally surprising. "You're a free woman. I know that, but Jake Pandora isn't the man you think he is."

"What do you mean?"

He shook his head gently, and his even tone was more convincing than any impassioned rhetoric. "I can't say more, but I'd hate to see you hurt by a man whose dealings would disgust you. He plays a deep game and——"

I didn't want to hear more and interrupted him without compunction. "I appreciate your concern, but it's completely unwarranted. Mr. Pandora and I share some common interests based in China and that's all there is to it. Now I need to go home. We'll talk later."

"Will we? Do you promise?" His tone had lost all its belligerence and held instead the quality of a little boy asking for a favor. I felt ashamed again. Colin O'Connor did indeed deserve more from me, deserved better. It was totally illogical to blame him for my failures, for the injustices of the legal system, or for the inconsistencies of human behavior. And it was especially unfair to hold Colin responsible for my ambivalent feelings about Jake Pandora. Colin never pretended to be anything other than what he was and never pretended to feel anything other than what his words admitted. I should appreciate his candor and his concern, even if his remarks about Jake Pandora made me question my own judgment and feelings. I didn't like appearing coquettish and callous before the honest emotion I saw in Colin's eyes and heard in his voice.

"I do promise. Maybe we could spend some time together Sunday afternoon."

"I'm on the beat that day, but I'll be in touch. Don't forget about me, Dinah. I'm not a man to take lightly."

"I know. I'd never do that."

"All right then, but keep it in mind for the future. Should I see you home?"

I shook my head. "No, please don't. I need some time by myself. You should get used to keeping your distance when I'm feeling cranky."

"I could never get used to keeping my distance from you. I'd have to be dead for that to happen." It may have been Colin's careful warning about Jake Pandora or simply that a cloud passed over the late afternoon sun as we said good-bye, but whatever the cause, I carried a chill with me all the way home.

When Casey picked me up Friday morning, I had completely recovered from Tuesday's bad temper. I had returned to the mission

Wednesday to donate an extra day that week because Ruth planned to be gone the greater part of the day at a meeting of a local charity board on which she served, and I didn't relish the prospect of being by myself. The exchange with Colin had troubled me more than I would admit to anyone, even—or especially—to myself. I knew my earlier conduct had given him every right to believe I was interested in him as more than a friend, and there were times I thought he was right. His open regard was flattering, and I admired much about him, including his impassioned allegiance to his police work and comrades and his determined ambition. I had no doubt he would make something of himself, could see him as the city's police commissioner one day or in some other prestigious position. I liked him as a person, too, enjoyed his humor, his gentle mockery of his own Irish roots, and his physical strength that made me feel safe and cherished. I thought he would be a good husband, a generous provider, and an impassioned lover. And yet lately I'd thought something important was missing between us. I didn't know what and I didn't know why but something seemed lacking. I feared the "something" was connected with my increased interaction with Jake Pandora, but that was as far as I could contemplate. I didn't think my interest had all that much to do with Pandora's extraordinary good looks because in our recent exchanges I hadn't given a thought to the perfection of his features. Truthfully, if—*when*— he annoyed me, he might as well have been Quasimodo of Notre Dame. I couldn't identify the source of his appeal, if appeal it was, except that I found in his attitude a kind of kindred spirit, strength and determination and self-confidence yet with an intangible air of vulnerability that I recognized in myself.

I couldn't dismiss Colin's warning about Pandora, however. Maybe it had been said only to denigrate a man Colin considered a rival, but his steady tone had seemed detached from his professed feelings for me. There had been steel behind the words.

In a perverse way, I hoped my interest in Jake Pandora was just because of that perfect face, though if that was the reason I thought of him with increasing frequency, how superficial did that make me? Dinah Hudson, my father's daughter and Donaldina Cameron's friend, enthralled with a man's handsome face and forget about character and morals and intentions—! Too much introspection is not healthy, I told myself firmly as I dressed Friday morning, and decided to give myself the benefit of the doubt. Whether Colin's warning was legitimate or not, Jake Pandora could still prove very useful to me. Surely it was the fact that he might have discovered something about the vile man who bore the responsibility for Suey Wah's fearsome journey and Mae Tao's disappearance that accounted for my good, my very good, mood as I contemplated spending the afternoon with him.

From his seat, Casey said, "Everything's quiet this morning, Miss. Jake told me I wasn't even to think about bringing you if there was a chance of trouble, but it'll be safe enough." His words added to the pleasure of a day lit by a perfect sun and loaded with more blue sky than any day should be allowed to possess.

"Good," I called to him before climbing into his cab. "Nothing should be permitted to spoil this lovely day." When he would have turned into the alley to deposit me immediately in front of the transport office, I protested.

"I can walk, Casey. Spare your poor beast the trek up the hill."

"But Jake told me—"

"Jake Pandora shouldn't always get his way. Set me down at the foot of the hill and allow me the opportunity for a walk."

Once I stood on the walk I tossed him a coin and he protested again. "But Jake already paid!"

"No doubt, but I can pay my own way. If your conscience bothers you, give Mr. Pandora his money back. Otherwise, consider it our secret." I gave him a grin to which he responded with one of his own.

"Keeping secrets from Jake Pandora can get a man into trouble."

"No doubt, but I'm not a man."

Casey gave me an admiring look. "No, ma'am, you aren't, and you won't get an argument from me about it, not in that outfit."

I dipped a quick, teasing curtsy. "The Irish is showing in you today. Thank you."

I stopped twice as I trudged up the hill toward the office, conscious of an uncomfortable, prickly feeling that made me think I was being watched. When I turned, however, and examined the few pedestrians around me, all of them had an ordinary look about them. I gave a brief thought to Jake's suggestion that because of my time with Suey Wah, someone might think I possessed information that threatened reputations and incomes. Could I really be in danger? A second look assured me that no menace lurked anywhere in my vicinity, but for all my confidence, the uneasy feeling did not disappear, and I picked up my pace the closer I got to the transport office.

When I pushed open the office door and stepped inside, Jake stood in the doorway at the back of the office with his back to me. He turned at my entrance and without a greeting, said, "I didn't hear the cab."

"I had Casey set me down at the foot of the hill. It was too pretty a day to forego a walk."

"That's not what I told him to do," the words said sternly, Casey and I apparently naughty children in need of a reprimand.

"This may come as a shock to you, but not everyone feels obligated to obey your every command."

The comment made him smile. "No shock at all, Miss Hudson. Trust me. You've taught me that lesson often enough."

He stepped toward me as I came farther into the room so that for a moment we stood very close, a fact that made my pulse take a sudden jerk at the proximity. Really, there was a strong and sensual allure to the man that could make a lesser woman light-headed. I casually stepped away from him and set my small bag down on the empty table where Eddie usually sat.

"All right, Mr. Pandora—"

"Didn't we decide on Jake?"

"All right, Jake, I've had enough mystery over the last few weeks. What have you found out?"

"Patience for just a little longer, Miss Hudson. If you haven't tired yourself out, are you up for another walk?"

"Yes. Why?"

"Lunch. What do you know about Greek food?"

"Nothing, I'm afraid." He took my arm and propelled me toward the door.

"Then you're in for an education and a treat. Come on."

"We could take Elena with us," I suggested, holding my ground, suddenly not at all sure I wanted to be alone with the man. I felt like iron filings exposed to a magnet.

"My niece has departed to be with her in-laws. When I broke the news that the dock strike would not allow her beloved's arrival, she very firmly sent me to the train station to buy a ticket south."

"And you meekly did what she said? Why do I have a hard time picturing you following a woman's orders?" Jake took my elbow and moved me along again, reaching for the door with his other hand.

"In my life I have learned never to argue with a woman who thinks she's in love."

"I bet you have learned that lesson," I murmured, stepping into the street. "I'll just bet you have." My words or their implication made him chuckle.

"I'm a quick learner, and I rarely forget what I've learned."

"Lucky for you, then."

"Lucky most of the time, anyway." He fell into step beside me and changed the subject. "I'm serious about you being on your own. I think you ought to be more careful."

I didn't take offense at his words, which were said sincerely and soberly and held a note of honest concern. Two men in a week implying anxiety for my well-being felt more gratifying than a woman with suffragette leanings should admit, so I asked quickly, "Because of something you know?"

"Something I've heard. I have my own spies and time on my hands, besides."

KAREN J. HASLEY

"Are you losing a lot because of the strike?" I detected a certain grim note in his last words.

"I lose money every day my steamers are docked, but I've heard the mayor is planning on sending in strike breakers."

"More violence, then," I commented sadly.

"Probably, but Phelan has to do something and neither party involved in the strike is willing to sit down and talk about the problems."

"I understand about that. All the bloodshed in China could have been avoided if only each side would have tried harder to understand the other." That thought made me remember Alfred Betterman and from there Pandora's literary advice. "I read that book you recommended, *The Red Badge of Courage*."

"What did you think?"

"It made me consider courage and cowardice differently, which is what I know you intended." I added awkwardly, "Thank you for that. It helped."

I expected to hear a flippant rejoinder of some kind from Pandora, something about how he knew better about a lot of things and I should listen to him more often, a retort I probably would have made under the same circumstances, but he remained quiet. When I looked over at him, I surprised an expression that was clearly, unmistakably tender, the same look he might give an endearing child.

Instead of shifting his glance, he said, "You're welcome," his voice low and as smooth as velvet. I felt a flare of warmth somewhere inside my chest, but the mood and wherever the mood might have led disappeared when Jake thrust out an arm to keep me from stepping into the street and the path of a dray wagon.

"Watch your step," he directed, and I thought to myself, Good advice. With this man, I had better watch my step indeed.

We stopped for lunch at a place so small there was no room for patrons to eat inside. Instead, in an unexpectedly charming way the owner, a man Jake introduced as Spiro, had clustered several small tables on the walk in front of his café, all of them covered with bright cloths and each set with a very small jar of fresh flowers.

"How lovely," I commented as I sat down and smiled despite the seriousness of the reason for our lunch. The perfect sun, bright colors, and perky flowers defied fear and suspicion. More prosaically, Jake gave his attention to the food.

"I haven't found anyone outside of my mother's kitchen that can make moussaka better than Spiro." In answer to my question, Jake explained, "Sliced eggplant, tomatoes, butter and eggs and cheese and I don't really know what else because Spiro is not about to give away his secrets"—the man standing next to our table smiled his agreement—"but you'll see what I mean. In the meanwhile, Spiro, bring us some of your famous dolmades and a bowl of tzatziki to tide us over while we wait for your masterpiece."

I was busy dipping torn pieces of heavy flatbread into the bowl of creamy tzatziki when Spiro delivered the dolmades to our table. When I tasted that dish—delectable vine leaves stuffed with rice that offered a delicate lemon flavor—I pronounced, "We can stop right here. I can't imagine anything more delicious than this."

"Just wait for the moussaka, and be sure to leave room for karidopita and coffee at the end of the meal or Spiro will consider it a personal insult."

I recall the afternoon and the time spent at a small table on the walk outside a tiny restaurant as one of the happiest interludes of that period of my life. How much was the food and how much my companion, I couldn't say, but I ate my way through lunch with abandon under Spiro's benevolent smile and Jake's smile that was something far different than benevolent but even more agreeable.

When Spiro set a small, long-handled brass pot on our table, I looked up at him with a faint feeling of shame and the need for an apology. "I don't usually eat as if I were starving," I explained, "but everything was just so—" I couldn't find the right word and had to settle for the commonplace"—just so delicious that I couldn't help myself." Spiro's mustache quivered over his smile.

"This humble fare? It was nothing. You are too kind, Miss," but I could tell he was pleased with the compliment. As he swept up the empty plates, he added, "I am going to bring you fresh karidopita, which to truly appreciate you must taste along with the coffee." To Jake, he said, "I brought it plain, the way you like it, but perhaps the lady would prefer something sweeter."

"No," I interjected. "Mr. Pandora's recommendations have been perfect so far, and I wouldn't think of disagreeing with his preferences." When Spiro left, I said to Jake, "Don't let that go to your head. I was talking only about the food." I spoke with a smile, however, feeling in perfect charity with a man who could introduce me to the kind of food in which I'd just indulged.

"I never dared to hope for anything else, Miss Hudson."

"Oh, stop calling me Miss Hudson. I'm not some ancient school-teacher doddering out of the classroom. I thought we decided *Dinah* was fine."

Jake grinned at that and would have made a flippant retort, but Spiro reappeared with slices of extraordinary cake, each piece rich with the flavor of walnuts, cinnamon, and cloves. Spiro was right about the coffee, too—its almost bitter flavor was the perfect complement to the flavorful pastry.

Finally, with both hands wrapped around a small cup of thick coffee and every last cake crumb devoured, I said with regret, "As much as I thoroughly enjoyed this meal, Jake, we did meet for a reason. You said you had some information, and it's probably time you satisfied my curiosity."

"I suppose, but I'm still absorbing the fact that a woman as slender as you can eat as much as a Greek regiment."

"Unkind and unfair. It was the attraction of novelty."

"So you think the next time we visit Spiro's you'll just pick at your food?"

I tried not to dwell on his assumption that there would be a next time and answered with a laugh, "No, of course, you're right. I'll probably shovel it in again, and I won't apologize then, either."

"Good. You're not at your best when you apologize. It doesn't seem to come easily or naturally to you."

"You should talk! I can't recall you making the effort."

"I can think of one or two times, but if I've overlooked an occasion, tell me what it is and I'll express my sincere regret for whatever offense I committed."

He had me there because at the moment I couldn't think of one single thing he should regret, not his handsome face, not his attitude, not the natural grace of his gestures, not the tone of his voice, not one single thing.

"I couldn't do that after this wonderful meal. All is forgiven."

"Really?" A seriousness to his tone that made my own smile fade.

I met his look with one of my own that did not falter and after a brief pause responded, "Yes. Really." The odd still moment passed when he leaned back in his chair.

"Good. I'm glad to hear it. Now, what do you know about Ralph Gallagher?"

I'm sure that for a moment I must have sat with my mouth literally and unbecomingly open until I found breath to reply, "My brother-in-law works at one of his banks. I met him the night of the cotillion. Why? What are you suggesting?"

Pandora chose his words carefully. "Gallagher's name has come up often enough in my inquiries that I've begun to wonder if he's quite as respectable as he pretends to be."

"That's a serious allegation, Jake." I pictured Gallagher the way I recalled him from the evening of the city's summer gala: confident, solid, pompous, and slightly flirtatious. I couldn't picture the man involved in anything the least bit shady. Abe Ruef, Eugene Schmitz, Justice Mackiver, and their compatriots fit my notion of degenerate scoundrels just fine but Ralph Gallagher— I shook my head at the idea. "I can't believe it. Martin always speaks of Mr. Gallagher very highly and my sister sits on a charity board with his wife. In fact, Martin, Ruth, and I have been invited to attend a small gathering at the Gallaghers' new home next week."

"A gathering you're planning to attend, right?" At my nod, he went on, "Then pay attention when you're there. See if anything curious develops. You're an intelligent woman."

"How kind of you to admit that fact. I feel like I've made real progress," I murmured, then asked, "Have you done business with Mr. Gallagher?"

"Nothing significant." Something about my tone made him ask, "Why do you ask?"

"I once saw you coming out of his house on Nob Hill."

"Did you?" He didn't explain his presence there. "You just happened to be strolling past the mansions on Nob Hill and spotted me? Quite a coincidence that we would both be there at the same time. Do you often spend your afternoons spying on the rich?"

"I wasn't spying! I was new to the city and a friend was showing me the sights."

I recalled Colin's attentions that day, my attraction to him, and that pleasant first kiss in the cab. In the intervening weeks, my feelings for Colin had subtly altered and while I didn't know exactly why and when, I realized the man sitting across the table from me had something—maybe everything—to do with the change. Pandora pulled me back from my musings.

"Your policeman?"

"Not mine."

"That's not what he'd say."

"How can you presume to know that? You met Colin once and briefly."

Jake smiled but without humor. "I know how he looked at you that day at the Cliff House."

I remembered that day, too, Colin's hand on my shoulder staking a claim and my unhappiness with the action. Was it that early gesture that had cooled my growing fondness for him? Now was not the time to consider it, but I thought Jake Pandora might have unknowingly put his finger on an answer for which I'd been searching. I shook my head slightly to banish those thoughts and changed the subject.

"I will keep my eyes and ears open at the Gallaghers' but I hardly think it likely that a social evening will be the forum for Ralph Gallagher to discuss his illegal or immoral pastimes."

"You think he has immoral pastimes, then?"

I gave the question more serious thought than I believe Jake expected and finally replied, "Ralph Gallagher is a man difficult to read. I admit he surprised me by flirting with me, but I don't see him as a man who would be involved in anything that didn't promise monetary benefit. I don't see him doing anything for the pure pleasure of it."

"An unfortunate man then. Pure pleasure has its place." I drew the line at pursuing his words and set my coffee cup down to gather up my gloves and bag.

"You would know about that, I'm sure, but at the risk of appearing uninterested in your opinion, is there anything more specific you can tell me about Ralph Gallagher that would help me know what to pay attention to?"

"If I'm right, Gallagher uses a code name for his smuggling enterprise. He calls it his Gold Mountain Interest, a play on a banking term that says something about the kind of man he is."

"Gold Mountain is what the Chinese call California. *Gam saan*, they say. There's a folk song I've heard in the villages." I slipped into the sing-song rhythms of the music and sang the English words in a low voice, "If you have a daughter, marry her quickly to a traveler to Gold Mountain / For when he gets off the boat, he will bring hundreds of pieces of silver."

"The Greeks have a similar song about the promise of California," Jake told me. "Too bad it's not always true." I thought of Suey Wah and Mae Tao, Fei Yen and Lu Chu, and all the girls who had come to America full of dreams for a hopeful future.

"Yes."

Jake reached across the little table to flick his index finger across my cheek. "Chin up, Miss Hudson. You can't change the past, but the future is always hopeful."

I stood and responded with a quick smile, "It is, isn't it?" To Spiro, now hovering in the doorway, I called, "Thank you, Spiro. Everything was superb. You're a genius."

He nodded in agreement, satisfied that at least two of us recognized that universal truth. "You have Jacobi bring you back soon, Miss. You appreciate greatness. You are always welcome."

Jake laughed out loud at the comment as we started to walk back toward the transport office. When we drew closer to our destination, I saw with unspoken regret that Casey's cab waited at the corner.

"Listen, Dinah," Jake said abruptly as he helped me into the cab, "don't do anything foolish when you visit the Gallaghers. Could you just be quiet and listen for a change?"

"Thank you for that, Jake. Are you saying I talk too much?"

"I didn't mean it that way. Exactly. Only don't underestimate the kind of men and the kind of money that are involved in the slave trade. Don't take any of it lightly. These are men who deal in children without a second thought. They're prepared to risk a great deal for lucrative earnings, and they'd easily sacrifice anyone who threatened their commerce or their anonymity. Your Miss Cameron remains unmolested because of the stature and the number of the people who support her and because she has learned how to use reticence to her advantage, but you are not at her level and her backing alone is not enough to protect you. Will you please remember all that and be careful? Just be careful."

I recognized his *please* for the concession it was and answered humbly, "I will. I promise."

"All right."

He seemed taken aback at my meek acquiescence and stepped away from the cab, gave a quick nod to Casey, and walked away without another word. I watched his retreating back before settling into the seat as Casey jerked the cab forward. The return to Grove Street passed quickly because I spent the whole trip deep in thought. About Jake Pandora and Colin O'Connor and Ralph Gallagher. About expectations and revelations and surprises. About life and how sometimes it took a direction a person didn't expect and could never have predicted.

Chapter Eleven

The invitation to the Gallaghers' dinner party had come only the week before, and my poor sister, unsure how I would accept the prospect of another evening spent in Irene Gallagher's company, shared it with her husband before she broached the subject to me. Ruth tried for a casual tone that was not convincing, and I felt an immediate pang of conscience at causing my sister discomfort at what ordinarily would have been a welcome and exciting prospect for her.

"You're named in the invitation specifically," Ruth told me, holding the ivory card of fine vellum in front of her. "Irene handwrote a small note. *Be sure to bring the charming Miss Hudson*, it says. Of course if you can't bear the idea, we'll all plead a prior engagement."

"And ruin Martin's chances for advancement? I wouldn't think of it. Poor Ruthie, do you fear I will break down and run shrieking out of the Gallaghers' fine dining room the same way I fled the summer cotillion? I promise I won't. I think I've come to grips with the Irene Gallaghers of this world, and I guarantee to be on my best behavior. I'm sorry my bad temper has the ability to spoil your happiness." I gave her a quick kiss on the cheek and added with a smile, "But will our budget support new gowns?"

"I've already thought about that. I'm going to refurbish old gowns and before you get worried that I'll embarrass you, come see what I've found in the latest McCall's. I admit that at first I was a little uncertain about proper attire for a dinner party, but the magazine shows just the right style."

"I trust you completely and would never dream of doubting your instinct for couture," I laughingly replied and allowed myself to be pulled along to Ruth's sewing room.

Before my afternoon with Jake Pandora, I had anticipated the evening at the Gallaghers' Nob Hill mansion with only a stoic sense of duty, something I had to do for my sister and brother-in-law, something to be endured. But because of Jake's suspicion about Ralph Gallagher, I actually looked forward to the evening as an opportunity to rejuvenate the search for Mae Tao. The few leads I had received about her whereabouts had all turned out to be dead ends, and I hoped that the evening held the promise of progress in my search for the girl I had abandoned so cavalierly months before. As unlikely as the idea was, my conscience found some comfort believing that an evening with the Gallaghers held the potential for unraveling the child's disappearance. I knew in an objective way that Mae Tao might be lost forever in the impenetrable maze that was Chinatown, but I was nowhere near admitting that fact, even—especially—to myself.

Martin was as excited as Ruth about the evening and endeared himself to me with a quiet thank you as we waited in the hallway for the carriage he'd ordered to carry us to the party. "I know you found Irene Gallagher difficult, Dinah, and I can't say I blame you. I thought she lacked good manners myself, and you know I don't usually notice that kind of thing." He gave me a quick smile, making a joke at his own expense, which I found even more endearing. "So thank you for agreeing to attend. Mr. Gallagher made it clear that I wasn't to come without you. You seem to have caught his fancy." Martin made the comment with complete innocence, and it was only my depraved and suspicious mind that attributed either a licentious or a corrupt reason for Mr. Gallagher's interest in me. Time would tell, I thought with satisfaction, and found myself looking forward to the seemingly unlimited prospects of the evening with happy anticipation.

The magnificence of the exterior of the Gallaghers' mansion dimmed before the absolute and unending grandeur of its interior. Servants took our wraps from us in the ornate hallway and when we entered the high-ceilinged drawing room ablaze with lights, Ruth's gasp was audible.

"How beautiful, Irene!" my sister exclaimed. "How very beautiful this room is!" Long and ornately framed mirrors bounced the light all over the room, set off the sparkling thread in the rich gold drapes, and illuminated the rich colors of a tapestry that covered one wall. To Irene Gallagher's credit, she remained properly modest and restrained in the face of her guests' admiration. She smiled with no trace of smugness in her expression and accepted compliments with just the right amount of modesty. Once in a while I saw her gaze slide to her husband, and I noticed that he was never too far away from her. If I'd had to guess, I would have said she was working under very specific instructions from her husband, and he had decided to stay close enough to be sure she did not step over any lines of propriety or good taste.

At dinner I sat next to Eugene Schmitz—"Handsome Gene" as I'd heard him called—an odd choice for Ralph Gallagher's guest list because of Schmitz's union activities. I recalled Gallagher's unequivocal opinion of what he termed the "socialist poison" of labor unions and the fact that the two men seemed on such convivial terms made me wonder what activities they could possibly have in common. On my other side sat Ben Ali Haggin, whose block-long mansion also on Nob Hill I recalled staring at in amazement in my earlier tour of the area. The size of Mr. Haggin's stables was legendary and although he was a perfect gentleman, as soon as he discovered that I didn't have one jot of equestrian knowledge, interest, or talent, he directed most of his attention to the woman on his right.

"You're quite the heroine," Schmitz commented during the meal, bringing up the old refrain, but this time the words did not have the power to make me uncomfortable.

"Don't believe everything you hear, Mr. Schmitz. Despite the embellishment of rumor, I spent most of my time in Pekin huddled in a small room, hot and hungry along with a crowd of people all similarly situated. Have you ever been to China?"

"No, I haven't had the pleasure. Surely with your unfortunate memories you don't recommend the place for travel?"

"Like every country on the globe, China is made up of some very bad and some very good people. San Francisco, too, if I'm not mistaken."

As white-gloved servants whisked away our dishes, Schmitz leaned back comfortably in his chair. "If I didn't know better, I'd say the young heroine, daughter of missionaries and defender of the helpless, possesses a cynical streak."

"A foot wide and a mile long," I agreed cheerfully. "Do you think it's unwarranted?"

As delicate goblets of fruit were placed before us, Schmitz shifted in his chair so he could look more directly at me. "I don't know if it's very becoming in a young woman of good breeding, but perhaps your past experiences would account for a suspicious nature." I believe he meant his words to tease and I allowed the intention.

"How understanding of you, Mr. Schmitz." We ate our iced fruit in silence, and then I asked casually, "Have you known the Gallaghers very long?"

"I've had several business dealings with Gallagher."

"Ah, the world of commerce. Always so impossible for my female mind to grasp. You have an interest in banking then?"

"Not in banking exactly."

"But from what you said, I thought—well, there you see how I tend to simplify the complicated world of business. Obviously, Mr. Gallagher must have commercial interests outside of banking."

"Ralph Gallagher is a successful man, Miss Hudson, and like all successful men, he has diversified interests." Reverting to a former topic, he said, "I understand you speak the Chinese language like a native."

"I have an ear for languages but how did you know that?"

Schmitz appeared discomfited for just a moment, then stated, "My wife must have mentioned it. She and Irene are friends. Or she may have heard your sister say something to that effect because they work together on some charitable board. I admit the Asian language sounds like gibberish to me."

"It did to me at first, too, but the Chinese language has an ambiguity to it that I enjoy. So much of its meaning is hidden beneath the surface. It's really full of surprises." For no reason I could identify, my words caused Eugene Schmitz to lose his smile.

"Surprises are not always welcome, Miss Hudson," was all he had time to say before Ralph Gallagher stood and invited all his guests to gather once more in the drawing room for conversation and digestifs.

I stood and made my way to Ruth's side. "Are you feeling all right?" I asked her. "You look a little flushed."

"I'm just warm."

"Shall I get Martin? We could leave, Ruthie, and no one would hold it against a woman in your condition."

"A woman in my condition does not get out all that often," Ruth responded, "and I intend to stay as long as I possibly can. I feel fine. But I see Irene Gallagher headed in our direction so you'd better make your escape now before you lose the opportunity."

I took Ruth's suggestion to heart and drifted with the other company into the glowing drawing room where servants holding silver trays of fine crystal glasses moved noiselessly among the guests offering brandy to the men and mellow Portugese Madeira to the women. I would have preferred the former but sipped the Madeira and pretended to enjoy it.

From behind me someone gently grasped my elbow, and I turned to face my host. Ralph Gallagher held out a glass of brandy, unmistakable by its rich caramel color, and lifted the glass of Madeira from my hand.

"You're a woman for brandy, I think. Try this. It's Armagnac from the south of France."

I exchanged glasses and took a sip of the liquor that burned its way down my throat with a sensation entirely agreeable. "Thank you. This is lovely."

"Not as lovely as you, Miss Hudson. I'm glad you forego the prim pastels of the season. They wouldn't suit you nearly as much as the scarlet you're wearing."

So Ralph Gallagher wanted to play at the game of flirtation again,

I thought with interest. Probably because of Jake's suspicions, my host had taken on a dangerous, almost villainous, look that he hadn't possessed the night of the summer cotillion. The power of suggestion, I realized, and smiled at Gallagher, all the while speculating wildly about both his personal and his business morals.

I looked down at the skirt of the gown Ruth had so painstakingly recreated from one of her last year's dresses. Covering its prim ecru underskirt with embroidered crimson silk, removing the sleeves, and draping the bodice with flowing swatches of the same bright silk had given the dress an entirely new and glamorous look. I had debated whether it was quite right for a dinner party, but my sister's unerring eye for fashion caused her to squelch my doubts immediately. Ruth had been right, of course. The dress flattered my figure and the plain underskirt offered an enticing illusion of skin beneath the fabric while remaining entirely appropriate.

"It's kind of you to notice," I responded to Ralph Gallagher. "Honesty forces me to admit, however, that if it weren't for my sister's sense of style, I would be completely baffled by society's code of fashion."

"No doubt because you are a woman to set trends, Miss Hudson, not follow them." This time I did not reply to the compliment, just met his glance over my glass and smiled again. Finally, I remarked, "I noticed a stunning portrait of a woman hanging in the hallway when I arrived. To my uninitiated eye, it had the look of a Sargent. And was that a family portrait in the foyer? I thought I recognized you and your wife but not the two boys."

"My sons, Douglas and Drew, are at school back East. They liked the Sargent painting, too. When they were boys, Drew nicknamed it The Warm Woman. He always had an eye for color."

"You must miss them."

"Must I?" He smiled without humor. "Douglas will inherit everything one day and he's doing well enough, I suppose, when he's not busy bailing his younger brother out of trouble."

"Oh, dear. A black sheep?" The expression on Gallagher's face when he spoke of his sons made him sympathetic, the first time I'd sensed anything even remotely, normally human about him.

"Drew's something, anyway. I don't know what. He seems destined to break his mother's heart."

"And his father's?"

A grim smile played around the man's lips. "My younger son is a charmer and I had hopes for him at one time, but those hopes vanished long ago."

"You speak as if he's a lost cause, but he must still be a young man. Maybe he just needs time to grow up. The Chinese have a saying: 'You won't help the new plants grow by pulling them up higher.'"

Gallagher thought about the words for a moment before smiling. "A wise people, the Chinese. I didn't realize."

"Realize what? That regardless of nationality or native language, humanity shares common loves and common fears? Shame on you, Mr. Gallagher. I wouldn't have thought you were so pedestrian in your views. The Chinese have feelings just like you. They love their children and want the best for them." Despite my good intentions, I invested the words with too much emotion and took a quick sip of brandy.

"I finally see the missionary's fervor, Miss Hudson. I couldn't quite picture you saving the unenlightened until just now. I'm sure you bring an admirable passion to your work at Miss Cameron's mission. I know very little about the Chinese people, and I admit I am not all that interested in them, but what those poor girls have had to endure I can only imagine." With those words, I had the certain feeling that Ralph Gallagher had in a way turned the tables on me and was either teasing or mocking me, I couldn't be quite sure which.

Because I'd promised Jake Pandora I'd be circumspect in my words, I swallowed my initial response and said gently, "Perhaps if you had daughters instead of sons, you would have a greater understanding of their circumstances. With so little knowledge of the Chinese people, I fear the girls may not seem much more than a commodity to you, but I assure you that before they came to the mission they were indeed "poor girls." The idea of their being taken advantage of by men who ought to know better is repugnant. I've always believed that men who lack both intelligence and integrity pose a serious threat to society. Besides being boring and vain, of course. What their poor wives have to endure I can only imagine." I mimicked his words and his tone on purpose, and he caught the message.

Gallagher smiled slightly and murmured, "You may remember I once told you that I know when I'm being mocked."

"Oh, I remember," I retorted in a similar low voice, then a bit more loudly added, "and I wouldn't dream of mocking anyone, least of all my host." I should have let the conversation end there, but I didn't, and I have no excuse except the brandy's intoxicating effect. Placing my empty glass on the tray of a passing servant, I turned back and looked directly into Ralph Gallagher's eyes. "You should take a greater interest in the Chinese, sir. In fact, I would guess you'd find great profit in Gold Mountain interest."

His eyes widened at that, and he grabbed my wrist firmly with one hand. "Are you speaking in riddles now, Miss Hudson?" I heard surprise and anger and an unexpected touch of what seemed like fear in his voice.

I shook my hand free of his grasp. "I haven't the temperament for riddles. I'm much too impatient and blunt."

"I mean this kindly, Miss Hudson, and more sincerely than you know, but you should be more circumspect in your speech and more careful. You should really be more careful." With the mockery gone, Ralph Gallagher seemed as honest and as human as I'd ever heard him, and because of that more likeable. Without putting specific words or meaning to it, he had moved the conversation to a more serious level, and I thought I detected true emotion in his voice.

"I'll try to be more careful in the future," I answered quietly. "I was only making conversation. If I've said something unsuitable, please forgive me. I've spent the greater part of my life out of ordinary society and can be inept in my speech. I have a passion for the girls at Miss Cameron's mission, though, a passion to keep them happy and safe."

Gallagher stepped to my side to walk past me and as he did so, he paused long enough to whisper against my ear, "I can tell that, Miss Hudson, but as a man I can only say that your passion is wasted on children. Please remember what I've told you. Not everyone finds you as charming as I do. Just be careful." He stepped farther to the side, called someone's name, and moved away in a manner that indicated he wanted to distance himself from me as quickly as possible. The purposeful intention of his action sent a shiver down my back as nothing else could have. Was someone watching us and listening to our conversation? I looked around with what I hoped was a casual disinterest. The beautiful, bright room was crowded with people, all reflected in the gilt mirrors on the walls. Conversation and laughter flowed as generously as the refreshments. A fancy crowd of fancy people and no one, as far as I could tell, paying me the least bit of attention. And yet Gallagher's *be careful* had echoed Jake Pandora's advice exactly and had held an edge that I couldn't ignore. Jake might be right about Gallagher's connection with illicit activities, but if Ralph Gallagher was involved in smuggling children into California, he was certainly not alone in the venture. Others were involved, too, and unless I was very mistaken, at least some of those others were among the well-bred guests who stood in conversation all around me.

Irene Gallagher and I exchanged few words during the evening, but as a servant dropped my cape around my shoulders in preparation for departure, she approached me and said, "I hope you enjoyed the evening, Miss Hudson."

"I did, very much, thank you. Your home is beautiful and your hospitality gracious. Ruth just went in search of you to relay our appreciation for the evening."

"My husband told me I embarrassed you the night of the cotillion and said I must be on better behavior tonight." Her words seemed forced, her tone brittle.

"Your husband was mistaken," I lied. "You did nothing of the sort."

"Perhaps you had the opportunity to share your opinion with Ralph when you were in such deep conversation with him earlier, such impassioned conversation. He admires you a great deal, you know." Her calculated words startled me, overt in a meaning that could not be misunderstood.

"He's very kind, as are you." Over her shoulder, I saw Ruth and raised my voice to say, "Here's our hostess, Ruth. I know you wanted to say good night."

Irene Gallagher turned around to face my sister, who was followed by Martin and Mr. Gallagher deep in conversation. Martin came forward to stand next to his wife and add to Ruth's murmured courtesies. For a moment Ralph Gallagher stood a dark and solitary figure in the background. His eyes were on me gravely, intently, with an emotion far different from admiration. I thought his serious look held a reminder of the warning he had voiced earlier in the evening. Gallagher nodded a good-night to me, dipping his head slowly in what seemed almost like a regal bow before he turned back to his guests. His wife, who had missed none of that exchange and was determined to put the worst construction on her husband's mute attention to me, saw us to the door. Ruth repeated her thank you and took Martin's arm before stepping outside. I followed them and turned to speak a final word to Irene Gallagher.

"You have nothing to be concerned about where I'm concerned," I told her, hoping she would hear my real message. "Nothing at all." Without giving her time to respond, I quickly slid past the servant holding open the door and hurried to catch up with Ruth and Martin.

The following week I returned to the final days of my routine at 920. Yuen Qui, whose interpreter's assignment I had taken on as she recuperated from an illness, had received permission from the doctor to return to the mission and her regular duties.

I heard the news with a wrench of dismay that must have been reflected on my face because Donaldina put an arm around my shoulders and said, "But that doesn't mean you must stop your visits or your work here, Dinah. There will always be a place for you at 920. Your classroom skills teaching English are the best I've seen, and the girls are fond of you. We all want you to stay part of our family."

"It won't be the same," I said with childlike petulance and then had to grin at myself. "Listen to me. I sound like a spoiled princess. I'm truly happy to hear Yuen Qui is back to good health and, of course, I'll continue with morning English lessons and anything else you can find for me to do. I can't argue with the timing, now that I think of it, because the baby isn't all that far away and for Ruth's sake I really should stay closer to home for the next few weeks." I stopped to search for the right words and finally concluded less than satisfactorily with, "Thank you, Dolly, for giving me the privilege of partnering with you, even for a short while. I don't believe I will ever know anything more worthwhile than my experiences here at 920. I'll never forget it."

"Save those fine words for my wake someday, Dinah," Miss Cameron responded dryly. "Having worked with you, I can guarantee that your life holds the potential for a great many more experiences of excitement and value. You are not a woman to sit idly and let adventure pass you by." She smiled. "Now wasn't your English class supposed to start ten minutes ago?"

I glanced at the hall clock, gave a little gasp at the time, and hurried toward the classroom, but behind me I'm sure I heard Miss Cameron say in a low voice, "We will not forget you either, Dinah. Depend on it."

I left 920 late that afternoon, crossed two streets, and was just about to cross another to reach a small alley I often used as a shortcut when someone called, "Missy! Missy!"

The only other people in my general vicinity were men, and they were all hurrying to whatever destination beckoned. Home, most likely, and supper, so I knew the caller must be trying to get my attention. Despite Jake Pandora's warnings and Ralph Gallagher's grave words, the idea that I might be in danger was never quite credible. Somehow it was hard to imagine that anyone would give me a second thought or consider me a threat. I knew that Suey Wah had no memory of the men involved in smuggling her into the state, and because that was the case, how could I possess knowledge that would be dangerous to anyone? The natural conclusion that I couldn't and didn't seemed so obvious that even with my unwise and provocative comment to Gallagher, I couldn't believe that anyone would think otherwise. I've taken time to think all this through because even today I am fairly dumbfounded by my own naiveté. I saw no threat, only a Chinese man standing by an ordinary cab that waited at the foot of the alley.

"Missy!" he called again and began to wave a piece of paper. "I have word for you about the girl you seek." I hurried across the empty street to where the man stood.

"About a girl named Mae Tao?" I asked eagerly. He nodded and handed the paper to me. I snatched the folded note out of his hand and opened it, but when I saw that the paper was blank, I lifted my head to say, "But there's nothing—" and after that I don't remember anything.

I can reconstruct what happened with fair accuracy, however. Someone came up behind me and pushed a cloth over my nose and mouth and something on the cloth—chloroform, most likely—caused me to lose consciousness almost immediately. I was quickly and inelegantly pushed into the waiting hands of an inhabitant of that not-so-innocent cab, which entered the alley with just the right amount of speed—not so fast as to appear suspicious and not so slowly that a pedestrian on the street would have had time to run up to see what had just occurred. Not that anyone did, as far as I know. If there were pedestrians they must have been busy with their own thoughts because I was abducted off a San Francisco street without anyone calling an alarm. Just like that I disappeared!

I remember nothing of the cab trip that followed, but I must have been manhandled and jostled and slung about like a sack of grain. That rough treatment certainly contributed to the pain I felt when I regained consciousness. I stirred slightly and turned my head, an action which caused me to be immediately and violently ill. I had felt wretched upon awakening but after that terrible bout of sickness, I felt far worse, still nauseated, my head pounding, and the slightest movement sending waves of dizziness crashing over me. I had never felt so completely and helplessly miserable as I did lying on that small, dirty bed in a dim room that reeked of human sweat and my own sickness. For the life of me, I couldn't recall what had happened or where I was, and I just barely knew who I was. Anything more complicated than that lay beyond my capabilities. Through the one small barred window halfway up the wall opposite me I could see the passing shadows of walking figures. Get up, Dinah, I told myself, get up and call for help, but if I moved any part of my body, I knew I would be sick again, and I couldn't bear that thought. All I could do was lie very still and stare at the window, what I needed just on the other side of those bars but unable to do anything about it.

I must have slept again and to my relief awoke to a clearer head. The light through the window had the look of early evening to it, and it seemed to me that the racket of street noises had increased. I moved my legs tentatively and slowly shifted them off the bed so that I lay in an awkward position: one foot on the floor, one foot close to the floor, and the rest of me still lying in a crooked and ungainly posture on the low bed. I took a deep breath, ignored the stomach-turning pain, and used an elbow to push myself to a sitting position, holding onto the side of the bed until the room stopped swirling. I was mesmerized by the small window and thought if I could just get to it, could thrust out my arms and cry for help, someone would be sure to come to my aid. At the time I had no way of knowing that the thoroughfare right outside was the infamous Morton Street—the street that came alive with saloons and sailors and brothels and brawls as soon as the sun set—and that cries for help for one reason or another were not all together uncommon but were generally ignored.

I pushed myself upright, teetered unsteadily, and took one step forward, and as I did so, a door on the wall behind me crashed open and a man called in Chinese, "Get back! Get back!" He hurried into the room, grasped me by one arm, and pulled me backwards. His tug made me fall inelegantly onto the bed again and moan with pain.

Unmoved, he stood over me and scolded, "You must not move. Not move at all. You must stay quiet or I will tie you to the bed."

I croaked out a few words from a throat and mouth that felt sticky and swollen. "I want some water. I am very thirsty. Please bring me some water." The man frowned at my request.

"I don't know. I'll see. But you may not move. You must stay still." By then he and I were in perfect agreement because all I truly wanted was to stay still, stop the throbbing in my head and the churning in my stomach, and drink something.

"Bring me water and I will be very still. But bring me something to drink."

The water he finally delivered was tepid with an odor about it that didn't bear scrutiny, but it was wonderful, nevertheless. I gulped down one glass, held it out to my captor with a mute demand for a refill, and drank the second glass he brought.

When I handed back the empty glass, I asked, "Why are you keeping me here? Who brought me here? Do you understand that you can hang for being involved in the abduction of a white woman?"

The man, who never stopped glaring at me, snatched the empty glass out of my hand and backed away from me. "Be still. Be quiet. You are to stay here until I have word otherwise."

"Please let me go. I can pay you a great deal of money."

He shook his head vigorously at that and repeated the same message, "You are to stay here until they send me word."

"Until who sends you word? Who brought me here?" I asked again, but I couldn't get any more information from him. From the look on his face my questions frightened him, and he quickly left the room. After his departure, I heard the noticeable click of a latch on the other side of the door fall into place.

I'm locked in this awful place, I thought hazily but without alarm, realized how weak and tired I still felt, and fell asleep again.

When I awoke next, I felt immeasurably better, achy but clear-headed and alert and ravenous. The light that filtered through the bars of the window was the light of early morning and the raucous street noises I recalled hearing intermittently through the night were gone. I swung into a sitting position on the bed and when my head and stomach did not respond to the motion, I stood upright. My arms and legs hurt in a way that indicated they'd been bumped and bruised, which they probably had been, but otherwise I felt whole. After taking two steps toward the window, I looked back over my shoulder at the door, expecting to see it thrown open by my jailer, who would then rush in and fling me unceremoniously back onto the bed. But nothing happened. Perhaps the fact that Morton Street was empty of both people and activity made my jailer think he had nothing to fear for the time being. Whatever the reason, I intended to take advantage of the unimpeded moment, however long it might last. At the window, I stood on tiptoe to peer out at what appeared to be an uninhabited street in an uninhabited city. No pedestrians and no danger lurked on Morton Street as the sun rose, wickedness and vice relegated to the dark anonymity of night. As I watched, a woman came into view on the other side of the street. She stepped off the walk onto the street, hurrying directly toward the window where I stood.

With another hasty look over my shoulder at the door, I dragged the small bed under the window, climbed on it, and thrust out both hands, all that would fit through the small opening. "Help me!" I cried. "I'm held here against my will!"

I could tell from the posture of the woman's shoulders that she didn't want to stop, that she regretted hearing my voice and was prepared to ignore my pale, waving hands. But if I let her pass without acknowledging me, I would lose the chance to get word to someone of my predicament and location.

"Please," I said again. "Please help me." At those words she looked over at the window opening and I knew I had won some kind of battle. "I've been kidnapped. I'm being held here against my will," I repeated hurriedly.

Though I could see her only partially, I thought the woman's face held the detritus of great beauty that had been ravaged by time and the abuse of life on the streets. Her fair hair was disheveled and her green eyes, which at one time must have shone brilliantly with the flash of emeralds, now looked only terribly, terribly weary, with no warmth to prove that this woman possessed any inner spark of life at all. A walking dead woman was my first thought at the gaze of those vacant green eyes sunk into a face that looked as old as time, and I felt a moment of despair. She will not help me, I told myself, but I had to try anyway because I feared she could be my only hope for rescue.

"There's nothing I can do for you. If I'm not back with the money from the night, he'll hurt me. Nothing I can do." Her voice, like her eyes, was expressionless. She may have been afraid, but it was only the words that told me so. The woman had passed beyond fear.

"Yes, you can do something. He doesn't have to know." I had no idea who the *he* was, but I had to say something. "Just tell someone you saw me here. Tell the authorities." But that was the wrong thing to say because she backed away, the idea of authorities possessing an intrinsic threat. I rushed on, not thinking, just talking to keep her attention and enlist her aid before my jailer spied me. "Or if not the authorities, tell my friend, Jake Pandora. He's at the Pandora Transport Company in the alley behind the Broadway Dock. Tell him you saw Dinah and tell him where. That's all I'm asking. He'll give you money, a lot of money, for the information." At her continuing indecision, I pleaded, "Please. They're going to kill me, I think. I don't know what else to do." My voice cracked on the last word and I believe it was that single syllable broken by desperate fear and panic that made her decision.

She spoke in a low voice. "All right. I'll do what I can. Dying isn't such a bad thing the way I live. Why would I care if he takes a knife to me?"

"Pandora will pay you. I'm sure he will. He'll give you whatever you ask. Just tell him I'm here."

At those words, the woman straightened her posture and stepped forward to look through the bars of the little window and stare straight into my face. "It's not about money. I got a girl of my own, a smart, good girl, and I don't know why, but there's something about you that reminds me of her. If she was in trouble, I'd want someone to do for her, and maybe my helping you means someone will help her some day. Maybe it does. Maybe that's how it works. God knows I'm no good to her as it is." She repeated Jake's name and his location. "I'll do what I can." Then, intending kindness, she advised in words that chilled me to the core, "Don't fight them. That's what I've learned. Don't talk back and don't fight them. Maybe then they won't kill you right away. Do whatever they tell you and act like you like it so I have time to get the word to this Pandora fella. I've got to go back to my loafer first and give him the night's earnings. I'm already late, and he'll beat me. He doesn't tolerate any of his girls coming back late with the money."

She pulled her shawl more tightly around her shoulders and started to walk away as I called after her, "Bless you! What's your name so I'll know who to thank when I'm free?" She stopped.

"All I've got to show for my life is a daughter and a name. That's all that belongs to me. My name is Bea." She spelled it for me, leaving the impression that spelling was something she did not do easily or well but proud of the little she could do. "B-E-A. That's my name."

After she moved out of view, I quickly stepped down and just managed to seat myself on the edge of the bed before the door opened with such force it smacked back against the wall. The same Chinese man from the night before stormed in shouting at me to get back, get back! He pushed me to the side and shoved the bed away from the window.

I said in Chinese and with as much dignity as I could muster, "I only wanted more air. I won't fit through that window, you know. Now I need to use the facility. Will you take me there?"

Without answering, he hurried out, carefully closing and locking the door behind him, and returned in a matter of minutes with a bucket that he placed in the corner behind the door. "Here facility," was his comment before exiting again.

I took a deep breath and sat back on the edge of the bed. I didn't really have to use the facility just then, I'd made it up as a distraction, but I supposed I would have to do so eventually and the bucket would have to do. I never thought I'd be grateful for my experiences during the Siege of Pekin, but at that particular moment I was. The stink of the room and a bucket in the corner were nothing new. I had endured them once before, and I would endure them again. Until Jake Pandora came for me, I would do what Bea advised—endure whatever it took to survive. I'd survived against the odds before and had lived to tell about it; I intended to repeat the experience.

For the rest of the morning I roamed that disgusting little room thinking and praying. I was very frightened, but my mind, recognizing the familiar sensation, adjusted to it and calmed. I didn't think the same could be said of my poor Ruthie, who would be worried to distraction. At first she wouldn't have been very concerned, but once Martin arrived home and I still wasn't there, she would have begun to feel a nagging worry. Perhaps she sent Martin to 920 to look for me; perhaps she went next door to use the neighbors' new telephone. Whatever action she took, she would eventually have discovered that I left the mission hours earlier, and then her vague anxiety would have blossomed into fear. My poor sister—and in her present condition, too. My job was to make her life easier, not add to her burdens.

I went over my conversation with Bea, too, and knew that I had instinctively asked for Jake Pandora because I trusted him. I thought first to send her to Colin, who with the full arm of the law behind him would have stormed wherever I was held and easily rescued me, but Bea's recoil at the mention of the authorities made me fear that regardless of what she agreed to do, once she was no longer confronted by my urgent pleading she would not willingly approach a policeman. I doubted she would enter the well-to-do, upstanding borders of Grove Street, either. Her profession showed too obviously in her dress and her face, and I thought she might hesitate before climbing the front steps of an affluent house in a prosperous and proper neighborhood.

Bea would know the dock area for a number of reasons, however, and feel quite comfortable with the likes of Jake Pandora. Not that I didn't understand why that should be so. I felt quite comfortable with Jake Pandora myself, comfortable on several levels and at that particular time especially comfortable that he would move heaven and earth to find me. I didn't dwell very long on why I believed—more than believed, felt absolutely confident—that Jake would find me. Nothing spoken between us, no promises, no protestations of devotion or fidelity, nothing concrete at all. I just knew, despite the lack of anything tangible in word or deed, that he would come.

When he did show up, the afternoon sky had just begun to dim; I had been imprisoned for a full day. My jailer brought me a bowl of a disgusting liquid in which floated solid but unrecognizable chunks of what might have been meat and while my first thought was to shove it right back at him, I was sensible enough not to do so. Instead, I took the bowl in both hands and tilted the contents into my mouth, trying not to give much thought to what exactly I was eating. I knew I might need my strength in the future and couldn't afford to be finicky. The man then threatened to tie me to the bed if I didn't stay away from the window, and I feared he would do exactly that. I thought I could best him if it was just the two of us, but if he brought in reinforcements, I didn't stand a chance, and I craved mobility, even in my limited space. Still, the small window held a mystical allure—freedom beckoned on the other side of those bars, freedom and safety and relief from fear. The street's traffic had increased as the day progressed, and I had the unfulfilled hope that another passer-by might come close enough to hear a call for help. Unfortunately, I was never left alone long enough to attempt another contact. August heat turned the room into a reeking oven, and I wanted to stay near the window for fresh air, too, even though the smells of Morton Street that breezed in were not much of an improvement. All I could do, however, was sit on the edge of the bed and stare at the window with the same fixed expression a cat might have assumed in front of a mouse hole.

Once that afternoon the door opened to allow a figure I recognized to enter—the man Jake and I had first seen at Wing Chee's, the one wearing two black armbands and his queue bound on the top of his head, the man who had followed Suey Wah and me the day of the dock strike. The highbinder Chong Lin. He stood in the open doorway legs akimbo, arms crossed across his chest, staring at me impassively. Only his eyes sparked with emotion. I found him terrifying, and to make up for that initial debilitating feeling of fear I took the offensive.

"How dare you keep me here against my will?!" I spoke sharply and with much more self-assurance than I really felt. "Kidnapping is an offense punishable by death. Do you really want to risk that? The men at whose bidding you have committed this crime will not be able to save you." Not a muscle moved on his face. I might as well have been speaking to granite. When I moved closer to him to speak again, he casually put his hand to the center of my chest and pushed me backwards with enough force that my legs caught on the edge of the bed and I sat down with an unceremonious grunt.

His action angered and frightened me at the same time, and I did not immediately try to stand again. Chong Lin maintained his posture and continued to stare at me. I didn't speak again but finally rose to my feet once more, not willing to sit before him any longer in a pose that indicated a slave before his master, but we both realized that for the time being he was indeed master of the situation. At his side he wore a long, curved saber, a Chinese *dao*, and to show he understood why I had risen to my feet, he rested his hand on the weapon's handle. His mute return message was clear to me: he could take off my head whenever and wherever he chose. I lifted my chin and met his look as fearlessly as I was able—probably not all that convincing a gesture because fright and panic were making my stomach churn and my heart beat so hard that its pounding threatened to cut off my air supply. I know he must have seen the fear in my expression and posture despite my intention to the contrary because he gave a small, self-satisfied smile before exiting. The fact that he had remained wordless the entire time intensified his superiority. I was the supplicant at his mercy and regardless of my false bravado, we both recognized the truth.

Just as I remembered the restless frustration of being forced to stay within an area too small for comfort, and as I recognized the smells of human habitation in the heat of summer, I also recalled the familiar, bitter, shameful taste of fear and the dead, staring eyes of Corporal Alfred Betterman. After Chong Lin's departure, I lay down on the bed and wept—just a little bit—offered an inarticulate prayer for rescue, and drifted into a brief and fitful sleep.

When the door next flew open, I must have been having a terrible dream because I fully expected to see Chong Lin standing in the doorway with his *dao* raised to lop off one of my body parts—my head if I were lucky. Because I stood too quickly, the room went black for a moment and when I could finally see who stood in front of me, it wasn't the terrifying turtle man of the black dragons, it was Jake Pandora. My Jake Pandora, for better or for worse, the man I'd known would come for me. Worry and anger made his face a little less perfect than usual but I was content with what I saw there. Those emotions were on my behalf, and the way he said my name told me even more than his expression. Hardly a time to feel a rush of romantic feeling and recognize that I loved the man, but there it was.

"I'm all right," I told him quickly. "I'm not hurt. How did you—?" I peered past him at a prone figure outstretched on the floor of the hallway. "Is he—?" Apparently unable to finish a sentence, I shrugged helplessly and to my surprise felt my eyes well up with tears.

"For God's sake, don't cry, Dinah, or I won't be able to focus on getting us out of here. How you ended up on Morton Street must be quite a story." His tone was nowhere near as rough as his words.

"I am not going to cry," I began and then over his shoulder caught the flash of something that made me shout, "Jake, behind you!"

He turned fast enough to escape the full strength of Chong Lin's blow but not so fast that the blade missed him entirely. The *dao* hacked across Jake's face, his perfectly beautiful face, slit open a gash that curved from the corner of his eyebrow to the edge of that classical mouth and with the same deadly intention continued down to connect with Jake's upraised forearm, cutting through cloth and skin. Blood splattered everywhere, Jake Pandora's bright red blood, and he stumbled against me.

I screamed Jake's name and threw myself between him and the *dao* that Chong Lin had raised for another slash. The turtle man repeated the humorless smile he'd given me earlier that day, the smile that said I am master here, and turned the direction of his blow toward me.

Injured as he was, Jake still tried to push me to the side, mumbling words I could not understand, but I refused to budge.

"I am not a coward," I said out loud and still standing between the unsteady Jake and the murderous Chong Ling, I stretched out my arms palms forward toward the poised knife with the same gesture I might have used to halt carriage traffic, my hands the only shield before that deadly, diabolical blade. I knew he meant to kill us both and waited to feel the slice of metal through skin and bone.

Jake, still losing blood, began to slump against me, and I remember feeling so tender toward him and so very sorry that he would die because of me. As if Alfred Betterman weren't enough to have on my conscience and carry into eternity, now I must drag along Jake Pandora, too. The thoughts seem lengthy in the writing, but in reality they were just a flash of something unarticulated and fragile as I prepared to die.

Obviously, I did not die. At the moment Chong Lin would have sliced through my neck, someone shot him from behind. For one quick moment, the deadly turtle man looked astonished and then he toppled forward, fell against Jake as I struggled to support him, and knocked both Jake and me backwards through the doorway and into my little prison of a room. I reached for Jake with both arms and purposefully fell with him so I could cradle his body and protect it from crashing against the floor. Surprisingly, I landed in a comfortable position, my legs under me, my skirts billowed out, and Jake's bleeding face and arm lying squarely in my lap.

"My darling," I said softly. "Don't you dare die," and then remembered that a shot—and thus a shooter—had rescued us. Lifting my head, I started to say thank you, but the words caught in my throat as I stared directly at Colin O'Connor. My heart leaped, literally leaped, with joy at the sight.

"Oh, Colin, how did you find me?" and then as Jake stirred in my lap, added, "Can you help me? He's terribly injured." I glanced down at Jake's bleeding face briefly and then looked back at Colin, who did not move a step from the open doorway where he stood still holding his gun, the shot's acrid smoke just beginning to dispel. Because I had been without food for a full day, because I'd been ill from the effects of chloroform, and because I believed the man I loved was bleeding to death in my lap, I was not quick to understand what was happening. I repeated Colin's name, only this time with hesitant uncertainty. He should be helping me, I thought with confusion, not standing with a look on his face that indicated he had just uncovered a disagreeable truth.

"Is he the one then?" Colin asked, his Irish brogue unmistakable.

"The one—?" I began, even more confused, then picked up strength to add, "I have no idea what you're talking about, but I need your help, Colin. I'm afraid Jake's going to bleed to death if we don't do something."

Colin came forward and crouched down next to me, Jake seemingly invisible to him, lifted my face with a finger under my chin, and stared into my face. Then he abruptly stood.

"I've thought there was someone else for a while, and I see there is. Dammit, Dinah, I didn't deserve for you to treat me like that."

Nothing in all my experience had prepared me for such a moment, and I had no idea what to say or how to act, didn't understand Colin's words or why he felt compelled to say them just then, didn't comprehend that he could ignore Jake Pandora's blood as it soaked into my skirt. Then Colin took a single step backward directly into a low shaft of late afternoon sunlight that stole between the bars of the window, and I suddenly understood everything so clearly it might as well have been written on the wall. The stream of sunlight gleamed off his hair and off the double rows of gold tone buttons on Colin's uniform and off the bright metal policeman's star he wore on his chest. Here was Suey Wah's shiny man. I could see it in his face and wondered if what was there had always been there and I had simply been too self-absorbed to notice it.

"Colin," I said gently, desperately, "you just did a very good thing. A noble thing. You saved our lives. Everything can be worked out. Don't spoil it for yourself."

Just as gently, Colin O'Connor replied, "I just saved *your* life, Dinah, because those were my orders. They don't want you dead. Not yet, anyway. I was told to make sure you stayed alive at all costs."

"Who told you?"

Colin shrugged. "To tell you the truth, I don't know. I have a contact who knows someone who knows someone. That's how the business works, how it's always worked."

I thought with despair that he was not going to do anything for Jake and allowed that despair to creep into my voice, "Help us get out of here, Colin. At least help Jake. Please. Do it for me. You saved his life. Please get us out of here."

"I'm sorry, Dinah, I can't do that. I wasn't told you were allowed to go anywhere, only that they don't want you dead." He spoke with slow, deliberate words so I wouldn't misunderstand. "But in my own way, I care about you, and I'm glad someone's fighting to keep you alive. I'm in so deep that I don't have the will or the way to argue about anything, but I don't believe I'd ever recover from having to hurt you. It worked out all right, my being here at the right time and being able to save your life, but you should understand that I don't give a damn what happens to him." To demonstrate his words, he nudged Jake's gashed arm with the toe of his boot hard enough to make Jake moan. "I guess that's what a man gets for loving you, gets to die in your arms. We should all be so lucky." He stepped into the hallway and pushed the door shut behind him. I heard sounds that I recognized as Colin dragging Chong Lin's body away down the hallway. The little man who'd been my jailer seemed to have completely disappeared.

Later, I told myself firmly, I will reflect on Colin O'Connor, the part he apparently played in the human smuggling business, and how I had managed to miss the level of depravity he must certainly possess. Later. What I intended to do first and foremost was keep Jake Pandora alive. Without conscious planning, I removed my shirtwaist, ripped off both sleeves at the seam—an old blouse, fortunately, and not as hard a job as I'd expected—and laid one piece over the cut in Jake's arm and the other over the slash that stretched from the corner of his eye, across his cheek, and down to the corner of his mouth. The fabric I wrapped tightly around his arm drew the edges of the cut together and had the same effect as impromptu stitches, but the injury to his face was harder to work with. I sat on the floor for what seemed a long, long time with the heel of my hand pressed hard against the material that I'd folded into a thick pad and placed against the bleeding wound, sat and prayed and willed the bleeding to stop. Head wounds bled a lot, I knew, but usually they appeared worse than they really were. Please God, let that be the case here, a terrible wound for sure, but one that looked worse than it really was. When my hand cramped from the strain of remaining motionless, I changed posture and resumed the pressure. At first I feared it was just wishful thinking, but after a while I could tell the bleeding had slowed. I looked regretfully at the rest of the blouse before tearing it into broad, bandage-like strips. When we're rescued, I'll be in my chemise, I thought, and ended up chuckling at the foolishness of vanity.

"What are you finding so funny about this situation?" Jake's voice came out weak and slurred, but any voice at all meant that he was alive with the strength to speak so for me the sound was more beautiful than angelic choirs.

"A woman's vanity," I said softly and then put a hand to his face. "Don't move. I believe the bleeding's stopped, and I don't have many more clothes to take off to use for bandages."

"Really? What a time for a man to be indisposed." He settled himself more comfortably into my lap. "I can't really remember what happened."

"I believe you came to rescue me and things were going relatively well until we were surprised by one of the black dragons." I proceeded to finish the story through Colin's departure.

"I'm sorry, Dinah."

"Sorry? For what exactly?" I thought Jake might be apologizing for the foiled rescue or for his being injured and incapacitated, but that's not where his thoughts were at all.

"Sorry that your friend turned out to be what he is."

"Yes, well, I suppose if I hadn't been so sure that he was smitten by my womanly charms, and if I hadn't been so busy basking in his spoken devotion, I might have noticed that something was lacking in his character."

"Your fault again, my love? When life is back to normal, I'm going to do whatever it takes to prove to you that not every bad thing that happens is your fault or your responsibility. At least, you don't sound like your heart is broken." I sat back with my shoulders against the edge of the bed.

"Say it again, please."

"Say what again?" I smiled at the bewilderment in his voice and despite the awkwardness of our postures and the blood encrusted rags at the side of his face, I leaned down to kiss Jake Pandora fully on the lips.

"What you just called me—*my love*. I'm afraid I didn't pay attention to anything you said after that." He did his best to return the kiss but finally had to relax back into my lap.

"Damn. My head in your lap and you sitting in your shift. I can't help but feel I'm missing out on an opportunity that may never present itself again." He was trying to make a joke, but his voice faded at the last words and his eyes closed. Asleep or unconscious, I couldn't tell which.

"Don't you believe it," I told him, but I knew he couldn't hear me. "I intend to enjoy opportunities with you that will make this look like a Sunday School outing. You live, and I'll guarantee it." I rested my hand against his poor wounded face and repeated in a whisper, "Just live."

Chapter Twelve

For the second time in as many days, I watched the late afternoon twilight creep across the sky outside the little window. Only now I had the responsibility for a wounded Jake Pandora and no idea what to do about the situation or about him. Blood still seeped into the fresh cloth I'd ripped from my petticoat and wrapped around Jake's arm. The pad of cloth on his face remained damp with blood, too, but I was relieved that what had been a steady flow of blood now had the appearance of a slow ooze.

When Jake awoke next, he pushed himself out of my lap and for all my argument would not be persuaded to stay where he was. I yanked the reeking, old mattress off the bed, propped it against the wall, and helped him shift his body so that he sat with his legs splayed out and his back resting against the mattress. I watched him worriedly for any sign that the exertion had caused the bleeding to resume and was relieved not to see a fresh trickle of blood.

With Jake out of my lap, I stood, stretched, took a quick brisk walk around the room's perimeter, and stopped to peer out the window into what was rapidly becoming night. Traffic had increased and I was busy trying to figure out how to get someone's attention through the window. More people did not necessarily mean more opportunities for rescue, not from the people that spent their nights on Morton Street. As our room's interior darkened, I could no longer see Jake's face, which was a mercy, perhaps, because seeing what would almost certainly be lasting damage to that perfect countenance made me feel like weeping.

"Dinah."

I sat down on the wooden edge of the bed frame and reached down for his hand. "I'm here. How do you feel?"

"Like hell." Pause. "Looks like you picked the wrong hero."

I squeezed his hand. "I don't think I ever thought of you as my hero."

"Thanks very much." His dry tone, more than the words, caused me to chuckle despite the serious situation.

"I mean I never needed a hero. I still don't."

"What do you need, then?"

I gave his question serious thought before answering. "Needing and wanting are two different things, Jake. I want a lot, probably too much, but what I need is someone I can count on for faithfulness and freedom and friendship."

He repeated the three words and I thought from his increasingly slurred speech that he was in worse condition than he let on or that I realized. "I'll give you that and more, Dinah, if you let me."

"Are you proposing to me?"

"I think I am."

"Well, you're delirious so it doesn't count."

"I may be delirious but it counts, anyway."

"When we're out of here, you won't remember you even asked."

"I'll forget a lot of things, darling girl, but I will never forget that. I thought maybe this—" he took my hand and laid it against the bandage on his face "—would clinch the deal."

"You *are* delirious! What in the world are you talking about?" He tried to laugh but caught his breath in pain when he did so.

"You said you'd never—how did you put it that afternoon?— throw yourself at a man who was more beautiful than you were. Won't this take care of that obstacle?"

"You are the most immodest and shameless man I have ever met."

"But I think you love me anyway."

The room was completely dark by then, and I couldn't see his face any more than he could see mine. All we had was the firm warmth of our hands together.

"Yes," I responded thoughtfully, "I think I do, but don't let it go to your head."

"Don't worry, love. My head has had about all it can handle for the time being." We sat in the darkness for a while longer before Jake spoke again in a weak and breathy voice that sounded nothing like him. Hearing him that feeble frightened me more than anything I had experienced over the last thirty hours. "I sent a message to your brother-in-law before I came here and to your Miss Cameron, too. I told them both where I was going and why. Someone will be here for you soon, Dinah."

"For us, you mean," I corrected, desperate to hear some of the old Jake's arrogance in his voice. Desperate for him to live. "Someone will be here for us. I'm not going anywhere without you."

As if on cue, the door opened to show Colin's bulky figure outlined in the doorway. In one hand he carried a lamp that he set down on the floor next to Jake.

"He isn't dead then."

I still held Jake's hand and felt it clench at Colin's words, in fury more than anything. I thought, He wanted to take a piece out of him and I couldn't blame him. So did I.

"No," I replied evenly, "he isn't, and he's not going to die, either, at least not in the near future."

"Dinah, I've come to take you home. That's the order I got: make sure she gets home. Someone must have talked a blue streak because at one time they wanted you to disappear completely, dead and in the Bay and no one the wiser. But that someone, whoever he is, must move in high circles and he wouldn't let that happen, so now I'm told to make sure you get home."

"I'm not going anywhere with you, Colin. I don't trust you any farther than I can throw you, and even if I did, I wouldn't leave Jake."

"I did everything for *us,* Dinah. It was all for us. Don't you see? I didn't have a choice. A woman like you would never be happy on a policeman's wage, and it was easy money. Carry messages, deliver the girls to wherever I was told, collect the money, and hand it to the waiting courier." The calm assumption of his words infuriated me.

"Don't you dare lay that on my shoulders, Colin O'Connor! Don't you dare! You were involved in the slave trade before you met me, and you know it. You're the one who wanted that mansion on Nob Hill, not me. What did I ever say or do to make you believe that I valued wealth more than the well-being of children? You're the greedy one, and I was just another thing you coveted."

"That's not—"

"Go away, Colin. I'm not leaving Jake." At the finality of my tone, Colin lifted the lamp so it shone fully on my face.

"I can see that. He's a lucky man. Even luckier if he lives. Well, I won't force you to come with me. Someone's bound to be along for you soon. Jesse Cook is looking for you, and I've never known him to fail when he's as hell bent as I saw him today." Colin moved toward the door, then stopped long enough to turn and explain, "I have to leave town, Dinah. My taking you home would have been the last you'd have seen of me, no matter what. The Chinaman I shot was a high level turtle man of the Black Dragons, and I'll be dead by morning if I don't run."

As perverse as it must sound, for just a moment I felt almost sorry for the man. He'd forfeited everything he valued: the brotherhood of the police, the city he loved and claimed as his home, his ambitions of promotion and prominence. Everything. Even me, although I wasn't sure that what Colin O'Connor felt for me had much connection to love. I didn't see how it could. Sitting in that stinking place in my shift with Jake's dried blood on my hands, I still had the sense to realize that a person didn't abandon his beloved. I wasn't leaving Jake.

"Go ahead and run, Colin. You'll be running your whole life so you might as well get started." He stepped into the hall without looking back but this time did not pull the door shut after him. I watched the light from the lantern Colin carried dance on the wall outside the door and then gradually fade until he had disappeared completely taking all the light with him, a man living in a personal darkness blacker than that hallway and all his own choice. I never saw or heard of him again.

"You sure know how to pick your men, Dinah."

Jake's faint words were meant lightly, but I didn't find them anything but true. I slipped off the edge of the bed and crouched beside him long enough to kiss his forehead—too hot from fever, I thought, and felt another desperate pang of something close to hysteria—before settling next to him on the floor shoulder to shoulder.

"I do, darling. You bet I do," I agreed and tried to give our situation objective consideration. I knew someone would come for us, but I couldn't be sure they'd arrive soon enough for Jake's well-being, which meant I should walk out the open door and find help. But a woman alone on Morton Street after dark couldn't be sure she would make it safely out of the rough neighborhood, especially if that woman was running around in her underclothing without a cent to her name. I wasn't even certain I could get safely out of the building where I was being held. Who knew what hobgoblins lurked at the end of the hall? At the same time, letting Jake Pandora die because I was frightened of the dark and the unknown and the street was unacceptable. I turned toward my companion, careful not to jostle him. He felt hotter than ever to the touch and had taken to mumbling random words and incomprehensible sentences, clear indicators that he needed medical care and needed it right away.

"I won't be gone long, Jake, but I have to get help. I'll be back. I promise. You won't die while I'm gone, will you?" Foolish question, I thought, but couldn't help repeating it. I had told Colin that I wouldn't leave Jake and I didn't want to, could hardly bear the idea of leaving him alone in this terrible place. I dreaded the idea of stepping out into a street renowned for its murders and assaults, its bawdy houses and taverns and criminals and whores. And yet somehow I did, I did, and in the end, it wasn't half as hard as I expected.

I met no one in the hallway as I carefully walked in the same direction the light from Colin's lamp had seemed to go, and at first I judged the shabby building to be empty. But I heard a commotion behind a door along the hall, a man and woman laughing very loudly, and realized I wasn't alone. I contemplated knocking on the door and asking the pair inside for help, heard more noises that indicated they would not appreciate being interrupted and would almost certainly not give a rip about me. I walked past the closed door toward the light that illuminated the end of the hallway. When I reached the source of light, I saw that it was an old oil lamp on a table by what appeared to be a front entrance. The lamp brightened an open doorway on the other side of the front door, and from that far room I heard more laughter, men and women both.

I weighed my chances: either sneak out the front door onto Morton Street or step into that room of rowdy strangers and hope someone would have pity on me. To this day, I can't say for sure which I would have chosen, a real-life dilemma strikingly reminiscent of Mr. Stockton's "The Lady, or the Tiger." Taking the time to process the risks of both alternatives and deciding which would give me the better chance of bringing quick aid to Jake took a moment and as I gathered my strength and said a quick prayer, the front door crashed open. One man who looked vaguely familiar stood directly in the doorway and behind him hovered several more men in uniform. The man and I exchanged stares, and I know I must have been a sight, half dressed, my hair in shambles, Jake's dried blood on my face and chest and hands, as wild-eyed and filthy a woman as I believe this man had ever seen for all his work among criminals. Finally locating his face in my memory, I smiled.

"You are the most beautiful thing I have ever seen, Sgt. Cook," I told him.

The words brought Jake's injured face to mind and forgetting how I must have appeared, I took several steps toward the sergeant. The door of the room toward which I'd been headed slammed shut, but from behind it I caught one or two muted cries and the shuffle of many hurrying feet before all was silence. The same Jesse Cook that had been instrumental in the rescue of several Chinese girls and who would later become San Francisco's respected and honored Chief of Police stood immobile and speechless.

"I'm Dinah Hudson," I continued, wanting to be helpful. "I think you might be looking for me. I'm not hurt, not really, but Jake Pandora is down the hall and he's terribly injured. He needs help right away." All the policemen remained still and staring, and I thought they were waiting for me to show them where Jake was. "He's this way," I said, but the grandiose motion I made with my hand, a woman leading the cavalry into battle, seemed to break the spell that held Sgt. Cook and his squad so unnaturally still.

"We are indeed looking for you, Miss Hudson. Here now, put this on. The night's too cool for a lady like yourself." He slid out of his uniform jacket and dropped it gently onto my shoulders before giving an abrupt nod to his officers in the direction of the hallway.

"I'll show you where Jake is," I volunteered.

"We'll find him, Miss. Everything's fine. Why don't you come with me outside so we can get some help for you?"

I realized that he supposed from the blood on me that I was injured or that I had been assaulted or abused in some shameful way. Certainly he thought I was, if not completely unbalanced and deranged, at least hysterical, and he was doing his best to pacify me. I took a deep breath in order to speak calmly.

"I don't need help, Sergeant. I'm starving and I'm filthy, but otherwise I'm right as rain, and I don't intend to let Jake Pandora out of my sight until I'm assured that he's getting the best medical care San Francisco has to offer." I pulled Sgt. Cook's jacket more tightly around me—he was right, the night was cool—and turned back into the same dark hallway I had crept down several minutes before. More to myself than to any of the policemen behind me, I muttered, "I think the man proposed marriage and I think I accepted and I intend to talk with him further about the idea. Now are you coming, Sergeant?"

"Yes, Ma'am, we're coming." The sergeant, a small smile of relief on his face, stepped beside me and added in a low voice meant only for me, "And if it isn't premature, let me be the first to offer my congratulations."

The next few hours passed as a blur. I sat next to an unconscious Jake as we were driven to St. Luke's Hospital. There I met the resident physician, Dr. Allen, who after a keen look at my face, did not ask a second time about my injuries. Instead, wise man that he was, he devoted the rest of his energies to taking care of Jake. When I attempted to follow him into a private room sealed off by a heavy wooden door, the doctor stopped, turned, and gave me a stern and unsmiling look.

"No, Miss Hudson, You may not come past this door. It's for doctors and nurses only."

"But—"

"I know you are concerned, and I can appreciate that, but in your present state of—" he gave me a long look and wrinkled his nose slightly in response to my close presence, a humbling gesture coming from the austere man in his pristine doctor's uniform— "dishevelment, shall we say, your current appearance would do the patient more harm than good. Go home, soak in a steaming bath, eat a hot meal, take a good nap, and then come back. Your Mr. Pandora has undoubtedly lost a great deal of blood, but from what I observed of his injuries and his constitution, I believe he will still be here when you return."

His words, the most positive thing I'd heard in a day and a half, made me feel like weeping. "You mean he won't die?"

"We will all die, Miss Hudson. Eventually. But barring a serious infection or some other unforeseen follow-up to his injuries—which can happen; I can't make guarantees at this point—I believe your Mr. Pandora will recover. From my brief examination, he seemed in overall excellent health, which is what will prove most helpful to his full recovery." Dr. Allen looked past me and added, "I see there's someone here to meet you. Come back later, Miss Hudson, and you may see the patient then."

When I turned to discover the doctor's meaning, I saw Ruth hurrying down the hallway, at least hurrying as much as her condition would allow—well, waddling really, but a beautiful sight nevertheless! When she caught sight of me, she stopped abruptly and tented both hands over her mouth to stifle a shriek. Martin, trying to keep hold of his wife's arm, stopped, too, and simply stared. By then I had become used to the reaction, however, and didn't give much thought to the way I looked. I couldn't really remember how it happened, but somewhere along the way I had exchanged Sgt. Cook's police coat for a fisherman's long sweater, much too large for me and with a smell hinting that several old salmon remained in its pockets. I didn't care at all that the sight and the smell of me was enough to stop cable cars in their tracks. What bothered me more was how all the color drained from Ruth's face in horror.

"Ruth!" I cried, rushing toward her. "I'm all right. I just look awful. I'm all right. Martin, for goodness sake, find a chair for your wife. She looks like she's going to topple over." I took hold of my sister by both of her upper arms to steady her. "I'm really fine, Ruthie. Don't look like that."

My sister took a shallow, strangled gasp, swallowed hard, and tried to smile. "If you say so," she said, valiantly trying to ignore my appearance.

"I do say so." After giving me a searching look, Ruth threw her arms around me and despite her protruding stomach and my reek of filth and fish managed to pull me into a firm hug.

"We didn't know what to do, did we, Martin?" My brother-in-law had returned to attempt to steer Ruth to a small side room that held a few uncomfortable looking chairs, but she was unwilling to move if it meant letting go of me. "When you weren't home for supper, I sent Martin to the mission, and he brought back the terrible news that you had left hours before. Miss Cameron sent word to the authorities right away, and Martin even went to see Mr. Gallagher. We didn't know what to do. Oh, Dinah, I was sick with worry. I prayed so hard for your safe return. We didn't know what to think or what to do. How do you get yourself into these situations?" Ruth tried to hide her sudden wave of emotion by fussing with my hair but quickly realized the futility of attempting to make any part of me presentable. She had never been one to misread a lost cause. Finally, she asked one more time, still needing to be reassured, "Are you certain you're all right?"

"Yes. I wasn't mistreated, just kept prisoner in a tiny room."

"But why? Why did someone abduct you and imprison you? And how did you escape?" Ruth's questions dwindled away and finally stopped altogether as she thought matters through. Then she asked the question slowly, "But if you're not at the hospital because you're injured, then why—?"

I started to explain as much as I could, told her about the woman named Bea who risked her own safety to find Jake and about Jake's arrival at the house on Morton Street, but when I tried to describe what it had been like to see Chong Lin's saber slice into Jake's perfect face, I couldn't finish.

"Oh, Dinah." Ruth, not any more used to seeing tears in my eyes than Jake had been, seemed speechless for a moment. "My dear, I am so sorry. Is Mr. Pandora—?"

"No," I interjected quickly. "Absolutely not. I won't allow it, and you know I always get my way. The doctor says he should recover, but his face, Ruthie, his beautiful face!" At that I began to cry in earnest and my sister once more wrapped me in her arms.

"Never you mind about his face, Dinah," she whispered in my ear. "If you love him, that won't matter. You do love him, don't you?"

"Yes," I whispered back. "I'm afraid I do. You were right all along."

Ruth wiped away my tears with her gloved fingers and linked her arm with mine as we began to walk down the hallway to the front doors of the hospital where a cab waited at the curb to take us home to Grove Street.

"Right about what?" she finally asked.

"About finding the right person. 'You just know,' you told me, and I do. I just know."

Ruth patted my hand and tried not to look too gratified at being proved right. Martin opened the doors for us, and we stepped out into the clear light of an early and unseasonably chilly August morning.

"Well, good," my sister said. "I can't wait to hear more, but I'll have to because first you're going to take a bath and wash your hair. I will ask Martin to burn every scrap of clothing you're wearing. You'll have a nourishing breakfast followed by a long sleep, and then you and I will have a much overdue sisterly chat. How does that sound?"

I had left Jake in the best care to be found in San Francisco and knew there was nothing I could do for him but pray. He would live or he would die. God knew. I didn't. But whatever happened, I had done the best I could. It was not my fault and his survival was no longer my responsibility. The knowledge caused an unexpected and comforting peace to settle somewhere in the general vicinity of my heart.

"It sounds perfect. Just perfect," I replied and meant every word.

Ruth followed through on everything she promised with ruthless precision. Bath. Meal. Sleep. I followed lamb-like behind her, dressed in the clothes she gave me, ate the food she put before me, and crawled into bed without protest, asleep before she pulled the covers under my chin. I slept nearly twenty-four hours straight through and awoke to the vague memory that something wasn't right before I remembered Jake lying in a hospital bed. The memory propelled me to dress and descend the stairs with lightning speed.

I found my sister sitting at the old kitchen table, a cup of steaming tea in her hand. When she saw me, she said with obvious relief, "Now you look like my sister again. Did you sleep well?" I poured myself a cup of tea from the pot on the table before sitting down across from her.

"Wonderfully. Not a dream. Not anything."

"Good." Ruth stood to gather a plate of warm breakfast from the pans on the stove, and when I tried to tell her that I didn't have time to eat, that I had to get to the hospital, she set the plate in front of me, saying as she did so, "I fully understand that you are concerned about Mr. Pandora's well-being, and I know that nothing could keep you from going to the hospital. I would feel the same way if it were Martin. I even understand that I will have to wait until you are back from the hospital to have my curiosity satisfied. However, you will eat breakfast before you go." She sat back down across from me, smiled, and took a sip of tea, sending me a glance over the rim of the cup that for some reason reminded me suddenly of our mother.

"All right." I was so hungry and the food so delicious that I couldn't remain sullen or act ungrateful. We talked about inconsequential matters and avoided my experiences of the past two days because we both understood that that particular conversation would take more time than I was willing to spend just then. I finished the meal, took a last sip of tea, and reached across the table to put my hand over Ruth's.

"You are the best sister in the world, Ruthie. I'm supposed to be taking care of you and look who's doing the work and the worrying. I'm sorry." She turned her hand palm up and clasped mine.

"Don't be. You have nothing to be sorry about. I'm a grown woman, and I don't need to be taken care of. When I didn't know if I'd ever see you again, I realized that it was my selfishness that had kept you here, that you never intended to stay and would have returned to China if I hadn't asked for your company. I felt guilty and grieved and when I asked God to bring you home safe, I promised myself and Him that I would stop trying to make you into what I wanted you to be. You say you're not a heroine and maybe that's true, maybe you only acted as any other woman in a similar situation would have acted. That I don't know. What I do know is that you are an exceptional woman and it's not your sister saying so, Dinah. Other people see something special in you, too. That's one reason you've always had male admirers. They get a glimpse of your energy and your passion and your intelligence and it catches them off guard. I hope your Mr. Pandora appreciates you."

I remembered the look on Jake's face when he first stepped into that awful room and saw me, the tone of his voice as he said, "I'll give you that and more, Dinah, if you let me," and thought that was about as close as any woman would ever come to knowing she was appreciated. More than that. To knowing she was loved.

"I think he does, Ruthie, but he's a man I expect will keep me guessing for the next fifty years or so." I gave her hand a squeeze and pushed away from the table. "He's already got me guessing because I have to assure myself he's all right. When I get home, we'll talk."

"Sgt. Cook wants to talk to you, Dinah. He mentioned something about Colin O'Connor and said he hoped to come by later today, and Miss Cameron has been very concerned, so I wouldn't be surprised if she put in an appearance, too. Please try not to leave me with a house full of company and no guest of honor." When I promised to return as quickly as possible, Ruth sighed. "That's no guarantee, but all right. I still want some time alone with you sister-to-sister because I don't understand everything that happened, but I can wait for now. I don't feel the same urgency because your face was so transparent when you talked about Jake Pandora that—well, you already answered my chief question."

I thought about Ruth's parting comments after I boarded the street car that would drop me off by the hospital's well-tended grounds on Valencia Street. The circumstances of Jake Pandora's proposal—if that's what it was—were dubious enough to make its validity suspect, and he had never once admitted that he cared for me, not in the way a woman usually wanted to be told. And yet I was as certain of his feelings for me as I was about my love for him. I couldn't hitch that certainty to anything specific, but I was content. It may take the man a while to discover that he couldn't live without me, I told myself, and I may have to help that realization along a little, but I accepted the fact. The time would come when Jake Pandora would admit he wanted me, and I could wait for that time because when it happened, the reward for my patience would be glorious.

I entered the hospital, headed in the general direction I recalled from my earlier visit, and serendipitously met Dr. Allen in the hallway. When he started to walk past me I startled him by grabbing his arm with a firm grip. I saw a slight irritation but no recognition in his eyes when he turned to face me and realized he didn't recognize me. How could he, I asked myself ruefully, since I was fully dressed and didn't drip blood? I hastened to remind the doctor how he knew me and watched the vague irritation disappear from his eyes when he finally remembered.

"Of course, I remember you now, Miss Hudson. You look considerably improved from the last time I saw you."

"I took your advice to bathe and eat and sleep, Dr. Allen. Will you take me to Mr. Pandora?"

At Jake's name, the doctor shrugged. "Unfortunately, Mr. Pandora lacked your good sense, Miss Hudson. He refused to take my advice. In fact, as I recall, he was adamant about not taking my advice."

"I don't understand. He's not—" I couldn't finish that particular thought and instead continued, "You said he wasn't in any overt danger, Dr. Allen. You said that Jake was young and healthy and barring anything unforeseen he would be just fine."

"I meant everything I said, and I diagnosed Mr. Pandora correctly. He had lost a lot of blood from those two wounds, but once he awoke there was nothing I could do to make him stay in the hospital."

"You let him out of bed?!" The doctor seemed to take offense at my tone because he drew himself up to a rigidly straight height.

"This is not an insane asylum, Miss Hudson, where people remain against their will—although I am beginning to wonder if that wouldn't be a more appropriate habitat for the two of you. Mr. Pandora insisted upon being released, and when I advised him against the wisdom of so precipitate an action, he was quite rude in his response. He was working under a very strong emotion that seemed to me to be plain and simple anger and when it became apparent that he was going to depart with or without his clothes, I advised the nurse to bring him something to wear and wished him well." Dr. Allen took pity on the fear and concern he must have seen in my eyes because he finished kindly, "He has two deep cuts, Miss Hudson, but they stitched up nicely. They will be sensitive and sore for a while and both will undoubtedly scar, but I have no reason to believe they will not heal just fine. From his description of the injuries it sounded like it was your quick thinking to stop the bleeding and keep him quiet that saved his life. You needn't look so worried. Mr. Pandora gave every indication that he is a man capable of taking care of himself. And before you ask, no, he did not tell me where he was headed and I did not ask. I had the definite impression that he felt he had something to accomplish and nothing I said was going to interfere with whatever that purpose was."

The doctor walked away, leaving me standing in the hospital corridor completely at a loss. I had been so sure of seeing Jake and assuring myself that he was well that for a moment I had no idea what to do. Then, annoyed with Jake because he had spoiled all my good intentions, I hurried outside and hailed one of the many cabs that waited around the hospital's doors. When the cabbie let me off at the Broadway Dock and asked if he should wait, I shook my head.

"No, thank you. I'll catch a cab home later." I tossed him his fare and stepped into the street to wave down another cab that had just begun to pull away from the curb on the other side of the street. This cab, driven by Casey's familiar figure, pulled up along the dock on the Bay side.

"Well, Miss, I haven't seen you in a while, not since the day of the strike as I recall. Looks like the mayor's going to bring in strike breakers. That'll liven things up around here. Are you here to see Jake?"

"Yes. Is he at the transport office, do you know?" I stood in the street and shaded my eyes as I looked up at Casey.

"I believe he is, but he's already got company."

"Really? Who?"

"Didn't know the man. I picked him up downtown. Jake sent me with a message and said I should wait because the fella would be coming back with me and he did. I dropped him off in front of the transport office a few minutes ago and Jake said not to wait." He eyed me. "Jake was looking pretty rough and if I read him right, three might be a crowd right now, if you take my meaning. How 'bout I take you home."

"Not on your life," I responded with an attempt at haughtiness. "I've come to see Jake Pandora, and he can just make room for me. Thank you, Casey."

"Should I wait for you?"

"I don't think you have to. I can take care of myself."

"No doubt, but maybe I'll take a breather anyway." He reached into his pocket for a small pipe and a pouch of tobacco and proceeded to prepare for a smoke with the ease of a man sitting in his parlor after supper.

I trudged up the alley, stopping midway to remove my hat and jacket. August could be deceptive in San Francisco and today promised to be warmer than usual. Just my luck because I'd dressed with a certain degree of formality, expecting as I had to be seated next to Jake's bed as his own personal angel of mercy, every hair in place and wearing the same shade of blue he'd complimented weeks before at the city's cotillion. That beatific picture of myself faltered under the glare of the August sun and the exertion of an alley with an incline that invariably winded me. I suppose I wasn't really cut out to be a heavenly vision, anyway, but the morning wasn't going the way I'd hoped and that knowledge coupled with the fact that I would once again appear in the door of the Pandora Transport Office disheveled and out of breath put me in a bad temper. I knew it was completely unreasonable, but I blamed Jake for not staying put in the hospital. Somehow I thought he should have realized I would come to him, and he should have waited for me. That's what I did when I'd been held on Morton Street. If that woman Bea managed to get a message to Jake, I'd known without a doubt that he would come for me and I'd waited. Of course, realistically I didn't have much choice about it, but still, would it have hurt him to wait a little while longer at the hospital this morning? Did he get some contrary enjoyment from seeing me perspiring and winded?

By the time I reached the front door of the transport office, I had talked myself into a bit of a temper and didn't bother knocking. I pushed open the door, stepped into the front room, saw that it was empty and almost called Jake's name before I heard his voice. And something about his voice, some tone I'd never heard from Jake before, something so cold and so fierce that I almost didn't recognize it as his voice, stopped me from making a sound. He was talking to someone in the back room and I stepped closer, somehow knowing I should do so quietly and without advanced notice.

"And you thought what, that she was expendable, that no one would miss her?"

"I have no idea what you're talking about, Pandora." I struggled to place the voice of the man responding to Jake's words, a familiar voice that I had heard somewhere before but for the life of me couldn't quite place.

"You know exactly what I'm talking about. Every trail led back to you. Where else would the money come from? The more I asked around the more your name came up."

"Envious people are always looking to blame a successful man and for what exactly? What are you really accusing me of? Indulging in a little smuggling now and then? As if half of San Francisco's men on the Hill aren't doing the same. It's a fact of life. I've even heard that you aren't above turning a little profit with your boats now and then, that you've brought in your share of girls."

"Is that what you've heard?" Jake's voice had lost the hiss of anger it had originally held. Now he sounded cool and amused and much, much more dangerous. "You should hire better informants, then."

I stood on the other side of the curtain that divided the two rooms and didn't move a step, didn't twitch and hardly breathed. I had finally placed the other man's voice and because of who he was, I knew why Jake wanted him there. I would have to do something about the situation because I was involved, too, but for now all I could do was listen.

Finally, after a pause, Ralph Gallagher said, "I'm leaving. Whatever you think I've done, Pandora, you have no proof. I should report your threatening behavior to the authorities."

"Yes," Jake replied slowly, still ostensibly amused, "you should. You really should. But right now I wouldn't move if I were you; I wouldn't take a step because I would very much like to kill you and I'm not sure I could resist that particular temptation."

"What have I ever done to you?" Gallagher's tone sounded honestly bewildered. "We haven't met more than three times that I know of. I recall that you once came to my home to propose a business venture, and I told you I was willing to talk further about it at my office, but I never heard from you again so I don't see why you'd blame me if the deal fell through. Did one of my bank managers refuse you a loan? Do you want money? Is that why I'm really here?" I had to credit Ralph Gallagher for his steady, reasonable tone because I had figured out that Jake must be holding some kind of weapon.

"You know why you're here. You read my note, and you didn't waste any time getting here."

"I choose to nip scurrilous accusations in the bud and what your note suggested was outrageous. I had nothing to do with Miss Hudson's abduction. If the idea wasn't so insulting and slanderous, it would be laughable."

"Laughable is not a word I'd use. You didn't see her. I did. Manhandled, frightened, ill, imprisoned in a stinking whore's crib. Did you really think I wouldn't call you to account for that?"

Ralph Gallagher's voice was as calm and unconcerned as if they discussed the weather, a man mildly curious and nothing more. I couldn't help but admire his control because if the look on Jake's face matched the tight fury in his voice, Gallagher's life was on the line.

"I didn't realize you even knew Miss Hudson. You're a fortunate man if I understand you correctly. Congratulations."

"I would never ask a woman like her to settle for a man like me, but that doesn't mean that I haven't made her safety and happiness my business. You made a serious misjudgment when you involved her in your nasty commerce."

"What you are accusing me of is ridiculous, but even if it weren't, even if there was truth to your allegations, we both know you aren't going to do anything to me."

"Is that what you think, Gallagher? Is that what you really think? Because the only person who knows you're here is a cabbie who probably scorns the likes of you more than I do. Who's going to hear the one shot it will take to kill you, and who'll notice when I load a sack onto one of my steamers and drop it into the ocean? And you know what I think makes it easiest for me? It's that no one will miss you or care that you're not around any more. Not your partners in crime and as far as I can tell, not your family. Nobody, Gallagher. What does it say about a man's life that no one will miss him when he's gone?"

Ralph Gallagher did not bother to refute Jake's contemptuous comments. Instead, he came back with a retort that told me Jake's words had stung. "Then from what I can see, we're more alike than you want to admit, Pandora. You live in the back room of a cheap office on an alley that hasn't even got a name. You have a two-bit business that will never amount to anything. And for all your noble talk, I don't believe a woman like Dinah Hudson would give you the time of day, so who will miss you when you're gone?" And that, I thought, was an entrance line not to be ignored.

"Actually," I said, pushing back the curtain and stepping into the room where the two men stood facing each other, "I would." I looked at Jake, winced at the sight of the bandage that hid half of his unnaturally pale face, and repeated, "I would, my darling. I would miss you very much, so please don't do this. I don't want to settle for a prison visit once a month or spend my life looking over my shoulder for fear the law has caught up with us. Send this little man away and let's get on with our lives."

Jake's eyes met mine and it seemed for a moment that he didn't recognize me. I almost didn't recognize him, either, not because of the bandages or the wound to his face, but because of what I saw in his look. I believe with complete certainty that Jake Pandora would have killed Ralph Gallagher without a second thought and done exactly what he described: dragged the banker's corpse out to sea—using just the one hand, apparently, since his injured arm was in a sling— and tossed the body overboard without a moment of remorse. I found that part of Jake Pandora almost frightening and took a deep breath before

I spoke. But by then whatever cold menace I thought I'd detected had melted completely away and what I saw in Jake's warm brown eyes was anything but frightening.

"Where did you come from?" It sounded like he was laughing at me. "Do you plan on making a habit of turning up in unexpected places and at inconvenient times?"

"Yes, my darling. I do. It's part of my charm and one of the reasons you love me to such distraction. But I wish you wouldn't murder Ralph Gallagher. I admit he deserves it, but let the law track him down. Human law or God's law, it will get him in the end." For the first time I turned to look at Gallagher, standing with a posture of elegant indifference to Jake, who stood in front of him with a pistol pointed at the banker's chest.

"I'm glad to see you well, Miss Hudson. You don't look any the worse for your shocking experience." We might as well have been exchanging pleasantries in the sumptuous front room of his Nob Hill mansion.

"For which I have you to thank, I believe."

He almost acknowledged my words with a nod but thought better of it and said without inflection, "I really don't understand your meaning."

"Saving my life doesn't balance out all the other lives you've ruined." I went on relentlessly, "I'm grateful, of course, but the truth is that I wouldn't have been at risk at all if it hadn't been for you and your unsavory cohorts. That fact makes me resist crediting you for my survival, but fair's fair."

"Dinah," Jake interjected, "what are you talking about?"

I continued to gaze at Ralph Gallagher gravely. "How did Colin O'Connor put it? 'Someone must have talked a blue streak,' he said, 'because at first they wanted you to disappear completely, dead and in the Bay and no one the wiser.' But Colin also said that my advocate moved in high circles and wouldn't let that happen. That advocate was you, wasn't it? So I suppose I should thank you, only I can't. I just can't."

Ralph Gallagher remained silent, and I continued to study him soberly, finally concluding, "You are a wicked man who preys on children
for selfish gain, and I will do everything in my power to see you held
accountable for your actions, but I won't let Jake kill you today. Not
today. Now we're even." As an afterthought, I added, "And by the way,
I plan to give Jake Pandora much more than the time of day."

I stepped toward Jake and took the gun from his hand, which he
allowed me to do without resistance. I placed the weapon on a stack
of boxes behind him and went to stand very close in front of Jake, my
back pressed against his chest. Almost with a will of its own, Jake's
good arm went around my waist and pulled me even closer. I felt him
inhale deeply, breathing me in—not like I was some fragrant elixir but
more like I was his oxygen, his life-giving air. We simply stood there,
two people so close we might have been mistaken for one figure.

In a very low voice, Jake asked, "Are you sure about this, Dinah?
Do we owe this man something?"

"His life for mine, Jake, but just this once."

All this time Ralph Gallagher had stood immobile, but with those
words, he picked at the edge of his suit coat and rearranged its folds,
then straightened his hat. What an inconvenience all this has been,
his actions telegraphed, but only an inconvenience. Inconsequential.
Trivial. A bother and nothing more.

"I imagine the chief of police would find your threatening my life
to be of interest, Pandora, but for your sake, Miss Hudson, I won't
mention this experience to anyone."

"Just our secret?" I asked and at his nod added, "Agreed. Martin
will continue with his job like this never happened, and Jake will run
his business without interference. My sister and your wife will sit on
the same charities and no one will hear—at least from us—what a
scoundrel you are. But I can't help but wonder, Ralph, if you ever think
about what you could have been and what you could have had and if
you ever wish you were more than the pathetic man you are."

He shrugged in answer and walked past me as I stood held tightly and very willingly by Jake's strong arm. Yet a part of me felt, perhaps shamefully, a grateful warmth to that cold man now departing. I lived and I was loved and for whatever reason, he had played a role in that. When I said Gallagher's name, he halted with one foot over the threshold, but he did not look back at Jake and me; he just stood there.

"I said you can't make up for all the damage you've done, for young girls scarred and young lives ruined, and I meant that, but it doesn't mean you couldn't try. You could see what it's like to be generous without expecting something in return. You could surprise someone with a totally selfless and unexpected act. You could change a life for the better. God's given you the power and the means to make a difference. How can you squander that opportunity?"

For just a moment, I saw his shoulders tighten. From the gesture, I might have thrust a dart into the small of his back, but then he stepped through the doorway and out of view without speaking or turning around.

"There's a cabbie waiting at the foot of the alley for you," I called before I heard the front door of the office open and then close. I never saw Ralph Gallagher or spoke to him again, and I have no reason to believe that my words had any effect on him at all.

At that moment, however, Ralph Gallagher was the farthest thing from my mind. I turned in Jake's embrace so that my face was very close to his. "You are such a blockhead," I said.

"Why? Because I wanted to kill a man who abused you?" The husky tenderness I heard in Jake's voice sent a small shiver down my back. What I heard there was promise enough for a lifetime.

"Well, perhaps that wasn't the wisest idea you've ever had, but no. Not that."

"What then?" He had lowered his mouth to my face so that when he spoke I could feel his breath against my skin.

"Because you said you refused to ask a woman like me to settle for a man like you. What does that mean, anyway? And who made it all your business? I have a say in my own future, you know."

"Do you?" he whispered, so close by then that only a breath separated our lips.

"Yes, I do. I—" My words were cut short at exactly that syllable and as far as I could tell, neither of us regretted the interruption.

Much later, I decided I hadn't been quite accurate in my prediction but that the miscalculation wasn't entirely my fault. From his words and actions that afternoon in the back room of the Pandora Transport Company, I was certain that Jake Pandora wanted me. Passionately. And I can honestly say that I have never had cause to doubt that certainty since. My mistake—made from ignorance and a perfectly understandable error under the circumstances—was expecting the word *glorious* to describe what it would be like to be loved by Jake Pandora because that experience held—and continues to offer—so much more than any one word could ever convey, even for a woman fluent in two languages. Not glorious and not perfect, but something better. Freedom and faithfulness and friendship and still more than that. When I discover the right word, I'll recognize it. But I haven't found it yet.

Epilogue

I can hardly believe it's true and, of course, I'm happy about it, but in an unforeseen way, the scar that gracefully curved down my husband's face did nothing to detract from his attractiveness. I would have loved him no matter how the wound healed and fully expected the result of his injury to mar his physical appearance. All it did, however, after healing quickly was give him the look of a dashing and dangerous pirate. He has my quick action at the time to thank for so smooth a scar, of course, and I am not shy about reminding him of that, but Jake is not usually suitably grateful, countering that he wouldn't have been injured at all were it not for me. A stalemate, I suppose, when it comes to that particular topic. Women still watch him covertly imagining heaven only knows what. Well, that's not exactly true. I knew what they were imagining because I married Jake Pandora, pirate extraordinaire, and enjoy the benefit of imagination become reality. Poor women. Nothing imagined, no matter how fanciful, could ever match the real thing.

Several things interrupted our wedding plans. In September, President McKinley was assassinated and the entire nation went into mourning. Walking down the aisle with a black armband woven into the ivory lace of my wedding gown would not do. I told Jake we would need to wait a little while, at least until the shock to the nation wore off, and was entertained by the expression on his face as he digested the fact that the wedding would be postponed. He is not a patient man.

Then my nephew was born and I couldn't leave Ruth to cope on her own. That's why I was in San Francisco in the first place, after all, and despite her protests and Jake's exaggerated sighs of longsuffering, I suggested we wait until Father could make the trip to California to meet both his new grandchild and his new son-in-law.

"I could abduct you," Jake said conversationally, seated before the fire in the Shandlings' front parlor. Ruth, Martin, and baby Teddy—my sister is a great fan of the new president—were all upstairs preparing for bed because Teddy had not yet mastered sleeping through the night and entertained us at odd and very early hours. I was half asleep myself, yawning unattractively and nestled comfortably against Jake's chest.

"I've already been abducted, thank you, or have you forgotten?" His arm, healed and strong, tightened around me.

"Forgotten what it felt like when that woman showed up in my doorway to tell me you were behind bars on Morton Street? Not hardly."

"Bea. Her name was Bea." I turned in his arms to ask, "You paid her something, didn't you, and you didn't skimp? I told her you'd be generous."

"Yes, love, I paid her. Not nearly enough for what she gave me, though."

"We should try to find her, Jake. Maybe we could help her."

"I did try, but I wasn't able to trace her. She seems to have disappeared."

I kissed him lightly. "What a good man you are!"

"That's an improvement."

"Over what?"

"Over being immodest and shameless. I distinctly recall you telling me I was the most shameless man you'd ever met."

"You were. You are. For which I am eternally grateful because I don't think I could love a man who was consistently and everlastingly correct."

"Do you, Dinah?" I had attempted a mild joke, but his words held no humor.

"Do I what?"

"Love me. I don't know why you would."

I had already learned that Jake Pandora was not a man given to a great deal of introspection and the slightly bemused tone of his voice made me push away from him to question, "Are you asking me to enumerate your virtues?"

The idea caused him to laugh low in his throat in the way that I had discovered caused an interesting physical reaction on my part. Before Jake, I had had no idea that a man's laugh could affect parts of one's body in such a delectable way.

"That would take a full ten seconds of your time at most. I'm not a virtuous man, Dinah, that's the problem. I got my education on the docks and some of my education would not be fit for your ears. I'm not all that different from the Ralph Gallaghers of the world, and I'm afraid that someday you'll realize that and want nothing to do with me."

"I can't stand it when you get humble. Thank goodness it happens so infrequently. You are nothing like Ralph Gallagher. Nothing at all." I felt very tender toward Jake at that moment and wanted to say all the right things but was caught off guard by another yawn. "I'm sorry, dearest. I'd recite Browning and explain all the reasons I love you, but I'm exhausted. As you probably know, Teddy—like babies everywhere—keeps to a schedule of his own, and there's no arguing with him."

"I don't know, and I'd like to discover about babies the natural way, with my wife participating," Jake muttered.

This time I laughed and leaned to whisper something into his ear that made him take a quick breath, turn toward me, and push me back onto the sofa cushion. "I'm not a patient man, Dinah, and you would be wise not to tease me."

"I'm not teasing," I retorted, made slightly breathless by his proximity. Really, I didn't think I would ever get used to the effect Jake Pandora had on my mind and body. "I mean it. Let's go to the justice of the peace tomorrow and get married."

"But your father—"

"—will understand, and he can respeak the ceremony when he

gets here if it would make him or you feel better. I'm no more happy with the situation than you are, Jake. Life is so short, and every night we spend apart seems a terrible waste. Let's get married tomorrow. Don't we need a license or something?"

"I've had a license—and a ring—for weeks." Jake pulled away from me. Despite the crackling fire, I was cold without his touch and suspected it would always be so. "Are you sure, Dinah?"

I gave one final yawn before struggling to my feet. "Yes, love. As sure as you are. Now go home. I promise that tomorrow night I will not send you away, but tonight I simply have to go to bed."

Jake rose, too, and reached for me one last time, saying into my ear before he kissed me good night, "Oh, you'll go to bed tomorrow night, too, my darling, but it won't be the same." And he was right about that. It wasn't.

I suppose what I've had with Jake Pandora these past years is a happy ending of sorts, though it doesn't feel like an ending. With Jake, with his energy and ambition and passion, every day since that afternoon at the justice of the peace has seemed like a beginning.

It hasn't always been happy, either, but that's not for Jake's lack of trying. Sometimes I lie awake in my husband's arms and remember Mae Tao, a plump and bossy little girl now all grown up—or more likely dead. I never found her, and I grieve for her loss. Some of the blame for her disappearance must be laid at my feet, but I've learned from Jake how to separate responsibility from guilt. I know in my heart of hearts that I didn't do all I could for her, and I wish I had acted differently, but I can't change the past, only learn from it. I lost track of my young friend, Johanna Swan, too. Time and children got in the way of all my good intentions, but I still wish her happy. She had so much grief in her young years I can only pray she found joy, as well.

One welcome reminder that life is not made up of only failures and disappointments is my little bird, my Suey Wah. She finished her schooling at Mission San Rafael and returned to 920 as a young lady, still petite and somewhat delicate but with a will of cheerful iron. She currently resides there as a resident teacher of English and always—in the sweet manner she retained from her childhood—credits me with her language skills. Not true, of course, but I have learned to smile my protest and change the subject. In any battle of wills, Suey Wah will always win. That she is alive proves the point.

Three years after my marriage, Ralph Gallagher dropped dead at his office. A shocked Martin brought the news to Ruth, who called me right away. I never shared what I knew about Ralph Gallagher with either Ruth or Martin and following his exit from the Pandora Transport Company never saw the man or talked to him again. I have no way of knowing if he ever managed to do even a single good, unselfish, and generous thing for anyone. I hope so but consider the prospect unlikely at best.

Jake and I were in China when the earthquake of 1906 knocked San Francisco to its knees, and I instantly feared for Ruth and her family. We rushed back to a ruined city of flames and rubble, an unbelievable sight. Many people died, but the only one I knew personally was Irene Gallagher, who refused to leave her Nob Hill mansion and died under its bricks. Ruth, Martin, and their two children were safe and came to live on board one of Jake's boats until we could get their house rebuilt. The docks stayed safe and the transport office was unscathed, but the beautiful city of San Francisco lay in shambles. Like the proverbial phoenix, however, it continues to rise from the ashes, and I suspect that one day it will be twice as magnificent as it was before the catastrophe

Providing proper but far too infrequent balance to the inequities of life, many of the men I'm certain were involved with Ralph Gallagher in the despicable practice of human smuggling have paid for their sins, one way or another. Abe Ruef currently sits in prison, convicted of extortion and Eugene Schmitz was recently found guilty of accepting bribes. Jake says Schmitz won't spend a day in jail, and sad to say, I fear Jake's right. The former mayor knows all the right people. To no one's regret, Judge Mackiver hanged himself in his chambers one afternoon.

Unfortunately only the actors—not the play itself—have changed. Until the United States repeals or alters the Chinese Exclusion Act and allows Chinese men to bring their wives and families legally into the country, the demand for Chinese women will continue, with a never-ending supply of villains eager to take advantage of the situation.

To this day, Donaldina Cameron remains the center and core of 920, a woman of indefatigable energy and surprising vulnerability. She led her girls through the earthquake to safety without turning a hair; I wish I'd been there to see it. We are friends now and I believe always will be, the mission our common bond. I have never met a woman more worthy of admiration and respect, and I fear that someday who she was and what she did will get lost among the wars and the legislation that passes for history nowadays. Will anyone remember her in a hundred years?

Recently when I voiced my concern to my husband, he merely shrugged. "Who will remember any of us in a hundred years, Dinah?"

"Our grandchildren will."

"Our grandchildren will look at pictures of us in an old album somewhere and wonder who we were and what we were like. They won't remember us. Not really."

"Memory is a funny thing," I replied quietly. "Who's to say that along with brown eyes and red hair and a love for water, we won't also pass along a thread of memory to our grandchildren, some spark of connection to this thing called family." I looked over at Jake, a touch of silver at his temples and the scar on his cheek showing pale and prominent against his brown skin. Still the most beautiful man I have ever seen in my life.

While neither Jake nor I could by any stretch of the imagination be considered meditative, whenever we strolled the beach around Cliff House, I was reminded of Colin O'Connor. He had completely disappeared, despite Jesse Cook's vigorous search for him, and I often wondered what became of the rugged Irishman. I couldn't help but think of him as "poor Colin," even as I acknowledged that he had been weak and greedy. I had almost loved him, and something about his memory still touches me, despite everything. *"As I hear the sweet lark sing / In the clear air of the day,"* Colin had crooned in that rich tenor voice, his breath on my cheek. I thought that if he had survived the vengeance of the Black Dragons, his life and future still could not have held much music these past years.

Unlike my life, filled as it has been with the music of family, music sometimes discordant and often much too loud—the Greeks have an exuberance for living that is never quiet—but rich and textured and beautiful, nevertheless. The thought reminds me of a recent family outing.

I recall our daughter Sophia standing at the water's edge staring at the Bay, mesmerized. She will inherit the transport company someday, and she will run it smart and hard because more than her brothers, it is Sophia who carries the force of her father. My two sons are good boys both, twins and alike as two peas in a pod, intelligent and curious and kind, but they are no match for their sister. Sophia has her father's dark beauty and my pragmatic nature and despite her tender years, she is already a force to be reckoned with.

As I watch my daughter, Jake reaches out to brush my cheek with the back of his hand. "I've been thinking about that thread of memory, and I hope you're right because our grandchildren should know their grandmother for sure, how the sun turned her red hair to gold and how the sea rested in her eyes. I want them to know that."

At his words, I am suddenly, momentarily, breathtakingly overwhelmed with love for this man. In every marriage, someone once said, one partner loves more than the other. If that's true, then I am the one that tips the scale. I know Jake loves me, but I know he also loves the sea and his boats and his good name. Loves them differently from me but loves each with a unique passion I have learned to accept. I must share his affection, but I don't care. Just a fraction of Jake Pandora holds more allure and excitement than any other whole man I know. I want to tell him all that he means to me, how he inhabits me

as tangibly as the blood that flows in my veins, how I treasure his faithfulness and his friendship, how he has freed me to love him without
restraint or regret. But Jake and I are not two people who comment on
such things very often. Neither of us feels the need or takes the time.
Our days are busy with travel and children and the transport business,
and our nights—well, our nights can be busy, too, but for us, words
are seldom necessary. More often than not they only get in the way.

"Look, Mama! Look, Papa! Look at the ship! Isn't she grand? Isn't
she beautiful? Look at her!"

I recognize the sharp excitement in Sophia's voice, which carries clearly through the muted conversations around us to where Jake
and I stand on the shore, and I understand what I hear in her voice.
The thrill that comes when the wind catches a vessel's sails just so
and pushes it powerfully, gracefully forward. The incoherent exhilaration of freedom. I follow my daughter's pointing, imperative hand to
a magnificent schooner that sits ready for adventure and poised on the
edge of the horizon, its sails bleached a blinding white in the sunlight.

"Yes, Soph," my husband calls, "I see her," but his dark eyes are
fixed on my face as he continues in a much softer voice, "and she is
beautiful. She is that."

From Jake the words are a sonnet, and the deep feeling I hear
behind them offers a rare look into something about which he speaks
only infrequently. I am speechless with surprise and pleasure and desire, a confusing combination. He smiles, confident and handsome,
clearly enjoying the unusual accomplishment of throwing me off balance. Shameless still and proud of it. A man who likes to have the last
word almost as much as I do and is not averse to employing a compliment to get it. Well, I am shameless, too, in my own way and because
his words pleased me, I kiss him lightly on the cheek without a rejoinder. He thinks he got the best of me in that exchange, but there will be
other times, and I don't always let him win. With no more to be said,
we join hands and continue our stroll down the sand side by side.